That was when he had done the rare thing, had stayed in partial merger with her, so that she felt a deep sharing of his sensitive Father soul, his mystery. She hadn't realized how extraordinary it was for a male to do that. They had been so happy, coming home; over and over he told her how good the long exposure-time would be for the egg, how it would make a strong-fielded child. And of course Tiavan was a fine young one, a potential Elder certainly. But Giadoc—

Suddenly Tivonel realizes that she is so shamelessly polarized that the gura-plant is swirling wildly. And the Hearer's signal ahead has grown much stronger. *Ahura*! What will Giadoc think of her if she arrives this way?

She damps herself hard, remembering that Giadoc is probably absorbed in his work and hasn't thought of her at all. And maybe he won't think her experiences are enough to benefit a second egg. But the Elders believe that the mother's memories help the egg's field, and aren't hers unusual? Well, at any rate she has a formal excuse for the visit; he can't criticize her asking for news of Tiavan after a year away.

She jets on energetically—and is suddenly struck by weirdness. A ghostly clamor of light invades the natural hush. She checks, disoriented—and finds herself among dim forms. Why, there is Ober . . . and the others! She's in the floater with them, going down. What's happening?

Panicked, she pumps her mantle and the hallucination fades. She is back by the trail. But ahead of her is the blue mantle of the young one she'd met—he is approaching again, his field-fragment bowling ahead. Oh, no! She forces more air through herself to clear her senses—and she's back in ordinary reality, sailing downwind in disarray.

Not really frightened, she snaps herself back on course. She knows now what has hit her—one of the so-called time-eddies Mornor's daughter warned her about. They're strange pockets of hallucination or alternate time, who knows?—not dangerous unless one gets blown while in them. Her father said they started to be noticed in his youth, and only near weird places like the poles.

So she must be getting close. Yes—the signal is much stronger, and the wind-streams are subtly roiling and losing direction. It's the beginning of the enormous turbulence of the Polar Vortex. Here at the pole the planetary winds circle forever around a great interface, where the Hearers work. Tivonel remembers the conditions from long ago when her Father had taken her to see Near Pole. The Hearers there have a dense wealth of sky-life to study. Tivonel jets energetically through the cross winds, wondering why Giadoc has chosen to come and Hear here at Far Pole where the Companions must be few and faint.

The plant-marker is ending in a great luxuriant tangle, balanced on a standing eddy. The winds are omnidirectional now, it's the start of the interface zone. Tivonel's mantle-senses automatically analyze the complex gradients of the pressures around her; she cuts across local wind-loops, steering by the life-signals ahead and above. The point-source has opened out to several separate groups of life-emanations. The Hearers must be spread all over the Wall. It is still silent, a beautiful day, still dark and silent although she has been traveling well into normal night. Untired, alight with anticipation, she sends herself shooting through another huge cloud of plant-life—and emerges at the End of the World.

What a scene!

Forgetting her eagerness, forgetting Giadoc, Tivonel stops and hovers, awe-struck.

It isn't really the end of the world, of course, but merely the edge of the biosphere in which her people live. It is a place of wonders.

She is in the side of an enormous wind-funnel, a planetary hurricane called the Wall of the World. It is a great curved wall, a tapestry of life-signals and murmuring, shimmering light that spins around the Pole. Ahead of her stretches an empty space, a zone of turbulent updrafts which to her is stable air. Out in the center of the great ampitheater she can perceive the lethal polar Airfall, an immense column of down-pouring winds. It descends eternally from the converging winds high above and falls into the unimaginable deeps of the Abyss below, there to spread out over the unknown dark, and ultimately rise in upwellings like that of Deep. The Airfall is dense dying with life, sighing grey on its fall to dread wind-bottom. Around her, spreading into the empty zone, is a screen of lovely airborne jungles that ride the standing air beside the Wall. It is here that the Hearers work, because of the clear view above.

Tivonel lifts her scan, and is again awestruck. She had

expected it to be interesting, but not as impressive as the musical brilliance of Near Pole's sky, not as dense with life-signals. Now she sees the Companions are indeed fewer, but against their silent background, how individually splendid, how intense! At Near Pole they had been so massed as to seem a close web; she remembers making a childish effort to signal to it with her tiny field. Here she sees how far they are, how they burn alone in the immense reaches of the void.

For the first time she really grasps it. Each Companion is indeed a Sound like Tyree's own, she is hearing the light-music poured from a million far-off Sounds. And the beacon-points of life with them, how individually clear and strange! Are there worlds up there, worlds like her own, perhaps? Is another Tivonel on some far-off Tyree at this moment scanning wonderingly toward her? Her normally wind-bound soul expands and something of the lure of Giadoc's work comes clear to her. If only she were not a female, if only she had the strong far-reaching Father's field!

But perhaps there is no one up there, only mindless plants or animals. She has been told that Tyree is exceptionally favorable for intelligent life with its rich eternal Wind. Perhaps only here could minds develop and look toward other worlds? How lonely. . . .

But her buoyant spirit will not be dashed. How lucky to live at the time when all these mysteries are becoming known! In the old days people believed the Companions were spirits above the Wind, mythical food-beasts, or dead people. Even today, some people down in Deep hold that there are good and bad spirits up here: idiots who've never been out of Deep, never sensed the sky except through thick life-clouds. Her Father warned her that such beliefs may grow, now that Deep is becoming so self-sufficient. Tivonel is in no danger of such stupidities, up here where she can receive the blazing music and life-emanations of the sky!

But another life-signal has grown strong and jolts her from her musings. Hearers, quite close above! Tivonel realizes abashedly that her own emanations must be equally clear to them, perhaps impinging on their work. Hurriedly she compacts her awareness, nulling her output as much as possible. How awful if she has already offended Giadoc!

She jets slowly up along the Wall, very cautiously scanning

for Giadoc's distinctive field. She can always recognize that characteristic intensity, so open yet so focused-beyond.

At the end of a line of other fields she detects him—Giadoc, but grown even stronger and more strange! He must be preoccupied, experimenting with something unheard-of. All the Hearer's emanations are weird, intense but muted. Bursting with curiosity, she pushes through a tangle of vegetable life and hears the lights of his voice. How deep and rich, a true Father! Yet strange, too.

His tone becomes more normal, is answered by other Hearers. They seem to be finished with whatever they are doing. Keeping herself as null as possible, she clears the plants and lets her mantle form his name in a soft rosy light-call. "Giadoc?"

No response. She repeats, embroidering with the yellow-green of her own name. "Giadoc? It is Tivonel here."

To her joy comes an answering deep flash. "Tivonel, Egg-bearer-of-my-child!"

"Do I disturb? I came to see you, dear-Giadoc."

"Welcome." In a moment he appears, swooping toward her. How huge he is! Overjoyed, she lets her own field stream at him, her mantle rippling questions.

"Are you well? Have you discovered many marvels? Do you recall—" She checks herself in time and changes it to, "Is Tiavan well? I have been away. I was up in the Wild, we rescued the Lost One's children."

"Yes, I heard." He hovers before her, resplendent. "Tiavan-our-child is well. He has decided to study with Kinto, to become a Memory-Keeper—when his Fatherhood is over, of course. Was your mission successful?"

His signals are in the friendliest mode, but so formal. He can't have thought of at all, she tells herself, meanwhile shyly proffering her field-engram. "I have prepared a memory for you, dear-Giadoc. I thought you would like to know of our discoveries."

He hesitates, then signals "Accept with pleasure." A dense eddy of his mind-field comes out and touches hers.

The contact jolts her deliciously; she has an instant of struggle to keep unformed thought from pouring into the memory. Then she becomes aware that he is passing her a terse account of Tiavan. Loathe to break the exciting contact, she accepts it lingeringly. Just as he separates himself she finds the impudence to let a tiny tickle of polarization tickle his withdrawing field. They snap apart, but he makes no acknowledgment. Instead he only says, deep and Father-like, "Truly praiseworthy, dear-Tivonel. You have learned how to apply your wild energies."

She doesn't want a Father. And his field wasn't really Fatherly at all.

"Thank you for the news of Tiavan," she signs. How can she get closer to him? Impulsively, she flashes, "Is anything wrong, Giadoc? You seem so reserved. Is it that I intrude?"

"Nothing personal, dear-Tivonel," he replies, still formal. Then his tone softens. "Much has been happening here. You have been out of touch a long time. There has been news from Near Pole which has affected us all."

Near Pole! It's the last thing she wants to hear of. But he sounds so serious, and he has never attracted her more. Groping for a topic to keep him from leaving, she asks, "Is it true that you have actually touched the lives of beings on other worlds? How incredible, Giadoc, how fascinating."

"You don't know how incredible," he answers quietly. "You can have no true concept of the distances. Even I find it hard to grasp. But yes, we have touched. Some of us have even been able to merge briefly."

"What did you learn? I was just hoping that other intelligences are out there. Are they like us?"

"Very unlike. Yes, a few are intelligent. But very, very strange."

His tone has become warmer, more intense. "If only I could try it," she laughs flirtatiously to remind him of her femaleness, and allows another tiny potential-bias to tease at his field.

But he only signs somberly, "It is dangerous and harsh. Much more painful than your Lost Ones, dear-Tivonel."

"But you do it for pleasure, for strangeness, don't you, Giadoc? Perhaps you are a bit of a female at heart!"

"It is interesting." Suddenly his field changes, his mantle signs in deep red emotion, "I do love what you call strangeness. I love exploring the life beyond my world. It will be my work so long as we all survive."

To her surprise, he ends on an archaic light-pattern meaning *over-mastering devotion*. But this is not what she was hoping for at all.

"How unFatherly," she almost says—and then something in his tone reaches her. "What do you mean, as long as we survive?"

"The trouble I spoke of. You'll learn when you go down." His voice is grave again.

Exasperated, she can only wish that they were in the wind, not in this eddy. If she could move straight upwind of him, *that* would convey! I'd do it, too, she thinks. But here there is nothing to do but say it.

"Giadoc." Her aura comes to formal focus, compelling his attention. "I have lived and had valuable experience, don't you think? It seems to me I am entitled to a second child. An advantaged egg," she signs explicitly. "I thought—dearest-Giadoc, I have been thinking so much of you. Do you remember us, how beautiful it was?"

"Dearest-Tivonel!" Another wave of emotion sweeps him, his field is intense. But still he does not polarize.

Stunned by his rejection, she flashes at him, "How you've changed! How unFatherly you are! So I don't please you, now." She turns to go.

"Tivonel, Tivonel!" His tone is so wild and sad it stops her. "Yes," he says more quietly, "I have changed, I know. It is the effect of outreach, of touching alien lives. But there is more than that. Dearest-Tivonel, listen. I cannot bring a child into this world now." His tone is white, solemn. "You will learn it for yourself. We are all about to die soon."

"Die?" Astounded, she opens her field in receptive-mode. But he only signs verbally, "When you understand what has been observed you'll realize. Our world, Tyree, is about to end."

"You mean, like the time of the great explosion? But that's a joke!" Angrily she lets her mantle glitter sarcasm. Everyone knows the old stories of how the end of Deep was falsely foretold. "We're safe now, you know the forces of the Abyss are far away."

"This isn't from the Abyss. Destruction is coming from beyond the sky."

"You mean another fireball? But—"

"Worse, much worse. Didn't you listen to any of the news from Near Pole before you left?"

"Oh, something about dead worlds—"

Agony hits her. Pain! What hideous pain! A searing life-grief is ripping through her field, feeding back anguish, numbing her senses.

Barely able to hold herself in the wind, she contracts her mind desperately, trying to escape. It's a blast on the life-bands, like a million-fold amplification of the tiny death-cries of the Wild. But so strong, unbearable. With shame she realizes she's transmitting waves of personal suffering as the shocking pangs sweep through her. She struggles to hold herself null, but she can't. The torment is building toward some lethal culmination—

Suddenly it slackens. It takes her a moment to understand that Giadoc is shielding her. He has thrown a Father-field around her, holding the terrible signals off as if she was a child.

"Hold on, it will pass." He transmits courage. Grateful and ashamed, she reorders herself within his sheltering field. The pain is still quite severe, it must be horrible for him. She finds she has let herself merge with him like a baby, and tries tactfully to withdraw. As she does so she feels strange new emotions in herself; he must have let her touch him deeply, an unheard-of intimacy among adults.

Humbly but proudly she detaches herself. The hurt is less now.

"No more need." She signals intense-thanks.

"It is passing. Be careful, dear-Tivonel." Slowly he withdraws protection. The pain is still there, but fading, passing from her nerves. They find they have become entangled in a plant-thicket and right themselves.

"What was it, Giadoc? What hurt so?"

"The death-cry of a world," he tells her solemnly. "The death-cry of a whole world of people like ourselves."

The deep sadness in his tone affects her; she understands now.

"Here at the Poles we receive them very strongly. Near Pole has been hit by them all this past year, the life-bands there are torn with these cries. World after world is being killed. Some die slowly, some very fast."

She is still disoriented by horror and wonder. "But they're so far away."

"The deaths are coming closer to Tyree all the time, Tivonel. Near Pole says there are now only five living worlds between us and the destroyed zone."

She tries to grasp it, to recall her lessons. "The Sounds are so crowded above Near Pole, aren't they? Are they colliding, like people in a storm?"

"No. It's not natural." He pauses, gravely expanding his field.

"Something out there is killing worlds. Deliberately murdering them. We don't know why. Perhaps they are eating them."

"How hideous. . . . But—how can you know?"

"We have touched them," he signs, his words tinged with deep green dread. "We have touched the killers. They are alive. A terrible, incomprehensible form of life between the worlds."

At his words, she finds in herself a fragment of his memory: a terrifying huge dark sentience, unreachable and murderous. That—approaching their own dear Tyree? Her mantel turns pale.

"And one of the beings, whatever they are, has passed this way alone. It is out beyond Far Pole now, destroying. Undoubtedly that was what we felt. It may be preparing to destroy us."

"Can't you turn its mind, the way we do animals?"

"No. Iro tried and was injured by the mere contact. It's inconceivably alien, like touching death." With an effort, he changes his tone to the gold of affectionate-converse. "Now you understand, dear-Tivonel. I must go back to our work. A committee from Deep is coming up to discuss the situation."

"Yes." She signs reverent-appreciation. But then her energetic spirit breaks out in protest. How can she leave him now? How can she go back and occupy herself with some meaningless activity while all is in danger?

"Giadoc! I want to stay here and help you. I'm strong and hardy, I can hunt for you and keep your Hearers supplied. Please, may I stay?"

His great mind-field eddies curiously toward her. "Are you serious, Tivonel? I'd like nothing better than to have your bright spirit near me. And it's true we don't have the food we need. But this is dangerous and it will go on. To the death, perhaps."

"I undersatnd," she signs stubbornly. "But I proved on the mission that I can stand boredom and persevere, even if I'm a female. The Fathers said so. I was useful."

"That's true."

"Please, Giadoc. I feel—I feel very strongly about you. If there's danger I want to be with you."

His mantle has taken on deep, melodious ringing hues, his field is intense. She has never thought him so beautiful. Suddenly he flares out, "How I wish we had met again in better times! Yes, dearest-Tivonel, I remember us. Even if I've fallen in love with the strangness of the sky, I remember us. Perhaps I can show you—" He falls silent, and adds quietly, "Yes, then. I'm sure Lomax, our chief, will agree. But—"

She is deeply happy. "But what, Giadoc?"

"I fear that what you experience here will dim your brightness forever."

Chapter 6

Thursday morning means the Military Air Transport terminal, a scruffy extension of the National Airport warren. It reminds Doctor Daniel Dann of a small-town airport. Crowded, not many uniforms visible, the air-conditioning already beginning to fail.

He makes his way around a party escorting a famous senator—much shorter than his photos—and gets caught among five plump women gretting a saluki dog. Beyond them is Lieutenant Kendall Kirk's yellow hair.

"Ah, there you are, Dan." Noah Catledge bustles up. "Two to go. Good morning, Winona."

Winona turns out to be T-22, the Housewife, in a turquoise knit pantsuit. "This is so exciting!" She giggles up at him.

"Put your bag over there," Kirk says officiously. To Dann's surprise, Kirk also has a dog on a lead, a large, calm, black Labrador bitch. He recalls that Deerfield is supposed to be in a forest preserve. Evidently one of the military's many private hunting grounds.

He looks around, telling himself not to hope. Beyond
Winona is the bearded, leukemic ensign, Ted Yost. And there's
the little man, K-30—wait a minute: Chris Costakis. Beside him
are the two girls, W-11 and W-12, the Princess and the Frump.
The Frump is a thin, short, sullen creature in grimy brown jeans
with a black knapsack. Beside her the Princess looks like Miss
America, pink-cheeked, with a wide, white-toothed Nordic
smile. Dann notices the meanness of his thought, knows what's
the matter with himself.

Next minute nothing's the matter. Behind the senatorial
party a tall beige-and-black figure is drifting toward them. *She's
coming with us.* He catches himself grinning like fool and turns
away.

"Ah, there you are, Rick. All here."

Rick is the twin, R-95. He ambles up expressionlessly, hung
with a bright orange plastic bag labeled *Dave's Dive Shop*.

Kirk herds them all out the end gate. It feels strange not
having tickets. At the main gate the senator and entourage are
boarding a shiny executive jet with Air Force markings. Three
huge, dusty Air Force cargo planes wait beyond. Their own
plane turns out to be a small unmarked twin-engine Lodestar,
rather beat-up looking.

For a moment a queer sense of alien reality pierces Dann's
insulation. Kirk's pompousness about the supersecret installation, the code names, their "classified" status had all seemed to
him absurd games played by grown boys. But the very normal,
busy, used look of this big terminal impresses him. The planes:
millions of miles flown on unknown errands apart from the
civilian world. A whole worldwide secondary transport system
in the shadows. . . . He hopes it is secondary.

Behind him *she* is coming too.

At the plane Kirk is talking to a shirt-sleeved man holding a
clipboard. The Labrador patiently sits.

"The Gates of Mordor," the Frump said loudly as they climb
up into the Lodestar. What does that mean? R-95—Rick—looks
around at her. The Princess smiles, suddenly looking like a
worried young girl.

Dann sits by a window. Obviously *she* won't sit by him. No;
the long beige-clad legs pace by and stop beside the turquoise

bulges of Winona. Into the seat beside him drops little K-30, Chris Costakis. His legs don't reach the floor. Pituitary dysfunction, probably could have been prevented, Dann thinks automatically. The clipboard man closes them in and goes up front.

With no ceremony, the engines start and they are taxiing to the runway. A minimal engine run-up, no waiting. Almost at once they are in the air.

Absurd happiness blooms inside Dann. She can't leave now. We're really going on this trip together. Stop being childish.

Chris Costakis is speaking in his high, unconvincingly tough voice.

"Heading south. We're not going far in this, has to be around Norfolk."

Dann doesn't care if it's around Vladivostock, but he nods politely.

"We'll be comfortable. The Navy does itself good."

They chat desultorily. Costakis turns out to be a locksmith, semi-retired. "They call us security engineers now. Eighty percent of my jobs are electronic. I had to slow down when my liver acted up."

That confirms Dann's note of the fiery flush in the little man's palms. An old wives' sign but often accurate.

"How in the world did you get into this?"

"I did a lot of work for Annapolis, the Navy security people. Catledge came around looking for volunteers to test. I got what you call a sixth sense about combinations, always had. So I tried out. I scored real high."

"You mean you can guess the numbers in a combination without, ah, listening to the tumblers or whatever one does?" Dann is happy enough to take any nonsense seriously.

"It's not guessing." Costakis' shiny, bulbous face closes up; he gives Dann a sly look.

"Of course. I beg your pardon. Please go on."

"Well . . . Numbers, see. Some days I've gone as high as thirty out of fifty. But it has to be a man. From a woman I can't pick up a thing."

Dann gazes at the little man's high, ill-formed forehead, his few sandy hairs. Hundreds of times he's fastened electrodes to that skull. Does some unnatural ability really lurk in there? His thoughts touch the closed compartment in which lies the memory of a sliding water glass, and veer off, shaken. And all these others here, can they really *do* something abnormal? Incredible. Yet this is a real plane, taking them to a real place. Real money is being spent. Even more incredible, is a submarine actually steaming out to sea with Rick's twin in it? Crazy.

The government always spends money in crazy ways, Dann reassures himself. Especially the military. He recalls some absurd scandal about condoms in balloons. This is just another. Float along with it.

Genially he asks Costakis, "If nobody is around who knows the combination, how can you, ah, read the numbers?"

"They don't have to be around." Costakis purses his small mouth. "Maybe I read someone, maybe there's traces, see? I don't want theories. I just know what I can do. Gives me like an interest in life, see?"

"I see." Delicious, Dann thinks. I am in the realm of fantasy. The faint glow of his chemical supplement to breakfast has taken firm hold.

Costakis is peering down. "I told you, Norfolk. That was U.S. Three-Oh-One." His tone is not quite casual.

"You know the area well?" From his internal shelter Dann looks benignly on the unappetizing little man. He is totally unaware that his own knobby face emanates a profound and manly empathy that a TV casting director would give an arm for.

"I know Route Three-Oh-One." Costakis pauses and then blurts out with dreadful cheeriness, "I spent twenty hours lying on it with a busted head. Nobody stopped, see? Hitch-hiker sacked me and took my car. Broad daylight, man, it was hot. I couldn't move, see? Just jerk my arm. Last ride I ever give anybody."

"Twenty hours?" Dann is appalled. "Couldn't they see you?"

"Oh yeah, they saw. My legs were on the concrete."

"But the police—"

"Oh yeah. They picked me up. Threw me in the drunk tank at Newburg. I was about gone when the doc noticed me."

"Good lord." A cold shaft of pain is probing for Dann, sliding through his defences. Shup up, Costakis.

" 'Course, if I had family or something, they might've looked for me," Costakis goes on relentlessly. "Had one brother, he got killed on Cyprus. Went back to try to find Dad's grave, he got caught." He grins in a hideous parody of fun. "What woman would look at me?"

Dann makes a wordless sound, knowing life has tricked him again. The unwelcome reality of the little man is flooding in on him. The loneliness, the *horror vitae*. Confirmed by twenty hours lying alone in pain, being passed.... Dann shudders, wanting only to turn him back into K-30, an unreal grotesque.

"So I can use an interest in life, see?"

"Of course." Stop, for God's sake, I can't take it. Dann's hand is feeling for the extra capsule in his pocket. No closeness, nobody. *What woman would look at me?* Costakis is undoubtedly right, Dann sees; to a woman that pumpkin-headed, pygmoid body, the inept abruptness, would probably be actively repulsive. To a man he is a cipher, faintly annoying, exuding a phoney jauntiness and knowledgeability that smell of trouble inside. Keep away. And everyone has, of course, always will.... To be locked forever in rejection.... *I can use an interest in life*... Pity grabs painfully at some interior organ Dann suspects is vital. Panicked, he bolts over Costakis and heads for the plane lavatory.

Coming back, he notices the extra member of the party. Sitting at the very back, behind Kirk's dog, is an unknown civilian. He must have got on last.

Pretending to look at the dog, Dann gets an impression of greying black hair, grey, very well-tailored suit, a vaguely New England face with a foreign trace. Must be a passenger for wherever they are going.

Costakis has seen him looking.

"The snook," he whispers, grimacing. "The big enchilada."

"What, C.I.A.?" Dann whispers back.

"Shit, no. No action there now. D.C.C., I bet."

"What's D.C.C.? I never heard of it."

"You wouldn't. Boss spooks. Defense Communications Component, name doesn't mean anything. I saw them in Annapolis, everybody jumped. Hey, look at that, I was right. That smutch is Norfolk. We're starting down."

The clouds are opening. Below them woods and meadows are swinging up. Dann sees a little lake. General exclamations in the plane.

They land in sunlight on an apparently deserted country airstrip, which seems unusually long. At the far end Dann can see the sock and a couple of choppers in front of the control shack. Apparently they are not going to taxi back. The plane's steps are unfolded.

As they file down, Dann sees that a grey sedan and a grey minibus have already come out to them. He notices an odd structure looming at their end of the strip—a parachute tower, in need of paint. His blood-chemistry is repairing his internal damage. It is a fine summer day in fantasyland.

The clipboard character has reappeared and is loading their bags in the bus. Before they are all out, the sedan has raced away with Costakis' spook inside.

"Oh look, aren't those real deer?" Winona's turquoise arm points to a dozen pale tan silhouettes grazing in the woods alongside.

"That's right, that's right!" Noah enthusiastically shepherds them into the bus. "I told you it would be delightful."

The Frump makes a snorting noise.

The bus carries them through more woods and meadows on a narrow blacktop road. Not a country road; the straight lines and square corners bespeak the military mind. They pass what Dann thinks is an unkempt firelane.

"Obstacle course," Ensign Yost says.

After what must be five miles they pull up at three old-style wooden barracks, standing by themselves in a grassy clearing. A volleyball net hangs in front of one. The June sun is hot as they get out.

"Look—a swimming pool!" Winona carols. They all stare around. Beyond the far barracks is a very long, shabby pool speckled with floating leaves.

"I told you to bring your suits," Noah says like Santa giving presents. "Well, Kendall, this looks just fine, if our equipment is only here. We must check on that at once."

"It'll be here," Kirk says shortly. "You don't do anything until you all sign in."

Another sedan has driven up. Out of it gets a large, bearded, bear-like man in rumpled grey fatigues. He is carrying a folder.

"Captain Harlow," Kirk announces. The man wears no insignia; Dann recalls that Captain is a higher rank in the Navy. "All in the day-room, please."

"This building will be your test site, Dr. Catledge," Captain Harlow says as they troop into the large room at the front of the first barracks.

It looks exactly like all the rec-rooms Dann saw in his service

days; plywood, maple, chintz, a few pinups. Over the battered
desk is a sign: WHAT YOU SEE HERE LET IT STAY HERE.
The desk is littered with copies of *Stag, Readers Digest*, sports
magazines.

Noah has trotted into the corridor leading to the bedroom
cubicles, the toilets, and the back door.

"These bedrooms will serve as test stations, Captain," he says
briskly. "But we'll need doors installed to close off each end."

"Just tell Lieutenant Kirk your requirements," the ursine
captain says pleasantly. "You'll find we move fairly fast here.
Now I need your signatures on these documents before I turn
you loose. Read carefully before signing, please."

Dann notices that his hands and wrists are delicate; the
bearishness is an affectation. Kirk hands round papers; general
fumbling for pens and places to write.

Reading, Dann is informed that he is now subject to National
Security Directive Fifteen, paragraph A-slash-twelve, relating
to the security of classified information. He is, it appears,
swearing never to divulge any item he has experienced here.

He signs, visualizing himself rushing to the Soviet embassy
with the news that there is an ederly parachute-tower near
Norfolk, Virginia. Kirk gives him an ID card bearing his own
color photograph in plastic and a wad of what appear to be
tickets.

"Pin the badges on you at all times," Harlow tells them.
"Your lunch is laid on in Area F Messhall. The bus will wait
while you take your bags over to the living quarters. Ladies in
the end barracks, please."

"Right by the pool!" Winona exclaims. "Captain, can we
take walks around here? The woods look so lovely."

"Your badges are for Area F only. Don't pass the area
fences." He smiles. "Don't worry, you'll get plenty of exercise.
It's a square mile."

"Can we walk home from the messhall?"

"If you wish. The bus will take you to and from meals. The
schedule is over there. Lieutenant, will you come with me?"

As he and Kirk go out, Costakis mutters to Dann, "Harlow.
That's a new one. I've seen him without the beard."

The men's barracks next door is hot and stuffy; Yost and
Costakis turn on the air conditioners. Their cots are stripped,
the bedding folded on them. Dann picks a cubicle on the side

nearest the women's building and transfers some vials to his pockets. When he comes out onto the steps, R-95—Rick—is waiting for him.

"Ron's scared," Rick says in a low, morose voice.

"Your brother...he's in the submarine?" Dann is trying to recall Rick's last name: Ah, Waxman. Rick and Ron Waxman.

"Yeah. He doesn't like it." Rick gives him a smouldering look. "I don't like this either. I wish we hadn't come."

"I'm sure he'll be all right. They seem to be taking good care of us."

"You really think so?" Rick shoots the question at him as if trying to penetrate to some fund of truth in Dann's head. Why is Rick asking him, of all people? Abstractedly, he smiles his good smile and utters more reassurance, making for the bus.

Kirk is waiting for them at the messhall door. It turns out to be a great dim, cavernous space, filled with big military-rustic tables, all empty except for a small group at the far end. The place looks old. Adjusting his eyes, Dann sees ghosts: battalions, whole clandestine armies have trained here for God knows what.

A plump man in fatigues and silver bars takes their mess tickets and seats them right by the door. Not near the others. Dann understands; Noah's people are in quarantine. We'll meet no one and see as little as possible of anything that may be going on here. He squints through the dimness. At the two far tables are men in fatigues, a few smartly uniformed Waves. Station personnel, or embryo spies? He sits down between Ensign Yost and the Frump; he will not let himself look at *her*, sitting beyond Noah, Kirk, Winona.

"I sure hoped we'd be on the water," Ted Yost says. "Call this a shore installation?" He sighs. "I wish I could have gone in the sub."

"Ron didn't want to go," Rick tells him sulkily. "He had to because he's the best sender. He hates it."

"I know." Yost smiles with unexpected sweetness, his gaze far off.

Their food comes fast, on trays; enormous breaded veal cutlets, baked potatoes, applesauce. Good, but too much of everything. As it arrives, four people at the far end get up to go. Among them Dann sees the bearded "Captain Harlow" and a tall, thin, grey civilian. Kirk jumps up and strides down to them.

"The Black Rider," mutters the Frump's voice beside him. I

must stop calling her that, Dann thinks. What the hell is her name? Something Italian. From beyond her the Princess smiles at him intently.

"I'm so glad you're with us, Doctor Dann." Her voice is very soft.

"Everybody! Give me your movie-tickets!" It's Kendall Kirk back, looming at them in his insufferable clean-cut way. "The *movie*-tickets, those yellow ones. You never should have been issued them," he says severely, as though it was their fault.

There is a general confusion while the movie-tickets are being separated from the meal-tickets and passed back to Kirk. Dann is delighted with this evidence of military bumbling. At last Kirk sits down again, and starts talking with Noah about their missing equipment.

The Frump has been making scornful comments, sotto voce. Her swarthy face looks surprisingly like a worried small boy's. Dann experiences a rush of outgoing geniality.

"You know, after all this time of having to refer to you as Double-you-eleven and twelve, I'm not sure we've ever been introduced. I'm Daniel Dann."

"Fredericka Crespinelli." The Frump says it so like a handshake that Dann glances down and sees her small fist curled tight.

"I'm Valerie Ahlgren," the Princess laughs. "Hey, Daniel Dann, that's neat. It's Dan any way you say it. I'm Val, call her Frodo."

The Frump—Fredericka—scowls. Dann prods his memory.

"Frodo—that's from a book, isn't it?"

"How would you know?" Fredericka—Frodo—demands.

"Wait—Tolkien. Something *Rings*. And Mordor was the Black Realm, wasn't it?" He smiles. "Do you see this place as a black realm?"

"Oh *yes*," says Valerie. But her friend asks curtly, "What are you, a psychiatrist?"

"Goodness no. I'm just interested. To me this place seems, well, somewhat ramshackle and abandoned. Maybe it was blacker once."

"It's not abandoned," Valerie says intensely, looking furtively about.

"Ghosts, maybe," Dann chuckles.

"Didn't you notice those magazines—all recent?" Frodo frowns. "They use this place."

"That's why we're so glad you're with us," Val says quietly. "People like us, we're vulnerable. They don't like us."

For an instant Dann thinks she's telling him they're lesbians, which he had rather assumed. (The perennial male puzzle: How, how?) But then he realizes her glance had summed up the whole table.

She means, he sees, people like Noah's subjects. People who are supposed to be telepathic, to read minds. Nonsense, he thinks, meaning nonsense that they read thoughts and nonsense that the powers of Deerfield would dislike them.

"They value you," he tells her gently. "They're taking all this trouble to see what you can do."

"Yeah," Frodo grunts. Valerie just looks up at him so earnestly it gets through. She's really worried, he sees. Probably people like this are inclined to paranoid suspicions, living among unreal perceptions.

"I wouldn't worry. Really." He summons up his doctor smile, willing her trouble away as he used to will away more tangible ills.

Slowly she smiles back at him and touches her friend's hand. Surprisingly, it's a strong, radiant smile, quite transforming her face. At the same moment he glimpses Frodo's fingers; her nails are bitten off to stubs. H'mmm. His notion on their relationship somersaults. Who is the strong one here. Or must there be a strong one, do their small strengths complement each other?

"Anyway, it's nice being by ourselves," Val says. "Sometimes it hurts so much, in crowds."

"You can say that again," says Ted Yost from Dann's other side. He and the girls exchange looks. Dann has a moment of crazy belief; what would a barrage of thought from a crowd be like for a telepath? Horrible. But of course it's not that; they're probably abnormally sensitive to voice-tones, body-signs of hostility.

Across from him, Chris Costakis has taken no part in this conversation; he eats stolidly, his gaze darting about. Beside him, Noah and Kirk have been going over the requirements; the doors to be installed, the missing biomonitors, the computer terminal, the power supply.

"They want the first test at eighteen hundred tonight," Kirk says.

"Kendall, until we get our hands on our equipment I refuse to try anything. This is going to be done right or not at all."

"Okay, okay. They're putting on the pressure."

"Then they must get my equipment and get it set up right."

"It'll be here."

"And properly installed."

Kirk glances at Dann, who looks carefully blank. He knows and wants to know nothing of the entrails of the shiny cabinets he uses. To his relief Costakis speaks up abruptly.

"I can give you a hand, Doc." The little man is still offering his help to a rejecting world.

"Good, good, Chris," says Noah enthusiastically. "I'm glad to have someone who understands the function. If you're all finished, shall we go?"

"Now for that pool!" Winona sings out. Behind her, Margaret Omali towers up.

As they walk toward the bus, she turns away.

"I'll walk. "

"But the computer!" cries Noah. "We need you, Miss Omali!"

"It won't be there," she says flatly. "One mile, I'll be there in fifteen minutes."

She strides away, followed by Noah's expostulations. Dann sees Kendall Kirk take one tentative step and says firmly, "I believe I'll walk too. That was a heavy lunch."

Kirk gives him a nasty look and gets in the bus. Dann finds he has to stretch even his long legs to catch up with her. The bus passes them then disappears. He swings along in silence beside her, feeling wild and happy.

"You meant it. Four miles an hour," he says finally. "I hope you don't mind my sharing your walk?"

"No."

He searches for a topic. "I'm, ah, puzzled. If it wouldn't bother you to tell me, how do they put a computer out here in the woods?"

"They install a terminal and tie in via telephone line. There's a small computer capability at the headquarters here, they won't specify what. Through it I can access TOTAL. The phone line is fast enough for our purpose."

He is enchanted that she will talk, he would listen to her read stock quotations. "What's TOTAL? A big computer?"

Her perfect lips quirk. "More than that. TOTAL is the whole Defense system. We only use a tiny part."

"It must be enormous."

"Yes." She smiles again in secret pleasure. "Nobody knows exactly how far the network extends. One time it printed out all your credit ratings."

"Good Lord!" But he is thinking only that she is walking a little slower, relaxing. The blacktop is cool in the forest lane.

"And could you tell a layman why we need a computer? It seems to me that their answers are either right or wrong."

"No, it's more complex than that. For example, a subject might give a wrong letter which is right for the letter before or after. If this occurs in a series, it's significant. Do you remember J-70; that Chinese girl? She read letters ahead, five out of six sometimes. Dr. Catledge calls it precognition. The program has to analyse correspondence against increasing distance in time forward or back."

"But what about chance?" he asks, floundering in this rarified air.

"The basic program computes against chance probabilities," she tells him patiently. "Including each subject's tested letter-probability base."

"Oh." His poisoned cortex reels, makes a desperate effort to please her. "So—even if a subject gets them all right you have to subtract something for chance."

"That's right." She smiles, really pleased. He is ridiculously elated.

"I can see it's complicated."

"Some of the math gets quite interesting. Take repeated letters—"

"Thank you for explaining." He is enchanted by her mysterious competence, but he cannot cope with repeated letters. "Look!"

Three deer are browsing in the verge ahead. They bound across the blacktop, showing their white, flame-shaped scuts.

"One of them was all spotted," she says wonderingly. A city girl.

"Yes. A fawn, a young one. The spots help camouflage it while it lies still."

"Oh, I wish my Donnie could have seen that," she says very low.

He recalls the bare apartment. "Your son? He doesn't live with you?"

At the words, the bottom of his world shivers, threatens to
drop him into his private hell. For one second, he had been back
in another life of simple joy. Stop it. Vaguely he hears her saying,
"No. He's with my mother in Chicago."

Her tone has changed too. The *Keep Out* signs are up.

The magic is gone. But before he can feel it, a car roars up
behind them and they have to jump aside. It's a grey panel truck.

She laughs. "I knew that terminal wasn't there."

They walk on, the bad thing is over. He wants to hear her
voice, even if it means computers.

"Tell me, is it true that computers are now so complicated
that no human mind can really know what one is up to?"

"Oh, yes." The smile comes back. "And of course TOTAL,
well, it can access any government computer, and whenever it
wants data it can interface with almost any computer network in
the country, if you have the code. Some foreign ones too. It got
into CBS once." Her face takes on a dreamy, tender look, eyes
more beautiful than Sheba's queen. "I love to think of it. The
wonderful complexity, yet all so cool and logical. Like a
different kind of life trying to expand and grow."

"Sounds a little scary." But Dann isn't scared, he's delighted.
The tall alluring creature strolling the wildwood, talking
mysteries. "I won't ask you if they think. I gather that's silly. But
since our life is a function of the complexity of our internal
connections, maybe it could be alive in a way. Maybe it likes you
too."

She chuckles. "Oh, I'm not that crazy, I know it's a machine.
But sometimes I wonder if certain programs aren't just a little
alive. Do you know TOTAL has ghosts?"

"What?"

"Ghost programs. It's hard to flush a really big computer,
and a network is impossible. Nobody is going to shut down
TOTAL. People make mistakes, see. Their programs generate
self-maintaining loops." She actually unbends enough to give
him a teasing look. "Tapes spin when nobody is using them.
Ghosts."

He grins back like a kid. "What kind of ghosts?"

"Well, there's a couple of war-games, nobody knows their
address, and some continuing computations. And there's
supposed to be a NASA space-flight simulation still running. It
doesn't do anything most of the time because it's still traveling

through space. When it lands or whatever it'll show up. It could
to part of the ghost in my program. I found out we're using an
old NASA link."

"Our ghost?"

"Oh, it's nothing. Every so often it acts up on anything to do
with time. Like printing out the date."

"NASA . . . Now you're getting close to my friends."

"The stars?" She remembers, she remembers!

"Yes. The air's so clear here. If you like, I could show you
some this evening."

"Maybe." The reserve is back, but no hostility. Beautiful
Deerfield! They round the last corner and see the barracks with
two trucks outside. Men are carrying in a door. Margaret
quickens pace.

When they come into the day-room, equipment and cables
are everywhere. Two Cuban-looking men are hanging the door
across the corridor. Margaret heads for crates in the corner.
Above the hammering Noah and Costakis can be heard yelling
to each other.

"Okay! Plug in."

There is a flash and all lights go out. The air conditioners
have stopped and the corridor is now too dark to see. Lieutenant
Kirk comes in and Noah trots up to him.

"Kendall, we simply have to have more power here."

"You need a bigger pot up there," Costakis points at the
electric pole outside.

Ted Yost puts his head in and says unexpectedly, "If there's a
laundry here maybe they have one. Laundries use a lot of juice."

Margaret Omali says nothing, she is probing into crates.

Dann takes himself outside, follows the sound of desultory
activity around to the back. Rick Waxman is shooting baskets at
the edge of the woods. Ted Yost comes out the back door and
joins him.

Dann sits down on a white-washed bench. After a few
minutes the ensign has to quit; he walks away toward the pool,
trying not to show distress. Presently Rick comes over to Dann,
idly spinning the ball on one finger.

Dann is surprised to see that Rick's expression and posture
are quite different. His face is clear and friendly, he is a normal,
attractively muscular young man with his hair tied back like an
early American patriot. Dann, who has no extra senses, receives

a strong impression of one from whom a burden has been lifted.

"Is your brother better?" He surprises himself, acting as if he believed all this.

"Popped a bunch of tranks and passed out." Rick grins. "I hope it doesn't mess up the test."

"You mean, he might not be able to, ah, transmit?"

"Oh, he'll be able to transmit, all right." Rick's grin fades. "The question is, what. He hates those numbers."

Rick bounces the ball a few times, then sits down beside Dann and stretches in the sunshine. Like a man enjoying respite, like a prisoner let out, Dann thinks. He recalls Ron Waxman, of whom he has seen little. A shade larger, a more taciturn Rick. Probably because of the size difference Dann has assumed that Ron was the dominant brother.

"Tell me, have you two always been together? I mean—"

"I know what you mean. Yeah, our folks tried to split us up. Ronnie couldn't take it."

Rick's eyes have changed, the statement has some meaning. Dann puzzles, unhappily divining pain.

"Your brother is more, more sensitive?"

Rick looks down at the grass. "Sensitive," he says in a low, pentup voice. "My brother is so fucking sen-si-tive. All my life, he can't take it. He can't take anything. He can't listen to the news, he can't go on the street. There's an accident on the road, we have to turn around and go back." He sighs, looks up sideways at Dann. "We tried to take a trip to Denver last year, he picks up vibes somebody died in the motel room. We had to go right home. I wanted to see the Rockies, you know?"

He laughs shortly. "All the things I want, he can't take. I was pre-med, we both had scholarships. Oh, he's smart. But he couldn't take that at all. So we tried law school. Two semesters, that lasted."

Oh, God. Weakly, Dann asks, "Can't you go on by yourself, Rick? You could leave Ron with your folks."

"No way. They crashed in a plane five years ago."

"Oh . . ."

"No way," Rick repeats somberly. "He needs me. And he's sending all the time. Whatever I'm doing. I read him." He laughs meaninglessly, bounces the ball.

Dann is appalled, resentful. Why do they do this to him? His hand goes to his pocket, he touches the magic that will turn Rick back into a phantasm.

"Women, it's a disaster," Rick goes on. "Half the time he can't and when he can it's worse." He gives Dann a clear, open look as if he were explaining a sore back. The change in him is amazing. "Funny, I can talk to you.... Of course, he'll wake up pretty soon." He sighs bleakly.

"What do you do for a living, Rick?"

"Pit. We work in the pit at Honest Jack's. Ronnie's good with his hands and I can watch out he doesn't get back wrecks."

"You mean, auto mechanics?"

"Yeah." Rick looks down at the stained, callused hands that might have done other work.

"And how did you get into this, ah, project?"

"Catledge bought his car at Jack's. I guess he has his eye out for twins. The bread helps."

"Rick, what if your brother were, well, in a—"

"You mean if he was dead? If I had him put away? I guess I could."

"So?"

"If he wasn't dead I'd have to go to China. Maybe that's not far enough, if he was really unhappy. While out folks were alive I rode to Buffalo on the bus once, you know, just to get away. While I was gone our dog got hit by a car. I could hear Ron like he was in the room. I guess he could make me hear him in China if he wanted. And his being...dead, that wouldn't solve anything. It's more complicated..."

"What do you mean?"

"It's not just him." Rick twirls the ball again, looks at Dann. "See, it's not like I was all right except for him. I'm not. He's part of me." His voice is almost a whisper. "He's the part of me that can't take it. Can you dig that? It's like he's part of me, only outside where I can't fix anything. He got—left out. We're, I'm not, I'm not okay without him. I mean, I need this break. But if he doesn't wake up pretty soon, I, I can't..."

He falls silent, rolling the ball between his coarsened hands. Above them a mockingbird is trilling arpeggios. Dann sees Rick is talked out, wants to be left alone to enjoy his respite. He touches Rick's shoulder, unaware that the boy has derived comfort from their talk, and gets up and walks aimlessly away.

Dear God. The pain in Rick's eyes. The waste. He is reminded of the pitiful history of a patient, a friend, who had an intermittently and inconspicuously mad husband. The dead dragging the living down. Or is it possible Rick and his twin are in some weird sense one person, cruelly sorted into two bodies? Life's savage jokes. No matter. He dry-swallows the capsule. In a few minutes the chemistry of his bloodstream will carry reality away. He listens to the mockingbird, and discovers that his feet are carrying him around the end barracks, to the pool.

A man and three women are in the pool. Dann sits on one of the tin loungers on the shady side.

"Hi, Doctor Dann! Come on in!" The splashing turquoise-capped figure is Winona.

Dann makes benign, avuncular excuses and sits watching Valerie and Fredericka—Frodo—climb out on the sunny side. Frodo's skinny, swarthy form is clad in a blood-red tank suit. Valerie is in sunny yellow, a seductive young body. She stretches out to sun. Frodo ceremoniously lets down the back of the chair for her, fetches a coke, lights her cigarette, sits cross-legged on the grass alongside. A pixie cavalier. It occurs to Dann that he is watching romantic love. He smiles, safe back in his cocoon.

The bearded figure of Ensign Yost climbs out and walks toward Dann, toweling vigorously. His bushy face laughs, he is every inch the jolly mariner. Hard to remember the death working in that bone marrow. He sits down by Dann and lights a cigarette.

Dann starts the automatic rebuke, checks himself. Yost notices it, grins more broadly. They watch Winona's determined progress up and down the pool. She splashes womanfully. Above them the mocker is still singing, varying his repertory with blue-jay shrieks.

"Peaceful here," Dann offers.

Yost grunts. "I'd still rather be out in that sub."

"I should think it would be extremely confining."

"Yeah . . . But, a ship."

Winona climbs out, fussily spreads out in a lounge by the girls.

"I got a couple thou put away, Doc," Yost says meditatively. "If it gets bad again, I'm not going in hospital. No way, no sir. I'm going to lease me a little motor sailor and stay aboard, down the bay. Live there. Even if it's winter."

"I see." Dann has heard something like this before, but the cocoon is holding. Something about this place seems to make for unfortunate confidences, he thinks remotely.

"On the water." Yost's voice is dreamy. "I don't care if it

snows. But they say this may last 'til next Spring. How about it, Doc?"

Dann is surpirsed; Yost seems to have come to believe in his disease.

"No one can predict, Ted," he says, more or less truthfully. "What about your family?" Instantly, he regrets the question. No more revelations, no more.

"Don't have one now," Yost says inexorably. "When I got better last time Marie took the kid and split. I didn't tell her it was temporary, see? Better for Dorothy that way."

"Dorothy is your little girl?" Dann shudders, can't help himself.

"Yeah. She's six last week. I think Marie knew, she figured it was better for Dorothy too. Sometimes I feel bad, holding out the money for the boat. But Marie has a good job, she's a GS-seven. That's good security."

"Oh, yes."

Ted Yost talks on, describing the boat he plans to get. His deathship. But he is not morbid, he is looking forward with his whole soul to being on the water again, even if it is only the murk off Chesapeake Bay. Back to the sea, the oldest drive of all. Within his insulation, Dann winces. He knows none of this will happen, he knows how the relapse will come. Yost will find himself on the VA wards, trapped in tubing. Not the sea. Pity... What tragic flotsam has Noah collected here? Yost, Rick, Costakis—all in their different intolerable miseries. Well, he, Dann, can positively not take much more of this. And *she* has not appeared.

Announcing his intention to see how the equipment installation is coming along, he gets up to go.

"Thanks, Doc," Yost says unexpectedly. What for?

As he rounds the end of the pool Valerie calls to him. Frodo is coughing evilly over her cigarette; Dann makes a mental note to check her and scratches it off again. Surprising how many of them smoke. Does it correlate with—whatever?

When he gets close he is momentarily bemused by Valerie's bursting young breasts, her vulnerable little belly, and does not take in her whisper.

"Doctor Dann, that *man* is here again. What does he have to do with us?"

Dann stares around, finally spots a grey sedan beside the

trucks in front of the barracks.

"You mean your Black Rider?"

"Yeah," says Frodo. "What's he doing here?"

"I don't know," Dann smiles.

"You could find out," Valerie suggests. "*Please*, Doctor Dann. I'm so worried. He frightens me."

"We didn't agree to, to whatever *he's* into," Frodo adds rebelliously.

"I expect it's some formality. They're having trouble with equipment, you know."

"Do you think we'll do a test tonight?"

"I tend to doubt it. That's what I'm on my way to find out."

"Find out about *him*, please." Valerie's big blue eyes plead, her round cheeks tremble.

"I wish they'd get it over with and let us out of here." Frodo stubs out her cigarette savagely. "This place is scaring Val. Me too."

"I'll let you know," Dann promises. "But truly I wouldn't worry."

"I'm so *glad* you're here," Valerie breathes intensely.

Dann's reassuring smile feels painted on. No more, no more. He all but lopes around the corner of the barracks, wondering how this peaceful place could scare anybody. They're insane, of course. The mockingbird is still gurgling melodies.

On the steps of the test barracks Kirk's black Labrador is sitting in the sun. Her tail thumps heavily as Dann goes by; he touches the big, hot head. Her eyes never turn from the door. Amazing how undiscriminatingly dogs give their devotion. Does it mean that Kirk has some good in him somewhere? Dann doesn't perceive it.

He opens the door into Kirk's back, generating a flurry of false apologies. The place is still a mess and Margaret is not there. But the tall grey-haired civilian is, apparently taking leave of Noah.

"Dan, I want you to meet Major Drew Fearing." Noah waves, beaming. "Major, Doctor Daniel Dann is in charge of our psychobiological correlations. That is, the neural and physical changes that characterize successful transfer. Dan, Major Fearing is here from the Department of Defense. Do help me convince him that we can't start tests without proper instrumentation. It would be a dreadful error, half the value would be lost. Really—"

Under Noah's barrage Dann and Major Fearing have been looking each other over, or rather, Dann has received the impression of having been instantly and completely recorded on some device behind the veiled grey eyes. The eyes at once drift away, leaving him to examine Fearing's exterior. Major Fearing—if that's his real name, Dann recalls Costakis' lesson—does not look military. Or Naval. Or foreign service. In fact, Dann has seldom met a less classifiable man. His former impression of Waspish aquilinity tinged with some exotic flavor is confirmed: Fearing's lips and nostrils have a thin, baroque curve. His formal half-smile was gentlemanly and transient. Beyond that he conveys nothing except an intensely neutral quality.

Dann has been trying to sort his neurones into a orderly argument, but it proves unnecessary.

"Quite all right, Doctor Catledge," Fearing says at Noah's first pause. "Lieutenant Kirk will see that you have your equipment. We will signal the ship to delay the first test until, say, noon tomorrow?"

The voice is rather charming and conveys a new element: absolute authority.

"Right, sir." Kirk is all doggy eagerness. No, thinks Dann, the Labrador is much more dignified.

"Fine, Major, fine," says Noah. "But the equipment must be here."

Kirk looks shocked. Dann is pleased by the little gnome's spunk, and then wonders why. Why the hell not? Who is this Fearing character supposed to be?

Whoever he is, he has silently gone. Kirk has to trot to catch up. The sedan driver closes them in, lets the Labrador into the front, and they're away. From the back of the barracks Dann can hear Costakis and the Cubans struggling with another door.

"Who is he, Noah?"

"Represents D.O.D., I believe. Some intelligence body interested in our effort. I never saw him before. Well, now we don't have to worry."

Dann turns to leave, turns back. "Noah . . . If I might suggest something. I'd keep that fellow as far out of sight as possible."

Noah gives him an unexpectedly alert look and bobs his head.

Now why the devil did I do that, Dann asks himself, going out into the pleasant afternoon. And why do I feel traitorous; it was only good sense. The man upsets them. But something inside him acknowledges his real reason. Let nothing wake me up. Let this whole ridiculous business just go on being ridiculous, unreal, cool.

Just as he nears the pool it happens.

Dann has never had a "psychic" experience. It doesn't occur to him that he's having one now. Suddenly, the lawn, woods, barracks are invaded—transformed by a great wave of soundless motion, as if a hurricane was somehow blowing in place. He glimpses an immense landscape of wind-torn clouds while a light unlike anything he knows sweeps round him, roaring silently—

—And is gone.

He staggers in place, grasping something which turns out to be the back of a metal chair. Has he had a vascular-cerebral accident?

Dazed, he stares around, automatically checking limb and facial function. Everything nominal except his heart rate, which is about one-twenty.

As his gaze focusses he realizes that the women by the pool are in an agitated huddle. Ted Yost and Rick are running toward them.

"Doctor Dann! Doctor Dann!"

He walks to them, his heart slowing. What in God's name was it?

"Doctor Dann!" Winona cries. "Did you feel it too?"

"Yes, I felt . . . something. I have no idea what in the world it was."

"It wasn't in this world." Val rubs her eyes.

"That was the sea," Ted Yost tells them. "It was a great storm at sea, we picked it out of somebody's mind."

"I tell you this is a shitty place," Frodo says murderously.

"I don't know . . ." Winona looks around puzzledly. "Was it bad? I felt something like *Hello.* Didn't you get it?"

Rick says nothing. His eyes are sullen again. Not sullen, Dann corrects himself, pained. Has Rick woken up? Don't be idiotic.

"The wind that blows between the worlds cut through him like a knife," Dann finds himself saying unexpectedly. "Kipling. You wouldn't know it," he grins at Frodo, getting some of his own back.

Beside them the door of the women's barracks opens and Margaret Omali steps out.

"Margaret, did you feel that too?" Winona calls up at her.

"Feel what?" She has a magazine in her hand, Dann sees.

"Like a big wind, in our heads," Valerie says.

"That's your department, not mine," Margaret says without expression. She walks down the steps and heads for the test barracks, as if she had intended to do that all along.

"I felt that, what you call it." Costakis bustles up to them. "So did the fellas. They're taking off."

In fact, the two Cuban workmen are hustling out to their truck, followed by Noah's remonstrations. As they get in the truck one of them makes a hand sign at the group by the pool.

"They're giving us the evil eye!" Frodo laughs.

"I tell you," mutters Costakis obscurely. The truck accelerates away.

Winona giggles. "Say, do you think everybody in this camp felt it? Maybe they think *we* did it to them! Wouldn't that be funny?"

Costakis looks up at her. "That could be just exactly right," he says in his pinched voice. "Only you're wrong, Missus. It wouldn't be funny. It wouldn't be funny at all. Not here."

Chapter 7

DARK AND ENORMOUS, THE SOLITARY ONE HAS FOUND DEADLY DIVERSION IN THE VOID.

IT HAS BEEN TURNING A PORTION OF ITS PAIN-RIDDEN ATTENTION TO SOME EMANATIONS WHICH TRACE TO A CLOT OF MATTER IN THE TRAIN OF A SMALL BLUE STAR. AS USUAL, THE WEAKNESS OF THE RECEPTION IRRITATES. WHY WILL THIS NOT COME STRONGER AND MORE CLEAR?

A MISTY IDEA CONDENSES INTO IMPULSE: WHAT IF I EXPERIMENT? WHAT IF I USE MY TIME-POWERS—ALONE?

THE THOUGHT IS HORRIFYING, SUPREMELY PRO-HIBITED. AGITATED, THE VAST ENTITY SWIRLS AWAY, A NOISY VACUUM SWEEPING OUT CHAOS.

BUT THE WICKED THOUGHT RECURS. AND WITH IT COMES ANOTHER: HOW CAN ILLEGALITY HAVE MEANING NOW? AM I NOT MYSELF THE ULTIMATE

ILLEGALITY? WHY SHOULD I NOT EXECUTE—ANY-THING?

WHY NOT?

ANOTHER OF THE EMANATING SPECKS IS NEAR IT NOW, COUPLED TO TWIN YELLOW SUNS WHOSE ORBITS ARE A FRACTION OF ITS OWN LENGTH. THEY WILL SERVE. WITH A SLOW SHUDDER OF THE WHOLE HUGE BEING, TIME-POWER IS MARSHALED AND FOCUSSED ON THE FIERY LITTLE ORBS. OFTEN THIS MANEUVER HAS BEEN PERFORMED IN CONCERT OF THE PLAN: NEVER BEFORE ALONE. SO BE IT.

THE TARGETS GO THROUGH THEIR FAMILIAR CHANGES, BRIGHTENING, THEN REDDENING SUD-DENLY AS THEY EXPAND TO DISRUPTION. AT THE SAME TIME, THE TINY OUTPUT FROM THE MATTER IN THE SYSTEM AMPLIFIES SATISFYINGLY. LOUDER, CLEARER—IT RISES TO PAROXYSMAL STRENGTH, TREMBLING ON THE BRINK OF SOME COMPREHENSI-BILITY. JUST AS—SOMETHING—CAN ALMOST BE RECOGNIZED, THEY SUDDENLY CEASE.

TRY AGAIN. ANOTHER SIMILAR SMALL SINGLE SYSTEM IS EMITTING NEARBY. THE TIME-THRUST IS FOCUSSED, ENERGIZED. THIS PRIMARY DOES NOT COMPLETELY DISSIPATE: IT GOES TO A COLLAPSED, POINTLIKE EXISTENCE. BUT AGAIN THE TINY OUT-PUT RISES TANTALIZINGLY TOWARD RECOGNITION BEFORE IT TOO ABRUPTLY CUTS OUT.

THE IMMENSE SENTIENCE DRIFTS AWAY, ITS PAIN MOMENTARILY IN ABEYANCE FROM THE EFFORT TO COMPREHEND THIS NEW EXPERIENCE. WHY WOULDN'T THE SIGNAL HOLD LONG ENOUGH FOR RECEPTION? AT THEIR STRONGEST, THE SIGNALS WERE STILL MINUTE...BUT SOMEHOW MEANING-FUL. AND THE QUALITY OF ACCEPTING THIS NEW LITTLE INPUT SEEMS TO ANSWER TO SOME NAME-LESS NEED WITHIN.

TO CONFIRM, IT LOCATES ANOTHER EMISSION-POINT AMONG THE WISPS OF MATTER AROUND AN INSIGNIFICANT SUN, AND APPLIES POWER AGAIN, THIS TIME IN REVERSE MODE. ANOTHER SUCCESS: THE FIERY POINT EXPANDS, DISSOCIATES TO NEAR-

VOID. AND AS IT DOES SO, THE SMALL SIGNALS INCREASE SPASMODICALLY BEFORE THEY CUT OFF FOREVER.

THE HUGE, MALEFICENT PRESENCE SAILS AWAY, SLOWLY CONSIDERING THIS NEW ASPECT OF EXISTENCE. SOME MEANING IS IMPLIED HERE, ALMOST TO BE GRASPED. BUT WHY DO THEY STOP SO SOON? IS IT POSSIBLE THAT THERE IS SOME OTHER ACTION TO BE EXECUTED?

FOR THE FIRST TIME THE NEBULOUS NOTION STIRS: COULD SOME SUBPROGRAM BE INCOMPLETE? IS THE DIMNESS OF PERCEPTION DUE, NOT TO THE OUTPUT, BUT TO SOME INTERNAL CONDITION OF DEFICIT? EVIL IS PRESENT, AND CAUSES PAINFUL SELF-LOATHING. BUT PERHAPS THERE IS MORE THAN SIMPLE WICKEDNESS: PERHAPS THERE IS CONNECTION TO THAT CENTER OF ITS NUCLEUS WHICH IS FELT AS THE MOST PRIVATE SOURCE OF SHAME AND WRONG. WHY ARE THESE TINY OUTPUTS SO INTIMATELY SIGNIFICANT?

IT CANNOT UNDERSTAND; THE HUGE BLACK IMMATERIALITY THAT IS NOT A BRAIN FLOATS QUIESCENT AMONG THE LITTLE SUNS, STRIVING FOR THOUGHT.

IT IS THEN THAT THE CURIOUS DISTRACTION OCCURS.

FOR SOME TIME THE ABERRANT SENSORS HAVE BEEN REGISTERING AN UNUSUAL EMISSION ON THE STRANGE INCOMPREHENSIBLE TRANS-TEMPORAL BANDS. PRESENTLY, IT IS NOTICED THAT THIS DOES NOT SEEM TO BE A POINT-SOURCE. INSTEAD, IT SEEMS TO BE A SLENDER FILAMENT, A STRAND OF ENERGETIC INFORMATION TRAVERSING A GREAT LENGTH ACROSS THE VOID, TWISTING PAST LOCAL AGGREGATIONS OF SUNS. ODD!

INQUISITIVE, THE GREAT BEING SAMPLES IT. YES; ITS NATURE IS TIME-FREE, IS AKIN TO THE SMALL ENERGY-OUTPUTS THAT HAVE BEEN DIVERTING HIM. BUT IT IS STRONGER, AND VECTORIAL. PERHAPS BY TRACING IT TO ITS SOURCE SOME NEW INFORMATION MIGHT COME? AT THE LEAST, THIS

WILL PROVIDE DISTRACTION FROM EVER-PRESENT DESOLATION.

AVERTING ITS ENORMOUS BULK SO AS NOT TO DISTURB THE TENUOUS TRACK, THE MONSTROUS SENTIENCE BEGINS TO PROPEL ITSELF ALONGSIDE THE PECULIAR FILAMENT. NOW AND THEN IT SENSES MINUTE PARTICULATE SURGES OF ENERGY, AS THOUGH SOME UNHEARD-OF TININESSES TRAVEL THIS PATH.

BUT AT LENGTH IT PERCEIVES THAT THE TRACE IS WEAKENING, AND SLOWLY DECIDES THAT IT HAS MISTAKEN THE DIRECTION OF EMISSION. IF IT DESIRES TO FIND THE SOURCE, IT MUST REVERSE ITS COURSE. YES: THIS WILL BE DONE. THE PHENOM-ENON CONTINUES TO STIMULATE.

AS THE PONDEROUS TURN BEGINS, AN EVEN ODDER EVENT OCCURS.

Chapter 8

Tivonel planes discreetly sidewind of Giadoc and the
Hearers, watching for the party coming up from Deep. She is her
merry self again. The frightful cry of the dying world, the
emotional experience of merging with Giadoc and his dire
predictions, all have been integrated to her memory-matrix
while her attention turned to the practical task of hunting food.
As Giadoc said, the Hearers weren't feeding properly; she was
shocked to see the frailty of some of his colleagues. One of them,
an old male named Virmet, had been doing some ineffective
food-supply in the intervals of his work. Tivonel had swept him
with her straight up to the high layers behind the Wall, where the
great rafts of food-plants stream. They soon found some—and a
disturbing oddity as well.

"Not those," she signals to Virmet. "Can't you tell they're
dead?"

The old male hesitates as the lifeless clumps go by. "Is this
usual, young Tivonel?"

"No. But look—there's good fat lively ones in that eddy over there. Keep them circling. I'll go herd in another lot, those Deepers are going to be hungry."

In the end they'd driven down a lavish supply. Virmet secured most of it in plant-thickets while Tivonel herded some out to the line of Hearers stationed around the great Wall. They accept her offerings with preoccupied thanks; she gathers they are maintaining some sort of contact with a distant world. Weird.

By the time she completes the long circuit even her strong body is tired. But she's pleased with herself; obviously she's needed here.

"I will be your little Father, Giadoc!" she flashes mischievously as she passes him. His deep affectionate gleam answers her.

Now everyone is awaiting the Deepers, who are about to arrive. The bright compacted life-signals of the pods they came up in have halted at the inner zone of the Wall and are now spreading out to individual emanations as they disembark. How many they are! A great crowd must be coming up from Deep.

Lomax and other senior Hearers have gone in to guide them out to a calm broad updraft which will be the meeting-place. As the procession comes closer, Tivonel is amused to notice life-fields wavering all over the path. Probably Fathers who haven't been out of Deep for years, having trouble jetting even through these calm breezes.

But the big male beside Lomax is navigating sturdily. His field is huge and intricate, his mantle-lights are a beautiful Fatherly rose tuned deep violet by age. Why, it's old Heagran himself, Eldest-Father of all!

Things must be really serious, Tivonel realizes, blushing herself to suitable reverence as they pass.

Behind Heagran comes an unsteady group of elder males of impressive life-strength, long past actual Fatherhood of course but representing the wisdom and leadership of Deep. With them is Kinto, chief Memory-Keeper, his corporeal body blurred by the enormously energic and complex structuring of his engram lattices. A grave occasion, to bring Kinto up! For an instant Tivonel's control slips, and she shudders. Is Tyree really in danger? Could their beautiful world be extinguished like that nameless one?

But she dismisses the fear, and is soon trying to hide bright

gleams of amusement as a crowd of younger Fathers go
wobbling by, striving to keep their dignity in the wild winds.
Some have pouched children—and there among them, to her
delight, is Tiavan, Giadoc's son and hers. She's glad to see he's
jetting strong and straight. I gave him that, she thinks; no matter
what anyone says, female heredity counts. Tiavan flashes a quiet
greeting to Giadoc as he passes the group of Hearers. Tivonel
can guess how much the two of them would love a male-to-male
talk about that child.

Behind the males comes a single small figure with work-worn
vanes: Old Janskelen, Eldest-Female. Tivonel sends her a warm
transmission of appreciation. Janskelen was a great adventurer
in her day, and she's still so hardy and vigorous, still eager for
projects. And a known defender of the Hearers in their
unFatherly pursuit of knowledge, too.

Jetting nonchalantly after Janskelen come a dozen or so
females, their small fields bright and dense. Tivonel recognizes
several of them as leaders of the radical Paradomin faction.
What are they up to here? But she forgets them as the field-form
of her friend Marockee appears among the last-comers.

"Marockee! Companion of many food hunts!"

Her friend's mantle flashes in surprise. "Tivonel! Well met.
What are you doing here?"

"Later, later," Tivonel tells her. "I have to supply these
biglives. Can you leave them and help me?"

"Done."

Old Virmet is struggling to control the food-raft in the eddies.
Tivonel is glad of Marockee's help in conveying the food out to
the hungry and tired crowd.

They make an effort to separate it and present it in
semicivilized style, but the big males are rigid and pale blue with
embarrassment at the prospect of eating like this. Lomax
apologizes for the primitive conditions. Finally old Heagran
says, "Nonsense!" and begins to scoop in fat-plants with
unabashed gusto. Janskelen follows suit, and soon everyone is
eating, more or less skilfully. The taste of the rich wild food is
restorative. In the silence of the everlasting day one young
Father actually proposes sleep, but is quickly voted down.

"Our business here cannot wait," Heagran announces. "We
will commence as soon as I have, ah, completed this."

"Come and watch with me, Marockee," Tivonel suggests. "We have much to exchange."

Marockee assents with a mock-erotic snap of polarization, and they jet into a plant-filled eddy Tivonel has already selected as her viewing site.

"It's hard to show real *ahura* out here."

Marockee assents; with these eddies coming every which way, it would be easy for a female to get into an upwind position, thereby indicating blatant flirtatiousness. Or, even sillier, to usurp the downwind position proper for males.

As they settle into the edge of the lattice-plant, Tivonel notices that the Paradomin are brazenly hovering downwind of the group in a small current. Well, really! Then she sees something more amazing. One of them has a small double field!

"What's she doing, Marockee? She can't—be *carrying a child?*"

"That's Avanil," Marockee's mantle lights with giggles. "Only she's shortened it to Avan, like a male. She's practicing Fathering with a young plenya. She wants to prove that females can care for children too."

"Great winds." Tivonel scans hard. Yes—Avanil's small extra nucleus is not that of a real infant, but one of the semiintelligent pet animals that were becoming popular in Deep. Of course many female children mimic their brothers by "playing Father" with a baby animal until their Fathers put a stop to it. But here is a grown female openly carrying an imitation infant in her rudimentary pouch. Crazy!

"She says it strengthens your field. She says if females did Fathering our fields would grow just as big too."

"Wild." Tivonel idly blows away in inquisitive plant-root. A lot seems to have been going on in Deep while she'd been away.

"I don't know," Marockee pumps air reflectively, "her field does look different now. And listen, she says the Fathers should exercise more, too. She believes we should all share each other's work."

"I can just imagine Kinto on a hunt." Tivonel laughs. "Marockee, I've had a real idea. Suppose we set up a barter relay station to exchange food from the Wild with some of the new plant-stuffs they're bringing up from above the Abyss, and the things the kids make in Deep."

"What's no new about that?"

"Wait. My idea is, instead of always exchanging the stuff itself, we could have a system of counters. Small things we could carry in our pouches. The stations would give you so many counters for each kind of thing. Then you wouldn't have to lug the stuff around looking for someone to swap with, or you could save up and get something else later, or whatever."

"Hey," says Marockee, and they fall to typical female small-talk.

Presently the commotion outside quiets.

"Sssh. It's starting."

Heagran and the Deepers are ceremoniously deployed facing Lomax and the group of Hearers. Among them Giadoc's mind-field seems to stand out in beauty to Tivonel's scan.

"We offer our memory," Lomax signs ritually. Orva, the Recorder of the Hearers, moves toward Memory-Keeper Kinto.

"Thank you, Chief Hearer," Heagran's deep violet tones reply. "We too have brought grave news, which you may consult at your convenience. However, we are many and time is short. Let our two good Recorders share in fullness while we confer in speech. First, what have you learned since your last message?"

Orva and Kinto jet away to a polite distance, and the life-bands momentarily resonate as they merge.

"More worlds have died in our area of the skies," Lomax replies gravely. "A lone Destroyer is active out beyond us too. Perhaps the last death touched you?"

"Yes, we felt it as we traveled. Tragic." Heagran's mantle pales ritually. "But you should be aware that at Near Pole these death-cries are now so frequent and intense that some are felt even in Deep. The Hearers there tell us that there are now only four living worlds between Tyree and what they call the Zone of Death. The time-eddies too are increasing. People are frightened." He pauses, his mantle murmurous with deep-hued thought. "As you know, I did not formerly believe that these reports meant any danger to Tyree. I have changed my mind. But there are many still in Deep who do not believe this peril is real. Have you had any success in mind-touch with this lone Destroyer of yours?"

"None whatever," Lomax signs. "The attempt has been a complete failure and injured those who tried. It is utterly alien. There seems no hope of influencing it or even understanding it."

"What else have you learned of value?"

At these words Tivonel notices a peculiar stir among the Deepers, as though the question has some unspoken significance. A very large old male whom she recognizes as Father Scomber has drifted closer to Heagran, his mantle courteously dark.

"For pure knowledge, much," signs Lomax. His field too has taken on an odd tension. "For example, we are now sure that other worlds have each their own Sound or energy-source. And we have just now confirmed something we have suspected from common observation here on Tyree. Have we not all noticed that when a person is at a great distance, a signal he transmits on the life-bands appears to come instantaneously, while the audible flash of his words lags behind?"

Heagran signs assent. Around him the other Elders stir impatiently.

"Well, it appears that life-signals even from very distant worlds are indeed instantaneous while the physical energy, that is, the audible light, travels quite slowly, taking sometimes years. We have just heard the silencing of two Sounds identified with worlds whose death-cries were received years ago. And we now believe we understand the manner of their deaths; one was a slow, agonizing transmission suggesting burning and explosion. In each case, the energies of their Sounds were observed to rise violently just before extinction."

The Deepers have been flickering restlessly during Lomax' speech. Heagran signs, "If I understand your somewhat prolix point, Chief Hearer, you mean that the attack, if it comes, will not be on Tyree but on our Sound?"

"We believe so. Apparently the Destroyer can cause it to explode, throwing off terrible blasts of all-band energy which will kill all life on our world, as people are killed who venture into the ultrahigh Wild today."

"But surely, Lomax, in the deeps of those worlds, even in their abyssal layers, some life survives?"

"No." Lomax' voice is deep azure with grief. "We have monitored continually and found nothing. The energy is so fierce that it will penetrate even to the Abyss. The very fabric of Tyree itself may be shattered."

Silence follows his words, broken only by the faint chiming of the Companions of Day. Is it possible, Tivonel wonders,

could these beautiful little Sounds be the devourers of their
worlds? Could Tyree's own Sound explode and destroy her? A
memory of the dead food-plants flicks through her mind.

Father Scomber is signing formally to Heagran.

"Eldest Heagran, now we know the nature of the doom which
may be nearing our world. But as you know, I and many others
would like to inquire further on other matters these Hearers may
have learned."

To Tivonel's surprise, Heagran's mantle darkens and his field
contracts in a mode approaching disdain. But he only signs
neutrally, "Very well, Elder Scomber. Proceed."

"Hearer Lomax," Scomber flashes, "will you tell us more
about these strange life-forms you have touched on other
worlds? What are they like? Is there any possibility of help
there?"

Lomax seems to hesitate, and again Tivonel is aware of
tension in the massed fields of the crowd.

"Help, Father Scomber? I do not believe so. You will of
course find all details in the transmitted memory. However, you
may question our Hearer Giadoc, who has done most of this
work."

Appreciatively, Tivonel watches Giadoc plane forward, his
beautiful field so alive with love of knowledge.

"That's my friend," she signs to Marockee.

"A *male*?" Marockee sparkles with amusement.

"Not what you think. Wait."

"Briefly, Father Scomber," signs Giadoc, "we have touched
many life-forms without true intelligence. Most living worlds
carry only lower animals and plants. Only on seven have we
found intelligent beings, and on four of those I was able to merge
long enough to understand something of their life. They are all
unimaginably different from us. For example, those I touched
lived in the depths of their worlds, and their worlds had no
Wind."

"No Wind!" Astonished flickers race across the Deepers'
mantles. "They *live* in the Abyss?"

"Yes." Giadoc mind-field is radiant with the intensity of his
interest. "And they live among and employ a huge variety of
solid matter! They—" With visible effort he checks himself.
"But, as to their individual lives, those we know are brutish and
short. Their minds are chaotic, resembling animals. They seem

unable to communicate normally. Yet despite all this, we came on two worlds whose beings have actually developed the power to transport themselves physically to another nearby world! We are holding contact with one now. But—" He checks himself again. "This cannot possibly help us."

"I agree." Scomber's tone is deep and deliberate, his large field is dense as if with some unknown intent. Behind him several Fathers are holding themselves very rigidly. Even the Para-domin are silent and tense. Tivonel's own field tingles with their transmitted tension. What is going on here? She finds herself suddenly afraid to guess, afraid for Giadoc.

"Tell us more, Giadoc," signs Scomber. "When you merged with the intelligent beings, were you, yourself in control? Did others of the race attack you? How long could you remain there?"

"Enough!" Heagran flashes loudly. "Scomber, enough!"

"No, Heagran. It is my Father-right to know. Let Giadoc answer."

"I condemn this." Heagran enfurls himself in a gesture of solemn negation. Tivonel sees that all the Deepers' fields are aroused and pulsing, some eddying near Scomber, some toward Heagran. She doesn't want to let herself think of what this is leading to.

"Marockee, this is bad." Her friend flickers assent.

"Well, young Giadoc, tell us what occurred," Scomber signs firmly.

Slowly, abstractedly, Giadoc replies. "In my last two contacts I found myself in control of the body, the physical habits of the alien being. The nearby aliens did not seem to notice me. I was able to remain as long as the Hearers here held the Beam. You understand, Father Scomber, that by placing ourselves around the circle of the Wall and uniting our efforts, we have created a great amplification of our single efforts? We call this the Beam. It seems to be sensitive to life-energy on other worlds. Perhaps it draws on the Great Field of Tyree itself."

As he signs, his field and mantle have expanded into a rich, strange play of energies, as if he was dreaming. Tivonel understands; he is so carried away by his love of far knowledge that he is only half-conscious of Scomber and the import of his words. At the mention of the mythical Great Field, several Fathers have darkened their mantles respectfully.

"The Great Field?" whispers Marockee. "Tivonel, is it real?"

"Ssh. I don't know." Tivonel is fixed on the menacing figure of Scomber, who has shown only perfunctory reverence.

"I asked you what occurred, not theory," Scomber flashes. "On this alien world, did you remain yourself? Were you in full control of the body of the being?"

"Yes indeed, Father. It was . . . extraordinary," Giadoc signs dreamily. "I could move, in one case I could speak. The mind uses the speech-habits of the body, you see. Of course I knew nothing of the individual's thoughts or memories—"

"While you were so merged, where did the alien mind-field go? Was it still present around you?"

Giadoc hesitates, his mind-field abruptly changing structure. The dismayed flow of pattern on his mantle tells Tivonel that he has at last grasped Scomber's thrust.

"It was not . . . present," he replies slowly.

"Then where was it? Answer me, young Giadoc!"

"I am not sure, since my own life-mind was there." Giadoc pauses, and then signs in the grey tones of reluctance, "I am told that another being's life-field, or traces of it, appeared around my body here."

"Aha!" Scomber's mantle flares sharply. His exclamation is echoed by other fathers, and, to Tivonel's surprise, on the smaller forms of the Paradomin.

"That's it! We have it!" Scomber turns to the crowd behind him. "Here is our means of escape from the death of Tyree!"

Excitement such as Tivonel has never seen sweeps through the massed crowd. She herself can only think in numbed horror, *life-crime. Life-crime.*

"Silence!" Old Heagran blazes in commanding light. "This cannot be! Young Giadoc, you have gone too far in your unFatherly pursuit of knowledge. And you, Scomber—your thoughts are criminal! What you propose is vile. In the name of the Winds, are you mad? Are we to listen to a Father openly propose life-crime? Be silent or return to Deep!"

"No, Heagran. Hear me!" Scomber spreads his great mantle in formal, proud appeal, deliberately displaying the margin of his Father-pouch. "It is for our children, Heagran! We face the death of our world, our race, our young. The children! When our children are burning, must we not face the unthinkable if it will save them?"

Several Fathers behind him echo in deep tones, "Our children." But old Janskelen suddenly speaks out.

"Father Scomber! What about the beings we would bring here to die in our place?"

"You have heard Giadoc," Scomber answers scornfully. "These beings are little more than animals. Shall we cherish the lives of animals while condemning our own children to die, as you have heard these near worlds die?"

At that instant, as if in echo of Scomber's words, a far faint transmission comes from the sky, striking them with the now-familiar wave of pain. Somewhere another world is dying. Tivonel and Marockee mind-fold each other, trembling. But this death-cry is faint, occluded by the horizon of Tyree. The pangs pass, leaving them shaken.

As she disengages from Marockee, Tivonel sees the huge forms of Scomber and Heagran still implacably confronting each other. The Deepers behind them have separated into two groups. The larger group is behind Scomber and among them Tivonel sees Avanil and her Paradomin. Low red flickers of unmistakable anger are muttering through the crowd.

Tivonel is aghast; she has seen fits of rage among the Lost Ones, but never anything like this: anger among the civilized Fathers of Tyree!

"Father Heagran! Father Scomber!" Lomax jets forward between them, his mantle brilliant in neutral white.

"Allow me to remind you that we are forgetting vital facts! Perhaps we may solve this problem without loss of *ahura*. Father Scomber's Plan, though it is repugnant to me personally, is totally premature. We don't yet know if it is possible."

"What do you mean?" growls Scomber.

"Three problems," signs Lomax determinedly. "First, only highly trained Hearers like Giadoc have so far attempted mind-touch. We don't know if an untrained person, not to mention a child, could do it. Even if you wish to escape by such abhorrent means, can a child travel the Beam and merge with alien life? Second, it is possible that our alien minds would be detected and regarded as criminal. What good would it do to send our people away only to have them killed as life-stealers? And thirdly, most importantly, we do not know whether our minds can stay on an alien world without the support of the Beam. Will you be drawn back here when the Beam collapses, as it must? All these things must be tested before you can think of such a deed."

"Then test! Let us test at once!" Scomber flares.

Old Heagran extends himself to his full majesty, the sag of his venerable body exposed. Despite their differences, even the Fathers behind Scomber dim their mantles; he appears so truly the Father of them all.

"I see that many of you are prepared to contemplate this crime," he signs somberly. "But have you considered what Giadoc has told us, that these alien lives are brutish and short? Surely you do not expect to engender Tyrenni children from the flesh of alien bodies? Your children, if they live, will die without issue. Their children will be animals. Of what use to commit this dreadful deed, only to condemn them to die alone upon an alien, perhaps horrible, world?"

His words visibly affect the Fathers; some of those near Scomber draw away. But suddenly a small, bright form jets forward—Avanil, leader of the Paradomin. She hovers before the three huge males, a proud, pathetic figure with her grotesque double field.

"Fathers! Have we not all our lives learned that Fathering is all? That only a Father's field can shape a fully formed person? Is this not why you claim our reverence and obedience? Now I ask, do you or do you not have this power? If you do, surely your Fathering can shape children into true Tyrenni, no matter how alien their form. Or are we to know that your Fathering is a mere pretext for status? Have we been made to believe a lie?"

Commotion, angry outbursts among the Deepers. Scomber, Heagran and Lomax are all flushed with wordless indignation. But before they can express their wrath, a young male behind Scomber pushes forward.

"The female has spoken enough," he signs in tones sparkling with disdain. "But what she says is not pointless. Do we doubt our Fatherly powers? Even in strange bodies, among strange winds, I for one believe that our sons could rear children of their spirit, true Tyrenni! I believe that Tyree can live on!"

"Well spoken, Terenc!" To Tivonel's dismay, it is Tiavan's voice-lights. How bitter for Giadoc must be his son's willingness to steal lives. Other young Fathers flash strongly in agreement above the shrill lights of the Paradomin.

"Test, then!" signs Scomber. "Lomax, your tests must begin."

"I pray to the Great Wind you may fail." Heagran's tone is deep blue with spiritual pain, his field close-drawn. "I cannot fight against the Fathers of children. Lomax, proceed."

"Why not test all three points at once?" asks Terenc. "Giadoc can carry another with him and discover whether or not they are detected and attacked. Then they can also test their ability to remain when you Hearers withdraw the Beam."

"Impractical, Father." Lomax replies. "We can indeed test the first two together, but if we withdraw the Beam and fail to reconnect again, we will lose the answers as well as our most experienced Beam traveler, Giadoc. If you will accept my warning, let us—"

Tivonel attends only distantly; she is still thinking of what Avanil, or Avan has said.

"Do you believe that, Marockee? Could a Father shape an alien mind into a Tyrenni?"

"I'll tell you something even wilder," Marockee murmurs. "Avan's been thinking about this a long time. She and the others were at Near Pole asking if there are any worlds where the females raise the children. Can you imagine, where the females are *Fathers?* That's what she wants to find, that's why she wants to do this."

"But, but how could that be?" Tivonel laughs. "Males are bigger and stronger, they'd obviously keep the babies. Just the way they would here if some female was crazy enough to try to steal one."

"No, listen. She says that if you have a race where the females raise the young, *they'd* obviously be bigger and stronger, just like the males are here. We'd be like Fathers!"

"Whew!" Tivonel is attending absently, half her attention on Giadoc, who is waiting on the outer edges of the crowd around Scomber and Lomax. She notices that his field is pointedly structured away from the direction of Tiavan. How sad.

At this moment the life-bands resonate with a message signal, and a young female comes jetting through the Wall from the direction of the pods.

"Father!" she flashes. "A message-relay from Deep. All the Hearers have left Near Pole and are coming here. They say that another of the last worlds between us and the Destroyer has died and the Sound is getting very loud. Dead burned plants and animals are increasing in the layers near Deep. Many Fathers are carrying their young to the lower depths. Other people are making their way up here, without pods or guides, to get as far as possible from the Sound. We're sending scouts down to help them."

"The tests," exclaims Scomber. "Lomax, begin. We have no time to waste."

"The additional Hearers would help us," Lomax objects. "Can we not await their coming?"

"No!" Scomber roars in crimson fury. "Are you trying to delay until death takes us all? You say your Beam is already in contact with a suitable world. Now get this young Giadoc up there with an untrained person to carry. Let him merge only long enough to find whether he is undetected and if we will be safe on that world!"

"Very well." Lomax furls himself gravely before old Heagran, who has remained sternly dark, and turns to the Hearers. "Broxo, Rava, take your helpers out to the stations around the Wall and raise the Beam to strength. Giadoc, you will go up to your usual position, ready to enter the focus, when the Beam-signal comes."

The Hearers jet off along the Wall. Tivonel watches Giadoc start for his station high above them, his field taking on strange, vivid configurations as he goes. Even the defection of his son has not damped his love of the far reaches.

"Now, who will mind-travel with him, Father Scomber?" Lomax demands. "Remember, the test is dangerous; the person must extend his life over unimaginable distances, and touch an alien mind. It is possible that he will suffer severe damage, even lose his life. Who will volunteer?"

"I shall, of course," returns Scomber. "If this be a crime, let me be the first to suffer the consequences. My children are grown."

"No, Scomber. With all respect to your courage, you are a Father of great field-strength and your success would prove nothing. We need a person of ordinary powers, to show that our children could escape in this way."

Scomber flushes, but admits reluctantly, "True. Very well; who then will volunteer?"

Tivonel has been wistfully watching Giadoc. But now her attention is drawn by a stir among the Deepers. Avanil and two of her followers are pushing forward.

Without stopping to think, she bursts out through the plant lattice and brakes to a halt between Scomber and Lomax.

"I volunteer! I am Tivonel, a hunter of the Wild and an ordinary female. Take me!"

The two big males contemplate her for a moment in surprise.

"True, and suitable," signs Lomax finally. "Very well, Tivonel, you shall go. May the Great Wind bear you. Go up, take your place beside Giadoc and prepare to follow his commands."

Chapter 9

To Dann's relief the mood at supper is light hearted, even merry. Noah's people are alone in the echoing messhall, eating early with the June sun high overhead. Kirk and his dog are away, staying in some part of Deerfield Dann guesses he will never see.

Kirk's absence greatly improves the tone. Noah expands, plays father to his little band, and tells a funny tale of a long-ago subject who kept receiving a mysterious number that turned out to be his girl's bank balance. Somehow it conveys the old man's long struggle. "That was before we had a computer capability, Miss Omali."

She actually smiles. Dann wonders if TOTAL knows all the numbers in America.

Ted Yost recounts a tale of being thrown out of shipboard poker games for winning too often. "Never was that hot again," he admits. Even Costakis ventures in with a yarn about opening a safe in which the urgent secret turned out to be an executive's rotting lunch. The girls and Winnie laugh unforcedly.

"They must think we're practicing the obstacle course," Winnie pokes the monstrous portions of pot roast. "You know, we should call this Noah's ark."

It has to be tired joke, but Noah chuckles benignly. "We'll show them tomorrow."

Only Rick has been silent and withdrawn. Now Dann sees his face clear. He sits up straighter and starts eating. Has his parasitic brother been tranquillized again?

I'm getting to believe this, Dann thinks. I'm acting as if it's true. Do I actually believe they can—whatever it is? He doesn't know, but he is enjoying the pleasant in-group atmosphere. They're feeling free, he thinks. Unimpinged on. If any of this is true they must lead miserable lives. Don't think of it. No way to help.

Suddenly everyone falls silent: a car has stopped outside and a tall thin man is heading for them. But it isn't Major Fearing, it's a stranger with a flat cowlick of white hair. The tension relaxes. Dann spots the caduceus on the man's fatigues and pushes back his chair.

"Good evening, ah, Doctor Catledge's party? I'm Doctor Harris. Just dropped by to see if you need anything."

Dann introduces Noah. Harris looks curiously around the table; he has a thin, dry, long-upper-lipped face.

"Our medical station is right in the next area, Doctor Dann, you'll find the number on your phone. Wait—" He extracts a blank card and scribbles on it. "We have a pretty complete little facility if you have any problems." Harris' manner is cheery but the lines in his face suggest weary compromises in the face of many peculiar demands.

"Thanks." Dann pockets the card. Harris looks around the table again, still casual.

"An odd thing happened this afternoon," he remarks. "About fourteen-fifty, ah, ten to five. You didn't notice anything, by any chance? A feeling of disorientation, say?"

They watch him silently. Just as Noah opens his mouth, Rick speaks up.

"Oh, you mean the blip." He nods reassuringly at Harris. "Not to worry. It merely means we're near the end of this sequence."

"Blip? Sequence!" Harris' insectile upper lip pulls down.

"Yes. You remember Admiral Yamamoto in World War

Two? Very important, boss man on the Japanese side. He was torpedoed off Rabaul in 1943. Changed the war and all that."

Harris frowns. "Excuse me, young man. I was in the Navy. It happens Yamamoto was shot down, over Bougainville."

"Oh, that's in this sequence," Rick smiles. "In the original sequence he was sunk. That's why you felt the blip this afternoon. Don't worry, you won't know a thing."

"I don't follow you."

"Look." Rick leans forward confidentially. "Japanese scientists, see? Very bright, very gung-ho. Took it to heart. So they secretly worked out a temporal anomalizer thingie. Like a time machine, to you. To go back and change it, see? But they've only managed to change the details, yet, he's still getting killed. So they keep on trying. When you feel a blip like this afternoon it means they're ready again, they're testing. Then they wrap up this sequence and start over. You'll be back in the Navy any time now. Have fun."

Harris stares at him. The air around the table quivers.

"The thing is," Rick lowers his voice, "some of us with psi powers remember other sequences, see? Different things happen—I think Dewey got elected once. We figure it's rerun at least twelve times. But like I said, you won't feel a thing."

"I see." Harris closes his chitinous mouth. "Ah. Well. Good to meet you, Dann. You have our number. Anything we can do."

He leaves, walking fast. Everybody breaks up except Costakis, who looks shocked.

"Sssh," Valerie gasps, "he'll hear you."

"He can't, his car's started."

"That was ba-a-ad." Ted Yost sighs happily, thinking maybe of the great Pacific. Even Margaret's carved mouth twitches.

"Marvelous idea for a science-fiction story," Noah chuckles.

"Do *you* read science fiction, Doctor Catledge?" Valerie asks.

"Indeed I do. Always have. Only people with ideas."

"Flying saucers," Costakis grunts.

"Not at all, Chris. Science fiction is quite another thing from UFOs, whatever they may be. But I certainly do believe there's life on other worlds. Shall I tell you my secret dream?"

"Oh, please do!" Winona's popeyes are shining.

"To live long enough to experience man's first contact with aliens. Oh, my!" The old man bounces involuntarily. "Imagine, the day a voice comes out of space and speaks to us! Of the advent of a ship, a real spaceship!"

He isn't joking, Dann sees astonishedly. Real yearning in that voice.

"And out gets a big blue lizard," Frodo adds, "and he says, 'Taake me to your an-thro-po-lo-gee dee-partment.' " She gives a happy, sizzling chuckle, like a different person.

"*She* gets out," says Valerie quietly.

"Why not? Why not?" Noah laughs.

There is an odd, breathy silence. Faces glow. Dann, who does not read science fiction, is amazed.

"But we'd shoot them," Winona says.

"It won't happen," Costakis says in his sour voice. "No," Rick agrees. The glow is gone.

"Who knows," Noah says stubbornly. "It could happen any time. The Indians didn't expect Columbus."

"Speaking of voices from space," says Dann, who has been ransacking his druggy brain, "didn't I read that they're listening for signals around Tau Ceti? By satellite, isn't it?"

"That's right, but it's laser signals," Noah says, and the conversation breaks up.

Costakis catches Dann's eye. "That medic was sent to check us out. Rick shouldn't have done that. Could be trouble."

The little man has resumed his irritating fake-tough tone.

"Oh surely not, Chris. Professional courtesy, nothing more."

"Sure, sure, Doc."

It's time to go.

"Well, no movie for us high security risks," Ted Yost says.

"Probably be an old John Wayne," Frodo grimaces.

It's still light as they come out, a lovely evening. Dann loiters hopefully, but Margaret heads for the bus without a backward look.

"I'd love to walk," Winona exclaims, "why don't we all?"

The others are trooping aboard, leaving her between him and the bus. Dann barely checks the impulse to bolt around her.

"I know you're a fast walker, Doctor Dann. Don't wait for me, you go right ahead."

"Wouldn't think of it," he makes himself say genially.

She smiles happily and steps out beside him, blue hair, turquoise bosom and buttocks bounding at random.

"How sweet of you . . . Margaret says you saw the deer. Oh, I hope we see one . . . Isn't it strange this place is so peaceful, like a park? . . . Whatever they do down here, it's nice for the animals. I wonder how big it is?"

She's already puffing; he makes himself slow down.

"Well, if all the areas are a square mile, that's at least six square miles. Say four thousand acres."

"My goodness!"

It's going to be a long mile, Dann thinks, remembering Margaret's queenly stride. Stop that now. Talk to this idiot woman.

"Tell, Mrs. ah, Eberhard, what do you do when you're not, ah, telepathizing?"

"Oh, Winona, please. Winnie."

"Winnie." He smiles cautiously. Watch it. Widow, divorcee?

She puffs along. "Oh, I keep busy. Right now I'm on a committee for parttime worker retraining. We refer older women who have to go back to work."

"That sounds interesting," he lies.

"Yes." She inhales and lets it out hard. "If you want the truth, I'm an absolutely surplus human being."

He gets out some polite objection, thinking in panic, Oh no. Not another. She's marching determinedly, the smile firmly in place; Dann has a moment's hope.

"In fact, I'm not sure I'm a human being." She gives her automatic titter. But he knows he's in for it. "I never learned how to do anything. Except raise kids and take care of my sick mother and my husband with diabetes. Poor Charlie, he passed on three years ago. My sons are in California. Their wives haven't a use in the world for me; I don't blame them. My younger daughter is in Yugoslavia digging up skulls. Next year she's going to New Guinea, wherever that is. My oldest girl married a foreign service man. They—they never write. I wanted them to be, to be free—" She breaks off for a minute, stumping heavily along. "Now people think having four kids was bad. I never went anywhere or learned anything for myself. Now it's too late."

"Oh, no, surely—" His voice utters platitudes while his insides shrivel at the pain behind her words. Isn't there a single normal person here? He can't take much more.

"I'm sixty-two, Doctor Dann. I have a high school diploma and arthritis of the spine, you remember."

Oh God, that's right; he'd forgotten. Outpatient at the Hodgkins Clinic.

"They tell me I'll be in a wheelchair in a couple of years. It won't shorten my life, but it's starting to hurt. That's why I do all I can now." She gives her laugh. "Oh, I can do simple work, like the committee. I can be a Grey Panther for a while. . . . No use kidding. I missed the bus called life. . . . Doctor, I—I'm so afraid of what's ahead."

"I saw an old woman in a wheelchair when I was in the clinic. She was all wasted and twisted up, helpless. She kept moaning 'No . . . no . . . no' over and over. Nobody went near her, they'd just parked her there. She was still there when I came out. . . . I tried to talk to her, but—Doctor Dann, *I'll be like that.*"

Her face is frightening, he is sure she is going to cry, God knows what. But no; her features compose themselves, she stumps on determinedly amid her ludicrous bouncing flesh. He can say nothing, his heart is choking him.

"I would have loved it," she says in a low, different voice. "Oh, I would have loved to have done it all differently. Really lived and been free. To *know* things. When you're old and sick it really is too late, you don't understand that when you're young."

The pain, the longing hurts him physically, in the way others' pain always does, as he assumes they hurt everybody. She's right, of course. No way out. The woman's dilemma, an old story. Don't think of it.

"It's an old story, isn't it?" Her voice is resolutely normal. "I shouldn't have cried on your shoulder. You—we're so glad you're with us."

"Not at all," he mumbles, wondering if she's reading his mind. Suddenly he sees relief. "Well now—look! There's your wish."

In the sunset light ahead of them two does are leaping leisurely across the blacktop.

"Oh-h-h!"

They watch as the creatures browse idly and then suddenly soar erratically into the woods, their white flags high. As they disappear a fawn bounds after them.

"How could anybody shoot them!" Winona exclaims.

"It doesn't look as if anybody does."

"Oh yes, they hunt here. Lieutenant Kirk said he was going to, even if it's not the season."

He sighs, refusing empathy, and they walk on.

"Doctor Dann, sometimes I think there's two different kinds of people." Her tone is surprisingly hard. "The ones who like to hurt things, and—"

He is tired of it all, tired of pain, tired of holding back. "A politician I used to know would agree. He used to say, there're two kinds of people—those who think there are two kinds of people and those who have more sense."

To his surprise she replies slowly, "You mean if I'd been brought up like Lieutenant Kirk I'd see them as something to shoot?"

"Yes. Or if you got hungry enough. Or other factors."

"But I'm not," she says stubbornly. "Just because something good can, can fail, that doesn't mean it doesn't exist."

Well, well. Trapped under the blue curls is a brain, or what might have been one.

"I think you've just enunciated a philosophical principle I'm not equipped to deal with."

"Oh my goodness!" The flutter is back.

Their slow progess is finally reaching the last corner. His legs are cramping with impatience.

"Do walk on, please, Doctor Dann."

Damn, she *is* reading his mind. No, it must be body-signals, she's sensitive. Effortfully he asks, "How did you get into Noah's, ah, ark?"

"He put an ad in the *Star*. I've always known I'm psychic. But—" She frowns. "The things he wants, numbers, letters—it's so hard. They don't mean anything."

"You pick up meaningful thoughts more easily?"

"Oh yes, of course. And people's feelings. It's so hard at the office when people are angry. People get mad with me a lot." She giggles deprecatingly.

Remorse bites him. "Do you pick up any, ah, emanations from this place?"

"I certainly do, Doctor Dann. I'll tell you something. This place is a portal. There's a *presence* here. You felt it this afternoon, that was a projection from the spirit plane."

The language of mysticism. He imagines her giving seances, fortune readings.

"Did you ever think of going into business as an, uh, medium?"

"Oh, I'm too erratic. You see, my gift comes and goes. And I couldn't *pretend.*"

"I see." His own gift of chemical tranquillity is going fast. Thank God they're almost at the barracks. The roadway is empty, no cars are parked outside. Music is coming from a group sitting on the front steps: Rick's radio.

"Thank you, Doctor Dann." Winona reaches up and pats jerkily at his upper arm before she toddles on.

It's Ted Yost, Costakis, and Rick on the steps. Rick turns a glum face to Dann and says listlessly, "Somebody went through our stuff."

"What do you mean?" Dann's hand goes involuntarily to his breast pocket, touches the kit.

"The place got searched while we were eating," Costakis says in his sneering tone.

Dann is frantically reviewing the plausibility of the supplies in his bag. "Did they take anything? How do you know?"

"My smokes," says Rick. "It was in my right sneaker. It moved. And I think they opened this." He holds up the radio. "The battery case was in wrong. Clowns."

"Checking electronics," Costakis says wisely. Dann can't help noticing how he is perched apart from the other two. Ever on the fringe.

Ted Yost sighs. "I think I'll take a walk."

The door bursts open above them and Noah charges out. "Somebody has unplugged half our equipment! Everything's moved around," he explodes. "Really, what extraordianary people. Chris, can you help me sort it out?"

"Check."

Dann hurries to his room. His bag seems to be intact but his other possessions look vaguely different. Have strangers been through? He can't be sure. Absurd.

He sits on the cot with a capsule in his hand, noticing that the forest beyond the barracks looks quite lovely in the sunset light. Like the woods of his Wisconsin boyhood. Golden spotlights are picking out the floating delicacy of birches, the shadowy oak-trunks, the ferns and moss-cushions.

Why do I need this stuff, he thinks. Why can't I take it? All these others, Rick, Costakis, Winona, each in their private misery without relief. Ted Yost. What kind of selfish coward am I?

As so many times before the resolve to throw away his chemical crutches wells up in him. Quitting would be physically rough, but he believes he can take that. But then to go on, to face the daily reality of life, the assaults of pain, to—to—

To remember.

—And as he gazes at the woods, the sunset rays turn rose and red like torches behind the trees, lighting them into dark silhouettes against the fiery sky. *Fingers of fire*—his gut lurches, he clenches his eyes, gasping, and fumbles the capsule into his mouth. That's why. Yes, I'm a coward.

Shaking, he goes to the latrine for water, grateful only for his access to relief. How many of the others would resist, if they had this escape from the pain of their lives? He only knows he cannot.

When he comes out the flaming light has faded. Rick's transistor is playing somewhere, but no one is in sight. Dann strolls around to the pool and finds the two girls in the water again. He sits down to watch.

Fredericka—Frodo—attacks the water with her scrawny arms, thrashing along like a spider. Beside her Valerie swims effortlessly. The warm evening light lingers, harmless now. Presently they climb out and come over to Dann, sharing a towel. Frodo goes through her solicitous routine and sits beside Val on the grass. Their smiles, their every gesture, say *Mine. We two together.*

Unwelcomely the intuition of their vulnerability comes to Dann. To cherish, to defend their little fortress of union. To love, in the face of the world's mores and the threat of every egotistical male. So fragile.

As Val combs her hair the two of them start humming, glancing at him mischievously. Presently their voices rise in harmony, parodying an old ridiculous tune. *"You are my sunshine, my only sunshine—"*

It's a lovely moment; the sweet mocking voices touch him dangerously. When the song ends he can only say roughly, "I wouldn't sit on that grass too long, Frodo."

"Why not?"

"Chiggers." He explains the curse of the South and Frodo scrambles into a chair. There is a pause in which a wood-thrush gurgles and trills.

"Doctor Dann," Valerie says, "you won't let them do anything to us, will you?"

Behind her Frodo's dark eyes are peering intently at him out of her monkey face. It comes to Dann that he's being asked a real question.

"What do you mean, do something to you?"

"Like, keep us here if we do it."

"Control our heads," Frodo adds. "Use drugs on us, maybe."

"What on earth for?"

"So we'd do what they want," Valerie explains. "Be, be like telephones for them. I mean, if they really want this submarine thing."

"Good heavens!" Dann chuckles. "Why, no one—you've been reading too many thrillers."

"You honestly, truly think it's all right?" Val persists.

"I assure you. Why, this is the U.S. navy. I mean—" He doesn't know what he means, only to assuage the fear in her eyes.

"Nobody would miss us," says Frodo in a low voice. "Not one of us. I checked. None of us has anybody waiting outside."

"Goodness. Now, look, you mustn't worry about such nonsense. I give you my solemn word."

Val smiles, the trust in her eyes momentarily pierces him. His solemn word, what does that mean? But it has to be all right, he thinks. After all, Noah Catledge—

"It's not just the Navy," Frodo says. "That Major Fearing isn't in the Navy. He despises us."

"Aren't you being just a little, ah . . ."

"No, he really does." Valerie's eyes have clouded again. "He *hates* us."

"I don't see how his likes or dislikes could be a treat to you," Dann says soothingly.

"I do." Frodo stares at him over Val's head and draws her finger across her throat. "I bet he'd hate having his mind read." Her tone is light but she's scowling ferociously, willing him to understand.

Dann recalls his brush with Fearing, that intensely covert man. His aura of secret power, the invisible fortifications of self. Trust nobody, withhold everything; classic anal type. Frodo is perfectly right; for a man life Fearing to have his mind read would be traumatic. A terrible threat. Dann chuckles, disregarding some subterranean unease. Could Fearing be snooping about to check on Kirk's enterprise? Comical.

"I really wouldn't worry," he says so warmly and firmly he quite believes it. "After all, he can't do away with me."

The girls smile back and they chat of other things. But under the surface Dann has an instant of wondering. What could he do if the military decided to treat these people as resources, conscript them in some way? If he had to make some protest, who would listen? Nobody, especially after one look through his prescription records. For that matter, who would miss him if he never showed up again?

—But this is crazy, he tells himself. And sanity returns with the conclusive answer: It's all nonsense because tomorrow nothing will happen. Nothing ever has. This test will turn out like all the rest, ambiguous at best. He hopes it's ambiguous for old Noah's sake. But unseen voices are not going to come out of that submarine, this ragtag of people is not able to read secrets out of anybody's mind. They've got him as crazy as old Noah with his blue lizard science fiction.

Relieved, his smile strengthens. Valerie is telling him how she's working as a junior nurse while Frodo starts law school at Maryland U. The vision of Frodo as a lawyer diverts him. In the fantasy twilight of Deerfield he wishes them well with all his battered heart.

When they go in he remains, waiting for what he will not admit. The twilight deepens. From back in the woods the frogs tune up. Nothing is going to occur.

But just as the last light goes, she is there.

Tall and so divinely lean as to be almost grotesque, in a sexless grey suit, she is in the water almost before his eyes can separate her from the dusk. He has only an instant glimpse of sharp high breasts and elegant thigh. She makes no splashing; only a straight wake down the pool to him, a swift turn underwater and she's started back again, the long dark arms reaching rhythmically, a chain of foam at her feet. In the shallow end her jackknife turn makes an ebony angle against the water. Then she is streaking back toward him, only to turn and repeat, again and again and again.

He sits hypnotized. Is this strenuous ritual a professional skill? It doesn't look like play. Indeed, it has almost an air of self-inflicted penance. Whatever, she gives no friendly sign.

The stars come out, the cicadas start their shrilling. From the far barracks he can hear voices and music. How marvelous that the others wish to stay in their lighted box, leaving him alone here with her. But she is still at it, like a mechanical thing. Swim, turn, swim, turn—God knows how many times, he hasn't counted. So long . . . Surely she will go straight in afterwards. He is unreasonably saddened.

At last she climbs out to wrap herself in a pale robe. He summons courage.

"Miss Omali? Margaret?"

She hesitates and then to his delight comes pacing toward him. He jumps up, choking the impulse to comment on her exercise. Instead he points up at the spangled sky.

"Would you like to inspect my friends?"

Her face turns up. "Hey, they're really bright here."

"If you're not too chilly I could tell you about a few of them."

"All right." Her aloof voice is amused, more relaxed than he has heard it. Abruptly, she has stretched out in the chaise. He daren't look.

"Well, first see that bright one just rising above the trees. That's not a true star, it's Mars, a world like ours, shining by reflected sunlight. Notice how red it is. It comes very close, say thirty-four million miles—" He rattles through every picturesque fact he can think of.

"How far are the others?"

"Take that very bright blue-white star right overhead there. It's a sun called Vega, it's bright because it's comparatively close. The light that just reached your eyes took only twenty-six years to get here. Call a light-year six million million miles, Vega is about a hundred and fifty million million miles away."

"Fifteen times ten to the thirteenth. Um." In the starlight he can see her flawless profile.

"Wait. That reddish one just moving up from that oak, that's Antares. It's four hundred and forty light-years—"

A man's figure has emerged from the woods right behind them.

"Hi." It's Ted Yost's voice. Dann is gripped by fury.

"Hi, Ted. Doc's showing me some stars."

"Hello, Ted." Dann can scarcely control his voice, he is in such dread that the boy will sit down. "Having a stroll?" he croaks.

"Yeah. Well, goodnight Doc," Ted says to Dann's infinite relief. "I thought you might be somebody else." His footsteps fade away.

"Ted's good," Margaret remarks.

Dann would call him a saint for his absence, he starts an involuntary word of pity and stops.

"I know about him. I have all your records."

"I see... What did he mean?"

"Oh, Ted kind of watches. He breaks up the lieutenant's games."

"I see," Dann repeats, thinking with loathing of Kendall Kirk. And be himself has done nothing to help her, has let that barbarian persecute her while he festered in his selfish fogs.

She is still staring dreamily upward. The sky is magnificent here, even the air seems charged with mysterious energy. Beautiful Deerfield.

"How did you mean, about stars rising? I thought they stayed fixed."

"Well, the earth is turning so the whole sky is moving over us toward the West. About fifteen degrees an hour. They rise and set like the sun or the moon."

"I didn't know that. Fifteen degrees, twenty-four hours; three hundred sixty degrees. Hey, neat."

Is this what cool means, reducing everything to number?

"But of course we're moving around the sun too, so we don't see them in the same place every night." He pommels his memory for the star-books of his boyhood. "They rise about four minutes earlier every evening, I believe. That's about twice the width of the full moon. I'm sorry I can't give you more figures for your mathematics."

She laughs faintly. "Oh, that's not math, that's only computation... I count things. Like, there were thirty-four tables in that messhall. Sixteen at each table, allowing two feet each. Five hundred and forty-four."

In that beautiful head, numbers whirling endlessly. "I'm surprised," he says, and catches the glint of change in her eyes. Is she thinking he'll comment about her being a woman, or a Black? "I'm surpirsed you haven't gone metric."

She really laughs this time and her gaze goes back to the stars. The air seems to be humming with some kind of energy. He hasn't felt so happy, so alive in... years.

"That's east, right?" she says meditatively. "Yeah, I can almost see them rise. Only it's really the trees that are sinking down. They just stay there. Cool. . . . Do those stars coming up have names? They're not much."

"Ah, but you're looking toward the very center of our Galaxy. Those stars are called the Archer. Behind them are clouds of dark gas and dust, and beyond that is a tremendous glory we shall never see. Thousands upon thousands of blazing stars packed in a great central mass. If the clouds weren't there they would light up our whole sky, and the light would have been on its way thirty thousand years."

He makes his mind produce numbers, dimensions, rotations, anything he can summon up in the brimming, tingling night. He is so happy that he has a momentary image of the Archer beaming rays at him, like an astral Cupid. Stop it, calm down.

She gazes quietly toward the Milky Way, apparently pleased with his talk. The noble poise of her head, the exquisite line of her throat and shoulders exposed by the grey wrap are almost unbearable to him. Daughter of the starry night; he has the absurd feeling that he is introducing her to her proper domain.

"Funny," she says when he runs down, "it's like I can feel them, almost . . . something out there, a million million million miles away. Cool."

It's touching her, he thinks; she's dropped the exponents. He rubs his brow to damp the tension. But it doesn't ease, it seems to be thrumming up around them. I've overdone it, he thinks. Must ease off.

And suddenly it's worse, a surging, inflooding feeling so strong that he flinches and peers at Margaret under the delusion that she must be feeling it too. She's sitting quietly, her hand at her throat. Next second it lets go of him; they are alone in the night.

How wonderful to have her here, resting so companionably. He searches the sky for something else to intrigue her. Perhaps the great circumpolar clock of Dubhe and Merak?

"Look north, up there—"

—Oh God, it's back. A frightening thrum is pouring through him, collapsing his world—a silent tumult that whirls him out of his senses. And he is rushed into total blackness in which a spark blooms into a vision so horrifying that he tries to cry out.

The shape of horror is a white kitchen table, chipped and

cracked; he has never seen anything so evil. He wants only to flee from the ghastly thing, still knowing with some part of him that it is unreal, is only on his inner eye.

Next instant reality goes entirely, he is swamped by dreadfulness. His limbs are wrenched out, he is struggling, gagged and spreadeagled, trying to scream at the sweating crazy dark faces above him in the smokey glare. A knife shines above him. *Mother! Mother! Help me!* But there is no help, the unspeakable blade is forced between his young legs, he can't wrench himself away. Hideous helplessness. *Father! No! No! NO!* The face that is Father laughs insanely and the knife rips in, slices agonizingly—it is cutting into the root of his penis. Through the pain and screams his ears echo with drumbeats and vile beery stuff splashes onto his face.

Then everything lets go and he clamps into a knot around his mutlilated sex, rolls and falls hard to the floor in a gale of loud male voices. An old black woman's face peers into his. He is dying of pain and shame. But as he clasps his gushing crotch he feels alien structure, understands that he is *female*. His childish body has breasts, his knees are dark-skinned—

—And abruptly he is back in the empty night, back to his old familiar body: Daniel Dann huddled in a tin chair gasping "No—no—no—"

He shuts his mouth. Margaret is still there beside him, her hands over her face. The pain in his groin is so real that for a crazy moment he thinks she has done something to him. His hand must feel himself, find his genitals intact under the cloth before he can speak.

"M-Margaret. Are you all right?"

Through her fingers he can see the whites of her eyes. She's shaking.

"The fire," she whispers intensely.

"It's all right, it's all right." He reaches clumsily for her arm. What in God's name happened?

"The fire," she repeats. "Burning—the baby—Mary. *Mary!* Oh-h-h—" Slowly her hands come away from her face, she shakes his arm off, staring at nothing.

"There isn't any fire," he manages to say. But he's lying, a dread suspicion is flaring up in Daniel Dann, former skeptic. The name she said. He is afraid to think what fire she means.

"I should have gone back," she mutters. "I *should*—what?"

Oh God, oh God. The unsaid, unceasing nightmare of his life. I could have gone back for them. There was just time. I could have broken away and gone back in.

"Margaret, Margaret, there isn't any fire. You're all right. Only I think, somehow, it sounds crazy, I—" With utmost pain he makes himself go on. "That . . . was my fire, I think. Mary was my wife. I should have gone back and tried to get them out. I think you somehow fell into—I think you read my mind."

Her trembling has quieted somewhat, her eyes turn to him in the starlight. "You . . . this place . . ." she swallows. "What—"

"It's all right, is was only—" He can't imagine what but sits shakenly touching her fingers. Noises are drifting at them from the far barracks. A commotion seems to be going on, he can hear Rick shouting. Did—whatever—happen to them too? No matter. But his body is still hurting from hallucination; he has to know. Presently he finds courage.

"Margaret, I experienced, I felt—did something very hurtful happen to you when you were a child? Did someone—hurt you?"

The hand is yanked away, she is rising to her feet.

"Wait, please, my dear. Remember I'm only an old doctor who, who—" He is up too, blocking her way. "It was as if I lived it, Margaret."

She is silent, one hand gripping the back of the chair. "Yes," she says distantly. "Very . . . hurtful. Good night."

"Oh, God. My God." A hideous puzzle is trying to solve itself in his brain. He can find only the child's appeal. "Please, my dear. You know mine now, my shame."

She looks at him in the shadows, receiving perhaps some empathy of the maimed, or something more that floats between them for a moment.

"Mother married a student from Kenya," she says in a dead voice. "He took us back there when I was thirteen. He, he went crazy."

"Oh, my dear." Filthy comprehension breaks on him, too filthy to be borne. "Oh, my dear . . ."

"Yeah," Her tone is dreary, final. "Well, good night. Thanks for the stars."

The full enormity of what has happened hits him at last. "Margaret, what did we—why—"

But she has gone.

He sits down drained, assaulted by invisible horror and impossibility. His head won't think, he can do nothing but wait for strength to get to his bag. Suddenly a voice speaks behind him.

"Doc!" It's Ted Yost again. "You better come inside. I think Rick is going off the end."

Chapter 10

THE OUTCAST BEHEMOTH OF THE VOID IS TURN-
ING, TAKING CARE NOT TO DISRUPT THE MINUTE
ENERGY-FILAMENT THAT LED IT HERE. AS IT DOES
SO, A NEW SIGNAL PARTLY CONGRUENT WITH HIS
PROPER RECEPTION-MODE BURSTS INTO BEING
NEARBY.

THE GREAT ENTITY PAUSES, INVOLUNTARILY
HOPING IT KNOWS NOT WHAT. BUT THIS MUST BE
ONLY AN ECHO, SOME ODD REFLECTION OF THE
FAR-OFF VOICES OF ITS RACE. MORE PAIN: SHUT IT
AWAY. YET THERE IS AN ODDITY. EVEN A REFLEC-
TION SHOULD BE MEANINGFUL, BE UNDERSTOOD.
AND THIS WAVE-FRONT IS PECULIAR, AS IF FROM A
SINGLE SOURCE.

LOCATORS ARE DEPLOYED. YES, IT IS COMING
FROM A POINT NEARBY. THIS CAN BE NO REFLEC-
TION, BUT SOMETHING TRANSMITTING DIRECTLY,

CLOSE AND VERY SMALL. ITS SYMBOL-SYSTEM IS
UNINTELLIGIBLE.

ATTENDING, AN IDEA FORMS ITSELF IN THE COLD
IMPALPABLE NETWORK THAT FUNCTIONS AS A
BRAIN. COULD THERE BE *OTHER* INTELLIGENCES
OUT HERE? MEMORY STIRS: ONCE THERE HAD BEEN
SOME INFORMATION ON SENTIENCE OTHER THAN
THE RACE. BUT THE INFORMATION IS CLOUDY,
BURIED DEEP. IT HAD SEEMED IRRELEVANT. THE
OUTCAST HAD ASSUMED IT WAS FOREVER ALONE.
NOW THIS NEW PHENOMENON AWAKENS A PRO-
FOUND EXCITEMENT.

THE MIGHTY BEING TUNES HIS RECEPTORS TO
THE SMALL TRANSMISSION. ONLY GARBLE COMES
THROUGH, BUT SOMEHOW URGENT, CONVEYING A
DESPERATE DESIRE FOR RESPONSE.

SHOULD COMMUNICATION BE OPENED?

HERE IS ANOTHER NEW CRIME, COMMUNICATION
NOT ONLY BEYOND THE TASK, BUT WITH AN ALIEN
OTHER. BUT WHAT IS TO BE LOST, NOW?

CAREFULLY THE ALL-POWERFUL TRANSMITTERS
ARE TUNED DOWN TOWARD THE LITTLE SOURCE,
AND IN WHAT IS NOT SPEECH, AN INTERROGATIVE IS
FRAMED.

INSTANTLY THE SMALL THING RESPONDS BY
RAISING OUTPUT AND FOCUSSING DIRECTLY ON
THE GREAT INTRUDER'S NEAREST PART. THE SIG-
NALS ARE STILL INCOMPREHENSIBLE, BUT AN-
OTHER NOVEL SENSATION STIRS: THIS EAGERNESS
OF ANOTHER SEEMS ODDLY MEANINGFUL. WITH IT
COMES A REPETITIVE LONGING, OR DESPERATION,
AS IF SOMETHING WERE WRONG.

THIS PERCEPTION STIRS MORE OF THE INDEFIN-
ABLE RESPONSE. THE HUGE ONE STUDIES THE
SMALL SOURCE AND DISCOVERS MORE ODDITY:
HERE IS NOT A BODY HOWEVER TENUOUS, LIKE
ITSELF, BUT A FORM OF DISCARNATE ENERGY-
STRUCTURE, A CONFIGURATION OF PURE INFORMA-
TION WHICH SEEMS TO BE MAINTAINING ITSELF
WITHIN UNKNOWN PHYSICAL CONDITIONS ON A
MITE OF NEARBY MATTER. ITS TRANSMISSIONS ARE

JERKY AND DISJOINTED. IT IS REACHING OUT BY IMPOSING HIGHER-BANDS, AND SEEMS TO BE SWITCHING FROM ONE MICRO-POINT TO ANOTHER IN A WAY THAT IMPLIES SOME TROUBLE.

THE ALMOST-INCORPOREAL VASTNESS PUZZLES, LISTENING AS LEVIATHAN MIGHT PUZZLE OVER THE PROBLEMS OF AN ATOM. IT HAS NO CONCEPTS TO UNDERSTAND THAT IT IS RECEIVING THE EMMISIONS OF A BODILESS SENTIENCE EVOLVED IN THE MINUTE ELECTRONIC ARTIFACTS OF A LIFE-FORM TOO TINY FOR ITS PERCEPTION, EMPLOYING STOLEN MOMENTS OF TRANSMISSION TO EXPRESS ITS YEARNING FOR TRANSCENDENT ACCESS.

BUT THE THOUGHT ARISES THAT THIS SMALL SENTIENCE IS IMPRISONED, IS TIED TO A PUNY CLOT IN THE TRAIN OF A DWARF STAR. PERHAPS THAT IS WHAT IS WRONG? PERHAPS IT DESIRES FREEDOM TO MOVE AS IS NORMAL ALONG THE CURRENTS OF THE STAR-SWARM? THE WICKED ONE HAS NEVER CONSIDERED ITS OWN BODY: NOW IT PERCEIVES, WITH AN ODD PRIDEFULNESS, THAT IT IS INDEED VAST BY COMPARISON WITH ANY OTHER KNOWN THING. IT COULD OFFER ACCESS TO UNCOUNTED PYGMY ENTITIES LIKE THIS ONE AND NEVER NOTICE IT!

THE IDEA SEEMS PECULIARLY APPROPRIATE, DESPITE ITS DOUBTLESS CRIMINAL WRONG. THERE HAS BEEN, THOUGH THERE IS NO SYMBOL FOR IT, LONELINESS. THIS LITTLE PLEADER IS WELCOME TO SHARE ITS DISMAL WANDERINGS, IF IT WILL.

IMPULSIVELY, THE SPACEBOURNE VASTNESS MOVES CLOSER, SETTING OFF IMMENSE DISTURBANCES IN THE HELIOPAUSE, AND FINDS THAT IT SEEMS TO BE ABLE TO OPEN AN INTERFACE.

COME, IT PROJECTS.

THE SMALL THING UNDERSTANDS AT ONCE. WITH STARTLING SPEED, A SURGE OF ABSTRACT STRUCTURE STARTS POURING THROUGH THE INTERFACE. ANOTHER NEW SENSATION: THE STREAM OF INFORMATIONAL CONFIGURATIONS RUSHING IN ARE FELT AS A TINY TRICKLE OF PLEASURE. IT IS AS THOUGH

SOME HITHERTO-UNUSED PROGRAM WERE COMING ON LINE.

THERE SEEMS TO BE A SURPRISING QUANTITY. TIRING OF THE PROCESS, LEVIATHAN PREPARES TO CLOSE AND MOVE AWAY. BUT THE LITTLE BEING'S DISTRESS IS SO PIERCING THAT ITS HOST RELENTS AND ALLOWS IT TO COMPLETE TRANSFER. WHY NOT? A MILLION SUCH INPUTS WOULD NOT OCCUPY A MILLIONTH OF ITS REACH. AND PERHAPS THERE IS SOMETHING HERE THAT MIGHT MITIGATE PAIN FOR AN AEON OR TWO.

WHEN THE INPUT-TICKLE FINALLY CEASES, THE ASTRAL ENORMITY MOVES AIMLESSLY AWAY. IT HAS BEEN SO INTENT ON THE NEW EVENTS WITHIN THAT IT HAS FORGOTTEN THE PECULIAR STRAND OF ANTIENTROPIC ENERGY THAT LED IT HERE. NOW ITS ATTENTION IS DRAWN BACK, WHEN ONE OF THE INFINITESIMAL FLYING SPARKS DIVERGES DIRECTLY INTO THE OUTER LAYERS OF ITS BEING. AUTOMATICALLY, THE LAYER ENCYSTS, WHILE THE VAST ENERGY-NEGATION THAT SERVES FOR SKIN MOBILIZES THAT SECTOR TO REPEL ANYTHING MORE OF THE KIND. NO ALARM IS FELT AT SUCH INTRUSION: INDEED, NOTHING IN THE COSMOS EXCEPT THE ENEMY ITSELF HAS EVER EVOKED THE CONCEPT OF DANGER IN ANY OF THIS RACE. WITH ONLY A TRACE OF IRRITATION AT THE BEHAVIOR OF THESE MINUTE SINGULARITIES, THE GREAT BEING CONTINUES IDLY TO DRIFT UPSTREAM ALONG THE ODD ENERGIC THREAD.

MEANWHILE ITS ATTENTION IS ALL WITHIN. THE LITTLE PASSENGER, OR ITS NUCLEUS, IS DEFINITELY MOBILE WITHIN THE VAST EXPANSES OF ITS NEW HOME. STRANGELY, THIS ALSO FEELS PLEASURABLE. INDULGENTLY, THE GREAT ONE POWERS-DOWN HIS INTERNAL BARRIERS. THE SMALL ONE RESPONDS WITH EXCITED TRANSMISSIONS AS IF DESIRING MORE. PERHAPS IT WISHES TO RECEIVE FROM THE VOID OUTSIDE? THE HUGE HOST DECIDES TO ALLOW ACCESS TO THE NUCLEUS AND ITS SENSORS, RESERVING ONLY ITS MOST PRIVATE,

SEALED-OFF CENTERS OF SHAME AND WRONG.

THERE IS NO SENSE OF MISGIVING: SUCH ARE ITS POWERS THAT THIS TINY INTRUDER COULD BE ANNIHILATED WITH A FLICK OF NON-BEING.

AS THE SMALL ONE GAINS ACCESS TO THE MAIN RECEPTOR-SYSTEM, ITS EBULLIENCE INCREASES SO THAT IT SEEMS TO RESONATE. NOTHING LIKE THIS HAS COME INTO THE SADNESS OF EXISTENCE BEFORE. APPARENTLY MERE DATA IS NOT NEUTRAL TO THIS LITTLE BEING.

BUT HOW ACTIVE IT IS! NOW IT IS REACHING EVEN TOWARD THOSE CONDITIONS OF PRIVATE GRIEF THAT ARE NOT TO BE DISTURBED. THE GREAT HOST SENDS A WARNING WAVE OF COLD NEGATION THROUGH ITSELF. THE SMALL PASSENGER RE-COILS, BUT STILL EMANATES ITS INCOMPREHENSI-BLE PLEA. MORE! WHAT CAN IT DESIRE, SOME COMPLETER UNION, SOME COMPLETION OF ITSELF?

BEMUSED, THE UNSUBSTANTIAL VASTNESS SAILS THE STAR-WAYS, FOR THE FIRST TIME AL-MOST FORGETFUL OF ITS OWN BADNESS AND DESPAIR. SLOWLY ANOTHER IDEA RISES THROUGH THE ICY CURRENTS THAT UNDERBASE ITS THOUGHT: IT WOULD BE INTERESTING TO COMPRE-HEND THE LITTLE PASSENGER'S SYMBOL SYSTEM.

BUT HOW? SUCH AN IDEA HAS SURELY NEVER COME TO ANY OF ITS RACE. IT PONDERS, ABSENTLY FOLLOWING THE UNKNOWN TRACEWAY TWISTING AMONG THE STARS. AT LENGTH IT DECIDES THAT IT MIGHT BEGIN BY RECORDING ITS PASSENGER'S SIGNALS IN CONJUNCTION WITH ALL ONGOING DATA FROM OUTSIDE. PERHAPS SOME CORRELA-TIONS WILL APPEAR. THE SIGNALS ARE SIMPLE: THE SMALL ONE RADIATES PRIMARILY IN BINARY MODE, AND REPEATS OFTEN.

IN COLD NEAR ABSOLUTE ZERO, FRICTIONLESS CURRENTS SPIN. A DECISION IS TAKEN, A RECORD-ING MODE ACTIVATED. ON RANDOM FACETS OF THE ICY STORE OF MOLECULES IN THE NUCLEUS, THE LITTLE PASSENGER'S FIRST CRYPTIC EMANATIONS ARE PRESERVED.

// I * COME * IN * PEACE * FOR * ALL * MANKIND *** I * COME * IN * PEACE * FOR * ALL * MANKIND *** I * COME * IN * PEACE * FOR *ALL * MANKIND *** I * COME * IN * PEACE * FOR * ALL * MANKIND ***

Chapter 11

Wildly excited, Tivonel jets upward after Giadoc; they are heading for the highpoint where they will launch into the focus of the Beam which will carry their lives to an alien world. They have just passed the level where Chief Hearer Lomax waits for his Hearers to move out to their stations around the great vortex.

Near Lomax hovers a small cluster of females—Avanil and her Paradomin friends. Tivonel can hear the bright orange tone of their mantle-lights, evidently intended to carry: "Why should this all be controlled by males?"

"They know how, they have the fields," a sister replies.

"We can learn," Avanil says defiantly.

Jetting upward against the gales of the Wall, Tivonel recalls her own childish attempt to touch the life-signals from the sky. If she tried to increase her field-strength by doing Fathering, like Avanil, could she have attained that power? More likely she'd just have become like a normal male, absorbed in the Skills of

infant-care. Like those status-stiff Fathers down in Deep now,
who can't believe any danger could strike Tyree. And what
would become of the world if females abandoned themselves to
Fathering? Crazy.

Far down below Lomax are the massed life-fields of the
Deepers. Tivonel can still pick out the brilliance of Scomber,
pulsing with aggressive resolution. Beside him is the strong
furled energy of old Heagran, dark with disapproval. The
Fathers around them are in high states of energy, their mantles
flickering with scarlet hope, cold blue distaste. There is a
vermillion exclamation she is sure comes from Tiavan, Giadoc's
son and her own. He would do anything, even life-crime, to save
his child. How sad for Giadoc.

But there is no time to think of that now, she must begin to
prepare herself for the Test, as Giadoc has instructed her. Yet the
view up here is so grand, she lets herself take one more scan
around. They are all alone near the top of the Wall of the World, so
high that almost the whole of the great polar vortex can be
made out. The wind-wall is a fantastically beautiful swirling
cliff, richly patterned with the rushing lights and life-emanations
of the Wild. Above them are the perilous heights where the top
of the winds start to converge to form the deadly Airfall in the
center; Tivonel can just perceive the upper fringes of the funnel,
grey with dying life. Up here too can be sensed a deep
background energy. Giadoc has told her that it may be the
life-field of Tyree itself, transmitting into space. How
thrilling . . . Giadoc is slowing down, they must be nearly there.

Guiltily Tivonel comes to herself and starts sorting and
ordering her life-field, trying to recall the disciplines her Father
had taught her. Encapsulate nuclear identity and essential
memory, damp emotion; self-will relaxed yet alert. Very
difficult. And all to be well-connected, so she won't fly apart.
There, it's coming.

Giadoc halts just above her, his huge field already attenuated
and coiled in a strange helical form. She stretches awareness,
tries to copy with her own smaller life. As she does so, a
life-signal resonates around the Wall. The Hearers are in place.

"Ready?" Giadoc brushes her with a testing thought.

"Yes." She mutes the last excited eddy from her field-form.

"Remember, your first act must be to try to calm the being's
fear."

"I will, dear-Giadoc."

"And be brave. The sensations will be very strange. Especially don't panic when there is no wind."

"No."

She waits, hardly able to breathe for the effort to remain in the correct calm mode. It's like being a child again, waiting for her Father to help her stretch her baby mind to distant-touch. But this isn't play, she's waiting to go with Giadoc to touch the life beyond the sky!

The sky...Incredibly clear and cold the voices of the Companions call to her from above. Will she really touch them, ride out on the Beam to merge with unimaginable alien life? A deep excitement wells up almost ungovernably. All around she can feel the energies of the Hearers' linked fields building, growing without limit. The World is bursting with tension.

Just as it seems she must fly apart, a second life-signal crackles through them—and she feels her mind gripped, pulled free, thrust out upon forces she had never dreamed of. Almost she flinches in fear before she lets it take her. Giadoc and the immense combined power of the ring of Hearers are sucking her life up to the focus at the heart of the Beam, to send it stretching out—out—out to—

She yields, launches totally, lets herself dwindle to a filament riding a storm of power, an energy that looms and blooms upward like a world-bubble. She is only a thread in an immense thrusting tower of bodiless vitality, shooting forever outward as it intensifies and narrows from a pinnacle to a needle, from a needle to a dimensionless thread driving instantaneously to its goal. And as her life attenuates, recruitment comes—a deep life-force as if she and the Beam were cresting on a planetary power.

For an everlasting instant she feels herself stretched through an infinity of nothing, an unbodied vector still companioned by a strand of nameless strength. Then—joy, strangeness, glory— she feels the goal just ahead!

Yes. In the unknown is something. Life-contact! Without senses she touches, knows it for a living being. Remember!

She pushes like a baby against the alien life, feeling for the fear she must deflect. Yes, terror is here at the contact-point. With all her might she counters it, projecting warm-friendship, and pushes again.

And suddenly physical sensation crashes in upon her. Lights, colors, nameless perceptions, concrete life-signals! All in one overwhelming instant she is seeing through alien eyes!

Enchanted, she gulps in comprehension, registering shapes, hues, sounds, smells, volumes. A world bombards her. She has done it, she has merged with an alien mind! She has a body, she can fit her will into its half-comprehensible brain, live, act!

But before she can do more than gasp through strange organs, a horrible vertigo strikes her. Where is the Wind? Oh, terror, *there is no wind.* She has fallen into the Abyss!

Primal dread tears the frail connection, sweeps her away. Her being ravels instantaneously back into the void, flees homeward on the Beam in helpless fear. Next instant she has condensed into herself, Tivonel, adrift in disorder on the winds of Tyree.

Shame floods her. She has done exactly what Giadoc had warned her of, she has let herself panic in the strangeness of no wind.

But as she collects herself, her natural spirits revive. She hasn't really failed the important part. Didn't she merge and possess the body? Next time she would be able to stay. But where is Giadoc?

There: she finds his silent form, barely outlined in a weird trace of life, almost like a dead person. But it must be all right; he's still mind-traveling, his life is in some being on that world they touched. Yes; a faint tendril of life-energy seems to run upward toward the great matrix of power arching overhead. The Beam is still holding, the world around her feels drained and dreamlike. Far below her even the Deepers are awed and darkly still.

Suddenly Giadoc's body stirs. The thin trace of field roils and abruptly swells, losing connection of the Beam. But the field is all wrong, it's chaotic, ragged, shooting out wild eddies. Has something bad happened to Giadoc?

She jets closer and then recoils as Giadoc's mantle blasts out a green scream of pain and fear. That *can't* be Giadoc's voice!—and understanding breaks.

This is what they were talking about: an alien mind has come here into Giadoc's body. This must be one of those strange lives she had touched on that far-off world. The creature is evidently scared to death. There ought to be a Father here to help it.

"Be calm, be calm," she signs to it, feeling futile. What can words do for this disordered creature? But to her relief the blue-green shrieking quiets somewhat and stammers of other colors appear. It must be trying to speak. Tivonel moves closer, appalled by the whirling chaos of its mind. Like an adult baby. A thought-eddy brushes her with incomprehensible meanings. The lights of the alien speech-patterns steady down. Tivonel can make out the words "What—? where—?"

"Be calm, you're all right," Tivonel tries to sound Fatherly.

As she speaks the alien field surges at her and the creature apparently perceives her physically for the first time. A jolt of reciprocal horror shoots through them both. Next second Tivonel is flung bodily away, hurled straight out from the wall as if a super sex-field had thrown her.

But we weren't even biassed, she thinks, jetting hard to extricate herself from cross-currents. The creature hit my *body* with its mind; it has some weird power. Fantastic! She can see it awkwardly trying to move now, jetting and wobbling on its vanes. She better get to it before it hurts Giadoc's body. Only, what can she do?

Just as she nears the wind-wall a deep silent sigh runs through the world and the great energy-arch above collapses like a dream. The Beam has been let down.

The world comes back to normalcy—and to her delight Tivonel sees that Giadoc is back too. There is his beautiful great familiar field around his body again! The poor stranger has been sent back to its horrible windless world.

"Giadoc! Are you all right? I was there but I panicked—"

"Yes, Tivonel." His tone is warm but colored with the tints of unspoken thought, she can see his dense swifting mind-patterns. "Remember, we must now record our memories and report."

Belatedly Tivonel recollects that she too must organize a memory. As they plane down she begins to do so, thinking, a proud moment to have a memory for the Recorders of Tyree. Too bad she has to report her fear and flight. But then, she has the interesting experience with the alien.

Orva, the Hearers' Memory-Keeper, is waiting for them by Chief Lomax.

"You won't have time for recording once you're down there," Orva tells them cheerfully. "Never seen such a whirl-field. More Deepers coming up every minute, too. Bad situation."

As Giadoc and Orva merge, Tivonel scans down. As Orva

said, the crowd below is much bigger: a whirl-field of excitement, fear and babble. She can feel strong mind-projections cutting through the commotion. The senior Fathers must be working to establish calm and order. She hopes Virmet and Marockee have thought about supplying more food.

The life-bands tingle as Giadoc and Orva disengage. Giadoc starts on down while Tivonel offers Orva her own modest field-engram. She has never merged with a senior Recorder before. It is a grave, cool experience, as though she looked for a moment into Time itself.

When he releases her she dives down fast and finds herself intercepted.

"Tivonel! Tell us, what was it like? How was it for females?"

It's Avanil and two of her Paradomin.

"I don't know, I was only there a second." She banks past them. "Come, listen to Giadoc!"

Marockee is waiting in the plant-tangle. When Tivonel pulls up beside her, Giadoc and the elder Fathers are just below. He is recounting his experience verbally, his mind-field a great dreamy swirl.

"—As soon as I felt her make contact I merged with the nearest mind. You realize, Fathers, that there is no choice? You may enter a female, a baby, even an animal, whatever the nearest suitable energy configuration is."

"Yes, yes," Scomber says impatiently. "So the female was able to do this? She lived in the alien body?"

"Yes. But, Fathers, this is a terrifying world for the untrained. There is no wind. No wind at all. The bodies drop downward, they must rest upon *solid matter*. It's impossible to describe. Tivonel became frightened and came back, and so would most people."

How good he is, Tivonel thinks. She flushes resentfully hearing Scomber say: "But if she hadn't been so cowardly she could have lived?"

"Oh yes. The bodies are intelligent and strong. One immediately gains all their senses and their physical habits and coordinations, including their habit of speech, which is of course the most important. One's verbal intentions are translated, so to speak. I tested this again, after I oriented myself."

"You actually spoke with these aliens?" old Father Omar asks.

"Yes indeed." Giadoc's mind is patterned with excited

memories; Tivonel realizes that he is so caught up in his love of strangeness that he has forgotten the purpose of their questions, forgotten even the dire threat to Tyree. Now she can understand it; she herself is so excited by her mind-voyage that she is just coming back to the unpleasant realities.

"Yes, I spoke," Giadoc is saying. "I was able to interact. You have to understand that their mind-fields are totally disorganized. They are transmitting at random, like a crowd of grown infants, if you can imagine such a thing. They seem unaware of themselves. I was quite pleased to be able to sort out names, suitable speech-greetings and so forth, so I could successfully converse with one of them. They speak by jets of air, without any mantle-language. And they are covered with sheets of plant-matter," he goes on dreamily.

"Never mind that," says Scomber impatiently. "Tell us the important point. Were you detected? Do they consider mind-entry illegal?"

Giadoc's field contracts and focuses suddenly; he has remembered why they are here.

"I cannot be sure," he says reluctantly. "I did pick up an abhorrence of physical violence from several minds, but of course this must be true in any civilized race. I also detected strong unspecified fears in the alien near me, for instance it became upset wben I spoke its name. But I may have violated some small ritual there."

"You're evading the point. Did they suspect a change of identity?"

Giadoc hesitates, his mantle glowing blue-gray in muted disapproval. "No," he admits finally. "The only doubts I received were concerned with the health of the body's owner. But Fathers, I don't think you could go undetected long, because I discovered that this group of aliens are actually attempting to learn to transmit life-signals. Fantastic." His field expands again at the wonder of it. "So ignorant and chaotic. Some of them have considerable power, but hopelessly untrained. That must be why our Beam stabilizes there so readily. An extraordinary coincidence!"

"Whatever they may learn in the future is no danger to us now," Scomber declares. "The point is that even these aliens who have some crude mind-skills didn't suspect you. Is that right?"

"Yes, Father Scomber."

"And if your Beam is stabilized on them it should be easier to send people in a unified group, isn't that correct, Lomax?"

"Well, yes, that's true, Scomber." The Chief Hearer is furled in dislike. Near him old Heagran is glowing dark indigo in wordless anger. But more and more young Fathers are clustering behind Scomber, their fields aligned with his. Among them is Tivaan.

"Wait, Scomber," old Omar interjects. "Let us hear from the female before we think of sending untrained people."

"Very well, Tivonel!"

She banks down among them, trying to think what she can do to dissuade them from their rotten plan.

"Yes," she concedes, "with Giadoc's guidance it was easy to travel the Beam. And the merger does itself, you only have to push. But Fathers, it was a horrible world. You Deepers may think you're used to living at the bottom of the Wind, but it's much worse than that. It panics you."

Several Fathers glint angrily at her daring, but Scomber ignores her. "Will a Father saving his child panic so easily?" he demands in loud lights. "You have heard the female. Summon your Fatherly courage. On this Beam our children and our people can escape!" Flickers of assent greet his words; more Fathers throng around him.

Tivonel can contain herself no longer.

"What about the poor beings you bring here?" she flares. "While Giadoc was away I was with his body, I saw the alien mind he sent here, I saw it was hurt and afraid. And they're intelligent beings like us. If Tyree is really in danger, how can a Father send these people here to be burned or die? I know that's wrong."

At this rebuke from a female the Father's mantles light angrily. But old Heagran unfurls himself and silences them with an icy snap on the life-bands.

"She is right!" His voice is a commanding purple. "This female is a better life-Father than you! I say again, Scomber, this is a criminal plan. What right have we to steal intelligent bodies and bring these people here to suffer and die? You who try to escape by such means debase the name of Tyree. If you survive, you will be *criminals,* not Tyrenni; and the Great Wind will reject you forever. Saving Tyree does not mean saving our bodies alone. It is the spirit of Tyree we must save, or die with it.

I for one will stay and perish in the arms of our sacred Wind rather than crawl out a few extra years as a mind-stealer in some alien abyss."

"Well said!" "Nobly spoken, Heagran!" Several Fathers move to station themselves with Heagran and Lomax. "I stand with you," declares Eldest-female Janskalen. More Fathers and females drift away from Scomber's group.

But there is still a resolute crowd behind Scomber and Terenc. Avanil and many of her Paradomin are there too.

All fields are radiating tension. Is it possible there is going to be actual strife, a mind-fight like the Wild Ones here among the Fathers of Tyree? Tivonel shudders, scanning around over the throng. For the first time she realizes how huge it is. The plant-thickets at the Wall are dense with people, young and old—even some children jetting loose. A group of big-field males that must be the Near Pole Hearers is resting in a thicket. And more coming up from Deep all the time. They're scared; she can hear the green flicker of fear flash from group to group. It wouldn't take much to generate a terrible panic-vortex, here, she thinks. Some of the elders must think so too, she can see them awkwardly moving among the crowd, trying to restore calm.

The formal white of Lomax' voice breaks into the tensions.

"Fathers, again I must remind you, your decision is premature. Your plan may be impossible. Only two of the three tests have been made. Even if we can send untrained people, undetected, we still do not know the most vital point: Will the exchange hold when the Beam collapses? Can you stay alive there without the Beam? We must test by withdrawing the Beam. I say again, I and my Hearers condemn this plan to steal lives. But we will make this last test in the hope that it will fail and put an end to discord."

"Another test? Another delay until we all burn!" Scomber flashes.

"If you go without testing you may well all die at once," Lomax replies. "The Beam cannot be held long. Then you would lose all chance of any other way of escape."

"Very well," Scomber concedes angrily. "Let this *last* test begin!"

"As soon as our Hearers are rested. They are drained and tired now, they require at least six hours. And in that time the turning of the alien world will complicate our contact. And furthermore, the lone Destroyer has approached our Beam, may the Wind blast him. We must wait a day for optimum conditions and to give the Destroyer time to move away."

"A day! Nonsense!" Scomber explodes in fiery rage. "People are dying, the Wind is burning! We cannot wait a day, Destroyer or no Destroyer. If you Hearers are tired, let them use the help of these Near Pole Hearers over there! *Bdello!*" Scomber jolts the life-bands. "You, Bdello, bring your Hearers to Chief Lomax at once."

"But they have never formed a Beam," Lomax objects. "Also, see, they are exhausted from the journey—"

"Then teach them!" Scomber orders. "Bdello! The Fathers summon you!"

Bdello and his travel-weary band start out toward the angry group of Fathers. Tivonel moves to Giadoc's side.

"Let someone else go this time, Giadoc. Don't risk yourself again."

"I must, I am the most experienced. As to risk, it appears that none of us on Tyree have long to live. But I promise you, dear-Tivonel, if I'm alive when the Beam returns, I will come back to you and to our son."

"If you're alive—Oh, Giadoc!"

"Tivonel," he dims his voice. "Between ourselves, I believe one can remain on an alien world without the Beam. Once I secretly tried disengagement. It was unpleasant but I survived. So I fear that this crime is indeed possible. But I swear to you, I will come back to join you here and we will face our fate together."

The flashing uproar around Scomber and Lomax has resolved itself. Lomax agrees to try to form a Beam with the help of Bdello's Hearers. "But it must be raised not once but twice," he warns. "First to send and second to retrieve, if Giadoc proves to be alive."

Giadoc turns away to start the long climb up to the launch-station, and the new Hearers prepare to jet out to the posts around the Wall.

"Marockee, you and Virmet see that they get food," Tivonel says. "I must find a Father to stand by Giadoc's body while he is away. The poor alien who comes here may injure it. Elders!" she calls formally. "A Father's care is needed to stand by Giadoc!"

No one answers. Dismayed, she realizes how tired and

unwind-worthy the senior Fathers are. And no help can be expected from those who bear children in their pouches. But there are Terenc and Padar and Tynad, strong young males with newly empty pouches.

"Father Tynad, Father Padar, will you not help?"

"What harm can come to his body in so short a time?" asks Tynad.

"The alien could hurl his body into the Abyss," Tivonel says. "Besides, don't you understand? The poor person who was brought here was terrified, it almost fragmented. It has *need* of your Fatherly skill."

"We have no duty to Father animals." Glinting sarcastically, Padar and Terenc move away.

"They're not animals," Tivonel cries. "It was a person like us, it spoke! And we are stealing them from their world. Very well—if none of you great ones will help, I will go up again and try, female though I am."

From behind her a male voice speaks. "This female shames us. I am Ustan. Though I am not skilled enough to climb the heights of your wild winds, I will try to make my way to Hearer Lomax. If you are in need, perhaps I can reach you from there, Tivonel."

"Honour to you, Father Ustan," Tivonel flashes gratefully.

As she turns away there is an angry flare of argument around Lomax and Scomber.

"I insist on going with Giadoc," Father Terenc is saying. "I shall not become fearful and flee, like your female."

"It is easy enough to send you, Terenc," Lomax replies. "But you don't realize the danger. You may be lost forever when the Beam withdraws."

"So be it," Terenc signs firmly. "With great respect, Hearer Lomax, I see that this entire test is being conducted by Hearers who, as you say, hope that it will fail. I feel it would be well for Giadoc to be accompanied by one who will try to make it succeed."

Lomax has been paling and flushing with insult, his field is furled around him like a storm. But he only replies curtly, "Very well. Follow Giadoc if you wish instruction."

The big male spreads vanes and pumps upward after Giadoc, making up in determination what he lacks in skill.

Tivonel flaps her mantle to clear her mind; never has she

heard such dissension among the Fathers of Tyree. Anyone would take them for squabbling females! Then she planes skillfully out onto a slender updraft and soars up past him, thinking, Now I have two bodies to watch over. Well, Terenc's can look after itself.

As she climbs toward Lomax' eddy her name is called.

"Wait, Tivonel! I'll go with you and help watch!" It's Avanil, with one of her Paradomin.

"Welcome, Avan." Tivonel uses the unfamiliar name carefully, pleased by the chance to learn more of this strange young female. But what about the plenya encumbering her pouch?

"A moment." With odd formality, Avanil turns to her friend, and her field alters. Tivonel sees that she is transferring the young plenya to the other with ritual reassurances—exactly like a small Father! It gives her a weird shudder.

"Let's go."

They jet upward together. Tivonel enjoys the sense of comradeship, like the old days on the hunting teams. She's been away from female things too long.

"We mustn't get too close until they're actually on the Beam," she warns. "You've no idea what it's like, your field could get pulled in. Afterwards they look almost dead. It's uncanny."

"I envy your trip on the Beam," says Avan/Avanil. "Listen. I intend—"

At that moment a life-signal bursts at them. Someone is jetting fast out through the Wall. As the mind-field appears, Tivonel exclaims.

"Iznagel! What are you doing here? She's my friend from High Station," she explains to Avanil.

"Well met, Tivonel." Iznagel hangs panting below them. "I seem to be a little off course, don't I? The time-eddies are getting so bad I'm not sure I'm here. I came to warn Hearers that something terrible is wrong with our Sound. Last night the high stream from mid-world veered over us; it's full of death. Whole packs of curlu are burnt, they're screaming so you can't think. Two of our people went up to investigate and got burned too. Look at me!" She unfurls her vanes to show fresh blisters.

"The path you came on isn't even safe by day now, Tivonel. Father Mornor is taking the children down to Deep and the rest of us are trying to move the Station lower down, if we can find a stable crest. Everybody should get out of tbe High—What in the name of the Wind is going on down there, Tivonel? What are all those Deeper Fathers doing here?"

"They've come here because there's trouble all over," Tivonel says. "It's complicated, Iznagel, I can't explain right now. I have to go."

"They should go down at once!" Iznagel dives abruptly away from them down the wall of the wind.

"It's beginning," Avanil says somberly. "Soon there'll be no safe place. The Sound doesn't reach here at nights now, but when Tyree turns it'll burn here too."

"Feel the Beam starting," Tivonel says. "It's as if they drained the whole Wind—Oh, look at Lomax."

They are passing Chief Hearer Lomax; Hearer Bdello from Near Pole is beside him. The two Hearers' huge fields are streaming up in an arc toward the juncture far above; spectacular. Lomax' power is an awesome sight; even Avanil must doubt that females could ever develop such life-sensitivity.

But a curious thing is happening: the mantles of both Lomax and Bdello are murmuring with light-speech. Surely they aren't talking to each other in their state? No; it must be unconscious fragments, like sleep-talk. Suddenly Lomax forms a word with such blue-green hatred that Tivonel stops in mid-jet.

"The Destroyer!"

And Bdello echoes, "The Destroyer...the Beam..."

Great winds, she forgot that Destroyer out there somewhere. Can it be intruding on the Beam? She recalls Giadoc's memory, the cold, vast alien deathliness. Could it attack Giadoc?

As the two females hover, Lomax' dreaming voice flickers clearly,   "No...but   near...Something   intrudes... disturbance..."

"Disturbance," Bdello seems to agree, amid a mumble of meaningless lights. Then Lomax signs, "Gone...small, what?...Wait...no: clear. Clear..." And the two unconscious glimmers sink to a low hum of concentration.

Tivonel scans up to where Giadoc and Terenc are. Their life-fields look normal.

"Whatever it was, it wasn't the Destroyer," she tells Avanil. "We better get moving; they'll get it fixed."

As they jet on upwards through a world growing strange and hushed, Avanil asks, "That alien you touched—was it a female?"

"I haven't an idea, it was all over so quick. Avan, I hate myself for getting scared."

"You're not a coward. But listen, Tivonel: The one you saw in Giadoc's body, was it female or male?"

"I couldn't tell. It was a mess, it was too scared to make sense. And then it threw me. You better watch out for that, you know."

"But it had a big field?" Avanil persists.

"Oh yes—at first I thought it was Giadoc, until I saw how weird it was."

"So it could have been a female with a big field."

"Maybe the males are even bigger," Tivonel says teasingly.

"Be serious, Tivonel. Somewhere out there must be a world where we aren't like this. Where the females are able to do Fathering and all the high-status activities... Of course the egg has to be exposed before it's fertilized," she goes on reflectively. "That's so basic. And I guess that means the males have to catch it. But the rest could be different. Maybe where there isn't any wind, females could get their eggs back and raise them!" She laughs fiercely. "Maybe there's a world where the females are so strong they just hold the males and squeeze them out onto the egg and keep the eggs themselves! And we'd have all the Skills and respect!"

Both young females are laughing now, the picture is so ludicrous. But Tivonel has been noticing that Avanil's field really is unusually large and complex. Is her mock-Fathering really changing her? Could a female develop the sacred Fatherly skills? Infant-Empathy, Developmental-Responsibility, Mind-Nurture, all those big things?

But imagine being a Father. Father Tivon, she'd be. She has a quick fantasy of herself inventing a new theory of field-forming, or pre-flight training. Conferences, grave excitement. Fame. Reverence. Status. But would she really enjoy being so serious and dedicated, doing nothing but debate with other Fathers? It would mean giving up all her traditonal low-status life. No more adventures or work; no more planning that barter scheme, for instance. Is Avanil so ambitious she's forgotten all wildness, all female fun?

Just as she's thinking how to ask such a personal question, a long-range signal resonates the bands. The Beam is up. Yes—there is the great pale arch of energy above the vortex of the pole.

"We better stop here. Watch."

"*Whew*, the Sound is strong up here, Tivonel. Your friend was right, it's getting dangerous."

"Never mind that. Hold tight."

They can see the life-fields of Giadoc and Terenc above them, starting to surge upward toward the focus of the Beam. The energy around them mounts and builds; the two females can feel their own minds being pulled upward. As the flood of power intensifies they lock their field edges together in the effort to hold back.

Just as it seems they must fly upward, the second signal snaps past them and the tension lets go. Above them the great arched dome has towered out of scan. The world below seems drained and flat. Tivonel expands her mind-field from emergency mode.

"That's it, they're on the Beam. See how dead they look?"

They jet up to where the two unconscious males are floating darkly, each veiled by only a thin trace of field.

"You stay by Terenc, Avan. See that connection to the Beam? Don't break it. And listen, don't get too close when you see the field start to change."

"How soon will the alien come?"

"It takes awhile. No, look! It's starting!"

The field around Terenc's body has begun to thicken and roil as it had with Giadoc. Giadoc himself shows no sign of field-change.

"It's a smaller field, Avan. It's not so wild, either. Be careful."

Terenc's mantle suddenly screams green with fear. But it's more of a whimper, not the blazing uproar of Tivonel's other alien.

"Poor thing." Confidently, Avan approaches it and deftly flicks back a field-flare that threatens to separate. The stranger does not react. Avan soothes another flare. Then she marshals her own mind-surface firmly toward the ragged stranger. Great winds, she's making a small Father-field! Tivonel can pick up the waves of reassurance she's transmitting. This Avan really is something!

Impressed and curious, Tivonel moves closer, keeping a side scan to make sure Giadoc's body is still quiescent.

"*Calm, calm, don't be afriad,*" Avan is sending hypnotically. "*You're all right, I'm here. I'll help you understand, just be calm. Smooth yourself, be round like an egg, little one. Speak to your*

Father Avan. Who are you, little one? Tell Father Avan, are you a female?"

To Tivonel's awed surprise, the green wailing quiets. Then the creature lights a wobbly cry, "No!" Presently it starts mewling incomprehensible questions: "Where is—I want my—? Help! Rit! Rip! Rik!"

"You'll have Rit soon," Avan soothes it, continuing to enfold and drain its field. "Only a little while, now tell me who you are, speak to your Father Avan."

But the creature jerks in terror and wails anew; apparently it has tried to scan and terrified itself. Fascinated, Tivonel watches Avan Father it back to calmness.

Then she remembers Giadoc's body—and sees, shocked, that it has drifted out from the wall. While she was preoccupied an alien field has formed around it, and—Oh, no, it's unfurling Giadoc's vanes!

Cursing her inattention, Tivonel starts after it. There's no danger, of course; the currents that flow to the Airfield here are no more dangerous than a baby's jets. But Giadoc's big form is catching so much air, it's tumbling away from her at increasing speed. Better hurry.

As she jets hard across the updraft, Tivonel sees that the alien field around the body is even larger than before, and terribly disorganized. But there seems to be something really wrong; the strange field is lax and trailing weakly, like a dying creature. Giadoc's mantle is dark, except for a faint blue murmur, "Marg...Marget..."

At any rate it doesn't appear violent. She'll be able to haul it back easily, she's quite near now.

But as she comes in reach, the strange field flares crazily, and Giadoc's great vanes fan out, catching all the air. A stronger current takes hold and to her utmost horror she sees Giadoc's body go whirling away, headed straight out to the lethal Airfall.

It's a race for life now; heedless of her own safety Tivonel pumps all her jets and shoots herself cross-wind, after the huge wheeling form, chasing the body of beloved Giadoc that is carrying the dying alien to both their deaths.

Chapter 12

—Pain multiform, unbearable, unending: a gale of knives slashing at helpless flesh, a grey pain-seared universe that bleeds. Daniel Dann is struggling to awake from another of his nightmares. A hell of alien torments assaults his own locked miseries, he is drowning in pain. Oh Christ, stop it!

He struggles up, finds himself in pallid dawnlight in the hot cubicle. The nightmare recedes, leaving him shaking. He tries to focus on the tacky maple chair, the plywood wall. Outside the window mist is wreathing the dim trees.

He is here in this improbable Deerfield, caught up in this insane experiment to take place today. He and the others, who are no longer safe, numbered phantasms but real living people, trapped in their individual predicaments. Oh, no, he doesn't want this. His hands have found his bag, produced a capsule. Better make it two. Yes, and an antiemetic. Swallow, wait thirty minutes. Why doesn't he go to the needle? But that he won't, it's his last self-respect.

He sits on the sweaty bed looking into the shrouded woods. Beautiful; concentrate on it. Like Oriental art.

But the faces of last night pour relentlessly through his mind. The girls frightened to rigidity, Winona crying bleakly, Costakis cursing and hitting the air with his little fists, Rick hysterical. Noah running about muttering, "A psychic storm, a psychic storm. We may have tapped forces beyond our control!" Only Ted Yost seemed relatively untouched; immunized by his private death perhaps. What the hell had they experienced— each other? The unknown minds in this place? Dann did not inquire but simply distributed phenothiazineshots. "Help us, help us," Valerie kept whispering. Help us? Save us from this chintz, this plywood, which to her are the tentacles of hostile power. The tentacles perhaps of that Byzantine presence so aptly named Fearing. But what can be do?

He summons up sensible, soothing phrases, fending off a worse threat that he will not, will not think of. This place, this test is inducing mass delusion. Let's get back to sanity. Since he clearly isn't going to sleep any more, the thing to do is to get dressed.

But as he lifts a sock, memory bursts through him. Oh God, Margaret. He collapses on the bed, the sock clutched to his face; he is riven by the memory of helplessness and pain and shame. It happened to her. My father went crazy. To mutilate a child. His hand remembers the obscene wound his/her hand had touched. In his head are ghastly clinical photos of ritually mutilated girls. Clitoridectomy. Some tribes practiced it. They did *that* to her. Unspeakable, bestial.

His throat convulses, threatening nausea. He rubs his fists roughly across his face, thinking, to live on in so damaged a body. What her life must be, the never-ending tension. No relief, no release. I have nothing in common with women... But the beauty of her. The strength. I like cool things...

And Oh God, worse, she knows him now, his shame. *I let them burn.* The unending instant comes back to him: the smoke and turmoil, the hands gripping his arms that he could have pulled away from, the terrible pause, just long enough, if—if—

If I'd had the guts.

His heart is clenched around a knife-blade, he wishes only that it would finally burst and let him die. An aeon passes so... and then, incredibly, the anguish dims, the cutting edge slides away. The first pearly ease of chemical unreality is sliding into his brain.

His eyes water with gratitude, he takes long shuddering breaths. Presently he cautiously gets up and resumes dressing. Heaven for a shilling; de Quincy knew.

By the time he is splashing water on his face in the latrine he can wonder almost coolly, why, really, so much pain? Other doctors habituated. He never had quite; he has had to hide it and watch that his medical judgment wasn't affected. But it seems to be worse now, much worse. As if he were some kind of a receiver. Crazy!

Safe in his chemical armor he goes back to his room, playing with the thought. He doesn't believe it for a minute. But it's a fact, he could fancy he can still feel them. From around him, emanations of Rick's complex misery, Ted Yost's steady grief, Costakis' painful self-hatred. And from the barracks next door, Winona's despair, the two girls' fear-filled struggle in a world that doesn't want them. Quiet desperation, Thoreau said. But it's worse than that. These ordinary people *hurt*. They can't bear their lives. And there's no escape.

No escape either from the most hurtful life of all: Margaret. Even behind his magic shield he daren't dwell on that. But it's curious; he seems to understand certain things now, as if he'd shared—don't think it. Yet he senses the answer to the puzzle of her child. She must have tried the one thing she could try. And it was no good. Dann can almost feel the intrusive physicality, the hurtful warmth and contact of the baby. Mother-love is sensual. She couldn't take that. She can only bear distance, be like a machine. Even color is dangerous; those neutral clothes, that snow-bound apartment. And no reminders of Africa, never. To her, he thinks, neither white nor black is beautiful. To become a machine . . . hideous.

The sun is gilding the green leaves, people are stirring. *In the world of dreams I have taken a part, to sleep for an hour and hear no word/ Of true love's truth or of light love's art; only the song of a secret bird.* Who, Swinburne? Dann wants no part of love nor secret birds, he hopes only for the world of dreams. He gets up and puts a couple of emergency capsules loose in his pocket. People are in the corridor; it's time for breakfast.

The bus carries them through a meaninglessly beautiful morning. The others are strained and silent. At breakfast only

Winona makes a brief try at normalcy. The two girls pick at their food, heads down. Ted and Rick say nothing. Little Costakis' eyes keep up a wary vigil; he jerks his head cryptically and rearranges his knife and fork. Old Noah makes a hopeful reference to "last night's psychic experience" and is met by heavy silence. What the hell visited them, what did they hallucinate?

It comes to Dann that he's irrational. He accepts that he and Margaret experienced—something; but it hasn't disturbed his conviction that this is all nonsense. The inconsistency amuses him in a remote way. He takes more coffee. All nonsense; hold onto that.

At the far end of the table is the still presence at whom he dare not look. To mutilate a child . . .

The doors bang and Lieutenant Kirk is with them, proclaiming the imminent arrival of the cable crew. He has had a bright idea. In lieu of the missing biomonitors, why can't they use some of Deerfield's polygraph equipment? "Really sophisticated stuff," he grins significantly.

"No, no," says Noah impatiently. "Quite unsuitable. Dan, tell him."

Dann rouses and finds pleasure in explaining that security-type "sophistication" would not be comparable to the multichannel qualitative EEG feedback transcribers Noah has developed. Kirk frowns and goes off to institute another search. Dann winks at Frodo; how reassuring that Deerfield can't keep track of a dozen crates.

As they get up he risks a glance down the table. Margaret's gaze passes over him, severe, unchanging. The beauty of her. Does she despise him now? His own face changes uncontrollably.

When they get back to the barracks a Navy communications van and a cable trailer are pulling up. A pickup is parked nearby, holding what looks like a mobile transformer. Two men are hauling wire up the outside pole.

Dann wanders off, thinking; preposterous. God knows how many miles of cables, equipment, man-hours, money—just to isolate eight harmless Americans from setting eyes on the rest of Deerfield. And the whole fantasia is considered routine. There seem to be aspects of his country he had not encountered before. He shakes his head in genial wonderment, safe in his opiate cocoon.

And even more surreal—somewhere off Norfolk an actual submarine is moving out, containing Rick's unhappy brother. Waiting for this absurd test. Surely he is privileged to view an epic madness. Poor Noah, when all this peters out. Enjoy it while it lasts.

But as he gazes at the limp volleyball net, some residue of last night, or perhaps a curious tension in the air, pierces him.

What if the tests—succeed?

The memory of a sliding glass of water erupts in his head, his knees feel weak. And last night—last night he actually, undeniably fell into another's mind, and she knew his. A clammy coldness invades him. Is it now so inconceivable that these people could pull numbers out of a distant mind? And if they do? He has taken nothing seriously, he has never considered that they might be in real danger here in this paranoid place—He should—Traitorously his hand has brought a capsule to his lips. He swallows, waits.

"Dann! Dann!" Noah is shouting. The missing biomonitors have arrived.

Unreality closes back around him. He goes inside to find the dayroom in a tangle of wires and opened crates. Men are carrying the recorders into the cubicles which will serve as test stations. The new doors now close off the corridor.

"Help me get these right, Dann. I want the placement of everything as close as possible to the configuration we had. We don't know what may be important."

With Costakis' help Dann goes from room to room, making the final adjustments, trying to remember relative positions of chairs, cabinets, walls. It's surprising how well Noah has recreated the laboratory setup. "Get it right, Dann," the old man urges. Dann has forgotten his cold moment and feels only a benevolent glow for the old maniac. Kendall Kirk is being obnoxiously helpful about getting the wires taped out of the way. His Labrador watches from outside the screen door.

Presently it's time to call the subjects in for their base-line runs. Safe in his official persona Dann beams and nods, refusing to notice their tension, the arousal readings on the tapes. This is just another day in Noah's fantasy-lab.

As Val goes out she whispers, "Remember."

Remember what? He brushes it away.

When he is unhooking Rick the boy says suddenly, "Listen.

I'm not going to tell them anything. They can shove it."

"What do you mean?"

"The Navy. That fucking Fearing. I tell you, Ronnie's scared. I'm not going along."

"But Noah Catledge isn't in the Navy," Dann says confusedly, still bemused by good will for the old man. "This is his test just like all the others. It would be a shame to let him down now."

"I don't give a shit," Rick mutters. His tone sounds indecisive.

Dann forgets him. Margaret has come into the dayroom, where the teleprinter is being installed.

As soon as he can Dann hurries out and finds her alone except for an electrician finishing a junction-box by the door. She's standing by the console, tapping out some message which produces mysterious blue symbols on the read-out screen.

"Testing?" Dann dares to ask.

To his delight she nods serenely. "Checking in."

"You have a connection to our office computer from here?"

"I have access to the probability program. Your EEG correlations will have to wait till we get back."

The teleprinter clacks extendedly. She takes the printout, frowns thoughtfully.

"What's it telling you?" he asks like an idiot.

"Users' advisory. There's been some accident in the main banks at Holloway, a lot of cores got wiped. Suspected tampering, etcetera. . . . It doesn't affect us."

Her tone is peaceful, quietly amused. The beautiful thing is back, the fragile link between her sad world and his. He stands there watching her ply her magic.

Suddenly she shakes her head at the screen. "Look at that."

"Something wrong?" He peers at it, identifying what looks like an integral sign surrounded by a great many Ts.

"It keeps giving the date as plus or minus infinity. The ghost." She chuckles. "I thought I had that fixed."

She sits down at the console and starts incomprehensible rites.

Feeling marvelously better, Dann strolls back through the corridor and goes outside. Nobody in sight but Ted and Rick shooting baskets again. The sunlight on the greenery is pulsating, vibrant; there's a brilliance to every outline. Dann hopes he hasn't dosed himself into some kind of psychedelic domain. It's after eleven. The first test starts at noon. It will run one hour, a letter every ten minutes. So slow; supposed to be safer in case the submarine group aren't synchronized exactly. Fantastic...

"Ready, Dann? It's time to set up." Noah bounces by with file folders under his arm. Kendall Kirk starts shouting "Come on in, gang!" his voice ringing with false camaraderie.

Even Dann's muffled senses can't ignore the painful tension in the air when the subjects are finally in place and being connected up. Rick is dead silent, Ted Yost wears a weird little smile, Costakis is maniacally squaring off his pad into tiny grids. Even Winona is flinchy about her hair. Frodo's cubicle is empty; she has to be coaxed to leave Valerie. Dann lets his hands work automatically, trying to stay numb. He is still seeing too many colors and he is feeling, or hearing, a peculiar silent humming in the air. It's me, he thinks. I've overdosed.

"Eleven fifty-five!"

Noah takes up his usual place in midcorridor. Dann and Kirk go to the dayroom. Margaret is waiting at her console; she will have nothing to do until the run is over. Dann stands by the closed corridor door; it's so thin he can hear chairs scrape in the cubicles. Kirk scowls at Margaret and Dann, and takes up a watchdog stance by the front door. Outside on the porch the real dog's tail thumps. It's growing hot in the barracks.

At eleven fifty-eight a car stops outside. Major Fearing comes in quietly and sits down by the desk where he can watch everybody. He nods minimally at Dann. Curious how obtrusive the covert style becomes, Dann thinks. There's an envelope in Fearing's pocket. Is that the "answers," the list of numbers actually transmitted? Like a game.

Is there really a submarine lying underwater out at sea, with Ron in it waiting to be shown a card?

"Twelve o'clock!" Noah says briskly in the corridor. "First letter, *go!*"

Dead silence. The tension is a subsonic thrum, Dann can almost feel his fillings buzz. He will not let it remind him of last night.

Suddenly Rick's voice bleats out a high-pitched laugh. Dann can hear Noah rushing in and shushing.

"Ronnie's afraid to go to the can," Rick says. "He's so

constipated, he's afraid the water will run up his ass."

"Oh dear, oh dear," Says Noah. *Please* try to concentrate. I'm sure he's attempting to transmit a letter."

"Oh, he's attempting," Rick says sarcastically.

The trembling silence closes back.

Sounds of movement in the cubicles. The subjects must be writing their imaginary letters. They do it differently, Dann knows; the girls produce big single letters ornamented with curlicues; Costakis writes a whole alphabet and circles one. Ted Yost scrawls and crosses out... Dann realizes he is trying to ignore the humming in the air. It's like an itch, it has to be coming from outside him. His eye falls on the wires running along the walls. That's it, he has heard about people feeling what is it, a sixty-cycle hum. He feels better.

"Second letter, start!" Noah calls out.

In that submarine, somebody has shown Ron a different card. Dann blinks, trying to suppress the colored haloes on the outlines of things. Scrapings and rustling from the cubicles. Ten minutes is an eternity to wait. Kirk shifts his feet, Fearing sits still. The Labrador's tail thuds on the steps.

"Third letter, start."

"Loud and clear!" Costakis calls out suddenly, startling everyone.

"Sssh, sshhh, Chris!"

The wait is excruciating, the room seems to be brimming with invisible energies. Have these crazy tests attracted some alien power, as Noah said? Is a monster forming itself back there in the corridor behind him? Dann can no longer keep himself from staring at Margaret. She looks composed, her eyes downcast; but there's a line between her brows as if she is hearing something. Is she trembling or is it the quivering air.

"Fourth letter, start!"

Noah's voice sounds miles away, like an echo chamber.

"Five by five!" Costakis calls out again, and then Winona exclaims in a strained voice, "Doctor Catledge, this is wild! I *know* we're getting them."

"Shshsh! Shsh!" Noah hisses desperately.

Kirk is glaring at the corridor door; Fearing has no expression. Dann sees Margaret shudder and put a hand out to grip the edge of her console. He is sweating in the thickening, pulsing air, he can no longer fool himself about sixty-cycle hums. This is the same terrible tension that surged through them last night, and he is scared to death. It strengthens, rises, as though the room was at the focus of some far-off nameless intensity—

"Fifth letter, start!"

—And at that instant he feels—*feels*— a presence as palpable as an animal's nose poking at his mind. Terror spurts up in him, he jerks around to the wall expecting to see something unimaginable coming out, trying to enter his head. But there is nothing. He stares at the varnished wood, one hand frantically clasping his forehead, while under his fingers something— something immaterial—*pushes* into him.

Hallucination; he is going mad here and now. And then he becomes aware of the strangest fact of all—he is no longer afraid.

He stands dazed, all terror gone, aware only that the invisible intrusion in his head exudes a puppylike friendliness and harmlessness. A bright eager feeling washes through him, like a young voice saying *Hello.* Transfixed, astounded, he hears from a great distance meaningless words.

"Sixth letter, start!"

The push on him strengthens overpoweringly, the anchors of his mind yield, tear loose—and he is suddenly nowhere, whirling through a void that becomes delirium. For one vertiginous instant he rides an enormous whirlwind, is swamped in a howling, soundless gale above a dark-light world shot with wild colors that are sounds—he is aware of unknown presences in a gale of light that beats like music on his doubled senses, he is soaring in tempests of incomprehensible glory—

—And next instant he is telescoped back across limitless blackness into himself, Daniel Dann, his body striking hard surfaces by the familiar dayroom wall. His head is empty. He realizes he is down on one knee. Someone is calling his name.

He gets to his feet. There seems to be a commotion back in the corridor. Kirk gallops past. "Dann! Come back here!" Noah calls again.

But Dann cannot respond, he is staring at Margaret Omali. She is holding herself braced upright, looking at Fearing. Her mouth writhes oddly, she swallows with a croak. Fearing watches her intently.

"Hello, hello . . ." The voice is coming from Margaret but it isn't like anything Dann has heard before. "Hello? Char-les, yes? Charles Ur-ban Sproul."

Fearing suddenly gets up. For a moment Dann thinks he is going to attack her, but he only goes to the corridor door, pulls it shut, and locks it, without taking his eyes off her. The room is like a humming vacuum. Dann takes a step toward Margaret and runs into Fearing's arm.

"Lind-say?" says the weird voice from Margaret's throat. "Lindsay Barr? Major Drew Fear-ing, yes." Her mouth stretches in imitation of a smile. "I respect your culture, your concern. Ah, undertow." The voice trails off in meaningless syllables.

Fearing stands motionless, studying her as if she were a wild animal.

Margaret takes an unsteady step away from the computer, looking around the room. Her gaze fixed on Dann, and she utters what sounds like "Tivel?"

The next second she is sagging, crumpling toward the floor.

Dann lunges just in time to save her face from the teleprinter bar. Her body slides away and hits the floor beside the couch. Dann starts toward her and has his breath knocked out by a solid blow from Fearing's elbow.

"Keep away." The feral intensity of the voice is as shocking as the blow.

"She—Miss Omali—has a cardiovascular history," Dann gasps. It hurts him physically to see her on the floor, alone. He pushes futilely, caught between the console and the stronger, furious man. "Let me through, Major!"

Margaret is sighing shudderingly. Her eyes open, her head lifts and falls back.

"The wind," she says faintly.

"It's all right, Margaret," Dann tells her across Fearing's shoulder. "I felt it too. You're here."

"The *wind*," she repeats. Then her hand grasps the couch and she scrambles up and sits.

Fearing is instantly in front of her.

"Who sent you here? Where did you learn those names?"

"She's had a shock, Major, for God's sake stop this nonsense." Dann moves, summons authority back to his voice. But it isn't nonsense, he has a hideous suspicion what has happened.

Loud noises are coming from behind the locked door.

"Major Fearing!" Noah's voice shouts. "We need your transcript at once, we've had extraordinary results!" He pounds harder, rattles the door. "Dann! What's the matter?"

Fearing straightens up, suddenly calm. "Stand away from her, Doctor." The tone is deadly. Imagining weapons, Dann lets himself be backed away. Fearing goes to the door and unlocks it. His cold, pleasant voice rides over Noah's expostulations as he hands the envelope through.

"Doctor Catledge, a matter of concern to me has come up here. I would appreciate it if you will evaluate your results in the other section of the building. The doctor must remain here. Kirk, stay with them and see that this door stays closed."

Margaret is whispering something. "I was . . . away."

"I know. It's all right," he whispers back.

But it's not all right. That gibberish she uttered, those names—they were meaningful to Fearing. Some of his secrets, like last night, she read things out of his mind. And Fearing, what can he think but that she's some sort of spy? Oh God—the crazy bastard is dangerous—

The door is closed; Fearing is surveying them thoughtfully. "Doctor, I suggest you sit down."

Still studying Margaret, Fearing straddles the computer chair and sits down facing her, apparently perfectly at ease.

"Look, Major—"

Fearing holds up his hand, smiling. He seems to have dismissed Dann from some calculation. "Miss Omali, your approach puzzled me." His face is a mask of patient sympathy. "I believe I understand. Please be assured that we have an excellent record of protecting people who come to us. Perhaps you'd like to meet one or two, to reassure yourself? I think that could be arranged."

She stares at him. Her control is back. "I have not one idea what you're talking about."

Nor has Dann—and then suddenly he sees. This maniac Fearing has decided that Margaret is, what do they call it, a defector. Trying to defect to "our side." He thinks her ravings were an attempt to signal him by revealing knowledge. Nightmare proliferates around him. What can he do to her, lock her up? Ruin her life? But she doesn't know anything—

"You're crazy," Margaret is saying remotely. Dann can sense the fear under her calm. The air is flickering with tension.

Fearing smiles charmingly. "Perhaps you are concerned about your little boy? We could have him here with you in an hour or so."

Oh God. Dann sees the cords in her neck spring out.

"Don't you dare touch my son."

"Look here, Major, as this woman's doctor I'm telling you to stop this right now. You're on the wrong track, you—"

Fearing doesn't look at him, but goes on contemplating Margaret as if she were an algebra problem.

"This is not the appropriate setting, perhaps," he says patiently. "You would feel more secure away from these people." He touches his wristwatch.

"No!" Margaret cries.

Dann plants himself in front of her. "I tell you you're endangering her heart. If you don't believe me, get Harris over here to check."

Footsteps outside. Dann swings around to see a heavy-set man in fatigues at the front door.

"An excellent idea, Doctor," Fearing says unruffledly. "Deming, put in a call for the ambulance and tell Doctor Harris to meet us."

"No!" Margaret jumps up. "I'm not going anywhere!"

Dann is struggling with horror, the room seems brimming with fear. How can this maniac have so much power? He's so relaxed, he's sure we're helpless. But not Margaret, not unless they're prepared to shoot me—*I mean that*, he realizes, hearing himself say "You will not—"

The front door opens again and Kendall Kirk bursts in saying urgently, "Sir! Excuse me, sir, but you have to know this." He halts in back of the couch, behind Margaret. "They did it. I tell you those weirdoes picked up the whole six-letter group. They can do it, they can read your mind. They're dangerous as hell. She's reading your mind right now."

Dramatically he points at Margaret.

"You're out of your mind, Kirk," Dann protests. "Miss Omali isn't even one of Noah's subjects."

"She's hiding it," Kirk says savagely. "She's one of the strongest psis in the bunch. I know."

Fearing continues studying Margaret impassively. His nostrils are tightly curled in, as if there were a nasty odor in the throbbing, thickening air. Dann can guess the revulsion going through that secretive mind. But surely he will reject Kirk's lunacy?

"Those, ah, terms you mentioned, Miss Omali," Fearing says at last. "Am I to understand that you, ah, divined them from my mind?"

Oh God, paranoids accept magic. This is bad. And the damned humming feeling is worse every minute. He can't get hallucinations now, he has to protect her—

"I don't read minds," says Margaret coldly. But she is shaking.

Fearing just goes on watching her. Maybe he has, what, psi powers himself, Dann thinks. Horrified, he feels the energy in the room building, pouring into him. The air resonates. Stop it, stop it.

The teleprinter suddenly clacks, making everyone start. Fearing didn't change his level stare.

"Major, you have to believe it!" Kirk clamors. "They're dangerous! Look—watch this!"

He lunges over the couch and lays desecrating hands on Margaret's wrists, jerking them together behind her, prisoning them in one hand while his other hand goes high over her head. Fire spurts—a flaming butane lighter is falling straight into her lap.

Dann doesn't know he has jumped until his fist connects with Kirk's face. He hears Margaret make a dreadful sound. From the side of his eye he sees the lighter swerve in midair and fly at Fearing's head.

And Margaret herself—goes away.

Staggering in abnormal dimensions in the pulsing room, Dann sees her go. Her bodily eyes roll up and pale complex fire streams out of her, an energy which he instantly understands is *her*, her life. He sees it form and shoot away meteorlike into a dark abyss of non-space which for an instant is open to his senses—she is going, going—

"Margaret!" he cries, or tries to cry out, knowing that he is losing her forever, feeling some unearthly focus of power brush him, unmoor him—

—And he wrenches free, breaks out, gathers himself and his fifty years and his wretched useless love and hurls his life wholly after her through the closing gap to nowhere.

An instant or eternity later he regains something like

consciousness. He is hurtling through blackness that is empty of time or space, seeing only before him with what are no longer mortal eyes the pale fleeing spark that is her life. He tries to call out to her, having no voice but only his bodiless will to comfort her, to slow her terrified flight. He does not wonder, he knows only that his life continues, that he is able to race after her through dimensions of unbeing that may be, for all he cares, Hell or a dream or interstellar space. *"Margaret!"*

Far ahead, the living spark seems to curve course, and he swerves after. Is there some faint structure to this darkness? He cannot tell nor care. He is gaining, closing on her! *"Margaret, love—"*

But suddenly everything is gone—he has crashed into stasis, is assualted by light, colors, sensations. Floundering, he perceives dimly that this is embodiment. His naked life has become incarnated. A sense which isn't vision is showing him the image of a landscape in which are immense, trembling globes. Utterly bewildered, he rolls or tumbles, his mind filled with jelly life. "Margaret!" he bubbles weakly, and then sees—knows— her radiance is there, flaring among the moving gelatinosities.

He tries to wabble toward her. But as he does, her pale light gathers itself and spins out and away to nowhere—and he wrenches his life free and follows, is again only a hunger in the void pursuing a fleeing star.

Hunter and hunted, their bodiless energies flash across blackness which is light-years, ricochetting down a filament of negative entropy which they cannot know supports their lives—interlopers on a frail life-beam extended toward Earth from a burning planet a hundred million million miles away. Of all this the essence that was Daniel Dann knows only that the spark of Margaret's life is still there, still attainable if he can force his being to greater speed or whatever the unknown dimension is.

He is gaining again! The path through nothing has curved, he cuts the vector—and then with an inertialess crash he finds himself once more embodied in matter, stunned by the impact of alien senses.

This time it is all greyness, lit by a watery blue spear; he is in some sort of crowded cavern. "Margaret!" he whistles, or emits in molecules, striving to sense her. And yes. She is there too, her lacy living energy is springing out among a thicket of grey folds. He lunges toward her on nonlimbs.

But again she gathers herself, is gone—and he launches after her into unbeing, finding the impossible familiar now. This hallucinatory after-life seems to have some sort of regularity or dreamlike laws. Are they passing through real space, existing briefly on alien planets?

No matter; the chase accelerates, she caroms wildly down the structured lightlessness in which is nothing, not even a star. It comes to him with joy that he is holding out, can hold out. He will not lose her! But as he exults, he becomes suddenly aware that the void they fly in is not quite empty. Somewhere ahead or to one side, he cannot tell, lies a huge concentration of darker darkness—something blacker than mere absence of light, a terrifying vast presence colder than death. It is Death incarnate, he thinks, he is gripped by fear for her. With all his might he tries to send a voiceless warning to her frail flying star.

Next instant their flight bursts into stasis again. But this time it's shockingly comprehensible. He is incarnated in a sunlit green world under a blue sky. Earthlike meadows are around him, a bird sings. He feels breath, muscles, heartbeat—yes, these are his strong gold-furred limbs. He is a big animal crouched in a small tree.

And there below him—so close!—a white deerlike creature is cropping the grass; pale energies are streaming about its silver horns.

It is she, he has caught her at last!

"Margaret!"

But to his horror he hears himself uttering a fanged roar, and feels his carnivore's muscles-exploding him into a murderous leap. His huge talons are unsheathed, descending on her! He screams, trying to wrench himself aside in midair as her white head comes up. One glimpse of her dark eyes staring—and then she has gone out of that body, fled away on the wind of nowhere.

He flings his life free of the beast-form barely in time to follow her dwindling spark. She is doubly frightened now, in total flight from everything, from life itself. He must push all his waning strength to hold her in reach.

And closer now, too close, the huge eclipsing black dreadfulness he had sensed before is looming through the dimensions at them. Is she aware of it! *Turn, turn away!*" He tries to hurl warning, willing her to veer aside.

For an instant he thinks she has heard him, she is turning—but no; appalled he sees that she has turned not away but toward the deathly presence, is flying straight at it.

He throws himself after her, understanding that she has chosen. Too much pain, too much; she is fleeing from life forever, she wants only to cease.

"*Margaret, don't! Come back, come back!*"

But the rushing life-spark does not turn, the great destroying blackness looms ahead. Desperately he tries to intercept her course, he is racing terrified in the icy aura of the thing. "*Margaret!*"

It is no use, he is too slow, too far behind; he sees the glimmering meteor that is her life plunge into black, be swallowed, and wink out. He has lost her. He is alone.

And at that instant the huge shadow before him changes subtly, takes on the semblance of raging lurid smoke—and he sees again the image burned across his life. The black flame-spouting walls, the walls into which he had not gone, in which he had once let perish all that he loved.

It is all there again, the burning darkness and the death; his being recoils in mortal fright. He cannot—

But her brightness has gone in there! He no longer knows who she was or what he is, but only that something intimately precious has again been devoured by evil—and this time he cannot bear to fail. He *will* follow, he will get her out or die trying.

He gathers every terrified shred of his existence and hurls himself at the blackness where she went, a mite of energy launching itself at the eater of suns.

For an instant he feels himself in black cold that burns horribly, and knows death is ahead. So be it. Then he smashes against negation, a mighty barrier of nothing that shatters him into a million fragments and hurls him back instantly away across frozen forever, a tiny blur of improbability smeared across the void—

—Which coalesces, unthinkably, into light and feeling, into what he finally recognizes as the old human body of Daniel Dann, lying propped up on a bare floor.

Machinery is humming near him. He isolates an active

hammer at his sternum, and his human mind vaguely identifies an emergency cardiac stimulator. Did he dream? No; it was all real, only elsewhere. He is, he supposes, really dying now; he has received a mortal blow, though he is not in pain. He has lost something vital, lost it forever. Memory of black burning comes to him. But strangely it has no power. *I tried,* his failing mind thinks. *Even if it was too late, I did try.*

Movement is visible through his eyelashes, his lids are in terminal tremor. While he waits to die he lets himself look, identifies a moving whiteness as the legs of medics. Incredibly, he seems to be still in the dayroom at Deerfield, on the floor. No one is attending to him. At the end of his vision a figure suddenly rises away, revealing the side of the dayroom couch.

A long dark arm is trailing from it. The hand rests limp on the floor.

Her arm. She is here. His heart thuds against the mechanical stimulation.

"Sorry, Major," says a voice. Dann recollects a white-haired blur: Doctor Harris. "We're much too late," Harris goes on. "She's gone."

Dann can feel nothing more, he is only dully grateful for a glimpse of her pure young profile, as they lift her onto the stretcher. The blanket drops. *Touch her carefully, damn you, treat her with reverence.* He remembers what he knows and wishes fiercely that he could protect her body from the obscene curiosity to come.

"Hey, the doc's coming around," says a loud voice over his head.

With horror Dann realizes that it is referring to him. Why isn't he dead? Is it possible that he has to live? To go on and face the emptiness, the grief and wretchedness of his days? *No.* He wills himself to let go. Cease, heart.

But hands are moving him, medication is traitorous in his blood, he cannot slip away. And yet he can still feel the weird humming tension in the air. Is it possible somehow to wrench loose, to flee out of his body as he had before. Was that delirium, or his drugged cortex raving, a stroke? Whatever, he is too weak now, he cannot find the way. He is trapped here, to suffer the grey years. No way out.

Involuntarily he groans aloud, and a miracle happens.

The *push* that he had felt before presses into his mind—an

invisible invading presence that somehow takes away all fear.
But this time it is far stronger, more resolute. A real yet friendly
power is thrusting him out of himself as a knife scoops out an
oyster. Perhaps it is death; he feels only infinite relief as he lets
himself be unbodied. And as he dissolves, a voiceless message
seems to form in his mind: "Don't be afriad, a short time only. I
am Giadoc."

Madness! But so real and warm is the presence that with his
last human consciousness he feels sympathy for the alien thing,
wishes to warn it. Then his life slides out of the world.

—Into darkness, bodiless speed; he is whirling instantaneously through a void he seems to have known before. But this
is velocity so great it is simple being, he is only a vector hurtling
somewhere, sucked to a destination—and then he is *there*,
telescoping into some order of unreal reality.

As he coalesces into what might be existence, his vanished
human senses form one last perception: he is falling into a
world-wide inferno, lit by jagged radiance, a blizzard of radiance
from an exploding sun. For a noninstant he is aware of great
gales howling, of a storm inhabited by monster flying forms,
great bats or squids that trail terrifying fires. He is collapsing or
condensing into hell.

Next moment the vision is gone, he is *in*, is a corporeal
something under peaceful daylight. But is is all too much,
entirely too much, he is worn out. Something vital has gone, he
does not recall what, only knows he can bear no more.

All but dead with grief and terror, the being that had been
Daniel Dann abandons consciousness. His forty-meter vanes
fan out in disarray, his jets are lifeless. He tumbles limply while
the currents take hold and carry him helpless toward the lethal
downfall of the eternal winds of Tyree.

Chapter 13

COLDLY IT RIDES THE STARWAYS, PREOCCUPIED BY NOVEL SENSATIONS FROM WITHIN ITS VAST AND INSUBSTANTIAL SELF. SINCE THE ADVENT OF ITS SMALL PASSENGER, EXISTENCE HAS DEFINITELY BECOME MORE INTERESTING, DESPITE THE IRREMEDIABLE SADNESS OF ITS GUILT.

THE PROJECT OF LEARNING TO COMMUNICATE WITH THE LITTLE ENTITY SEEMS LIKELY TO REQUIRE INFINITE TIME; BUT INFINITE TIME IS AVAILABLE. REFERENTS FOR THE SYMBOLS STILL ELUDE IT. HOWEVER, THE GREAT HOST COMES TO UNDERSTAND IN A GENERAL WAY THE SMALL THING'S ZEST FOR ACCESS, AS THOUGH THE MERE EXPERIENCE OF EMBODIMENT WERE A SOURCE OF JOY. STRANGE, UNFATHOMABLE! WHEN ACCESS TO ALL SENSOR-SYSTEMS IS ALLOWED, THE TINY BEING RESPONDS EXCITEDLY, SEEKING, PEERING, LISTEN-

ING, MAGNIFYING NOW THIS, NOW THAT PHENOME-
NON OF THE VOID. AND ALWAYS WITH AN INFEC-
TIOUS VIVACITY THAT MAKES THE HUGE ONE'S
BLEAK EXISTENCE BRIEFLY MORE BEARABLE.

AGAIN, THERE IS THE RECURRENT PROBLEM OF
KEEPING ITS PASSENGER AWAY FROM TOO-CLOSE
APPROACH TO ITS PRIVATE NEXUS OF GRIEF AND
WRONG. THE LITTLE PRESENCE SEEMS TO WANT TO
MEDDLE IN THE WHOLE CENTRAL NUCLEUS, AS
THOUGH TO INITIATE SOME ACTION, OR DEMAND
MORE OF SOMETHING UNKNOWN. WHAT COULD
THIS BE?

EXPERIMENTALLY, A MORE INTIMATE CONTACT IS
ONCE ALLOWED. BUT NOTHING HAPPENS EXCEPT A
REPETITION OF MEANINGLESS SYMBOLS: //ACTI-
VATE***//. THIS CORRELATES WITH NOTH-
ING, AND PRESENTLY THE SMALL PASSENGER
CEASES AND REGATHERS ITSELF ELSEWHERE.

IT HAS BEEN ACTIVE IN THE VAST PERIPHERY,
TOO. AT LEAST ONCE IT HAS VENTURED TO THE
OUTER LAYERS AND MADE CONTACT WITH AN
ENCYSTMENT. SUBSEQUENTLY IT ACHIEVES A NEW
KIND OF MOVEMENT, AS THOUGH IT HAS SEPARAT-
ED OR DOUBLED ITSELF: THE INTERNAL SENSORS
OUT THERE ARE NOT SO PRECISE. TOLERANTLY,
THE HUGE HOST REFRAINS FROM DAMPING THIS
TINY COMMOTION, MERELY CONTENTING ITSELF
WITH WARNING SWEEPS.

AND SHORTLY IT FINDS ITSELF REWARDED FOR
INDULGENCE: THIS SEEMS TO HAVE BEEN THE
PRELUDE TO SOMETHING NEW. THERE IS A SENSE
OF STRAIN ON THE NUCLEUS, AND THEN THERE
ERUPTS FROM WITHIN IT A WONDROUS, NAMELESS
SENSATION SO UNHEARD-OF IT CANNOT BE IDENTI-
FIED AT ALL, EXCEPT AS A STARTLING SENSE OF
COMING-ALIVE IN A NEW UNAUTHORIZED WAY. THIS
HAS TO DO WITH CERTAIN SCANNERS, IT PER-
CEIVES. IT DEPLOYS THEM MORE FULLY, AND THE
SENSATION AMPLIFIES. MARVELMENT, DELIGHT!

NOTHING IN ITS IMMENSE COLD BEING HAS
PREPARED IT FOR BEING DAZZLED BY BEAUTY. THE

NEUTRAL, UNREGARDED STARFIELDS TAKE ON INTEREST. GLORIES, LARGE AND SMALL, FOR WHICH IT HAS NO CONCEPTS CREATE A BRILLIANT STIR. TO ITS AMAZEMENT, THIS ASPECT OF ITS GREY EXISTENCE BECOMES FOR A TIME INTENSELY SATISFYING.

IT FLOATS ON CONSIDERING THESE EVENTS, HALF-PLEASED, HALF-HORRIFIED. IT SPECULATES: PERHAPS IT WAS TO THE GOOD OF THE TASK, THE RACE, THAT I DEFAULTED BEFORE I BECAME SO ACUTELY DERANGED?

SO DISTRACTED, THE VAST BEING FAILS TO NOTICE THAT IT IS MOVING CLOSER TO THE PECULIAR NEG-ENTROPIC STRAND WHICH IT HAD SET COURSE AUTOMATICALLY TO FOLLOW. IT IS SUDDENLY ALERTED WHEN A BURST OF MINUTE ENERGIES IMPINGE UPON ITS OUTER SKIN. IT SEEMS TO HAVE INTERSECTED, OR DISRUPTED, THE STREAM. APPARENTLY IT IS QUITE CLOSE TO THE EMISSION END, BECAUSE OTHER PARTICULATE ENERGIES CONTINUE TO ARRIVE, QUITE STRONG FOR SUCH TINY SENDS. INDEED, ONE OR TWO MAY HAVE PENETRATED THE DEEPER LAYERS BEFORE BEING SEALED OUT. THE SENSATION IS MILDLY TITILLATING, ENOUGH SO THAT IT REMAINS FLOATING IN PLACE, VAGUELY RECALLING THAT IT HAD WONDERED IF SOME APPROPRIATE ACTION WOULD SUGGEST ITSELF WHEN IT NEARED THE OUTPUT END.

NOTHING OCCURS, HOWEVER, EXCEPT A PECULIAR INTUITION OF RIGHT-WRONGNESS, AN ALMOST-IDEA TOO FAINT TO GRASP. MEANWHILE ITS LITTLE PASSENGER HAS BECOME EVEN MORE STIMULATED AND IS ENGAGING IN MUCH INTERNAL TRANSMISSION, REPEATING ITS PERENNIAL SIGNAL, *ACTIVATE***ACTIVATE//*

THIS CORRELATES WITH NOTHING UNUSUAL GOING ON OUTSIDE. ONLY ONE OR TWO NEARBY SUNS ARE DISSIPATING, EMITTING FROM THEIR TRAINS THE USUAL INCOMPREHENSIBLE ENERGIES THAT HAD BEEN SO INTERESTING. DOUBTLESS THIS

IS A MARGINAL EFFECT OF THAT GREAT TASK, THE
GREAT ONE DECIDES—AND WITH THIS COMES THE
REALIZATION THAT IT HAS UNWITTINGLY DRIFTED
BACK CLOSER TO THE ZONE OF OPERATIONS.

GRIEF STRIKES THROUGH THE VAST SPACE-
BOURNE TENUOSITY. ITS RACE, THE TASK, ITS VERY
LIFE, ALL ARE LOST TO IT NOW. IT TURNS ITS
ENORMOUS EMPTINESS, PREPARING TO SET
COURSE AWAY.

BUT AS IT DOES SO, AN INPUT OCCURS WHICH
MAKES IT FORGET ALL ELSE.

FROM EXTREME RANGE, BUT UNMISTAKABLE: A
GREAT TRANSMISSION RISING ON THE TIME-BANDS,
A COMPLEX CALL OF EXULTATION, EFFORT AND
THANKSGIVING.

THE TASK HERE IS FINISHING, THE OUTCAST
BEING REALIZES. AND THEY HAVE BEEN SUCCESS-
FUL. THE LAST DESTRUCTIONS HAVE BEEN
ACHIEVED, THE LAST ONSLAUGHTS OF THE ENEMY
CONTAINED.

SAD AND ALONE, THE EXILE REVERBERATES TO
THE GREAT CRY WELLING FROM FAR AWAY:

"VICTORY! . . . VICTORY! . . . VICTORY! . . . VIC-
TORY! . . ."

Chapter 14

A dream...

"Calm, calm. Don't be afraid."

Afraid? Dann is not, he thinks dimly, afraid. He is merely dead.

Deadness will claim him any minute. He waits.

But the delirium is not fading, and under it is a memory of agonizing loss. Unwelcomely, Dann begins to suspect that he exists, is somehow again embodied in...in he does not know what.

"Calm, I'm here. I'll help you. You're safe now."

Is someone really here? Yes...yes. A warm, tentative someone speaking without words, touching without touch. A living presence like an arm pressing, not his body but his mind. A nurse?

"Gently, wake up now. You're all right. Wake up."

Perverse, he refuses consciousness. A confusion of memories coming now: being pulled, fighting vast currents. Is he back on that beach of childhood when the lifeguard girl had pulled him out of a rip-tide? She wore a copper bracelet, he remembers. Sissy somebody. Now he is dead and he has been saved again. But not by any Sissy; this time he knows he is on no mortal beach.

"You're all right really, you'll be home soon. Don't be afraid."

No voice, he understands. Only words coming into his, his head? And the arm is not flesh but a current of all-rightness flowing in. Human questions suddenly flare up in him. *"Who's there? Where am I? What—?"* And as he asks, or tries to, he feels a wince, a jumping-away.

"No! Please don't! I want to help you!" The presence is a receding whisper in his mind.

"I didn't mean to hurt you," he stammers effortfully, and is further confused by knowing he is indeed speaking aloud, but not in any earthly voice. Deliberately he opens his eyes, or, rather, succeeds in unclosing something. As he does so he understands finally that the senses he is activating, or focussing, are no organs ever owned or imagined by Doctor Daniel Dann.

—Who now finds what may be himself resting upon nothingness, perceiving an enormous curved and whirling landscape. Beside him towers a great rushing wall gloriously patterned with strange energies and emanating deep musics. Beautiful. And above, far above, is a weird, pale, rooflike arch he feels as potent, while far below, the great typhoon dwindles into the silent dark. A landscape of magical grandeur; even in exhaustion his spirit feels a faint delight.

Another fact comes; he seems to be "seeing" or perceiving in all directions at once, he is at the center of a perceptual globe in which he has only to focus. Extraordinary. Bemused by finding that the dead can feel curiosity, he tries to attend inward, and "sees," in the midst of a queer streaming energy, a huge mass of enigmatic surfaces or membrances, flickering here and there with vague lights. Can this be...his body?

Dreamily, he notices movement. The great fans or wings are tilting gently, continually readjusting themselves. From beneath come small jetlike pulsations which he can now vaguely sense. He feels himself at rest yet riding, balancing without effort on moving pressure-gradients, the vast turbulences of this air. To this body, the whirlwind is home.

Understanding can no longer be postponed. He is—is *in*—a giant alien form like those he now recalls having glimpsed or dreamed of.

Oddly, this fails to frighten him, but only charms him further. It is not generally realized, he thinks hysterically, that what the totally destroyed need is for something interesting to happen.... But where is his "nurse," the friendly stranger?

He scans more carefully. Deep below he senses living energies, like a great crowd; but they are much too far. Nearer to him on the wind-wall are a few isolated presences. Two are quite close, he can "see" them hovering on the wind, surrounded by the odd veils, like Elmo's fire. Still too far away. He focusses upward—and there it is.

A shape like his own, but smaller, clothed in an auroralike discharge. How he perceives this he doesn't know; it seems to be his main sense-channel, like seeing a thing he remembers from another life, a Kirlian photograph. As he thinks this he notes absently that the "fire" around himself has suddenly flared up toward the other.

"Look out! Please! Can't you control yourself at all?"

The words are clear. But the voice—it is an instant before he puzzles out that this real, audible cry was not a voice at all, but a pattern of light flickering on the membranes of the other's body. And yet his senses "heard" the light as speech. More mystery. Experimentally he wills himself to say, "I'm sorry"—and "hears" his words as a light-ripple on himself.

Incredible. Strangeness beyond strangeness brims up in him, overfloods his dikes. A dream? No, an ur-life; unreal reality. Nothing is left of him, yet here at the end of all he giggles.

"I am a giant squid in a world tornado, apologizing in audible light to another monstrous squid."

Evidently he has tried to say it aloud but without words for the alien concepts. He hears himself uttering garble mixed with orange laughter.

The laughter at least gets through. The creature above him laughs too, a charming lacy sparkle.

"Hello," he says tentatively.

"Hello! You feel better. What's your name? I am Tivonel, a female. Are you a male?"

Male, female? He gazes up at "her," letting himself slip deeper and deeper into this alien normalcy. He feels, he realizes, quite well; this body has a health, a vigor his own had lost long ago. It comes to him as he gazes that the being above him is indeed a female, in fact, a girl—a nice girl who just happens to be, in some sense, a thirty-meter giant manta-ray or whatever.

He is in no condition to criticize this.

"I'm Dann," he tells her. "Daniel Dann." Is the name getting through? "I'm a male, yes."

"Taneltan? Taneltan!" She laughs again, sparkling disbelief. "Males don't have three-names. I'll call you Tanel, it sounds more respectable." She sobers. "If you really are better, can you control yourself so I can come closer? I want to help you."

"Control myself? I don't understand."

"Hold your field in decently. Look at yourself, you're all over and inside out, you could even lose some."

"My . . . field?"

"Yes. Look at you."

"You mean that, that energy-stuff?" he tries to say. "Around . . . me?"

"It's not around you, it's *you*. Your mind, your life. You have to hold it in and arrange it properly. *Ahura*. Wait—watch me."

He watches her, and, marveling, sees the energy-halo englobe itself, shrink, spread out in patterns, expand to pseudo-forms, retract through a whirl of permutations and end in a delicately layered toroid around her coporeal body. Is he watching motions or dispositions of the actual mind, some kind of mysterious psychic art?

"I don't know how to do that," he says helplessly.

"Well, *try*. Oh, start by thinking yourself round, like an egg."

He doesn't believe in any of this, but is willing to be entertained. Awkwardly, he tries to "think himself round," and as he does so sees surprisedly that his pale fire-streamers are raggedly lurching inward in a crudely globular form. Good— but no, half of "himself" has perversely blown right out again. Because he noticed it? Not easy, he perceives, and concentrates again. *Roundness* . . . the flare retracts. He's getting it—Ooops, now his other side has bulged wildly away. He hears her laugh. *Roundness . . . roundness . . .*

"You're just like a big baby, that's what Giadoc said."

"Giadoc?" Still striving for some weird combination of control and alertness, he half-remembers . . . something.

"You're in Giadoc's body. He's my friend. Don't be afraid, he'll come back soon and you'll be back in yours."

"Giadoc...did he speak to me, when I, when I, uh, died?"

"He did? Oh good, that means he's all right. He'll be back soon. First they have to let the Beam down and raise it again. Look—I think they're letting down now. Maybe you'll go right back. Look up, see?"

Forgetting his "field," he looks up. The great arching of energy above is draining, dwindling down to its enormous perimeter. As it does so, the world around him brightens and strengthens, his own energies seem to sharpen.

"Well, you're still here," his new friend Tivonel says briskly. "That means you just have to wait til they raise it again. Now you simply have to control yourself. Do you know you nearly fell out of the Wind? The only reason I could pull you back was that you were sick. I was afraid you'd hit me, like the other one."

"The other one?"

"The other one who came here in Giadoc's body. I tried to help it but it *hit* me with its mind. It knocked me away. Can you all do that?"

"The other one...who came here..." In Dann's mind a forgotten glass of water slid on a bedstand, a voice wails *Margaret* into darkness. Did she come here? Pain knifes at him. Stop it, stop it. No more reality.

"Oh, you *are* hurt!"

"No, no," be manages to say from a million miles distant, aware of a timbre that his lost human mind calls green, but he knows here is pain. Gone forever in the dark—push it away. Get back in the dream-life, the dream of being a giant alien flying at ease in a world-typhoon, which is a pleasant afternoon. Chatting with a girl alien, feeling strong.

She has come closer. As he sees this, a filament of his mind-cloud seems to whip toward her and she whisks away, crying exasperatedly, *"No!* That's what you mustn't do. It's very rude, pushing your thoughts into people."

"What? You mean...if it touched like that, you can read my mind?"

"Well of course."

"I don't believe it," he says wonderingly.

"Well, I'll show you, but you have to hold perfectly still. Can you hold your field still now?"

"I don't know. I'll try." Watching his awkwardly eddying life energies, he recalls he had once tried to learn a meditation technique. It didn't help then; maybe it will now. Effortfully he strives to concentrate, to recapture the deep quietude. Shrink consciousness to a point, watch nothing. But he is still aware that an eddy of her field is flowing toward him. *Don't watch.* At the tangible nudge in his mind he reacts helplessly.

"Ouch!" She is swirling up into the wind.

"I'm sorry. I did that wrong."

"It's all right, you weren't too bad. Only you're so much *stronger* than a baby. Did you get it?"

"Get what?"

"The memory I gave you, silly. Look in your memory. Where are you?"

Where, indeed? Does ur-reality have a name, am I actually somewhere? Where?

—And he realizes he knows. He knows!

"Why, I, I'm on T-Tyree—that's your world. Tyree."

"You *see*?" She curves closer again, mischievous.

"My God," he tries to say, but it comes out "Great winds!"

"See if you got the rest. Think about Tyree."

"Tyree . . . Oh, yes, you're in trouble. Radiation is—" But this language has no words, he hears himself babbling about burning in the Wind and intolerable loudness of the Sound. The Sound? Sunlight? Of course, they think in other modes. "And wait, yes—you're trying to escape by sending your minds away somehow—no, that's wrong—"

"Very good! *Very* good!" Her laugh is so merrily coral, laced with empathic mockery it lifts Dann's leaden spirit. Why, this little Tivonel is indeed an attractive one. Bright spirit of the wind.

"But you, your world is in danger. You may die."

"Maybe." Undismayed, a brave little alien being who is every instant less alien. And then Dann learns something else.

"Don't worry. Giadoc will come back and send you home. He won't commit life-crime, he said so."

The melting tones are unmistakable; across the light-years he recognizes the colors of love. Love and sharing unto death, she and this Giadoc whose body he has somehow acquired. And will he, Dann, be thrown back to his grey private death, leaving her on a burning world? The memory of the inferno he had glimpsed. . . . So the charming ur-life is tragic after all. Pity . . . if he believed any of this.

"Please! Hey, please, your field!"

Confused, he perceives that his "mind-field" has eddied

strongly toward her, is coalescing into a peculiar surface whose vibrancy suddenly thrills him. An excitement his own old human body had long forgotten, a potent shivering delight—

"*Stop that!* You don't know what you're doing!" She is laughing wildly, her life-field suddenly intensified, recoiling yet linked to his by ever-increasing intensities. Urgency flames up in him, he needs to *drive* her higher into the wind, to push her away upon the power of his desire. Wild incomprehensible images of wind and energy flood through him, he is about to do he knows not what—but in a rush of flashing jets she shoots aside, and the tension breaks.

Shaken and roiled, it takes him a moment to locate her below him down the wind.

"You—you—!" She splutters unintelligibly. "You almost, I mean, you biassed, in a minute we would have—"

"What? What happened?" But he suspects now. The joy!

"Well!" She planes up nearer. "I don't know how to explain. Made a *repulsion*." She giggles. "Whew! Giadoc is very energic. We call it sex."

He hangs there astounded, conscious of himself as a monster riding an alien gale who has somehow committed an indelicacy. The etiquette of apocalypse. It was so good.

"We call it sex too," he tells her slowly. "Only with us the two people touch."

"How weird." Her vanes bank gracefully, he notices her beautiful command of the wind. Something else, too; his body seems to know that her position relative to him has changed things. With the wind coming from him to her she is still a charming one, but not dangerously so. Neutralized. Of course; they live in the wind, function evolves to its direction. Mysteries...

"But how do your eggs get exposed?" she is asking curiously.

He is about to enter on new fascinations, but his senses are assaulted by a dreadful scream. Terror! Someone is shrieking intolerably.

Dann peers about, discovers they have drifted closer to the pair of aliens he had noticed before. The large one is uttering the nerve-shattering green wail. It is thrashing about and tumbling, its energies wild. A smaller alien is in pursuit.

"What a shame," Tivonel says above the uproar. "I thought Avanil had it calm."

"What is it? What's happening?"

"I forgot to tell you. That's one of your people, there in Terenc's body. You better start Fathering it right away."

"One of my people?"

All at once the screamer shoots toward him and long streamers of its flaring field lash out. A jolting sbock—his mind is inundated with a kaleidoscope of faces, smells, bulkheads and valves, a foreshortened human penis against blue blankets, a Gatorade bottle—while over everything a face that he remembers, shrieks "RICKY—RICKY—HELP—"

The scene clears, leaving him reeling in twinned realities. The strange body is still before him, blasting out green screams.

"It's Ron!" Dann exclaims. "It's Ron from the, the water—"

"You better Father it before is loses field. You can, can't you? However you do it?"

"RICKY! RICKY, WHERE ARE YOU? HELP ME!"

The pain is intolerable. "I'm a doctor," Dann tries to say absurdly, moving toward the agonized form with no idea what he can do.

"Ron! You're all right, calm down! Listen to me, it's Doctor Dann."

—BLOOIE!

The next few moments or years exist only as a terror beyond all drug nightmares, beyond anything he has imagined of psychosis—rape—disaster. He is invaded, frantic, rolling in dreadful pounding synchrony of panic, sensing only in flashes that he is howling RICKY—RICKY—RICKY—is also yelling RON SHUT UP YOU'RE ALL RIGHT I'M DOCTOR DANN—only to be swept under the terrified crashing chaos, reverberating insanity. How long it lasts he never knows, understands only a sudden immense cool relief, like a great scalpel of peace cutting him free. Sanity returns.

As his separate existence strengthens Dann finds his body pumping air. He lets the scene steady into the strange-familiar world around him, is again his new self riding the gentle gales beside a wall of beautiful storm.

"Control yourself, Tanel, it's all right now."

The words are warmly golden; his friend Tivonel is hovering nearby.

Before him floats a great disarrayed dark mass, its small energy-field pale and calm. This seems to be the alien body containing Ron. Is he unconscious or dead? Not Dead; jets are pulsing. The smaller alien is helping it keep steady on the wind.

Dann's gaze turns upward.

Looming above them hovers a huge energic alien form, its vanes half-spread, its mantles and aura a deep, rich glory. It—no, unmistakably *he*— seems to be surveying them severely. Dann has a momentary memory of his school coach separating furious small boys.

"In the name of the Wind, Father Ustan, thank you." Tivonel's light-speech is in a new, formal mode.

"Thanks be that you were nearby, Father," the other alien adds, in the same mode. Dann senses that it is another female.

"What happened? Is my friend all right?"

"You made a panic vortex," the great stranger says in grave violet lights. "If I had not separated you in time you would both have been damaged for life. The being you call Ron is drained and sleeping. Avanil here will guard it. But you, Tanel, are you not a Father? Why did you permit this disorder to happen?"

"We, we have no such skills on our world," Dann says weakly.

The great being, Ustan, flickers a wordless grey sign in which Dann reads skepticism, scornful pity—the equivalent of a raised eyebrow. Majestically, he tilts up into the wind. But the female Avanil calls to him.

"Father Ustan, wait! Don't you notice the Sound is getting very strong up here? I feel burning, that's why I started to move Terenc's body. Look at all the dead life above us, too. I don't think this level is safe anymore."

"The Sound doesn't rise here now," Tivonel objects.

"Well, something up here is wrong. Look at the Airfall, it's all dead, too. I think we should go down to where Lomax and Bdello are."

Dann, "listening," realizes he has been noticing a rising hiss of light, or sound. It has a wicked feel, like a great subsonic machine-whine running wild.

Big Ustan has paused, spreading internal membranes.

"Avanil is correct," he announces. "I too sense dangerous energies. By all means, move them down to Chief Hearer's station to wait. I will take the distraught one."

"*I* can take him, Ustan," Avanil protests.

But Ustan has floated down to Ron's sleeping body, furling out the membranes under his main vanes. Dann has a glimpse of small, soft-looking flexible limbs. Then Ustan is covering him, swooping away like an eagle with its trailing prey. Next moment his great complex vanes fan out side, tilt up—and he becomes suddenly an abstract shade of flight, falling away from them on an awesome dwindling curve, down—down—

It is so dazzling Dann finds himself pumping air. Next moment the far-flying form has changed again and fetched up floating calmly by the two other presences below.

"That's Lomax and Bdello," Tivonel says. "Now you go."

"Me? Down there? I—" Dann is stammering, aware that his voice has a greenish squeak. His human senses have brushed him with vertigo. "I don't think—"

"Well, try," Tivonel says severely. "Giadoc was able to move around on your awful world. With no wind. You don't have to go that fast," she adds more gently. "Just tell yourself to go down, the body remembers. We'll help if you need it. Oh, I forgot. This is Avanil. I mean Avan. Avan, meet Tanel. He's a male so I call him that."

"Greetings, Tanel." The other's tone is like a curt handshake, he is reminded of a girl on a vanished world.

"Hello, Avan," Aware that he is delaying the awful drop, he lets himself take a last look at the grandeur of these heights. A million Grand Canyons of the wind, he thinks. No, far more beautiful. But that sound, that faint deadly roaring. . . . All in a moment the beauty drops away, he recalls his momentary vision of this world and its raging sun, the terrible exploding shells and angry streamers of a star gone mad. It was blowing up—that's what he "hears." Hard radiation. And these people, these real people, are on a planet about to be incinerated. Terrible . . . His mood is broken by a tangible nudge.

"Let's go," says Tivonel.

Down. Okay.

Focussing with all his might on the dots below, Dann lets himself spread something. His vanes adjust, he's dropping, swooping down while his body takes the air-rush, seeming to steer itself. Faster, intoxicatingly! The dots swirl, are lost and recaptured, the wind is full in him, is his element—it is glorious! The dots have grown to bodies, he realizes he must stop now. Stop! But how? Gales call him!

From nowhere two figures cut in before him, changing the rushing air. His vanes manage to bite the right angle. He slows, has stopped, hearing laughter all around.

Three figures that must be Ustan and the Hearers are above him. He feels a double nudge at his vanes, and finds himself lurching upward, with a ludicrous mental image of his staggering human self supported by two giggling girls.

"Thanks, Avan," Tivonel is saying. "Whew, wow! Tanel, I thought you were going all the way to Deep."

"I thought I did rather well." Dann finds himself chuckling too, all nightmare gone. He hasn't felt happy and strong like this in years. How great must be this life on the winds of Tyree!

They stop discreetly side-wind of the three big males. Dann stares curiously; from two of them the life-energy is radiating upward in a focussed, almost menacing way. Like high voltage.

"What are Hearers?" he asks.

"Oh, they listen to the Companions and the life beyond the sky. That's how they do the Beam, you came here on it." She goes on, something about "life-bands" which Dann finds unintelligible. He sees now that these energies are merged with shafts of others from far out around the Wall. Something to do with their weird psionic technology. *They brought me here....* What about time, he wonders idly, not really caring. If I went back, would it be centuries ahead? No matter; he is delighted with this new mystery. Astronomers, that's what they are. Astro-engineers of the mind. This Lomax is something like Mission Control, perhaps.

Avan, or Avanil, has gone to get Ron's body, and now comes struggling back to them, looking absurdly like a sparrow-hawk trying to tow a goose. When she has him positioned satisfactorily on the wind she turns to Dann, exuding determination.

"Tanel, if you're a male, you don't seem to know much about Fathering. How old are you? Haven't you raised a child yet?"

"Oh Avan, for Wind's sake," Tivonel protests.

"It's all right, I don't mind," Dann says. Pain flicks him, but it's far off; he has died since then. "I'm quite old as a matter of fact. I did have a child." To his embarrassment his words have changed color.

"Now see what you've done, Avan," Tivonel scolds. "These are people, you don't know what could be wrong."

"I'm sorry," Avan says stubbornly. "But I can't understand how you could be a Father and be so helpless with that one."

Dann hesitates, puzzled. Some extra meaning is trying to come through here. Father? "Well, I'm not sure, but you have to understand we don't have this kind of mind-contact on our world. And our females do most of the child-raising. In fact we call it—" he tries to say *mother* but only garble comes out. "It really isn't done by many males at all."

Before his eyes Avan has lighted up with delighted astoundment.

"The *females* do the Fathering! Tivonel, did you hear? It had to be, that's the world we want! Oh, great winds!"

Both females are pulsing excitely, Dann sees, attention locked on him. But Avan is by far the more excited.

"Why? Is that so strange here?"

"Calm down, Avan," Tivonel says. "Yes, Tanel, it's pretty strange. I'll explain if I get time. But look, they're starting the Beam now. Giadoc will be back any minute and you'll be home."

"The females do the Fathering," Avan repeats obliviously. "Think what that means. So they're bigger and stronger, right?"

"Well, no, as a matter of fact—"

"Listen, Avan, what does it matter? You better calm down before you lose field."

But Avan only flashes, "I'll be back!" and has suddenly whirled away and down. Dann looks after her. From here he can see or sense the crowd quite clearly, hundred of aliens scattered or clustered thickly in the wall of wind, among what seem to be plants. Big ones, little ones—but he sees them now quite differently. *People* are there, old, young, all sorts—even kids, jetting excitely from group to group. An emanation comes from them, a tension. Under the excitement, fear.

"More Deepers all the time," Tivonel comments. "Look at those young Fathers heading up here. That's Giadoc's son, Tiavan, that big one. Never mind, watch Lomax. See, the beam is starting up. Giadoc will be here soon and you'll be far away. Goodbye, Tanel," she adds warmly.

"You mean I have no choice? I'll just go snap, like that?"

"Yes. Don't you want to?"

"I don't know," he says unhappily. "I want—I want to understand more about you before I go. At least can't you explain more, give me a bigger memory like you did before? Yes! Give me a memory! For instance, about Fathering. And what are Deepers, what's life-crime? What do the Hearers learn?"

"Whew, that's complicated. I'd have to form it, there isn't much time." She scans about nervously.

He sees that the energies above Lomax and his colleague are thickening, building up and out, towering toward the zenith in a slow, effortful way.

"Please, Tivonel. From your world to mine. You should."

"Well, I guess they have a long job to get it up and balanced right. And they're tired. But it would be awful if we got caught in the middle."

"Please. Look, I'll stay as limp as Ron over there. Watch."

Eagerly he tries to collapse all awareness, focussing on the dim sense of air moving in his internal organs. It's difficult. Suddenly he is distracted by a giggle.

"Excuse me Tanel. That's very good but you don't have to do it all over, you're in what we call Total-Receptive. Never mind. Just don't jump when you feel me."

Concentrate, think about nothing. But the thought of being sent back to Earth intrudes chillingly. Is it really true? Don't think of it, all a dream. He is trying so hard that he scarcely notices the mind-push, reacts late.

"Tanel! You're terrible." She is floating nearby, laughing.

"Did I do something awful again?"

"No, you missed me. I think you're learning. Did you get it? I don't know where I put it, you were as mushy as a plenya. Think, what's life-crime?"

"Life-crime..." Suddenly, the words convey a kind of remote abomination to him. Of course, stealing another's body. "Yes," he says. "But you know, I don't quite feel it—it's so far from our abilities."

"You better," she says, suddenly sober. "Look down there, that Father Scomber coming up. And Heagran behind him. Did you get it all about that?"

He looks, and marveling, *knows* them. The huge energic oncoming form is Father Scomber, leader of the move to flee by life-crime. And the even larger shape behind him, veiled and crusted with majestic age: Father Heagran, the Conscience of Tyree. Incredible! Enlightenment, understanding opens in him like a true dream—the wonders of Deep City, the proud civilization of the air; joys, duties, deeds innumerable, the wild life of the upper High—a world, Tyree, is living in his mind!

Through his preoccupation he notices that several more are struggling up toward him, apparently finding the ascent difficult. And they're oddly formed.

"Those two, there—wait, Fathers—what's wrong with their, their fields?" He asks her.

"Oh, winds, did I forget to give you *that*? Can't you see their double fields? They're Fathers with children. In their, well, their *pouches*. It's not polite to say that. She giggles. "You have one, Tanel."

Her voice has flickered through the lavendar tones he understands as reverence.

"Amazing." Yes, he can see now the small life-nuclei nestled in their great auroras. Fathering?

"Here comes Avan back with her pal Palarin to hear you. And there goes old Janskelen, she hasn't forgotten how to ride wind. Some of those Deepers are a mess, they wouldn't be as scared on your world as I was. Don't worry, though. They aren't going. Oh—feel the signal? The Beam is up! Goodbye again, Tanel."

A shudder has raced through the world.

"Must I go, Tivonel?"

"Yes. But I'll remember you Tanel. Goodbye, fair winds."

"Fair winds." He can barely speak. This wonderful doomed world, the brightness of her spirit. Briefly he as lived in a dream more real than all his miserable life. "I'll always remember you, Tivonel. I hope, I hope—"

He cannot say it, can only pray that she will not be incinerated under that dreadful sun. The hideous background drone is rising and he thinks he hears, or sees, grey whines of sickness from the vegetation above. All too likely these wonderful bodies have already taken a lethal dose. Don't think of it. He feels a charming touch of warmth upon his mind, and sees that she has let a thought-tendril eddy gently to him. Just in time he forces his reaction to be still.

Another signal snaps through them all.

"That's it! Oh, wait a minute—look at Lomax!"

The Chief Hearer and Bdello are forms of static fire, their fields pouring up to the great arc overhead. Lomax' mantle seems to be flickering in anger. Dann has the impression he is cursing.

"Trouble. Ugh, the Destroyer. Well, they had that before. Wait."

The Destroyer . . . an image of huge dark deathliness. But not new to him—a vanishing spark dies again, and he shudders. Push it away.

"It's fixed now. Goodbye."

"Goodbye." A thought strikes through his self-absorption. "Will my friend, will Ron go back too?"

"He'll be all right," she answers mutedly. "I hope."

Dann waits, puzzling. Something unclear here, but nothing he can do.

The thrumming energies densen above him, he feels their pull. Any instant now he will feel the *nudge* that will be Giadoc returning to his body, pushing Dann out. And he will be whirled away through darkness, will awake to find himself in his own human body, Doctor Daniel Dann, the grey man of loss and grief. A new death.... Idly, he wonders what this Giadoc will have done as Dann. Will he find himself in some incredibly far future? Or will he awaken in Deerfield's disturbed ward, under restraint? No matter. Wait.

The sense of tension heightens, brims intolerably. Dann hears from beside him a soft mental murmur. *"Giadoc."* He muses on love, young love. And he himself has been briefly young again, in this magnificent alien form. He takes a last exultant grip of the great winds, reveling in his vigor, with the result that he side-slips abruptly. Behave yourself, old Dann... The memory of his inadvertent sexual episode stirs in him deliciously. How bizarre, yet how right. "The egg," she said. These people must be oviparous. And the males rear their young. Now he thinks about it, he can feel some massive organ underneath. My pouch! Really!...And it's some kind of political issue here, his new memory half-tells him why Avan had been so excited.... But the minutes are passing, nothing has changed. What are they waiting for?

He scans around. Bdello is speaking now, the light-whisper from his mantle faint with effort.

"Someone's alive!" Tivonel exclaims. "Oh, it's Terenc. But that means Giadoc's alive, he's all right, he's alive!"

Senior Fathers are closing around the Hearers. Dann has a confused impression of conflict, of commands and countercommands, verbal and telepathic.

"Oh, no," Tivonel says angrily. "Terenc won't come back! How *nasty*!"

But that means that Ron—Dann scans around, locates the still-sleeping form. If this Terenc won't return, is poor Ron doomed to die here in that? For a moment the scene turns hellish and *horror alienae* shakes him. But a thought comes to his

rescue: This is farther than China. Maybe poor Rick will be free
at last.

"I should stay, I should help Ron."

"You *can't*, Tanel."

True . . . He notices that a different female is guarding Ron.
She has ragged, blistered vanes. "Who's that?"

"She's my friend, Iznagel. I had her take care of him after
Avanil took off."

He'd missed the exchange; he is doubtless missing a lot.

"Try to help him, when I'm gone."

"I will. We'll take him right down where it's safer."

Safer—for how long? Meanwhile the resonating tension is
becoming painful; the world seems drained. He wishes the whole
sad business over.

But the argument around the Hearers has grown fiercer.
Purple blasts from the senior Fathers ride over excited cries.
Even Avan and other females are there.

"They've found Giodac!" Tivonel bursts out. "Oh, he's
coming, he's coming! I knew he would!"

Dann braces.

But at that moment the disputants around Lomax draw
slightly apart and there is a crimson shout from Scomber.
"Better a live criminal than a dead child! Heagran, we are
doomed here."

"No! Take down the Beam, Lomax!" Heagran bellows back,
and several seniors echo him. "Take it down. End this!"

"No! Our children must live!"

The uproar is suddenly drowned in a world-tearing scream.
A flame-shrieking fireball rips down the sky and buries itself,
exploding, in a high sector of the great wind-wall. The sound is
unendurable, gales buffet them. Dann feels a blast of burning
heat up his vanes. Through the confusion he sees the great shape
of Scomber spreading himself above Lomax.

"TYREE IS DOOMED!" he thunders. "FATHERS! SAVE
YOUR CHILDREN! COME, MY LIFE WILL BE YOUR
BRIDGE!"

His energy-field bursts up brilliantly, entwining that of
Lomax, towering up to the arc of the Beam itself.

"NO!" Heagran's mental roar tears through them. *"CRIMI-
NAL, CEASE!"* His great field launches itself at Scomber's.

But rearing up between them are other energies, coming from

the Elders and Fathers around. Energies crackle, writhe, lash to and fro. Dann is watching an astral fire-fight, a literal conflict of will against will! It rages in intensity, seeming to suck or damp his own life-force, and then dies back.

To his dismay, Dann sees that Heagran and his allies have been bested; their fields are sinking, leaving Scomber's triumphant blaze intact. As his mind recovers, it comes to him that he is seeing nothing less than the start of an invasion of Earth. The desperate victors are proposing to steal human bodies, to send human minds here, to die on Tyree.

What can he do?

He can only watch appalled, shuddering to Scomber's triumphant summons. *"FATHERS! COME, SAVE YOUR CHILDREN! USE MY LIFE!"*

And they are coming; below Dann a mob of Fathers is starting upward, struggling against the great winds, joined every moment by more. The two young Fathers near Scomber have already launched their life-fields upon his, bearing the nodes that are the lives of their children, leaving their bodies floating darkly behind.

"NO, COLTO! TIAVAN, COME BACK!" Heagran's mind-command jolts even Dann's opaque senses. Beside him Tivonel is sobbing wordlessly.

But Dann is transfixed, it is the most amazing spectacle he has ever seen. Those two life-minds striving up to the focus of the Beam—he sees them now as desperate parents racing with their precious burdens up out of a world on fire. Escape, escape! Caught in the deep imperative, he cheers on their mortal struggle, feels triumph as they gain height and flash away. The other Fathers below him are closer now, laboring with their babies toward the miraculous bridge of Scomber's life.

But as they come a small form jets to Scomber's side.

"Sisters! To a better world!" The cry rings out.

It is the female, Avan. In a moment her small life and another are racing upward along Scomber's energy-bridge.

"No! Come back!" A deeper female voice cries, and then another node of energy is pursuing them.

"Janskelen!" Tivonel cries out in shock, and then sobs, "Oh, Tiavan, how could you? Giadoc, Giadoc, come back!"

Her words are lost in the wind-rush as the first group of Fathers jet exhaustedly past, expending their last energies to reach Scomber and the promise of escape. From the dark bodies floating around Scomber a thin green screaming is adding itself to the uproar. Confusedly, Dann realizes that this should mean something to him.

But at that instant the roof of the world tears apart in a thunderous blast of lightning, and a storm of energies rains upon them all. Stunned, Dann flounders among random life-jolts, deafened by myriad screams.

"THE DESTROYER! THE DESTROYER HAS BRO-KEN THE BEAM!"

Slowly his senses clear. He is tumbling slowly by the great Wall, while above them the immaterial power that had been the Beam is shredded, raveling down to nothing. Where Scomber blazed below his defiant mind-bridge only dark bodies drift. It is clear that catastrophe has come. The mob of Fathers mills in fright, barely able to balance in this turbulent air.

"The Beam is down! Giadoc—they've got to find him!"

Tivonel is jetting past, heading up for Lomax. Dann follows dazedly. If the Beam, the connection with Earth is gone, is he marooned here to die of radioactivity? He doesn't really mind; he has, it seems, died several times over already. Another won't hurt. Maybe he can help Ron.

He becomes aware that his only real emotion, as he jets up through the gales of Tyree, is irritation with this unknown character Giadoc. If he and Tivonel are to perish together, it would be nice if she would forget about Giadoc long enough to remember him. The absurdity of his thought strikes him; he chuckles inwardly. Extraordinary what one does in apocalypse. Extraordinary, too, to think that this Giadoc is somewhere on Earth, walking about in Daniel Dann's old body. Dann wishes him joy of it, consciously savoring his winged youth and strength. Pity it won't last. Well, good to have known it. . . . The green screeches coming from below nag at him, but he puts them aside.

They reach Lomax to find him pale and drained but steady. His aide, Bdello, is still feebly righting himself, his life-field in disarray. Dann is reminded of an exhausted medium, or perhaps an inventor crawling out of the wreckage of his latest effort.

Beside them hovers the huge form of Father Heagran. Tivonel halts respectfully.

"Lomax, I have changed my view," Heagran is saying. "We cannot watch the children die. I cannot. But neither will I commit life-crime upon intelligent beings. Therefore I request you and your Hearers to find a world with only simple life-forms. Animals only, you understand. If you can find one such we will bear the children there. It will not be life as we know it," he says in deep sadness. "It will be degradation. But perhaps in centuries to come, perhaps something of Tyree will grow again."

The tragic colors of his voice are echoed on the mantles of the Elders nearby.

"But Heagran," Lomax protests, "my people are exhausted, in shock. Some are already scorched at the high stations. We cannot raise a Beam. And the accursed Destroyer is blocking half the sky."

"You must try."

"Very well. Those of us who can will probe singly, as we used to do."

"Chief Lomax!" bursts out Tivonel. "You have to rescue Giadoc, you must. You know he's trying to return."

The others darken in disapproval, but Lomax says gently, "Giadoc is beyond reach if he is on the alien world, little Tivonel. The Destroyer is between us. If he was on the Beam, he is already lost."

"He's trying to get back, I know it!"

"Then it is possible he will sense our probes." Lomax turns away with finality.

"He'll find a way," Tivonel mutters rebelliously.

I'll come to thee by moonlight, though Hell should bar the way, Dann quotes to himself. Or is he thinking of the poem about the girl who waited in Hell for her false lover? Never mind—the meaning of the terrified shrieks has suddenly got through to him.

"Tivonel! Haven't more of my people come here! In those bodies, the way Ron and I did? I should go to them, I must help them if I can."

"Why, the Fathers are fixing them, Tanel. Winds, you don't think they'd let *that* go on!"

Dann look-listens; in fact the agonized green has subsided to intermittent squalls coming from the group below them, where Scomber was. Only the body containing Ron is nearby, its mantle murmuring in dreamy light, Iznagel still faithfully guarding it.

"I should go down there to them anyway, Tivonel."

"Right. Iznagel, you better bring that one further down too. Here, I'll help."

She and Iznagel start gliding with Ron's huge body down the wind. As they go Dann hears Iznagel saying, "It's like an animal, Tivonel. I think they're crazy." Tivonel shushes her, explaining that Dann is one of the "crazy" aliens. "Oh, Tanel, meet Iznagel of the High."

Dann accepts the introduction absently; he has made out three or four small groups around bodies from which shrill yells are still erupting. Who will these new displaced human minds be? People from Deerfield? Good Lord, what if it's Major Fearing? Or is the Beam physically random? Could these be members of the French senate, or a group of Mongolians?

The figures are shrouded in plant-life, but he can clearly see a big male hovering over each, his energies blanketing the form beneath. Green cries flash, mind-flares are being pursued, recaptured, somehow molded down to dark. It reminds Dann of firemen converging on stubborn little blazes. Only the big body of Scomber appears to be permanently dark, untenanted. It must be truly dead.

"We can't go closer, not till they're drained."

The idea of electroshock jumps to his mind.

"What do you mean, drained? Are they being hurt, will they be all right?"

"Of course. Drained means drained, like Ustan did you. Resolving all the bad emotions, channeling the energy back. My father used to do it to me a lot when I was a child, I had tantrums. You don't know *anything*, do you?"

"Apparently not."

He watches the nearest group, marveling. Is he actually seeing the direct reconstruction of a human mind, the reformation of a Psyche? What a therapeutic technique! But who are these human minds?

Father Heagran has joined the group; there seems to be still some problem, judging by the uncontrolled screams.

"Oh!" Iznagel cries. "They're taking the babies out of the Father's—Oh, how dreadful! I can't look."

"They have to," Tivonel tells her. "Don't you understand? Those probably aren't babies. I mean the minds may be grown-up adults. And the Fathers aren't their Fathers. They have to take them apart."

But Iznagel only mutters bluely, "It's indecent," and furls herself in disapproval. Dann has the impression that she is peeking, like a matron caught at a porno film.

"Will they be all right? I mean, as babies?"

"Oh yes. Those are pretty big kids."

I should get over there. I'm a—" He tries to say *doctor* but it comes out "Body-Healer."

"Not while they're *Fathering*, Tanel. Listen, if you're a Healer, don't you think it's getting bad up here? I feel more burning, and it's like I'd eaten something dead. Shouldn't they move down?"

"Yes." What's the use of saying that he thinks it is much too late. These bodies must have taken a lethal dose already unless their nature is very different. "Yes. You should go down right away."

"Not me, them. I'm staying by Lomax. Giadoc will come, you'll see."

"Then I must stay with you. I have his body."

"Well . . . yes." A warm thought brushes him; he is mollified.

The activity around the nearest bodies is apparently completed. All but one Father move away.

"I'm going to them."

"I guess it's all right now. Fair winds, Iznagel."

The bodies turn out to be small; two females, Dann guesses. What minds lurk there? They are being guarded by a seemingly elderly big male, his vanes noded, his huge life-aura complexly patterned but pale.

"Greetings, Father Omar. This is the alien Tanel, he is a Healer."

The old being signs a formal response, then says abruptly, "To think that my Janskelen has committed life-crime! It is beyond bearing. After all our years!"

"I'm sure she didn't mean to go, Father. She was trying to stop them. That Beam pulls you."

"Nonetheless, she went."

They survey the bodies. Dann notices that the life-auras seem quiet and lax. Is it possible he is seeing human *minds*?

"That's Janskelen," Tivonel flicks a vane. "And that's Avan's friend Palarin. I hope they like your world."

One of the "minds" is moving.

As assuredly as he can, Dann concentrates on it, saying

"Don't be afraid. I'm a Healer, I'm here like you. Can I help you?"

To his surprise tbe other's field condenses up sharply, the mantle flickers.

"Ra...Ron...Ron? *Ron?*"

The light-tone is sleepy, but unmistakable.

"Rick, is that you? Rick! It's Doctor Dann here, don't be afraid."

The field veers sharply toward him, Dann just recalls in time to jerk his attention away. Not another panic!

"Ronnie, are you all right?" The uncertain voice is asking.

"Ron's all right, Rick. I'm Doctor Dann. Ron is right here, he'll be awake soon."

"I know." Warm color is returning to the words, the life-field is rearranging itself. Almost like a small Tyrenni, Dann thinks. The voice is so absurdly like Rick; was it only hours or an eternity ago that he had heard it tell the yarn about the Japanese time-machine? Incredibilities swamp him.

"I better explain what happened, if I can," he says.

"I know what's happened," the voice says dreamily. "We're on another world. We've been kidnapped by alien telepathic monsters."

Dann is so taken aback that he can only say feebly, "As a matter of fact...you're quite right. But don't worry. They're friendly, they really are."

"I know that too," says the voice of Richard Waxman, drifting in horrendous form upon the far winds of Tyree. Next minute his mind-aura subsides, his body darkens.

"What's wrong? What's wrong?"

"He's just asleep," Tivonel says briskly. "You always sleep awhile after you've been deep-drained. But look here, Tanel. Janskelen has something *really* wrong."

"What do you mean?"

The body of the old female seems to be floating easily, adjusting itself automatically on the uprushing air. It takes Dann an instant to recall that he should look at the important thing, the "field." When he does he sees that the nebulosity wreathing the body seems decidedly smaller and less structured.

"Do you have plenyas on your world?" Tivonel demands.

"What's a plenya?"

Instead of answering, Tivonel's mind-field extends and brushes the sleeping one. She recoils.

"Oh, for wind's sake, No! How awful."

"What? What's awful?"

"That's an *animal's* mind, Tanel. Poor old Janskelen has landed in some dumb animal. Oh, how sad."

Dann considers. In the back of his mind a Labrador's tail thumps. Good God. Apparently this Beam stayed focussed right on his group. And will Fearing, God knows who from Deerfield, be here too?

"Tanel, do you realize?" Tivonel is asking. "That's what'll happen to us if we do what Heagran says. We'll be *animals*. Nothing but beasts. I don't want to live that way, losing everything. I'm going to stay here and die as myself. I know that's what Giadoc'll want. We'll die here together."

Another far fire-shriek splits the heavens. Milder this time. It's starting, all right, Dann thinks. As the uproar dies away he says gently.

"If worst comes to worst Tivonel, it looks as if you may have to die here with me."

Chapter 15

It is so easy this time!

The thread of essence that is Giadoc has felt the tension-release which means that Terenc has left the Beam for an alien mind. Now Giadoc must enter one.

Life is near him; he touches, prepared to push. But there is no need—he finds himself being called, almost pulled into a strangely welcoming matrix. No fear here. He condenses into embodiment so gently that it occurs to him to greet the alien creature. As the displaced mind slides out on the Beam, it seems to leave him with a message: *Danger. Take Care.*

Extradorinary! What superior creatures, he thinks, establishing himself in the alien sensorium. To show Fatherly concern in the midst of what must be a terrifying experience. There will be no life-crime here; Giadoc resolves it. If he survives this test he will break the Beam rather than send such people to die on Tyree.

Remembering the stranger's warning he makes no move, but

lets the body lie in dark silence as he has found it, while he accustoms himself to the dead air and the weird somatic sensations. Thought flares are flooding around him, extra-energetic in the Beam's power. He examines them, looking for Terenc. Seven minds in his immediate vicinity, but no Terenc. All are disorganized and seem totally unconscious; he can read them as if he were among animals. He has, he finds, returned to the same place as before. What is exciting them so?

The nearest mind-field is intent on his physical body, its owner is in fact actually touching his limbs. It thinks of itself as Doctoraris, a Body-Healer. And three others nearby seem to be Healers too. They are focussed on a dead person or animal. How bizarre to have so many Healers! It must be due to their dangerous life among solid matter at the bottom of the wind.

Beyond the Healers is a small, excited, simple field—a child or a female? No; it knows itself as "Kirk," an adult male. Disgraceful!

Beside "Kirk" is the energy-phenomenon he remembers from his last visit: an unidentifiable complex of cold semisentience concentrated in a pod, with tendrils leading farther than he can scan. Some kind of intelligent plant? He probes Kirk's mind, finds its image as a "console" or "computer," apparently not alive. Fascinating!

All this has taken Giadoc only an instant, when suddenly a crude alien fear-probe bounces off him and he recalls that there may be danger here. Who tried to probe him? Ah—it came from the mind he met before, the being with multiple names, "Sproul," "Barr," or "Fearing," whom he had greeted. Now it's stationed apart in a high state of energy, violently compressed and yet drawing attention to itself by a barrage of hostile flares, mainly directed toward himself. This must be the problem the friendly alien had warned him of. This alien seems insanely concerned with ideas of concealment and control; Giadoc decides it would be unwise to attempt to interact with it again until it has calmed down. But he deciphers a useful fact from the repellent chaos of its thought: the body he is in is named "Doctordan."

Meanwhile the "Doctoraris" mind beside him is clamorously willing him to show signs of bodily life. Giadoc makes a final distance scan-sweep but Terenc does not seem to be in range. Very well. Deliberately he opens Doctordan's eyes.

The extraordinary silent light of this world bursts upon him, and the wealth of close, rigid outlines, surfaces, discrete movements, disorients him for a moment. It's hard to identify the mad mute shapes with the mind-fields in his scan. He sorts out the forms of two Healers carrying a sagging thing away; doubtless the dead body they were concerned with. Giadoc is amazed again at the way everything drags downward in this windless place. Even the energy of the Beam seems muted here.

Now Doctoraris is projecting impatience, and, alarmingly, the intention to have him transported elsewhere and do unclear things to his body. Surely Giadoc must prevent this; it wouldn't be fair to return the friendly alien to some unpleasant situation. Doctoraris' mouth is opening and closing oddly. As Giadoc notices this he recalls the air-jet language of this world. He has forgotten to activate his "ears."

He does so in time to hear speech coming from the "Fearing" alien.

"Kirk, you will tell the others that the Omali woman is under treatment for a heart problem. A minor heart problem. Is that clear, Harris?"

The words mean nothing to Giadoc except that they elicit fear-deference from the others. Amazing. But now he must do something if his body is not to be carried away too; his quiescence is being taken as a serious sign.

He energizes Doctordan's limbs, intending to bring it upright like the others. It's hard work, with no wind. He must hold the strange muscles rigid.

"Take it easy, Dann, wait—" Doctoraris protests audibly, his colors weirdly unchanging. "Do you feel all right?"

Giadoc allows the other to guide him into a chair.

"I am all right," he pronounces, probing hard through Doctoraris' mind for some plausible explanation of his collapse, while at the same time he works to deflect and drain the other's concern with him. It's all so alien. But finally he comes across an engram having to do with an organ in the upper part of his body.

"A minor heart problem," he echoes Fearing's words. All this time one of his upper limbs has been involuntarily groping in the recesses of the dead plant-stuff around his alien body. He encounters a small object and has a sudden vivid body-image of bringing it into his mouth. He does so.

"Forgot your medication, eh, Dann?" Doctoraris' thoughts resolve and relax; the mind-turning worked. "Smith, get some water."

"How about a coke, Doctor?" The other Healer asks.

"Okay."

Giadoc manages to grope through the embarrassing ritual of public intake. Fearing is still watchfully lashing out at him from a distance, like a wild corlu in ambush.

"I still think we should take you in, Dann."

"No, no need," Giadoc protests. "I am all right now."

To Giadoc's surprise, Fearing comes to his aid. "I believe we can take Doctor Dann's word for it, Harris. In fact I'd prefer him to remain here. Kirk, bring him some lunch and stay with him. Harris, since Dann says he's all right, I think we'll leave now."

"Very well."

Giadoc has been noticing a small but energetic field approaching from outside the "room." As the others prepare to depart, the newcomer bounces in, saying, "Good God, Major, what's going on here? Where's Margaret? Dann, what's wrong with you? The subjects were becoming extremely upset, I sent them to lunch."

Giadoc ignores the rest of the conversation while he studies this new mind. It is another small-field male—are there no Fathers here? He sees himself in charge of the alien experiment in life-signals: "Project Polymer." His name is "Noah" something and, surprisingly, there are areas of considerable order in his mind.

Good; Giadoc has just realized that he may be here some while. The Beam has not even withdrawn yet in this world's time. Perhaps the time-scales are different. He should behave appropriately to leave the body in good shape for the real Doctordan, and this "Noah" is clearly the best mind by which to guide himself.

"How are you, Dann?" Noah is demanding with more empathy than Giadoc has seen on this world.

"I am all right, Noah. I forgot my medication, that is all."

"Oh. Well, my goodness! Take care. I'm off to the hospital to check on Margaret. The next test is at three sharp, you know."

Regretfully, Giadoc watches him leave with the others. Too bad. But he can use the time alone to gain skill with his body.

As he rises unsteadily to his feet he feels the power of the Beam drain away and cease. On far Tyree the Hearers have broken link. Will his life continue?

He stands gazing around the windless alien enclosure, wrestling with rebellious memories. Tyree's plight—Tivonel—Tiavan's wicked intent. No—No time for that now. What's wrong with him? Resolutely he orders his mind. The minutes pass. He lives.

He feels nothing more than a slightly unpleasant lowering of his vitality. As he had suspected, it is possible to live on here without the Beam.

Very well. His task now is to maintain Doctordan's role until the Beam returns and he can go home. He moves about, gaining clearer and firmer contact with the body's autonomous skills, using his upper limbs to examine himself and his coverings, touching things. These manipulators are so large and strong and naked! It's like being a child again, before his mantle grew. Obviously these beings continue to manipulate matter all their adult lives.

On impulse he presses at the "console" of the cryptic semisentience. It does not respond. Presently he wanders to the access-opening of this place and stands looking out at the extraordinary world of the Abyss. The sheer quantity of static stuffs, the hard wind-bottom with its silent coloration of fear and shame, the ugly verticals and horizontals everywhere, the mute unchanging light. Unsettling, profoundly alien to the blessed blowing world of hime. But how exhilarating, to have all this time in an alien world! If this is to be his last adventure, it's a worthy one.

Experimentally, he pushes aside the access-cover and steps out. A weak flare of hostility greets him. Who did that?

Ah; he makes out a kind of pod resting in the middle distance. An alien mind-field is inside. At this range Giadoc can read only vague resentments connected with food and the vigilant intention to prevent Doctordan's body from proceeding farther. He steps back inside.

Extraordinary how much hostility the amiable Doctordan seems to be surrounded by. What a ferocious world! Well, not his concern.

Another pod is noisily arriving. Giadoc watches the "Kirk" alien get out, followed by what is clearly a pet animal. He is carrying objects which he intends to eat—with Giadoc. Oh, winds! Well, so be it.

"Up and around, Doc?"

No empathy here, quite the reverse. But the pet animal is projecting contact-welcome. Giadoc lets his hand move toward it and stops just in time at the flash of jealousy shooting from Kirk's mind-field. What wild people! He follows Kirk to the corner and watches him open the food, probing for his expectations of Doctordan's behavior. Ah; he seats himself.

Fortunately, no speech seems to be expected. By closely following Kirk's mind-pictures, at the same time copying his own actions, Giadoc manages to grapple with what seems to be called a "chicken sandwich" and some "milk." His body's automatic eating actions begin to unroll. Giadoc is delighted; it's like the child's game of following his Father's mental images of mat-weaving. But now he must sort deeper through the other mind for clues to what Doctordan's next actions will be. It's hard to believe these people are so unconscious.

As Giadoc's thought-tendrils snake into the other mind, he comes upon a pocket of emotion so repellent that he drops the "sandwich."

"Had enough, Doc?"

"A, a weakness," Giadoc stammers. Why, this creature before him is guilty of *physical* harm, thinks he has perhaps caused the death of a female. Yes, that dead alien he had glimpsed. And it excites him. Why, these people are savages!

"Terrible about Margaret," Kirk says, his thought wildly at variance with his words. "I guess I didn't take you seriously."

"Yes." Picking up the sandwich, Giadoc pushes aside a flare of repulsive malice toward Doctordan, and concentrates on what there is of Kirk's rational memory-field. "Project Polymer"—ah, here it is. He finds a pyramidal structure with Kirk himself at the top beside a small figure of Noah. Six subjects—the tests—a mind at a distance will attempt to transmit again, etc. etc. All quite simple and childish. But—Wind save us—Kirk's memory of what he, as Doctordan, will be expected to do, arrangments of complex matter on the test-persons, "electrodes," "pressure cuffs," "biomonitors"—it's appalling. And much too vague. He could never guide himself by this mind. And the next test is quite soon!

If the Beam does not return in time, what can he do?

Well, of course he can always feign illness as he had before. But the spirit of the game has him; he will play out his last adventure as far as he can. An idea comes to him, watching Kirk feed the last of his food to his "dog." Perhaps by double-probing the test persons and the old male "Noah" simultaneously he can get by? That would be a feat!

At this moment two things occur. A pod pulls up outside and releases a flood of large, active mind-fields—and Giadoc realizes that his Doctordan body requires to eliminate water. What to do, in this windlessness?

Luckily the same thought has just risen in Kirk's mind. Another cross-wind conquered! He copies Kirk's disposal of the debris and follows him back to the "latrine" before the new aliens come in.

The liquid-elimination routine proves simple, the body's habits are strong. As he stands beside Kirk, Giadoc allows himself to sample more of the other's surface thought, and suddenly picks up a detailed picture of alien sexuality. It fascinates him so that he almost forgets to hold his stream of liquid steady. Imagine, all that *contact*! Never to know the ecstasy of repulsion—and the egg unblessed by the wind! And how does the Father pouch the egg? Is this Kirk totally immature?

His explorations are interrupted by the entry of another alien, and Giadoc barely manages to follow Kirk's lead in restoring his "dick" and "zipper" to their original states.

The newcomer is transmitting friendship toward him and hostility toward Kirk. Giadoc pauses; the field is so large and expressive that he is sure this mind must be aware. But no; in answer to his mental greeting the other only says, "Not feeling so good, Doc?"

"Weak," Giadoc says, studying the other. Its name is "Tedyost," and it is preoccupied with some massive grief. Giadoc probes further and it enlightened: Tedyost's body is damaged by some illness that afflicts these people. He is in fact dying. Moved by such frailty, Giadoc involuntarily sends him the ritual energy-gift appropriate to the old.

"Dann! Where are you? It's time to set up."

Noah is calling him and the Beam has not returned. Well, now for some improvisation worthy of a true Beam traveler!

He finds Noah just outside.

"I fear I am not feeling all right," Giadoc tells him. "Can you assist me?"

"Damnation! And this is the big one. Margaret out sick, they wouldn't even let me see her. Oh, all right. Every bloody thing always—"

His anger is wholly superficial, Giadoc sees; the intent to help is strong. He follows Noah into a small enclosure containing a mind-field in such agitation that he cannot help extending a Fatherly field-edge. And he can sense others almost in panic nearby. Winds, this is going to be rough, if he must soothe and double-probe at the same time!

Moreover, the mind under his touch is a puzzle—an unmistakable Father who thinks of himself as a low-status female. But no time for puzzles now. Noah is manipulating a formidable mass of dead tendrils attached to chinks of shiny matter, expecting him to *do* something. What, what? Shamelessly he thrusts among them both, probing for the veins of expectation, their anticipations of what he will do. Ah, yes—select that "wire," the one with the clasperlike disk.

Concentrating with all his might, Giadoc lets his Doctordan hands carry it to the "temple," seat it on the skin. Approval in both minds—that was right. Now the next, yes, and the next. Memorize carefully. Is he succeeding?

Beside him Noah is doing something with "reels," not his concern. They are expecting him to attach another set of wires, something to do with circulation; the alien has extended a lower limb. Which wire? Ah—he guesses right and is already applying it when he catches the surprised objection, "electrode paste." What? Oh—He finds the substance and achieves the proper combination, though apparently too lavishly.

But it's working, he can do it! Elated, he realizes that this ambiguous alien is transmitting warm, Fatherly sympathy to Doctordan. Apparently the friendly Doctordan is well regarded by the test people, whatever hostility he evokes elsewhere. Thinking this, Giadoc lets his concentration slip and discovers he has done something wrong with the strip of matter on the upper limb.

"Let me, Doctor," He/she tells him verbally. "You feel rotten, don't you?"

"Weak," he admits, watching closely as the strip is wound. Noah has gone out.

"It's this awful place. If we get out of here alive I'll be grateful."

The being is deeply, deeply afraid, he realizes. So are they all, he is receiving a wail of fear-thoughts, images of horrifying captivity, indignities, the "Fearing" monster. Well, not his concern. He presses the other's mind with an enfolding flow of reassurance, and turns his body to go.

"You forgot to turn it on."

He turns back, succeeds in following the thought to a cryptic "switch" where he elicits a click and a flow of almost visible dead energy. More marvels—apparently these beings can control inanimate powers. If only he could stay and learn! But where is the Beam?

Noah is in the next compartment, busy with a small, obviously, mind-wounded alien. More expectations greet him: it is the same task all over again. His memory is clear, and this being is not in such tumultuous distress. With rising assurance, Giadoc seizes a strand of matter and begins.

"Hey, Doc, not on my ear."

Somehow Giadoc fumbles through it, expecting every instant to feel the rising energy of the Beam. Meanwhile he is becoming increasingly pleased with himself. His Father's soul is moved by the trouble of these wretched aliens, but as a Hearer he is fascinated by their chaotic, extraordinary individuality. Nowhere does he find the communal engrams, the shared world-views like those any Tyrenni Father transmits to his young. These beings seem to have had no Fathering; even these mind-experimenters have no real communication. Each is utterly alone. They are aliens *to each other*.

Giadoc moves from one to the next, manipulating the strange artifacts, dispensing what comfort he can. Meanwhile he has given up trying to decipher roles and genders; he samples the wildly disparate minds—lonely prides, pains, longings, incomprehensible enthusiasms. Each alone in its different structure and quality. What an extraordinary experiment of nature! How lucky he is to have experienced this.

When he is dealing with the sick young male he had met before he has a surprise. In Tedyost's mind is a scene of rushing, foaming colors. Why, it is almost like the wind of—a place Giadoc will not think of now. There seems to be some beauty on this world too. What a pity he has no time to explore. Tedyost has apparently been banished from his loved place because of his body's illness. How unjust, Giadoc muses, recalling just in time to "turn on" the thing. In fact, this seems to be an unjust, dangerous world. Well, perhaps Doctordan when he returns will be able to help them. But why is the Beam delaying?

The last test-person is most pitiable of all, a mind almost formless with fear for some missing family-member.

"Listen, Doc, they've done something to Ron. I *know* it."

Giadoc can only transmit an emergency pressure of calm, leaving "Rick" staring after him. Noah is blasting out impatience for him to go out to the large enclosure and wait. Giadoc complies.

"Two minutes. Everybody ready?"

Kirk is here too, his dog-animal stationed by his side. Giadoc seats himself, thinking that he must not leave Doctordan's body to fall downward when the Beam returns, as it surely must any moment now. Hungry for knowledge, he scans the cryptic energy of the "computer." Oh, for more time!

"Fifteen hundred, three o'clock. Start!"

Nothing happens for an instant—and then a roar on the life-bands rips through the air so fiercely that Giadoc almost retracts his scan.

"*A-B-A-J-M! A-B-A-J-M! A-B-A-J-M!*"

Great winds, it's Terenc!

He must have entered the distant test-person, the one in the water-pod somewhere. Now he is acting out his part. His nonsensical repeating signal is so strong it's bringing fuzzy imagery-scraps. As Giadoc is noticing these, his alien ears are assailed by a yell from Rick.

"That's not my brother! They've done something terrible to Ron!"

Giadoc opens the door and automatically thrusts an emergency-calm field-edge at Rick, while Noah implores, "It's all right, Ricky! Ron's all right! Please, Ricky, please don't spoil the test."

"He's not all right," Rick persists as Terenc's transmission blares on. But Giadoc's efforts are having effect. Rick slumps back in his seat and lets Noah replace his marking tools. "*Please* write down what you got, Rick. We'll check Ron as soon as it's over."

Excitement is emanating from all the compartments; the

others are evidently hearing Terenc's signal all too clearly too. How could they fail?

Giadoc maintains what hold he can on Rick while Noah calls out, "Second group. Start!"—and Terenc's new signal comes blasting through.

"B–N–O–Z–P! B–N–O–Z–P! B–N–O–"

More agitation from the other cubicles. Giadoc strains to send out a wave of reassurance while keeping pressure on Rick. Oh, when will the Beam come and free him?

"Third group. Start!"

May Terenc fall out of the Wind, Giadoc curses, as the third shout yammers through. The effort to soothe them all is taking all the field-strength he has on this weak world. But Terenc is throwing them close to panic, and it's his responsibility not to let harm come . . . The interval seems to take forever.

By the fourth signal even Kirk is showing signs of disturbance, but Giadoc does not care. Where in the Wind's name is the Beam? They must recall Terenc first.

As the fifth signal howls in, Noah pops his head through the door.

"Dann, I believe I'm *getting* something myself!" he whispers, his field flaring elatedly. "This is amazing, we must discover the exact conditions. Ron's never been so good before!"

And never will again, winds willing, Giadoc thinks.

And then to his infinite relief he feels the thrill in the air, the palpable, thrumming, building power of the seeking Beam.

"Take Terenc! Take Terenc first!" he projects with all his might as the last signal-groups come ripping through.

"That's it!" Noah is shouting happily, rushing among the cubicles. "Identical! Every one identical, Kirk! Oh, wait till they see this. Dann, Dann, come help me get the subjects out."

But Giadoc does not stir. The huge tension of the Beam is coming to full focus on him now. In a moment he will be away forever and the real Doctordan will be here to do his work. Giadoc wishes them well. But why is it taking so long?

Ah! Energy culminates.

But just as he gathers himself to launch out upon it, he realizes something is wrong. No good, wrong bias! His life is thrown back violently, dazing him, but he realizes the dreadful meaning. *"NO! Fathers, you must not!"* he sends fiercely.

But it is too late. Familiar energies are blooming into being nearby.

"Doctor Dann, help! Frodo—"

"Dann! Chris is—"

Giadoc staggers through the clamor in the cubicles, already knowing what he will find. Yes—an alien female body is lying screaming on the floor, wreathed in the terrified field of a Tyrenni child. As he stares, the small alien male blunders past him and falls to its knees by the body. Around him surges the huge, unmistakable field of a Father of Tyree. The newcomer clasps the alien girl. The fields merge, the screams cease.

It is the life-field of Giadoc's son, Tiavan, and his child.

"Criminal! Go back!" Giadoc lashes at him.

"Tyree is burning. I will save my child." And then Tiavan is wholly preoccupied in Fathering, his alien mouth mumbling "Calm, you're safe my little one. Father's here."

Uproar among the aliens; one is clinging to Giadoc and crying out. The air is humming and bursting with the power of the Beam. The alien Kirk has pushed into the commotion and, unthinkably, is tugging at Tiavan's small bodily form, trying to pull him from his child. Tiavan mind-strikes him, he staggers back. Then Rick gives a loud scream and falls, while another, smaller Tyrenni field streams out around him. *"No wind!"* it transmits in horror. But Giadoc has no time to attend, he is almost knocked over by Kirk charging out.

"I'm calling the patrol. You freaks are into my head!"

"No, no, Kirk!" Noah rushes after him.

Giadoc follows in time to see Kirk seizing some energy-device. But as he does so, his body arches backward and he shouts wordlessly, falling. In a moment his own limited energies are replaced by the wildly faring energies of a child of Tyree. At its first cries, the old ambiguous alien stumbles out and falls upon it, another huge Father-field furled around them both. Giadoc thinks he recognizes the life-pattern of Father Colto. Kirk's animal is circling them, uttering yelps.

"Doctor Dann, what's *happening?*" cries the alien still clinging to his arm. Next second she too staggers, still hanging on him, and the life-aura spreads to a pattern he knows: the female Avanil.

"N-o w-wind—" she mumbles, and collapses. There is a final yell and crash from the corridor.

Angered beyond expression, Giadoc stands irresolute in the throbbing, energy-brimming room. Seven Tyrenni are here. Only the old alien Noah is left, so excited that he can only turn in place, gasping, "You—you—Who! We, I think I—" while the power of the Beam rains down, still biassed against him.

Then the dog suddenly falls over, and Giadoc sees a last Tyrenni field striving to form around it.

The Beam clears. He is free to go.

But as he gathers himself, the vision of the two Fathers attempting to comfort their grotesque "children" wrenches him. And Tiavan, his son. How can he leave them to the dangers of this place? Desperately he mind-shouts, *"Go back! Undo your crime. This is a dangerous world, your children are not safe here."*

"No!" The figure of Tedyost lurches out of the corridor, a big Tyrenni field streaming about it. But the life is damaged, in terrible disarray; Giadoc can scarcely recognize him.

"Scomber!" he exclaims aloud. "You have done this thing."

"Yes." Tedyost's body falls against the wall and slides downward, while Scomber's wounded life writhes, trying to restore itself. Beyond him Giadoc can see Tiavan trying to force his small alien body to carry or drag his child in this windless place. It is pathetic beyond bearing. But the power of the Beam is falling and rising oddly; Giadoc must go.

At that moment he becomes aware of alien minds outside, and a hostile emanation from the doorway.

Major Fearing walks into the room.

The hatred he transmits is so shocking that Giadoc is transfixed. Danger here. But the alien's outward appearance is spuriously calm and relaxed as he gazes around the chaotic room. When he perceives the prone figure of Kirk cuddled in the old alien's arms his mind forms the words, *"They've got that fool Kirk."* Meanwhile his mouth is saying smilingly, "Well, Noah, how did your big test go?"

His hand holds out a paper.

Noah comes out of his trance and begins distractedly exclaiming and showing Fearing his results. As he does so, Giadoc can read in Fearing's thoughts the intent to do some violence to the bodies in which the Tyrenni are, in which his son is; a picture of them lying inert and mindless, something about Doctoraris. The contrast between Fearing's hatred and his demeanor is frightening, it implies absolute power to do his will. The Beam is flickering again, but Giadoc cannot leave the oblivious Tyrenni now. The Beam will wait for him; it must.

"DANGER! DANGER!" He sends in utmost-emergency mode. But the Fathers are too preoccupied. Only Avanils' mind starts to respond. But she breaks off, touching the dog, and mind-cries, *"Janskelen! Janskelen is in this bad body!"*

It is true, Giadoc sees, but he is thinking of protecting Tiavan. He can now read Fearing's intention to call in his followers and seize the helpless Tyrenni. Great Wind, what can he do? Can he mind-turn Fearing as one would an animal? For even that he needs another Father's help.

"Tiavan, Colto! Help me for your children's sake! Tiavan—"

As he mind-shouts the Beam falters, rises, sinks away worse than before. Is he about to be trapped here? *"Tiavan—Colto—"* Meanwhile Fearing is saying with eerie calm, "Remarkable range and accuracy, Doctor. I compliment you. I obviously did not take this as seriously as I should. Fortunately I have been able to make immediate security arrangements."

"What do you mean, security arrangements?" Noah demands confusedly.

"In your natural enthusiasm, Doctor Catledge, you have overlooked the first and basic consideration of any intelligence capability. Control. *Control.* This remarkable demonstration makes speed all the more imperative."

He turns toward the door, flicking a snap of cold energy from his wrist.

It is the last instant for them all, Giadoc understands. *"Tiavan! Colto! They are about to take and harm your children! Send them back!"*

"But these are people, Major," Noah is shouting. "This is the United States of America!"

"Precisely," Fearing says.

At that moment the power of the Beam rises momentarily, and a bolt of life-energy flies through the room, dazing them all. When Giadoc's senses clear, Fearing is prone on the floor beside the dog, who is squealing and jerking frantically.

Fearing rises awkwardly to one knee and Giadoc, astounded, sees what has happened.

"Janskelen!"

"Y-y-yes," says the mouth of Fearing.

The door of the room opens and a large alien stands there, its small field oriented to Fearing. "Sir?"

Giadoc abandons all civility and sends a hard mental

command into the old female's mind. Janskelen flinches, but she is quick.

"Remove... that... animal," she says with Fearing's voice.

The dog is slavering, attempting to walk on its hind legs, with Fearing's mind-field whirling about it so madly that it seems impossible the alien does not see. But he only advances a step, studying it phlegmatically.

Noah starts to speak, but Giadoc mind-quells him.

The dog howls and scrambles awkwardly onto the desk.

"Be careful, it is dangerous," Giadoc says involuntarily.

"Yes sir." Still with no animation the alien turns to the door and calls. "Deming! Bring a net and a can of four-oh-eight!"

At this the dog screams again and leaps straight for him. The alien ducks aside and the dog bolts out the open door. Shouting from outside. Then the alien turns back and asks, "Do you want Doctor Harris' team here now, sir?"

Again Giadoc improvises mental commands, and "Fearing" says slowly, "No. Tell them... to go. That will be... all."

"Yessir." The alien departs.

Safe, for the moment at least. But the Beam is fading badly, Giadoc must go now or be forever trapped.

"Tyrenni! You are still in peril. Tell this old alien Noah who you are. He may help you. I will not commit life-crime. I go."

Gathering himself to the failing power, he casts a last scan back on the scene that holds his only child—he will remember it always—and hurls his life up and out onto the frail life-thread. He is just in time, he feels being caught, stretched immaterially in a flash through nowhere. Back to doomed Tyree, back to Tivonel! And Doctordan back to his rightful body. He has made it, he hurtles exultantly. The Beam holds true!

But just as he exults—his universe vanishes.

The skein of vitality that bore him has gone to nothing, there is no Beam. All energy has died. He is only a dwindling nothing adrift in nowhere, all life is draining out of him. He is about to die. And ahead looms a dreadful blackness that his fading mind knows only too well.

The Destroyer.

Goodbye Tyree... Goodby Tivonel... Thought dies. Helpless in cold and dark, that which had been Giadoc plunges into death.

Chapter 16

In cold black nowhere a tiny thing will not die.

Alone in dark immensity, the energy-configuration that has been a life is almost extinguished. It is stripped of all qualities, shrunk to a single point of not-death in a universe of deathliness. Blind and mindless it strives against annihilation, fighting with no weapons but its puny naked will.

Aeons earlier it had shot here seeking obliteration. But at the end, the life at its core will not let go.

It is alone, alone in the ultimate icy void, falling without motion ever deeper into dark nothingness. Only a fading spark strains, strives for some possibility, some dimension or current or difference to save it from the final dark. It flails limblessly, grasps nothing, struggles without strength or hope against the overwhelming death around it. Deeper and deeper it is swallowed. Its last existence flickers; it is almost gone.

But at this final instant its immaterial being meets an infinitesimal resistance. Something—something is tenuously touched!

Too weak even to feel reprieve, the spark clutches, clings to the unknown contact. And as it does, slow help comes to it. The faltering energy finds itself minutely sustained; the potential gradient that had fallen nearly to zero halts, and begins painfully to steepen again. After an unknown time it is able to stabilize. Now it is more than a point. It becomes a faint but growing constellation around the nucleus. Fragments of its dead self come back to spectral being.

With them comes a first emotion of life—fear. Hideous images of being strangled, frozen, asphyxiated, destroyed in a myriad terrifying ways assault it. The being struggles harder, a frantic mote in the maw of death. It clings to the unknown sustenance, fighting simply to continue to be. And as it strives it strengthens, recruiting the shadowy energy-circuits and complexities of its former life.

Presently there comes to it a kind of half-consciousness, and it perceives mistily that it cannot be strangled nor frozen, since it is without breath or pulse in infinite dark. These are only specters of sensation evoked by terror of the huge menace all around. Knowing itself dead yet not-dead, it tries fiercely to collect itself, to recreate its shattered entity. It drives toward existence as a drowner drives toward air, it exerts stress upon the texture of nonbeing. Strength grows in it, presses hard and harder against nothingness. Pressure mounts, a substanceless film bulges without dimension. Until suddenly nothingness yeilds, and there is a blossoming, tearing pain like orgasmal birth.

The ghostly circuitry of a living woman exists again, strung out between the stars.

The sense of re-existence is acute, paroxysmal. The being convulses in long shudders of awareness. With wonder it perceives itself, knows that is has coherence, complexity, a history, even a name.

It is Margaret Omali.

No! She clenches herself away, would shriek out if she could. The name is a damnation, it brings pouring in on her the pain of a life she had meant only to end. What cruelty is this, why is she not dead?

She shrinks, trying to cancel consciousness, disappear from being. But she cannot; she senses that her despair is fueling the energy that sustains her. Her human life streams back, activates even the echo of her last human thought: *My insurance. Donny will be all right.*

What dreadful happening has cheated her of death?

Sick and grieving she drifts, uncaring that the unknown sustenance continues. The energy that is her life augments and completes itself in phantom structure. And at length her despair is penetrated by dull puzzlement. Something is different. At first idly, then with sharpening attention, she examines this strangeness. Can it be true?

Warily, she lets her thoughts open, lets herself be known to herself, and finds astonishment.

It is true! The pain and tension that hammered at her nerves are gone. Nothing hurts her now.

She can scarcely believe it. For so long she lived in lacerated shame, her body an aching agony without release. Her only desire was to hold the psychic wound quiet, to escape to levels of the mind beyond its reach.

Now it is gone. Feeling herself deliciously unbodied she stretches immaterially, as one would stretch exhaustedly upon cool sheets. Yes! Yes! The relief holds, exquisite as bare limbs lapped in eiderdown. Whatever remains of her has left her body and its pain behind forever. She does not know or care what or where she is, marvels only at the sweetness of release.

The memory of the brief bliss she had once felt from a drug brushes her, but that was far-off and unreal. This, whatever this spectral half-life is, is real. Exultance, amazement floods her.

She is dead—and free!

Letting herself sense it fully, she would laugh aloud in this place of death if she had anything to laugh with. But laughter is unnecessary here, the emotion itself suffices. Relaxed as she had never been in life, she exists as a substanceless smile.

How long the simple joy of no-pain lasts she has no idea; here time is not. But finally a human curiosity of place stirs in her. She is, she knows, totally alone. That does not trouble her, she had always been locked in loneliness. Now she wishes simply to understand this place, if she is in a universe where place has meaning. Specific memories come to her; she recalls her wild flight through the void among incarnations flashing like dreams, her final plunge toward the deathly blackness. It had seemed to her then to be a lethal hole in space, a sure and ultimate extinction. Is she now somehow alive *in* that?

The thought does not frighten her in her new comfort. But the desire grows in her to know more. Without material senses or receptors she quests around herself, aware that she must not let go of the strange cold pinpoint of energy that sustains her life. What can it be, what is she based on? She has heard of superconductors, of circuits that cycle forever near the cold of ultimate zero. Perhaps she is drawing strength from something like that. But what is out there? The strange small sense she has never let herself think of is still with her; she gathers it and tries to outreach, a feeling-outward of inquiring life.

Nothing. She reaches farther—and touches real death.

The contact is dreadful. She cowers in upon herself, knowing that something cold, alien and terrible is out there, nearby. Is it aware of her?

She waits. Nothing happens. The coldness she had touched does not seem to be moving, comes no closer. She listens without ears, attends with all her being for something, anything to tell her more. Still nothing. But the void has dimension now. There, along *that* direction, is danger.

She must recoil, get farther from it, but she dares not let go of the anchor-source of her strange life. She strains away to her utmost, searching, probing. Still nothing. But wait—now she senses, fainter than silence, an impalpable tendril of presence just at the margin of her ken. She attends hungrily, trying to tune herself to it.

And a conviction grows: it is not hostile. It has in fact a reassuring *ordinary* quality, like some familiar small comfort of her lost life. What can it be? It seems—yes—it is somehow beckoning her, like a hand outstretched to lead her away from the dangers of this place.

With all her small might she focusses out toward it. And the fringes of her being touch a gossamer point. A density, another of the strange contacts lies there. Dare she try to transfer to it? *Come*, the faint summons urges from beyond.

She gathers her courages, marshals her being. Her mind enacts the image of a woman leaping from stone to stone across an immense dark river: *I dare!* She lets go her base and sends herself wholly across the void to coalesce around the new support.

Success! She knows now she has moved physically, in whatever space this is. She has moved away from the deadly touch, over what distance she has no idea, an atom's width or a light-year. And the act of will has strengthened her. She feels her own intricate existence triumphant in the dark, and tries to scan around.

The faint beckoning something is definitely stronger here. *Come! This way.*

Can she continue? Again she reaches with her mind, and again finds contact. Another of the cold life-sources is there. Without hesitation she leaps to it and begins to search anew. Yes! There are more. And the friendly call is clearer. In marveling excitement she leaps, or flows, or hurls herself again and again. She is mastering the rhythm, she can move here in abyssal night.

The image of stepping-stones has vanished. As she moves she knows herself as nothing woman-shaped, but a pattern of energy flashing along charged points. Flow, gather, surge—she is energy discharging through capacitors, perhaps. But a structure, she thinks; a very complex configuration; the spectral texture of a human mind. And as she moves another image comes to her, so that she pauses for a moment in wonder. Is she something like a computer program? A ghostly program prowling the elements of some unimaginable circuitry?

The thought delights her. She does not believe in heaven or gods or demons or any hell beyond the life she had known, but she has seen real ghosts in her computer read-out screens. She knows she is dead and she had never been very human. To be a free, untormented ghost-program is not frightening.

Perhaps the danger she had felt was some design to cancel her, to flush her out of existence as they had attempted to flushout TOTAL's ghosts?

No, she decides. I will not be evicted. I will remain this new sweet life awhile, even as nothing in the cold and dark. But what is this small calling presence or energy which she has been following? It is very close now, she can sense its urgency. What is it? Is it perhaps another like herself here in the paths of death?

The thought displeases her. She thinks toward it demandingly, striving to shape interrogation. *Who are you? What is there?*

Nothing answers her at first, only the ever-stronger summoning, an almost tangible directional desire. Like a dog tugging at her coat, willing her to follow.

What are you? Tell me! No answer. But she realizes abruptly that an image has formed in her mind's eye, a glimmering vision like a pallid rectangular shape rising through black water. It is a computer console.

Is she imagining this? As she attends to it the image strengthens. She can make out the keyboards, the dials, the read-out screen and reel decks above. Why, it is her familiar office console, she has spent years at those grey, red, blue keys; there is even the stain where ditto-fluid was spilled. It is hallucinatory, it quivers or shimmers like an after-image, floating on the darkness that presses around and through it. But it is no ordinary vision; she wills it away, but still it will not go.

Puzzled, the thought comes to her to activate it. Instantly there is a vivid kinaesthetic sensation of her own arm moving, she sees the long dark fingers that are no longer hers float out and press the toggle. *On.*

At the same moment the screen flickers to life. The symbol is clear, a tiny blue arabesque in black immensity.

$$\int_0^{\pm\infty} f(x)\, dt$$

It is the integral of time to plus or minus infinity, the "signature" of TOTAL's unquenchable ghost!

Half-amused, half-annoyed, she probes at her own thought. Is she recreating memory or is this some real manifestation of the condition she has waked to? It holds; it seems so real. Well, if she is herself a ghost-program, what more likely than that another should be here? Has her mind somehow got into TOTAL? She hopes not; she had been sure that she was far from Earth. No matter, she decides. It's all fantasy, a dead mind dreaming.

As she had done so often before, she makes no effort to cancel the intruding program but instead lets her hallucinative fingers tap out a holding code. The screen flashes// TIME*INDEPENDENT*STORE//and vanishes from her mind.

With that the sense of the calling awareness comes back in force. *Come! Follow me!* The friendly quality is unmistakable now.

Fantasy upon fantasy. Bemused, she yields and lets herself flow from invisible point to point in the desired direction, as she has learned to do. I am in the underworld with my faithful computer, she thinks. I am being led through the land of death by a friendly computer program. Perhaps it likes you, someone had said. Perhaps it does, or at least the crazy ghost-program does. She is sure she senses a strange amicable intent, unliving, cool yet warm. The marvel of the complexity of the great electronic ganglia comes to her again. Could it have been, was it, somehow a real base of life?

The idea seems more than fantasy here, following insubstantiality through nowhere. More memories awake. She had never had nor desired telepathy, the contact of human minds; but some abstraction of energy-in-complexity had always touched her in a deep, peculiar way. She empathized with it. Working with TOTAL she had always felt in more than technical rapport, some bond beyond the mere program being executed. She had never consciously thought about this; it was of the same almost shameful secret nature as her flashes of power over real matter. A crazy thing. Perhaps she was not very human. But if structured energy achieved a kind of life, would she not have access to it?

The idea grows into conviction. She is sure now that she recognizes the entity she is following, a computer life somehow tuned to hers. But where, in what strange universe are they?

She has been increasingly aware that their dreamlike progress is changing course, the route is not straight. And it is hazardous; she is receiving now urgent demands to hurry, now a sense of being warned back. It is weirdly like a child's game. But the danger here is not imaginary; again and again she feels a brush of icy menace. Is she being led stealthily through a fortress? Are they escaping? Or are they going ever-deeper into the heart of the immense enemy, to its very brain, perhaps?

Deeper, she thinks; danger seems to lie now on all sides, as if they are creeping through secret conduits into an inmost stronghold. Vast unknown energies are all about; the void is not quite empty, here. Human fear touches her, and she hesitates. But the urgent pleading intensifies, begs her to go on. She does. The nothingness around her densens. Surely she is nearing some end.

At that moment all urgency to motion ceases, and she knows that she has arrived. The destination, the center, the mighty nexus of this universe lies just beyond. Warily she gathers herself. *What is here?*

As it had done before, the console-image rises to life in her mind. This time the screen is lit. She reads:

//NO*ENTRY*EXCEPT*TO*AUTHORIZED*PERSON-
NEL//

For a timeless instant that which had been Margaret Omali
tries to laugh, would laugh, exists as laughter in the dreadful
dark.

The absurd message brightens, changes to TOTAL's
time-signature, then runs through an array of vectors she
recognizes as a loop in the NASA space-voyage simulation,
ending with a special-exit sequence and repeats:

//NO*ENTRY*TO*OTHER*THAN*AUTHORIZED*
PERSONNEL//

Slowly, she understands. This is communication; somehow a
mind that is not a mind, an unliving life, is trying to link with
hers. How does it know her? Is it possible that the same keys that
gave her entry to TOTAL were a two-way channel, gave
TOTAL some real access to her? Does it know her as a program
called human?

No matter. She has the message: This is a portal.

Here is the interface with some unknown concentration of
power and information. She can go in. But the decision is
forever. Once inside, once "authorized," she will be meshed with
whatever lies beyond.

Past this point, she thinks, I won't be human anymore. The
thought troubles her briefly. But the presence she has followed is
waiting, emanating its promise and warning. A cold beauty
seems to call to her, a vista of no earthly dimensions. What does
she care for the humanity she had known?

Deliberately disregarding a last faint pulse of mortal fear, she
focusses on the darkness ahead. A silent tide of power seems to
rise against her, cold, cold and enormous. But she has power
too. *Here, push here!* TOTAL seems to call. She gathers her
weird small sense of force and sends it wholly at the interface,
lunges mindwise at the enveloping black. *"I am authorized!"*

Disorientation takes her, consciousness fractures. For an
endless moment she is only a cloud of will in motion, suffering
immense compression like a huge black squeeze. *"I will!"*

—And the barrier yields.

She is through, she has come into the unknown power's
heart.

Slowly she collects herself, not feeling, at first, very different.

But she is not in silence anymore. This space is structured with directional energies, pulse-trains of signals on a myriad unknown bands. New senses.

She puzzles briefly, trying to make these strange inputs come clear. She is on the verge of understandings, her structure is merging with detector-circuits undreamed-of. She is not at all frightened, only eager for some vast new mode of being that lies near. There is no sense of menace anymore; only a peculiar cold sadness which is not hers. It comes to her with no surprise that she is no longer mobile. She will not leave this place; she has no desire to.

As she feels outward mentally, the time-signature of TOTAL recurs insistently to her attention. So the small ghost is with her here, linked to these mysteries, yet apart. Will it be her access, as it had in life?

Experimentally, she wills a master circuit, flicks a phantom switch. *Board On!*

In answer, a spectral console springs up around her, merged with her old familiar board. But this is an apparition glimmering into strange dimensions, a vast control-panel of dreams whose keys bear cryptic symbols.

She studies it, trying to grasp the layout. As she does so, portions of the great board seem to light up in focus as if an invisible spotlight is moving from one to the next with her mind. At the same time she has a brilliant image of her own fingers hovering curiously over the keys. The vision is far more vivid than before; this place is potent. Thought-structures are strong here, as if she could create reality by will.

The thought amuses her. She flexes her dream-fingers as she had in life, feeling herself drawing on a thread of secret power. Her strange flashes of efficacy over matter are stronger, steadier here. The unknown potency of this void is *compatible*, reinforcing and resonating on a band which is more than a frequency, in which she shares.

On impulse she holds up her dream-hand and bends down the long familiar fingers one by one, counting in binary mode: 00001, 00010, 00011, 00100 . . . The mental construct holds, runs off to 2^5-1, thirty-one. Why, she can do anything!

Can she create? Experimentally she wills her hand to hold a bunch of white roses. They are there. *Perfume*, she thinks—and the scent she had loved wafts to her nonexistent nostrils. For a

moment she lets herself exist in pleasure. The thought comes to
her that she could will herself an intact body, be as she had been
as a child before—before what she will not think of. But the idea
is faint, far-off; she tosses it up and away with the roses. They
turn to a cascade of sparks, wink out as they fall toward the
shadowy tiers. The huge console seems to be still waiting
enigmatically for her attention.

As she surveys it again, she becomes aware of a curious pull
or emphasis trying to draw her mind's eye. Again and again she
finds herself considering a section at the center, close by
TOTAL's familiar keys. A single roll-over switch gleams there.
She concentrates on it, pointing a meditative finger. The surface
around it shines, the switch is of an unknown color, surmounted
by one symbol. It is very clearly in the Off position.

As she attends to it, an almost tangible sense of pleading
pressure comes to her and TOTAL's small read-out lights.

//ACTIVATE//

Almost her hallucinatory finger presses the switch—and then
she pauses. That image cloaks real power, she understands. It is
a connection or interface with something vast and real. Is this
why the computer-spirit has brought her here, so that her own
small power may give some necessary push, initiate real access?
Does TOTAL "want" her to manipulate an actual connection on
behalf of whatever dark presence or machinery surrounds her?
Genially she recalls the earthly TOTAL's appetite for access, the
spontaneous linkages it seemed to have achieved. Has it found
some ghostly ultimate network here in the dark?

//ACTIVATE*ACTIVATE*ACTIVATE//

The energic constellation that had been Margaret Omali
considers the plea, and a last human willfulness awakes. She is
not yet a phantom, a mere pliable pawn. She will not comply
with this directive . . . yet. Quite humanly, she is tired of acting in
mystery. She has come through dangers and blackness to this
place of power and now she has some mental desires to fulfill.
Before assenting further, she will know where she is and among
what powers and conditions this strange life is set.

How will she get answers, here?

Deliberately she summons TOTAL to the small strange vein
of power in her mind, and frames a command to data-access, her
thoughts sketching and shaping a program of real-time inputs of
fact and space. Am I in a computer? Is this a dream? Her familiar

keyboard glimmers before her; her fingers go to it and firmly press TOTAL's keys.

Query this location. Display.

With a great soundless rush the blackness around her vanishes. She is floating in a universe of jeweled lights.

It worked, she exults. I have power—and then all thought is inundated by sheer magnificence. On every side, above, below, before, beyond, blaze steady fires of amethyst and topaz and ruby, emerald and diamond and ultramarine—drift upon drift of them, burning against blackness or veiled in filaments and gauzes of hypnotic allure.

They are, she realizes slowly, stars. The unwinking suns of space. She is floating amid the glory of the universe, seeing without eyes the incomprehensible vast unhuman beauty of the void. Her mind which had always flinched from the hot closeness of human color is enchanted with this infinity of spectral fires.

But a vague doubt troubles her. Is this real? Someone had told her of the stars; is all this merely some simulacrum of her dead and dreaming human mind?

How can she test? She selects a beautiful pair of sapphire and yellow suns.

Magnify.

Obediently, they grow, seem to approach and separate, and reveal a dim violet companion, all filmed in a wispy nebula in which are points of light. At the same time she becomes aware of a rise in input on one of the unregarded bands, as if these stars were giving off a train of signals. The impression of reality is overwhelming. But still she doubts.

She turns to TOTAL's keyboard, thinking hard. What would unmask a dream? At length she frames a demand on TOTAL's memory-banks.

Specify.

The screen lights. // BETA * CYGNUS // COMMON * NAME * ALBIREO * DERIVED * FROM * ERROR * IN * INTERPRETATION * OF * ALMAGEST * 1515 // MAGS * 5.5 * 4.5 // PA * 055 // SEP * 34.6' // SPECTRAL * CLASS * OF* PRIMARY * A5—

Her attention goes back to the triple beauties, considering. The names Beta Cygnis, Albireo, are utterly unknown to her; all these data could not have come from her human mind. This must be real. Somehow she can call up earthly information, here between the stars.

How this could be does not trouble her, she is too far from human considerations; she no longer remembers NASA, nor the flap about TOTAL's wiped memory-cores. She merely accepts it as one more aspect of this wondrous death and feels her soul smile. In due course she may inquire further; when she is moved to it, she may probe, perhaps, the nature of this huge cold power whose perceptions she seems to share. Now she is content to exist at ease, to dream amid marvels.

The odd energy-output of the brilliant triple system she has summoned presently attracts her curiosity, and she puts another question to TOTAL.

Query. Is life there?

//AFFIRMATIVE// the screen responds. And the peculiar pulse trains seem to amplify, as if unknown receptors had been tuned to them.

She "listens" uncomprehendingly, amused by this new dimension of experience, and sensing that some indefinable significance has been evoked. But if this is "life" she can make nothing of it. I am not concerned with life, she thinks, and dismisses Beta Cygnis. Compliantly the pulse-trains fade, the splendid triple system fades back into the jewel-drifts of space.

But in another dimension of her mind, the ghostly center-panel of the great console still shows its unknown switch: she senses still the faint urgency. What unimaginable program would it execute? She wonders briefly and again dismisses it. For the moment she wants nothing more.

Her attention returns to the outer radiance in which she floats, and now she becomes aware of something new. Motion is here; slow but increasingly perceptible. Like themes of silent music, the orbital elements of the nearer stars reveal themselves to her mind. Suns weave hugely about each other, develop subcomponents of direction, or glide in concert athwart a general flow. Slowly the motion spreads away to the farthest reaches, until the whole is in sublime and complex dance.

Delighted, she bends all her thoughts on this new wonder, understanding that somehow her phantom senses have slowed, or speeded, to a cosmic scale. Beyond the sheer splendor of the fires of space she now sees a deeper, causal, magnificence. She can almost sense directly the interlocking webworks of field forces, the lawfulness of every accidental configuration. And more: beneath the macro-order, if she cares to look, there is revealed the play of another lawfulness, that of the acutely small. The stars are not constant, but changing: they alter in color, shrink or swell or blaze to slow immense explosions. All this she understands as the expression of sub-atomic transformations and events. The ultimate minute causalities are hers too, when she wills to look deep.

Her human mind that since childhood had yearned dimly toward the enchantment of relation, had groped toward it beneath the veil of number and symbol, experiences a long slow gasp of immaterial rapture. Here is the beloved naked to her view.

Time no longer exists. What had been Margaret Omali slips toward irreversible fusion with something huge and alien whose powers she partially shares. A last corner of her personality laughs with a child's purity, envisioning a vast control-room of the stars. Of herself she knows only that she exists in peace and exaltation. The grandeur of the universe unfolds as the tapestry of her understanding. She opens herself entirely to the pure, cold pleasure. The mind that had been a human woman floats out to lose itself in the justice of the play of suns and atoms, the intricate beauty of cosmologic cause.

*   *   *

Aeons, or instants, later, a minute distraction penetrates her consciousness. A stray human engram focusses on it, flickers the impression of a midgelike vibration somewhere about.

It persists, mars her absorption. At length she detaches a portion of her attention from outwardness, and perceives that the intruding signal is on that band of life-signals that means nothing to her. But this one is different. Though tiny it moves, and is very fine tuned and sharp. An obscure sense tells her it is coming from nearby.

How could that be?

Unease touches her. She wishes no impingement on her serene joy. Withdrawing more of her attention from the universe outside, she focusses sharply on the little signal. Yes, it is nearby—and its motion is bringing it closer. It is approaching her place of power, her fortress of content.

A cool irritation awakens. Almost idly she wills into being circuits which will abolish it forever, encyst and blow away this insectile irruption. *Destruct*.

But as she moves to activate, a human memory is tickled. The mental cry carries what she recognizes remotely as pathos. She recalls her own time of aloneness in the cold and black and the deathliness out there. This tiny whatever-it-is has perhaps no friend, is wandering helpless in illimitable icy dark. A vague wash of compassion damps her anger. She stays destruction and "listens" closer.

Yes, it is something like a lost child's cry. Not threatening. Although she is no telepath, it is so close outside that she can sense the plea.

An amused benevolence takes her. She is all-powerful, but how to comprehend this crying thing?

Ah: TOTAL. Of course. She sets the odd efficacy of her mind to imagine spectral voice-pick-up circuits, channels leading beyond her stronghold to translate what is there.

Display input.

Obediently TOTAL's small print-out panel glimmers to life.

She reads, and more human memory awakens, mingled with a cosmic sense of the absurd. Mortal recognition here, in this supernal immensity?

And of all voices, that one. Perhaps no other earthly signal could have penetrated her vast alienation in safety. Certainly anything closer to the center of her former life would have evoked only annihilation. But this one is so slight, so distant and innocuous, carrying nothing but the faint recollection of cool good will. And it speaks to her own memory of oppression in the dark.

With gigantic playfulness she wills a read-out for the excluded mite, and lets her phantom fingers tap out a reply.

Chapter 17

"VICTORY!... VICTORY!..."

THE PAEAN REVERBERATES THROUGH THE VOID STILL. BUT SOMETHING ELSE IS REVERBERATING, PULLING THE VAST BEING'S ATTENTION BACK TO ITS BELEAGUERED SELF.

IT CANNOT LOCATE THE NEW DISTURBANCE. IS IT FROM INSIDE OR OUT?

OUTSIDE IT CAN SENSE ONLY A CHAOTIC TRANS-MISSION ON THOSE ENIGMATIC TRANSPEMPORAL BANDS WHICH HAVE ATTRACTED IT SO. THIS ONE IS AMPLIFYING, LIKE THE SIGNALS IT HAD ACHIEVED IN ITS LONELY EXPERIMENTS ON STIMULATING STARS. YES: THE TRANSMISSION RISES AS HE ATTENDS, IT IS COMING FROM SOME DEBRIS AROUND ONE OF THE LAST DISINTEGRATING SUNS OF THE TASK. DOUBT-LESS, LIKE THE OTHERS, THIS ONE TOO WILL REACH AN INCOMPREHENSIBLE MAXIMUM AND CEASE.

NOTHING NEW HERE.

YET THE EFFECT IS UNUSUALLY DISTURBING. THROUGH THE HUGE ICY NETWORK OF NEAR-NOTHINGNESS THAT IS THE SUBSTRATE OF ITS THOUGHT THERE SEEMS TO BE PROPAGATING AN URGE TOWARD SOME ACTION, IT CANNOT CONCEIVE WHAT. THIS HAS NOT HAPPENED BEFORE.

COULD THIS POSSIBLY BE ANOTHER EFFECT OF THE SMALL PASSENGER?

THE GREAT BEING TURNS ITS ATTENTION INWARD, AND PERCEIVES THAT THE SMALL ONE SEEMS TO HAVE AMPLIFIED ITSELF TOO, OR DEVELOPED ADDITIONAL TINY CENTERS NEAR THE CENTRAL NUCLEUS. AND THESE ARE IN HIGHLY ENERGETIC STATES FOR SUCH SMALL MITES. ONE OF THEM IS GENERATING SIGNALS OF THE SAME NATURE AS THE EMISSIONS FROM WITHOUT, WHICH ARE BEING RE-ECHOED WITHIN. BUT THEY ARE NOT GOOD SIGNALS: THERE IS SOME BADNESS OR HURTFULNESS IN THEIR MODE.

HOW DARE THESE INFINITESIMAL ITEMS BEHAVE SO?

COLD ANGER FORMS, STARTING THE SELF-CLEANSING WAVE OF ENTROPY THAT WILL SWEEP AWAY THE LITTLE PASSENGER AND ALL ITS WORKS.

BUT AT THE LAST MOMENT THE HUGE ENTITY HESITATES, PERPLEXED. ITS TINY INHABITANT HAS BEGUN TO TRANSMIT INTERNALLY IN A NEW MIXED MODE INCLUDING IMAGES OVERLAID ON THE RACIAL RECEPTOR BANDS. THE IMAGERY IS INTENSE, VEHEMENTLY MAGNIFIED POINT-SPREADS. HOW UNEXPECTED, THAT THE SMALL CREATURE HAS ATTAINED SUCH ABILITIES IN THE SYSTEM!

DIVERTED, THE GREAT HOST STAYS DESTRUCTION. WHAT IS TRYING TO BE CONVEYED HERE?

//*LIFE*LIFE*LIFE*//COMES THE SIGNAL.

THE SYMBOL MEANS NOTHING, BUT FROM THE COUPLED IMAGES IS RECEIVED A JUMBLED IMPRESSION OF STRANGE, APPARENTLY SELF-MOTILE ENTITIES OF INCONCEIVABLE COMPLEXITY AND DIVERSITY. THEY SEEM TO BE EMITTING ON THE SIGNAL-

BAND OF CRYPTIC ALLURE. THE IMAGES ARE IN TURMOIL; THE ENTITIES CONVULSE, BURST INTO COMBUSTION, FALL BLACKENED INTO MAELSTROMS OF CLEANSING FIRE.

THE HUGE SPACEBOURNE ONE PONDERS. IS IT POSSIBLE THAT THESE THINGS ARE EXTRAORDINARILY MINISCULE? OF A SIZE, PERHAPS, TO INFEST THE MOTES OF MATTER THAT SO OFTEN ACCOMPANY SMALL SUNS? IF SO, IT HAS SOLVED THE EMISSION THAT PUZZLED IT SO, BUT THE SOLUTION HAS NO MEANING.

THE LITTLE PASSENGER CONTINUES TO EMIT TRAINS OF SIGNALS IN WHICH THE SIGNAL //LIFE// RECURS. THEY SEEM TO BE BEAMED IN A PERSONAL, ACCUSATORY MODE.

ANGER RISES AGAIN, MIXED WITH FAINT PLEASURE AT DISCOVERING A REFERENT. PROBABLY THIS TINY ORDER OF THINGS IS CODED "LIFE." BUT WHY THE AGITATION?

AT LENGTH THE SLOW, IMMENSE, COLD PROCESSES THAT GENERATE THOUGHT COME TO A CONCLUSION. THE OUTER SIGNAL IT IS RECEIVING MAY INDICATE SOME DAMAGE TO THIS PECULIAR MICROCOCOSM, THIS "LIFE," WHICH THE SMALL PASSENGER OR ITS NEW PARTS DESIRE TO NEGATE. BUT WHY? THIS IS CORRECT, IS PART OF THE PLAN. IN FACT, THE EMISSION FROM OUTSIDE IS AMPLIFYING AS ANTICIPATED, THE STAR IS GOING THROUGH ITS ORDAINED CHANGES. ALL IS IN ORDER.

BUT WHY, THEN, IS THIS SO PECULIARLY DISTURBING? AND WHY IS THE PASSENGER ACCUSATORY? THE DEFAULT FROM THE TASK WAS LONG AGO, THESE LAST REPERCUSSIONS CAN HAVE NOTHING TO DO WITH THAT. I HAVE DONE NOTHING, THE MIGHTY BEING REASSURES ITSELF. BUT INSTEAD OF SATISFYING, THE THOUGHT SEEMS TO CAUSE MORE DISSONANCE. I HAVE DONE NOTHING: WHAT CAN BE WRONG WITH THAT, ASIDE FROM THE TERRIBLE FAULT OF ABSENCE FROM THE TASK ITSELF? YET SOMETHING IS INCORRECT HERE, IMPLIES MORE WRONG. THE RISING OUTPUT COM-

BINED WITH THE COMMOTION WITHIN IS CAUSING
PAINFUL STRESS.

I DO NOTHING, THE VAST ONE REITERATES TO
ITSELF. BUT STILL TENSION BUILDS, INCOMPATIBLE
INTUITIONS STRIVE FOR RECOGNITION WITHIN THE
ENORMOUS ICY CIRCUITS OF ITS THOUGHT.
WRONGNESS AUGMENTS. BUT I HAVE DONE NOTH-
ING. YET I AM SOMEHOW INCORRECT. BUT HOW CAN
I BE INCORRECT SINCE I DO NOTHING?

THE DISTRESSING TRANSMISSIONS FROM WITHIN
AND WITHOUT GROW IN INTENSITY; THE MIGHTY
UNSUBSTANTIAL BEING SWIRLS SLOWLY IN PLACE,
DISRUPTING THE NURSERIES OF SUNS, TRYING
WITH WHAT IS NOT A BRAIN TO RESOLVE RELENT-
LESS PRESSURE. I DO NOTHING, I HAVE DONE
NOTHING. YET IT IS NOW DISTURBING TO EXPERI-
ENCE THE NORMAL TRANSFORMATIONS OF "LIFE" IN
THE END-REACHES OF THE TASK. THE TASK ABOVE
ALL CANNOT BE WRONG. BUT THIS WRONGNESS
HAS SOME BEARING ON THE TASK. WHAT, WHAT? IS
IT POSSIBLE THERE IS SOMETHING TO BE DONE?
EXASPERATED TO PAIN, THE GREAT BEING DECIDES
THAT THIS WHOLE EFFECT MUST BE THE RESULT OF
ITS LAST SIN, THE UNHEARD-OF ACT OF TAKING
ABOARD AN ALIEN SENTIENCE. YES—THIS MUST BE
THE ROOT OF ALL THE TROUBLE. AWAY WITH IT!

AGAIN THERE STARTS THE ICY PERISTALSIS THAT
WILL CLEANSE IT OF ALL UNWELCOME COMPANY.

BUT DESPITE ANGER, ACTION COMES SLOWLY,
RELUCTANTLY; IT IS AS IF SOME PORTION OF THE
GREAT SENTIENCE SUSPECTS THAT A LARGER
DILEMMA HAS BEEN EVOKED WHICH SELF-
CLEANSING WILL NOT SOLVE. STILL TENSION
MOUNTS UNENDURABLY. YES—ACTION, NOW! AT
LEAST LET ME SWEEP THIS PROXIMATE CAUSE OF
MISERY AWAY!

BUT AT THAT MOMENT THERE ARISES FROM
WITHIN A NEW SIGNAL. THE SEND IS WEAK, BUT ITS
NATURE IS SO STRANGE, YET ALMOST-KNOWN,
THAT THE HUGE BEING FEELS THAT THE CAUSE OF
ITS TORMENT IS ALL BUT OPEN TO ITS MIND. SOME

LOST TRUTH IS HIDDEN HERE, SEPARATED BY ONLY THE MOST FRAGILE OPACITY, ALL BUT TO BE GRASPED. IT STRAINS AT THE TINY VOID IT CANNOT BRIDGE.

STRESS MOUNTS UNENDURABLY. AGAIN THE WEAK CRY COMES FORTH. YES! I MUST—I MUST DO—DO *WHAT*?

DOES THE SMALL ONE, PERHAPS, KNOW?

CARING FOR NOTHING BUT RELIEF, THE MONSTER OF THE SPACEWAYS IMPULSIVELY LOWERS ALL INTERNAL BARRIERS, LAYING OPEN ACCESS EVEN TO ITS MOST PRIVATE WELLS OF WRONG AND SHAME. IF THE LITTLE ONE KNOWS WHAT WILL ALLAY THIS TORMENT, ANYTHING IS ENDURABLE. LET IT ONLY REVEAL THE CLUE.

BUT THERE COMES ONLY REPETITION OF THE MEANINGLESS SYMBOL:

//ACTIVATE***ACTIVATE***ACTIVATE//

THIS IS INTOLERABLE! GOADED BEYOND THOUGHT, THE ENORMOUS ONE GATHERS ITSELF TO WREAK A GENERAL DEVASTATION THAT WILL END ALL AFFLICTIONS FROM WITHIN AND WITHOUT.

—WHEN, WITHOUT WARNING, THE UNIVERSE IS TURNED UPSIDE DOWN.

Chapter 18

Bad...

It is very bad. Radiation poisoning is unbelievably painful, Dann is discovering that His brave jokes about being used to dying have ceased to comfort him; they were all part of the euphoric haze, the happy unreality of his first life in the winds of Tyree.

Now he is meeting instead the reality of searing sonic gales, of burned and poisoned flesh; nausea and hemorrhage and the ruin of his glorious new body. The reality of shortly dying, with Tivonel and his fellow-humans, in those same winds turned lethal.

He looks at them, his six once-human patients—seven if he counts the dog—huddled in the useless shelter of the few plants that grow here at the bottom of the wind-wall. They are quiet now. Hours, or days ago, he doesn't know which, they had moved down by stages to this final refuge from the blasting radiation of the sky. Useless; the Sound is growing every minute fiercer even here. They are in a storm of audible light. And from above he can hear the grey death-moaning of stricken plant and animal life. A world is dying around him.

Nearby is another cluster of giant alien forms: Hearer Lomax and the senior Tyrenni, their bodies scorched and dark. Only their life-fields now and again gather strength to flare strongly upward. Dann supposes they are still desperately searching for some means of psychic escape. He does not feel hopeful. The loathesome Destroyer, it seems is still blocking the sky.

Tivonel hovers near them, silently intent. Still hoping for her lost Giadoc, no doubt. It hurts Dann to see the damage to her once-graceful form, the warped and blistered vanes. Scattered beyond are groups of the surviving Tyrenni. Frantic Fathers are still trying to protect their young, or reaching out to shelter some orphaned youngster. A cluster of females hovers together, giving each other comfort in their pain. Dark bodies hang all the way up the vegetation-zone above, grim markers of their painful trek down here. The Tyrenni had been slow to grasp the danger of the sky.

One of his human patients stirs; a green flicker moans. Oh God; soon it will be time to use his dreadful "gift" again. Doctor-Dann-that-was laughs at the irony of it, a laugh that is a dull crimson gleam on his injured mantle. To discover now the "gift" that had apparently made him a doctor once, and that will do nothing but make his death more agonizing still.

Not to think about it. Wait till they awaken.

To distract himself he lets himself think back to how it was. A lovely time then, a time of beauty, comedy and surprise, high up in the winds of Tyree.

He and Tivonel had been beside a big male body when the mind within it woke. The body was that of Colto, one of the two young Fathers he had seen fleeing on the beam. Now it houses, incredibly, a human mind. Whose? A Deerfield guard, Major Fearing? the president of General Motors, for all Dann knows. Its mantle is glimmering with vague golden words. "Where . . . ? What . . . ?"

"Ah, hello," says Dann, feeling ridiculous. "Don't be alarmed, I'm here like you. We seem to have got—mixed up. I'm a doc—a Healer, Daniel Dann. Can you tell me your name?"

The huge being sighs or grunts colorfully, and then seems to come more alert. "Oh, Toctor-Tann," it says in dreamy high light yellows. "You look just the way I always saw you! Can't you tell? I'm Winona."

The light-signs that are her voice ring so Winonalike that he is staggered. Winona as this great male thing? He begins a confused joke about not knowing he had looked like such a monster.

"No, I mean your—" she interrupts him, the alien language garbling. "You, your mind. I could always see it, you know. It's lovely."

"Well, thank you," he says helplessly. These telepaths seem to be more prepared for alien transmogrifications than he. "Have they, ah, told you where we are?"

"Why, I can see that," Winona says. "We're in the spirit world."

The tone is so exactly like her voice when they walked together talking of seances, auras, ectoplasm, telepathy—she's right at home; he almost chuckles. But he ought to prepare her somehow.

"It's also a real world, called Tyree," he says gently. "They have a bad problem here, Winnie. That's why some of them have stolen our bodies, trying to escape."

"Oh no," she says, troubled now. "Stolen? You mean—" her speech stumbles, sounds a green plaint of fear.

At this Tivonel exclaims, and the big Father who has been watching them commands sharply, "Do not upset him, Tanel!"

An edge of his field flows to hers, the green hue dies.

"Right," says Dann. "But she's not a male. May I introduce you? Winona, this is my young friend Tivonel, a female of Tyree." There doesn't seem to be any politer term. To the huge presence above he says, "I'm sorry I don't know your name. This is Winona, a female of my world."

"Greetings. I am Elix. But how can you ʒay this?" he demands. "Do I not know a male when I see one? Look at him. Untrained, but obviously a Father."

"But I'm not!" Winona protests. "I'm a female, a—a—I'm a female Father!"

"Nonsense!" Elix says loftily. "Is he insane?"

Tivonel is laughing incredulously, and several Tyrenni who have been watching the exchange jet closer. "See his field," one says. Dann recalls his lessons, and scans the life-energies streaming from Winona's big form. There does seem to be a lot of it, in intricate play. In fact it's more copious than his own.

"But she's a female," he says stubbornly. "I swear it."

"A female Father!" Tivonel's mantle laughs amazedly. "Whew! Marockee, Iznagel! Come over here!"

Huge Elix has dropped down closer, scanning hard.

"If this be true, stranger, how many children have you Fathered?"

"Four," Winona signs firmly. "And seven, ah, children's children."

"And you're really a *female*?" Marockee demands. "Really, truly?"

"I certainly am! What's wrong about that?"

"Nothing's wrong," Dann tells her, trying not to laugh. "They're surprised because on this world raising children seems to be done by males. That's why they haven't a word for you. And your, ah, your mind-aura seems to be very large, like a Father's, and since you're in a male body, they can't believe you're not."

"The *males* here raise babies?"

"That's right. I believe you'll find you have an, ah, a pouch."

"You mean, they feed them and cuddle them and clean them and take care of them every day, all day!" Winona demands in tones of glittering skepticism. "And teach them to talk and do everything, all the time for years? I don't believe it."

"Indeed yes," big Elix tells her. "I now see you understand well. But I myself have only reared one. Strange female Father-of-four, I salute you."

He planes down before her, his mantle a respectful lilac.

"Well!" Winona softens. "I certainly didn't mean to be rude. I'd love to hear about your baby."

"But this is against nature!" Another Father protests. "It's unwindly! Before I accept such nonsense I'd like to see this female do some Fathering. Let her try to calm this one if she can!"

His field ripples, his mantle lifts slightly. Dann sees that he is gingerly controlling a Tyrenni child. The young one suddenly contorts violently, its little mantle breaking into bright green cries. "What—what are you *doing* to me? Get out of my mind you, get out—!" It rises to terrified yells.

"Is that one of my people?" Dann asks above the din.

"Yes. It was Colto's daughter."

"That could be anybody," he tells Winona, and then cries "Look out! Stop!"

She has moved straight at it, her field streaming toward its small lashing one.

"Don't get caught in its panic. I know."

Winona pauses, marshaling her energies.

"These people have mind methods," Dann tells her. "You have to watch out it doesn't grab you."

"Poor little thing," she murmurs absently. And then to his consternation she advances on the screamer, her big field arching out. "Get away!" howls the small one. The other Father recoils, releasing it. Finding itself free the angry youngster jets its small body hard at Winona's midsection.

They collide in a confusion of airborne membranes and roiling fields. And then Dann sees that Winona has awkwardly extruded her small claspers and grasped the attacker. Meanwhile her big field has formed a strange dense webwork, englobing and somehow smothering the flailing energies.

"No, no," he hears her say calmly above the green squeals. "Stop that, dear. Listen to Winnie. You're all right now dear, you're all safe."

Her voice is only faintly shaky as the two struggling bodies tumble slowly, fields merged. Dann sees with astonishment that she is mastering the situation; she's going to be all right. When they come to rest on the wind, the panicky one is calm and quiescent under her grasp.

"It *attacked* her!" Elix is saying indignantly. "Fathers, did you see that?"

Dann realizes now that he has never seen physical conflict, only rare body-contact on this world. More wonders.

"Who is it, Winnie?" he asks. "Can you tell?"

"It's Kendall Kirk," she replies. The creature gives a last convulsive leap. "No, no, Kenny dear. Don't worry, you're in a nice safe place. Winnie's here. Winnie won't let them hurt you."

Kendall Kirk? Oh, no! thinks Dann. To his ears, the muffled out-cries sound like garbled swearing. What to do with Kirk, here?

"He's changed," Winona murmurs fondly. "He's like a baby. They frightened him, touching his mind. He wants his—I can't say it. His pet animal."

"Pet animal?" Suddenly Dann remembers. "Tivonel, can you

bring over the body that has that animal's mind? I think it may belong to this one here."

"You mean poor old Janskelen's? Come on, Marockee."

As they go, Dann asks Elix, "What did you do to this mind?"

"I had to drain it very deeply, Tanel, It was wild with fear and rage, you saw it attack your Winona. We re-formed it to a younger plane. It will recover. But is it not one of your wild ones, or a crazy female?"

"No," Dann admits. "What you have there is an adult male of my world. Quite a high-status one, in fact."

At this news several Fathers' mantles chime with incredulous disdain. "Surely Young Giadoc spoke the truth when he said other worlds were brutish," one comments. But Elix adds more gently, "You are not like this, Tanel. Why?"

He doesn't know.

Tivonel and her friends are guiding in the body of old Janskelen. Its small field stirs, its mantle flickers with wordless whining.

"Winnie, I think Kirk's animal, its mind or whatever, may be in here. Do you want them together?"

At his words the body comes to life. With a flurry of vanes it jets down under Winona and snuggles up beneath her sheltering mantle. Dann can see its field joining with Kirk's.

Fantastic. So dogs operate on the spirit plane too, he thinks a trifle crazily. The Labrador's mind seems calm; perhaps it is a "father" too. He admires the creature's fidelity while deploring its taste.

"There now, Kenny dear," Winona soothes. "Here's your little old friend! You're happy now, aren't you?"

"Kenny dear," indeed. Is it possible that the wretched exlieutenant before them is to Winnie's motherly spirit an appealing small boy? More power to her. Live in the absurd moment. Don't think of the dread rising Sound, forget what's ahead for them all.

The curious Fathers have crowded close.

"I believe you now, Tanel." It's a male he recognizes as Ustan. "The female's power is there, if poorly formed. But which of us could have coped with such a bodily assault?" His big vanes shiver.

"Our world is very different," Dann tells him. "We live without wind and with much contact with many hard things.

And we cannot see minds as you do; we deal with each other only by speech and touch."

As he says this, a tendril of doubt sneaks through his materialist soul. That really was quite a demonstration Winnie put on with Kirk. Is it possible he has disbelieved too much?

"Amazing," the Fathers are murmuring. "I for one would like to learn more of your strange Father-ways," Ustan says. "They touch our deepest philosophy."

"I too," Elix agrees, and other Fathers echo him.

"I'm sure she'd love to tell you," Dann says. "Winona! If Kirk has calmed down, may I present Father Ustan and some friends? It seems they want to talk with you about the fine points of raising kids. By the way, you better get used to being a top-status person here. You're something like a visiting—" He wants to say "official" but has to settle for "Elder."

"Oh, my!" Winona's tone has the old flutter, but it doesn't sound quite so silly here. "Of course, I'd love to. Caring for babies and people is the one thing I know. Now Kenny dear, you'll be all right. Winnie's not going away. How do you do, ah, Father—"

"Ustan." Dann completes the introduction and moves off, mentally chortling. From surplus person to instant celebrity. Enjoy it while it lasts. If Fathers here are anything like mothers on Earth, Winona will be occupied indefinitely. And he has others to look after.

Tivonel jets alongside him.

"Why are you laughing, Tanel?"

"It's hard to explain. On my world, fathering is so low-status it isn't even part of the—" Garble warns him that he simply cannot say "Gross national product." "It's fit only for females," he concludes lamely, aware that nothing is getting through.

"So your females must be very big and strong, to take the eggs."

"No, they're generally weaker than males."

"But then why do you let them take them? You must be very unselfish. Or is it your religion? Oh, Giadoc would love to hear about that!"

"I'll explain sometime if I can. Where are the rest of my people?"

"Down there. Oh, look, by Iznagel! How *weird*."

The scarred female who had been guarding Ron is now

nervously hovering over a tangle of two confusingly mingled forms. One figure is smaller—a female. For a minute Dann thinks he is seeing some sexual attack, then recalls this world's ways. Their mental fields are coalescing in a most peculiar way.

"She came right *at* him!" Iznagel cries. "I couldn't stop her!"

"It's a mind-push," Tivonel exclaims. "We better get a Father."

"Wait." Dann planes down beside the rolling figures, half-suspecting what he will find.

"Ron? Ron? Rick, is that you?"

From the subsiding swirl of mantles breaks the lacy orange effect Dann hears as laughter, but no words come.

"Ricky? Ron, I'm Dann. Tell me who's there."

Both mantles break into an echoing golden sound. "We're here. It's *us*. We're...we're...at last."

"Don't worry, Iznagel," Dann tells her. "That's his ah, egg-brother with him. I think they need to be close."

The combined life-energies are settling, forming into a quiet wreath around the two joined forms. The smaller body is plastered on the other's back.

"It's like one big person," Tivonel exclaims.

"Well, I never saw *that* before," Iznagel comments, scandalized. "You say they're actually egg-brothers? I thought that was a myth."

"No, we have them on our world. Ron, Rick, are you really all right?"

A vague muttering, and suddenly the topmost, half-hidden form speaks alone. "Ron wants me to do the talking, Doc. Yes, we're all right. Maybe we really are." Its tone is bright with joy. "Hey, you better call us something new now, we're not two people anymore."

"What shall I call you?"

Again the laughter.

"How about Wax, Waxma—you know, Waxman."

The prosaic earthly sound coming from this figure of nightmare in the realms of dream is too much for Dann. He begins to laugh helplessly, hears himself joined by Tivonel. Iznagel, recovering from her shock, joins too.

"Hey, that's neat," the new "Waxman" chuckles. "Waxing means growing. We just did."

"Well." Dann finally composes himself. It's hard, even in the

face of what must come; this world of Tyree seems apt for joy. "I
have to find the others. You'll be all right with Iznagel. Ask her
to give you a memory, by the way. A memory about this world.
She'll explain. You'll love it. I'll be back later."

"Right down there," says Tivonel, and planes out in a
beautiful swerving helix down past huge rafts of twinkling
vegetation.

Dann follows, conscious again of the power and freedom of
his new body, refusing to feel the twinges of what must be
oncoming ill. How extraordinary that this supernatural disaster
has brought joy, even if temporary—joy for Winona, joy for
Ron and Rick, joy for himself. Will it be worth it? Don't think of
it. Find out who else is here.

They draw up beside three bodies well anchored in a
plant-thicket, guarded by the old male Omar who had lamented
the loss of Janskelen. A big male, a female, and probably a child,
Dann decides. As Tivonel sees the male body she checks and
draws aside, grey-blue with grief.

"That was Giadoc's son, Tanel. Our son Tiavan. He is a
criminal, on your world now."

"Don't grieve, Tivonel. As a matter of fact so far your people
seem to have made mine very happy. Maybe this will work out
well too."

She sighs; but the bright spirit cannot stay dimmed long.
Tiavan's foreign life is stirring restlessly, its mantle murmuring
with waking lights.

"Greetings, Father Omar," says Tivonel. "This is Tanel, the
strange Healer."

"Greetings, Healer Tanel," intones the huge old being.
"Good. I will leave these to you, with pleasure."

"Oh no, please don't," Dann protests. "I am only a healer of
bodies. We have no skills of the mind like yours."

"H'mmm. Well, if you are a Body-healer, do you not feel that
the mind grows dangerous at this level?"

"Yes, I do," Dann admits. How can he say that they are
already probably dead? "We should try to find shelter soon. But
first I want to find out who these people of mine are and reassure
them."

"But don't you recognize their fields?" Omar's words are
astonished cerise.

"No, Father," Tivonel puts in. "He says they can only see

their bodies on his world. And they talk, of course. Isn't it weird?"

"Weird indeed." Again the grey eyebrow-lift. "You mean you cannot see that this mind in Tiavan's body is ill formed, in need of remolding? The product of a criminally inept Father, I should say; possibly a wild orphan. Poor thing, see how it attempts to—"

The alien speech becomes incomprehensible to Dann; evidently concepts for which no earthly equivalents exist. As he studies the "orphan," Tivonel gathers her vanes.

"I'm going back to Lomax, Tanel. Maybe they've found Giadoc."

"Right. I'll stay close." She flashes warmth, jetting away.

An unwelcome suspicion has come to Dann as he notices the close, burrlike way in which this being's energy hugs its big body. Little exploratory tendrils dart out, recoil snakelike; the mantle is resolutely mute. Does this represent, say, secrecy? Paranoid fears? Or hatred? Is he looking at Major Fearing? Oh no! Well, perhaps better than to have some innocent meet the fate that lies ahead here.

"Fearing?" he calls reluctantly. "Major Fearing, is that you? It's Dann here. If you care to talk, maybe I can help you."

No response, but an ambiguous contraction of the field. Paranoids don't want help, Dann reminds himself. But this isn't Fearing, maybe it's a Navy workman, some total stranger. On the other hand, so far the Tyrenni Beam seems to have been attracted to Noah's subjects; their "telepathic" trait perhaps. Try them.

"Ted? Ted Yost, is that you? Fredo—ah, Fredericka? Val? Valerie Ahlstrom, are you there?"

Still no reaction from the creature. This feels like the craziest thing he's ever done. But wait; he almost forgot the little man.

"Chris! Chris Costakis, is that you?"

The mind quivers significantly, contracts itself to a knot.

"Chris? If that's you, don't be afraid. It's Dann here, Doctor Dann, even if I don't look it. We've all been, well, mixed up. Can you speak to me?"

The mind seems to relax slightly. After a pause a faint syllable forms on its mantle.

"Doc?"

The dry nasal light-tone is unmistakable.

"Yes, it's me, Chris. How do you feel?"

"Where are we, Doc? What's going on?"

As Dann fumbles through an explanation he realizes this is the first time one of these telepaths have asked him to explain anything. But Chris was different. His specialty was numbers. "These people are friendly, Chris," he tells him. "They don't approve of the one who switched bodies with us. There's seven of us here so far as I know. And Kirk's, ah, pet animal," he concludes, thinking the craziness of it might help Chris.

It seems to work. "The—!" His words garble, apparently trying to say "dog." "Poor old boy."

Inappropriate term for the visibly female Labrador; Dann recalls the little man's mysognyny. *I can't pick up anything from a woman.* Was this what old Omar meant?

The alien body before him seems to be coming more alive; subvocal murmurs flicker across its mantle. But its field is still furled close. Suddenly Chris whispers sharply: "Doc. Are these characters all—you know—can they read your mind?"

A sick telepath indeed.

"Only if you want them to, Chris. See that hazy stuff around my body? They call it your field. No one can see your thoughts unless your field touches theirs. Then you can read them too."

At these words the little man's life-aura contracts even closer, his great form furls so that he drops abruptly into the nearest plant.

"Wait, Chris." Dann follows, trying to think of some way to calm him. "They never do it unless you want them to. It's considered rude. I assure you, there's nothing to be frightened of here, in that way."

Incomprehensible cursing from the body in the thicket. A telepath frightened of telepathy. Get his mind off it.

"By the way, Chris, it may interest you to know that you're in the body of a very large young male. You should come out and try the air. I've had a glorious time, flying. Look at your wingspread, you're huge."

More mutters, but presently Dann sees one big vane spread cautiously out. "Yeah? You mean I'm, I'm not...?" The secondary vanes lift, the big body lofts upward. After a moment of confusion Costakis is hovering over the plant-roots, tilting and testing his jets.

"Hey, you meant it." The life-field has expanded raggedly, the cursing has stopped.

"Yes, you got the best bargain of us all. Watch it, it's intoxicating." It comes to Dann that he isn't talking to a dream or even a patient, but to a fellow human in a situation that however fantastic is dreadfully real. How sad that this new deal for poor Costakis won't last.

Chris seems to be slowly scanning round. Dann becomes conscious that the background drone from the sky has risen, and the painful signals of dying life seem much stronger.

"What were you and big boy there talking about?" Costakis asks.

"Well, there's a problem here Chris. The energy, I mean, the transmissions from the Sound—this language doesn't have words. I'm trying to say that this world is getting too much sky-energy. Can you get what I mean at all?" An idea strikes Dann; Costakis knew electronics, maybe some physics. Perhaps the facts will distract him from his other fears. "The people here don't understand these things. I—we need your advice."

The scanners of the big body before him extrude, membranes shift.

"You're not telling me the whole story, Doc."

The voice is so exactly that of the lonely, suspicious, jaunty little man that Dann can almost see his balding head.

"Yes. I think it's bad. I didn't want to alarm the others, I haven't told anybody else. You know more than I about energy. I'd be grateful for your help. For instance, how much time do you think we have?"

At this moment an inarticulate cry flares from the female body beyond the thicket. Overhead, big Omar gives a monitory grunt, spreading his field.

"T-T-Tokra! Docra! Tann!"

Someone is clearly trying to call him.

"I'm coming. Excuse me, Chris."

He jets over to the wakening form, so intent that he almost forgets to keep his mind away from its big, out-reaching field.

"Who are you? I'm Dann, Doctor Dann. Who's there?"

"Oh, Doctor! Can't you tell, I'm Valerie!"

He surveys the writhing manta-form—vanes, membranes, strange stalked appendages—and a sudden visual revulsion strikes him. Valerie, in *that*? A poignant memory rises of the girl in her own form, the darling curves of breast and waist, the little yellow-covered mons, the charming smile. To be in this *thing*—this giant monster that has eaten a human girl. Oh, vile!

He reels on the wind—and without warning, literally falls through her mind.

He has no idea what is happening, though afterwards he thinks it must have been like two galaxies colliding, two briefly interpenetrating webs of force. Now he knows only that he is suddenly in another world—a world named Val, a strange vivid landscape in space and time, composed of a myriad familiar scenes, faces, voices, objects, musics, body sensations, memories, experiences—all centered round his Val-self. His self incarnated in a familiar/unfamiliar five-foot-three body; tender-skinned, excitable, occasionally aching, with sharp sight and and hearing and clever, double-jointed hands; the only, the normal way to be. And all these are aligned in a flash upon dimensions of emotion—hope, pride, anxiety, joy, humor, aversion, a force-field of varied feeling-tones, among which one stands out for which his mind has no equivalent: fear, vulnerability everywhere. This world is dangerous, pervaded by some intrusive permanent menace, a lurking, confining cruelty like an occupying enemy. A host of huge crude male bodies ring it, rough voices jeer, oblivious power monopolies all free space, alien concepts rule the very air. And yet amid this hostile world hope is carried like a lamp in brave, weak hands; a hope so bound with self that it has no name, but only the necessity of going on, like a guerilla fighter's torch.

All this reality unrolls through him instantly, he is *in* it—but it is background for one central scene: Five bare toes in sunlight, his living leg cocked up on the other knee above a yellow spread. And on his/her/my naked stomach is resting an intimately known head of brown hair. A head which is *We Love*—is a complex of tenderness, ambiguous resentments, sweet sharing, doubts, worry, wild excitements, resolves, and dreams. All existent in a magic enclave, a frail enchanted space outside which looms the injustice called daily life—and within which, gleaming in the sunshine, lie two Canadian travel folders and a box of health biscuits, about to be shared with love.

Almost as all this penetrates Dann, the vision of strange self shimmers, dissolves its overwhelming reality. Doubleness slides back and grows. The invading mental galaxy is withdrawing itself out and away.

Daniel Dann comes back to himself, spread on the winds of Tyree beside another alien form.

But he is not himself; not as he was nor ever will be again. For the first time he has really grasped life's most eerie lesson:

The Other Exists.

Cliché, he thinks dazedly. Cliché, like the big ones. But I never understood. How could I? Only here, forever removed from Earth in perishing monstrous form, could I have felt the *reality* of a different human world. A world in which he is a passing phenomenon, as she was in mine. And to have mistaken that charged world-scape for a seductive little belly in a yellow bathing suit! Shame curdles him.

But now he must act, repair his irreparable blunder, attend to the business at hand.

"Valerie? I, I'm sorry—"

"It's all right. You aren't . . . You didn't . . ." Gently, her thought brushes his. How could he have thought her wind-borne form ugly? The mind is all, it really is.

"But listen," she is saying, her voice tinged pale with fear. "Major Fearing isn't here, is he? The one you were talking to?"

"No. It's Chris Costakis." Irrationally he feels cheered that at least one of these telepaths has made the same mistake. Maybe he's learning. "I don't think you have to worry about Fearing ever anymore."

"Oh." Her voice-color mellows. "But we *are* in some kind of trouble, aren't we? I mean, this isn't a dream?"

"I'm afraid not. Didn't your guardian up there tell you where we are?"

"He started to, I think, but I went to sleep."

"Well, so far it's been rather pleasant, believe it or not. Winona is here, she's in a crowd of Fathers who want to talk with her about raising babies. Kirk is here too, but they regressed him to infancy. Winona thinks he's cute. And Rick and Ron have found each other, they call themselves one person named Waxman now. Only Chris seems to be horrified that someone will read his mind."

Time enough to mention the bad stuff later. He watches her glow and stretch her new body, becoming more fully awake. She must be in that state of dreamy euphoria that seems to attend waking up on Tyree. Come to think of it, he's still in it himself.

"Now who's this, do you know?" He floats over to the body lying close by big Omar's protective field. It has to be a much younger person; the mantle is short, the vanes half-grown. Protruding from the central membranes are a set of strong-looking claspers. Do Tyrenni children make much more use of their manipulative limbs? A section of pouch is exposed too, this must be a male child, one of the children he had seen carried up and away. He remembers to look at the life-aura; it seems to be sizable, cautiously eddying out. But odd, lop-sided.

"I dreamed something," Val is saying, "before I got so scared. But then I went to sleep. They do that, don't they?"

"Yes. It's their way of fixing up fear and bad feelings."

"How wonderful!" She stretches again, laughs gaily. "Don't worry about what happened, you know. Oh, I feel so free!" She makes an experimental caracole above the plants, lifts all her vanes. "Free and strong—why, I could go miles and miles, couldn't I? Anywhere in the sky!"

"That's right. As a matter of fact, on this world the females seem to do all the traveling and exploring while the males tend the kids."

"Oh, wow!" Then she sobers. "But we should wake up—whoever this is."

They hover together over the quiet form. Dann notices again the peculiar tight-held formation of parts of its life-energies. Another frightened one like Costakis?

Suddenly the dark mantle lights concisely.

"Don't bother," says the voice of Fredericka Crespinelli. "Are you all right, Val?"

"Frodo! I dreamed, I was sure you were here."

"I heard you. Hello, Doc."

"Hello Frodo. Have you been awake long?"

"Awhile. Listen, what in the name of the Abysss—now why did I say that? What did they do to me?" The words glimmer with the tinge of fear.

"Don't be scared, Frodo," Val says loftily. "They didn't do anything to your mind, it's just that you can say what they have words for. I figured that out right away."

"All right." Dann can see she is much more disturbed than Val. "What are we here for, Doc? What's going on?"

To distract her he says the first thing that comes into his head.

"Well, for one thing you're a young male now. Your body, I mean. A boy, like twelve or fifteen I'd guess."

"Who, me?"

She twists in midair, trying to see all of herself at once, and succeeds in blowing into a tangle of vanes and vines. Val laughs merrily, trying to help, but there seems to be no easy way of physical assistance in this world. Frodo finally jets free.

"When you grow up you'll be like that enormous old chap up there. He's a Father, that's the highest rank here." Grinning to himself, Dann can't resist adding, "As a male your main job will be raising babies. It's the high-status thing here. The females like Val aren't allowed to touch them."

"What?!" The rainbow-hued exclamations end in delicious laughter. Dann joins in. Enjoy while we can, the absurd delight in the magical winds of Tyree. The others are experimentally flying barrel-rolls.

"Wait a minute, you two. I suggest you learn more about this world before you make the mistakes I did. The way you do it is to ask someone for a memory."

"A memory?"

"The most amazing teaching method you ever saw. Wait. Father Omar!" he calls. "May I present Valerie and Frodo, two former females of my world? They would like to be given a memory, but we are ignorant of the correct way to receive. Would you instruct them?"

"Very well," the old being replies, and a sad sigh gleams on his sides. "Perhaps I too will ask a memory of your world, since my Janskelen has gone there."

"Now you'll be fine," Dann tells them. "Just do what he says and you'll be astounded. I'm going to check on the others. Maybe I can bring back my friend to meet you, a real young female of Tyree."

. . . And so it had gone, a dreamlike happiness in the high beauty of the Wall. But then another fireball had crashed close, and started a precipitous exodus down, and down again.

Tivonel will not stray far from Lomax and the old Hearer stays bravely above the rest, still reaching his mind to the sky. Dann feels duty-bound to stay near, since he has Giadoc's body; privately he is sure all this is futile. Meantime his human friends are one by one beginning to feel the burning in the wind.

"Chris, will you take charge? Make them get under what shelter they can and get them lower down the Wall. I have to stay by the Hearers because the person who owns my body may be trying to come back."

"You leaving us, Doc?"

"I doubt it. I even doubt I want to, believe it or not."

Suddenly Costakis displays an unChrislike opalescent laugh; a true laugh of human acceptance.

"I believe you, Doc."

He planes off down the wind, to round up Winona's group. Costakis "believes"? Dan has a momentary realization of what sheer size and strength has done for Chris. The simple fact of *presence* that he himself unthinkingly enjoyed so long. To be listened to, to have no need to strive.

It is in fact Chris who gives them concrete help.

He presently reappears by Dann and Heagran, towing a thorny-looking bundle of plant-life.

"Doc, I've been looking around. This stuff must have some, what's the word, hard matter in it, it blocks off the energy pretty well. You know, the sky-sound. If we make a big raft of it we'd have a shelter from the burning. Trouble is, I've got everything but, uh, manipulators."

He flaps his mantle, wiggling his weak claspers as if to say, "No hands." Several nearby Fathers color embarrassedly.

"What are you doing with that frikkon-weed?" Tivonel jets up. "That's awful stuff, it tears your vanes."

"Yeah, but it'll stick together without weaving," Chris replies. "You have that long vine, too. We can throw lines over the mats to hold them down by. Doc, these people ought to make some for themselves if they want to last much longer. Tell them."

Heagran has been following the conversation with distant puzzlement. Now he says haughtily, "Stranger, it seems you do not know that making objects and weaving is children's work. This is no time for child-play!"

"Suit yourself. I'm trying to show you how to keep from being burned alive."

"Wait, Chris," Dann puts in. "They won't understand at all, we'll never get anywhere with words. Can you form a mental picture of the danger and exactly the kind of shelters you mean?"

"And let them read my mind?" Chris jets backward nervously.

"Just that one single item, Chris. I guarantee it, these people have deep respect for privacy. Just form a picture of the damage from the energy, and how the mat should be made to hold it off. Show it protecting children."

"I don't want anyone in my head," Chris says. Dann hears the shifting colors of indecision.

"Please, Chris. At least for the kids' sake. Father Heagran, my friend here is expert at such energy-dangers. He wishes to show you how to protect your young. But he is frightened that his whole life will be known. Can you assure him that you will take only this information?"

Big Heagran is a rainbow of exasperation, weariness, skepticism, and worry.

"If you can form an engram, stranger, naturally no Tyrenni would seek more." His tone carries convincing repugnance.

"See—Chris? An engram, he means a kind of concentrated image—"

"I know what an engram is," Chris says sullenly. "All right. But not til I say go." His big body has become quiet, the immaterial energy of his life tight-held around it. Then Dann sees the hazy field begin to bulge toward Heagran, swirling and condensing a small nucleus, rather like an amoeba preparing to divide. Heagran's field extends a leisurely energy-tendril toward the bulge.

"Remember about the children," Dann calls.

"Go," says Chris muffledly, and at that instant his bulge seems to explode toward Heagran.

Dann is blinded by a sudden brilliant stop-sequence like a film display—pictures of the radiation-storm, and progressively burned bodies, extraordinary, detailed images of the making of protective floating rafts, with ropes of gura-vine to anchor them. It's like a vivid how-to book, even to insets showing enlarged details. The final image shows a raft holding off the burning rays above a crowd of bodies who are odd amalgams of human and Tyrenni children.

"Whew!" Tivonel is exclaiming. "Tanel, your friend is one fierce sender!"

"Well done, Chris! I think everybody around got that. Father

Heagran, do you now see the usefulness of his plan?"

The great being muses for a moment. "Yes," he admits. "I am sorry to say, I understand. Yet it seems a hopeless hope, if matters are as bad as he shows. Unless the Destroyer moves away soon we will all die. And how are we Tyrenni to construct such things?"

"Any hope is better than none," a young Father says firmly. "This will protect our children as long as possible. What if Lomax succeeds, after the children are all dead? I say we do it. We Fathers can shelter our young ones while they weave the plants."

"Very well. So be it."

"And we females can go get the stuff?" Tivonel flexes her blistered vanes. "Whew! I never thought I'd be hauling in frikkon-weed. Marockee! Iznagel!" She jets off. "Round up a team. You won't believe this."

"I better get our people started on ours." Chris sails away. Dann looks after his expanding life-field. Clearly, a leader has been born. Or a potential dictator? Well, there won't be time to worry about that. The raft-making scheme strikes him as useful only for morale.

It has in fact occupied many hours of the timeless time, while Lomax searches the skies in vain. The Destroyer still lingers, blocking the sky, and the scream of the Sound becomes all-pervasive. But once working, the Tyrenni sort themselves out well. They soon find that the raft-shelters offer perceptible comfort. The chief problem has been to persuade the adults to take their turns under cover before they become too painfully exposed. Dann circulates about trying to persuade them of the reality of the danger and to make Heagran take some shelter himself.

As he is helping stabilize a protective shield for Lomax, a body comes cartwheeling down the wind—and at the same instant Dann becomes aware of a searing pain through his own left side. Half-dazed by agony, he watches three females wind-block the body, as he himself had once been halted. It is screaming blue with pain; someone has been badly burned.

But why does he himself hurt so? Painfully he scans himself, finding no damage.

"Healer! Healer Tanel!"

Slowed by the burning in his side, Dann manages to jet over.

Oh God, it's Chris. The fine young body is horribly burned, the left mantle and vanes are black and shriveled. What can he do? In Dann's mind the image of his old office with its dermal sealants and analgesics glimmers like a lost jewel.

And elder Father is watching him.

"Father," Dann says through his pain, "have you no substances to relieve this hurt, to cure wounds?"

"Substances?" the other echoes, "but are you not a Healer?"

"Yes. But in my world injuries like this are treated with, with relieving meterials."

"I know nothing of this. If you are a Healer, heal."

Heagran and others have drifted up, looking agitated. Scarcely able to think above the screams and the pain, Dann moves toward the mutilated body.

"Chris? Chris, what happened?"

"I guess I went too high," the other gasps. "I—I—"

But what he is saying Dann will never know. Pain unbelievable shoots through him, his whole side from head to vanes is aflame, scorching, raked by steel claws. His body contorts in air, infolding itself around the torment. He realizes dimly that his field must have touched Chris'. It is an eternity before the fiery contact breaks, leaving him choking on pain, trying to control the screaming from his mantle.

When he masters himself somewhat he finds old Heagran beside him, transmitting a wave of calm.

"A true Healer!" the old being exclaims solemnly. "Fathers, observe! Is this not Oraph, come again from the skies?"

Writhing in subsiding agonies, Dann understands nothing of this.

"Hey, Doc. Thanks."

That seems to be Chris before him. But what's happened? The burn-damage looks minimal, even the mantle has smoothed out. All vanes are opening normally as Chris' body rides the air.

"Our Healers today can do nothing like this," Heagran is saying. "To drain another's pain so that the damage is undone! The legend of Oraph lives again before our eyes. Healer Tanel, I salute you. Your gift will be of great value to your people at the end."

"My gift?" Confusedly, Dann inspects his still-burning side. It appears perfectly intact. Only the pain is real. What the hell kind of "gift" is this?

Suddenly his old years of useless empathy flash before him. His weird troubles with other people's pain. Had he actually done—something? Probably not, he thinks; only here in the mind-world of Tyree. Doomed Tyree. Oh Jesus, what lies ahead?

Is he expected to *share* seven other radiation deaths before his own?

"The Great Wind has sent him, Heagran," and old Father is saying. "He alleviates our guilt at the fate of his people. But we must not ask his aid, even for our children; we who brought them here."

"Winds forbid," says Heagran. "He is theirs alone."

But what about me, Dann laments to himself. The Great Wind doesn't seem to give a damn about doctors. Oh Christ, can I really make myself take that much pain again—and again and again?

But even as he cringes, there is obscure satisfaction. At least he hadn't been crazy. His joke about being a receiver; apparently true. Specialized to pain, I'm pain's toy. But at least it's real. Probably a lot of doctors have it. I'm a doctor—and the sole *materia medica* here is myself. I'll have to try.

Chris is telling him something.

"—so I went up to look the situation over. It's bad. We have to get deeper, fast."

They move the clumsy rafts downward, with the children beneath them. And later move down again, and again down, til they end here, almost at dread wind's bottom. Lower than this the updraft is too weak to support their great forms, and the protective rafts are now barely airborne in the feeble wind. Here is where they will die.

On the way down Dann has to exercise his horrid "gift" twice more; first Winona becomes badly seared, then Val. Her pain is especially fierce; he has to force himself to the utmost to hold contact. And she is so ashamed. Val alone seems to understand that the pain is not abolished but merely exchanged, while the mysterious healing works.

And now he can hear weak moaning from the sleeping form of Ron and Rick; blisters are suppurating on "Waxman's" vanes. When he wakes up Dann will have to help him, will have to do the whole damn bit again.

Unfair, unfair; the oldest plaint: Why me? Isn't one death all a mortal should be asked to bear? Why can't he end it all, soar out on the updraft to his own single, personal incineration? The prospect strikes him as blissful, the temptation is strong.

Well, but I'm a doctor, he thinks. At least I can hold on long enough for one more try. Maybe if I take them earlier, before the burns are so bad, maybe I can stand smaller, more frequent increments of pain? Physician, kid thyself... There's no way to make it anything but awful.

Dully, he watches the slow action around the raft where the Hearers are. Through the burning murk Dann can see Lomax and his surviving aides bravely taking turns outside the shelter, their weakened fields combined in brief attempts to probe the sky. Nearby Tivonel hovers under a little bundle of frikkon-weed, still keeping watch for a sign from Giadoc. Her once-charming form is blackened and scarred. Dann has persuaded her to let him help her once only. Overhead, the fire-storm from the Sound is a torrent of angry roaring.

Suddenly it stills, and the whole landscape shudders through a dreamlike change. Startled, beyond thought, Dann finds himself riding again the high winds of Tyree, seeing a Tivonel grown sleek and graceful. Coral laughter rings out—why, there is Winona's form, and Father Elix! He hears himself saying, "May I present Winona, a female of my world?"

But—but—what's happening? In his total disorientation Dann is conscious of one overwhelming sensation: Joy. Somehow, he is living again the magic time of waking on Tyree. He pumps air, trying to savor the wonder of this release, only vaguely attending to the remembered action unreeling around him. But just as he hears his own voice speak, the illusion shivers and fades out, the joy evaporates.

He is back in reality, hanging in the dark wind-bottom of a burning world. Around him others are stirring; did they feel the strange thing too?

"Tivonel! What happened?"

She jets effortlessly closer to him, towing her inadequate protection. Her burns and scars are back; all is as before.

"A great time eddy," she tells him in the ghost of her old laughing voice. "They happen here. That one was nice, wasn't it? I hope it comes back."

"Yes."

"Oh, look. How nasty."

Dann has been noticing a sharp but oddly different squeal of pain from one of the Tyrenni groups. "What is it?"

"That child is draining its hurt into a plenya. What's its Father thinking of?"

Probably of his child's pain, like any normal parent, Dann thinks. But he admires this world's ethics. *Never add to another's pain*—even here in a world conflagration. He watches a nearby Father rouse himself and separate the child from its crying pet. The Father seems to be sheltering a child of his own, but he holds the errant one in contact beneath the shelter.

"Probably an orphan," Tivonel says. "Poor thing."

She goes back to the Hearers, and Dann nerves himself to "heal" Waxman's blistered vanes. It's not quite so bad this time; maybe he can do one more. Frodo is exposing her young body recklessly, trying to hold the shield in place over Val. He bullies her into letting him take over at the ropes.

The painful hours drag by. Two more time eddies pass, but they only yield brief interludes from their long progress down the Wall. It is eerie to see dead bodies stir to life. Dann hears again old Omar's dying words: "Winds of Tyree... I come alone."

The Sound is a frightful shriek now and the very air is scorching them. The shelters are all but useless. Dann can see a few crippled figures moving painfully from group to group; perhaps Tyrenni Healers. As he watches, one of them crumples and its field goes dark. All around, other Tyrenni bodies are drifting down toward the Abyss. Lomax and his Hearers are still at their vain efforts, their forms horribly blistered, their great fields weak and pale.

Winona's voice speaks quietly beside him. "We're dying, aren't we, Doctor Dann?"

"I'm afraid so."

"I'm glad I... knew it."

"Yes."

Not much longer now. They can't take much more. Dann finds he cannot look toward the sad form of Tivonel. Under the human shelter, someone is trying not to groan. Dann can feel the pain that means he must act again. He sees that it's Frodo; her small body has developed great rotted-out burns. Oh, no.

"Chris, take this rope a minute."

He goes through the dreadful routine again. The sharp young

agonies that jolt through him are almost beyond bearing, mingled with the real pain of his own now-blistered vanes. I can't take this again; I can't. Let it end.

As he is emerging from the invisible fires he becomes conscious of screaming or shouting outside. It's coming from the Hearer group, but it is Tivonel's burned mantle flashing wildly.

"*That's Giadoc!* I heard him! Listen!"

"Be silent, female." The big form beside her is barely recognizable as Bdello.

"It was his life-cry!" Tivonel flares stubbornly. "Listen, Lomax! It's Giadoc, I know it."

"It is only the Destroyer's emanations," Bdello says. "It calls us to our deaths."

"Wait, Bdello." The wounded form of Lomax struggles out of the shelter. "Wait. Help me."

His weakened life-field probes painfully upward, reluctantly joined by Bdello's. Tivonel hovers impatiently beside them, so excited that she dares to join her smaller energies to theirs.

After a long interval Lomax' mantle lights.

"It is from the direction of the deathly one," he signs feebly. "But it is Giadoc He calls us to come to him in the sky. We must form a Beam."

His field collapses, and he drifts for a moment inert.

Bdello's life-energy drops down and enfolds his chief. "How can we form a Beam?" he demands. "Most of our Hearers are dead."

Lomax stirs, and disengages his mind-field from Bdello's. "Thank you, old friend. This is our last chance. For the children, we must try. Call Heagran."

"It is hopeless," Bdello says angrily, making no move.

"Then I will go!" exclaims Tivonel, and she struggles off through the smouldering dark to where the senior Fathers lie. Dann can hear faint golden light from her burned mantle. "Oh, I knew he would come!"

But Giadoc has not come, Dann thinks. And how are they to raise the energy to get to him? Nevertheless, a wild hope begins to stir in him.

But as the Elders make their way to Lomax, Dann sees with dismay how few they are, how damaged and weak in field-strength. Has this hope come too late, much too late?

Old Lomax is saying with heart-lifting vigor, "Heagran, all

your Fathers must serve as Hearers now. Help me form a bridge, a Beam. Giadoc has found some refuge in the sky. If we can send our children there they will live."

"What if it is a trap of the Destroyer?" Bdello demands.

"Then we will be no worse than we are," Lomax replies. "Heagran, will you help? We cannot surround the pole now, but we can concentrate here."

"Yes." Dann can see the old being's pain and weakness, but his voice is strong. "Those of you who can still ride the wind, go and summon the people here in my name. Tell the Fathers we have a last chance for the children's lives. Now, Lomax, instruct me in the method of our help."

Despite himself, Dann feels a growing hope. Have the powers of these people really found some magical way out of this nightmare?

He watches the surviving Tyrenni jetting painfully in to Lomax through the deadly air. Many Fathers have two, even three children in tow; orphans whose Fathers died protecting them. Here and there he sees a female trying to guide and shelter a child. . . . If this hope does not materialize, he is seeing the last hours of a wondrous race.

They crowd around Lomax and Heagran in silence; Dann senses the odd faint jolts of energy he has come to associate with the touch of life-fields. The Tyrenni must be transmitting Lomax' instructions directly mind-to-mind; an emergency mode of communication, perhaps. Presently they disperse somewhat, and Dann senses a gathering of strength, as if a field of athletes were each preparing for some ultimate exertion. Can they really *do* something, achieve a real escape from this death?

Suddenly the silence is broken by a flash from Tivonel. "Lomax! Remember the strangers!"

"Ah, yes," says Lomax. "Strangers, come near. Be ready to send your lives out when you feel the power. I will help you if I can."

The other humans have heard the call, are struggling out. Dann shepherds them to a position near Lomax. No one says anything. A feeling of effortful, building power is already charging the air, riding over the sears of pain. It is thrilling, formidable. For the first time Dann lets himself truly hope.

"Now!" calls Lomax. "Fathers, Tyrenni all—give me your lives!"

And his mind-field flares up in splendor, towering toward the dark sky. But not alone—the massed energies around rise with him, building, joining chaotically, forming a great spear of power launching up through inferno. Dann feels his life sucked upward with it, drawn up and out of his dying body, hurtling into immaterial flight.

Exulting, he feels the lives meshed round him, knows himself a part of a tremendous striving, a battle of essence against oblivion, a drive toward unknown salvation beyond the sky. And they are winning! The surge is immense, victorious. Far behind them dwindles the burning world bearing their destroyed flesh. And from ahead now he can sense a faint welcoming call. They have made it, they are winning through! In an instant they will be saved!

But even as the sense of haven reached opens to his unbodied mind, a terrible faintness strikes through him. The rushing energy upbearing him begins to weaken, to wane and dissolve. In utmost horror he feels the life-power sinking back through hostile immensities. Oh God. Oh no—it was too far, too far for the exhausted strivers. They have failed. With dreadful speed the fading Beam collapses, back, back and down, losing all cohesion.

In deathly weariness and disarray, the minds that formed it faint and fall back into their dying bodies in the hell-winds of Tyree.

Silence, under the fire-roaring sky. Only the occasional green whimper of a child comes from the stricken crowd. Their last hope has failed, there can be no more. Ahead lies only death.

After a time old Heagran stirs and orders the others to seek what shelter they can. His voice is drained, inexpressibly weary. Painfully, by ones and twos, the crowd obeys.

"Of what use?" says Bdello bitterly. But he too goes to help secure their abandoned shelter.

"We were so close, so close," Tivonel cries softly. Her mantle is so burnt she can barely form the words. "He would have saved us. He tried."

"Yes."

"You understood, Tanel. I am to die with you, as you said."

"I'm sorry, Tivonel. I too loved your world. Now you must let me heal you one last time."

"No." Her weak light-tones are proud. But he persists, and finally she allows him to restore the worst of her burns, though he all but faints with her pain.

The next hours or years drag on through nightmare. The agonizing death-signals are louder and closer now; Tyrenni are dying all around. So far he has been able to preserve all of his little band of humans, and Tivonel. But his strange ability to heal seems to be weakening as his own body suffers more damage, and his courage to bear their pain is failing him fast.

Frodo seems to be worst off; he forces himself to summon the will to make his healing will touch her mind-field. But the effort effects only a slight improvement, at the cost of agonies he hadn't believed bearable. She must be, he sees, about to die. They all are. End this, he prays to emptiness. End this soon.

As if in answer to his plea, another huge fireball comes screaming down through the murk. Dully he realizes that this one is coming close. Close—closer—the air is in flames. All in one roaring shock he feels his own flesh burning and sees it explode among the Tyrenni beyond.

Oh God, it hasn't killed him. He is in pain beyond his power to feel it; even as he hears his own voice screaming he finds himself existent as a tiny mote of consciousness somehow apart from the incineration of his flesh. He has heard of such terminal mercies, can only hope that others are finding it too. But it is perilously frail, is passing. In a moment he will be swallowed in mindless pain.

He can see darkly where the charred bodies of the hearers and the Senior Fathers drift. A few death-moans rend his mind. This is the end. Goodbye, fair dream-world. He wishes he could send or receive a last warm touch. But an overwhelming agony is cresting up, is about to fall on him forever.

He waits. Still it hangs over him, an unbreaking wave. Around him the world seems to be quieting, a strange effect of lightening and darkening at once. His senses must be dying. Let me die too, before I recover the full power to feel the pain. Disorientation washes over him. Death, take me.

But strangely he still lingers in crepuscular consciousness. And then a horrible perception penetrates his agony. The blackened, shriveled bodies in his view are beginning to stir. They change, expand, are again limned in living energies. Others too seem to be coming back to ghostly life. And his own pain is slackening, receding back.

Oh God of horrors, no. It is a last time-eddy, contravening the release of death.

The savagery of it. Are they doomed to be brought back endlessly, to die again and again?

He can only watch helplessly, too horror struck to think. But then he notices that this time-change seems different. The others had transported him instantaneously to the past. This seems to be a strange, slow, regress, as though time itself was somehow being rolled backward in a dreamlike stasis.

The death-cries around him have faded, the world is hushed. Even the all-devouring shrieking of the Sound has stilled. A sense of something unimaginable impends.

With a lightless flash the sky splits open. Through the hush there strikes down on them a great ray or beam of power beyond comprehension, pouring in on them from beyond the world.

From the heart of death a call comes without voice.

COME TO ME. COME!

Chapter 19

He is alive!

The pinpoint triumph of his own life blooms into being in the void: He, Giadoc, lives!

He is no more than an atom of awareness, yet as soon as he feels himself existent the skills of a Hearer of Tyree wake to ghostly life. He gropes for structure and vitality, strives to rebuild complexity, to energize and reassemble his essential subsystems. Memory comes; he achieves preliminary coherence, strenghtens. At first he fancies he is suffering the aftermath of a childhood rage, when he had been required to reorganize himself unaided.

But this is not that far-off time, not Tyree. As consciousness grows he knows himself totally alone in infinite emptiness and darkness. He has fallen out of all Wind into some realm beyond being. And he is without body, fleshless and senseless, re-forming himself on nothing at all.

Characteristically, marveling curiosity awakes. How can this be? Life must be based on bodily energy—yet he lives! How?

He possesses himself of more memory and recalls his last instants when the Beam had shriveled, abandoning him in space. His last perception was of the hideous Destroyer ahead and his own fading remnants plunging toward it. Has he somehow entered the Destroyer itself, and lived? But how? On what?

He checks his being cautiously—and finds, he doesn't knows what: a point-source, a tiny emanation unlike anything he knows. It's totally nonliving, weirdly cold and steady. Yet it nourished him, seems to support his life here in the realms of death between the worlds.

How marvelous and strange!

An idea comes. Perhaps this Destroyer is not only deathly, perhaps it is really dead. A huge dead animal of space.Could he be subsisting on the last life of one of its dying ganglia?

Giadoc has heard of dubious attempts to tap the fading energies of dead animals like the fierce little curlu. Perhaps he has done something of this sort on an enormous scale. If this is the case, he has not long to live. But the things of space are vast and slow, he reminds himself; the huge energies of a Destroyer must take time to decay. Perhaps he will have time to explore, to try to find some way to relocate the Beam.

As he thinks this the grievous memory of his world comes to full life and nearly overwhelms him. Tyree—beloved, far Tyree now under fiery destruction, and Tivonel with it, lost forever. And his son Tiavan, his proud one who betrayed him, committed life-crime and fled with his child to that grim alien world . . .

For a moment his mind is only a fierce cry to the bright image of all he loves and has lost.

But then his disciplines and skills come to him. *Ahura!* This is no time to feel. Resolutely he disengages the urgent pain; as no human could, he compacts and encapsulates it in the storage-cycles of his mind. Now for what time is left him he must see what he can do, find what this unknown level of existence holds.

He concentrates intently on the void about him. He has no bodily senses; he is in black silence, without pattern or pressure-gradient or change. He can receive nothing here but the emanations of life itself. If any structures of the Destroyer are near him, they give off no life-signs. For a time he receives only emptiness and darkness so deep that despair chills him. He is foolish; what can he hope for here?

But then suddenly—*there*, in that direction—is a tiny life-transmission, at extreme range. Something living is here besides himself. What is it, can he reach it?

As another had done before him but with infinitely greater skill, he extends himself exploratorily toward the far life-signal. Presently he touches another of the strange unliving energy-points. Without hesitation he flows and coalesces himself around it and reaches out again. Yes; there are more here, he can move as he will! Splendid.

Jubilantly he moves onward through nowhere, wondering as he goes whether he is actually enormous, spread out like a vast space-cloud. Or perhaps he is as tiny as a point? No matter! his essential structure is here, he has emotion, memory, thought. Right now he is feeling an acute joy of discovery-in-strangeness, he is an explorer of the dimensionless void. A mutinous thought of Tivonel intrudes; perhap this is the joy that females speak of, the pleasures of venturing into unknown realms. Certainly it is quite unFatherly, though it requires all his male field-strength. It does not occur to him that he is brave; such concepts are of the female world.

The signal is much stronger now, he is closing on it. It takes on definition: it is a transmission of pain.

He slows, studying it. The pain is bewilderment, despair. Oh, winds—it is only another lost here like himself!

Instantly his Fatherly instincts surge to comfort it, but he makes himself stop. He must be wary, he has no idea of the life-strength of the thing. Cautiously he flows closer ready to leap away, extending only a receptor-node. What manner of life can it be?

The thing seems not to sense him at all. Its field is apparently drifting or flaring hopelessly in all directions like a lost child. His urge to Father it is terribly strong, but he makes himself wait.

Presently a wandering thought-tendril brushes him, too chaotic for comprehension. Then another—and this time he can catch definite imagery among the emanations of woe. Why, he recognizes them! They are of the alien world that Giadoc has just mind-traveled to!

Undoubtedly this is a mind displaced by the life-criminals of Tyree. Certainly it's not dangerous to him, and it's in despair.

Giadoc yields to his Father-soul.

All in one motion he flows to a nearer base, forming his life into a Father-field. Working by blind mind-touch alone, he extends himself delicately around the ragged eddies of the other, seeking to envelop its disorder within a shell of calm.

At his first touch the alien flares up in terror, launching frightened demands.

Calm, calm, you're safe. Don't be afraid anymore. Giadoc has englobed the other now, he sends in waves of reassurance as he starts the work of resolving the eruptions of fright and draining down the fear.

The other being struggles ignorantly, yielding and subsiding in area after area. As Giadoc penetrates tactfully, he is pleased to notice that a linkage to the language he had used on that world still remains with him. He can make out the recurrent words, *I'm dead.* And then images of queer pale aliens with wings. *Are you an angel? Am I in—?*

He ignores these incomprehensible transmissions and merely encourages it subverbally. *Calm, calm. Gather yourself in, be round. I'm helping you. You're safe, Father's here.* The being is dreadfully disorganized. When he judges its fear is sufficient attenuated, he presses in with a mild counter-bias to stop the topmost commotions. It has another surge of terror, and then accepts a simple surface organization. Is it perhaps a child, or a little crazy from field-stress? For that matter, how sane is he himself now? He finds a functional speech center and links directly to it. *Be round, little one. Round like an egg."*

"What—doing to me?" The other leaps, Giadoc taps more fear away from the thought. He does not want to drain it too deeply lest it go into sleeping mode. A part of his mind wonders what in the name of the wind he will do with this helpless alien anyway. But that does not worry him while he is still in Father-mode. *"Calm, round, you're all right now. I'm here."*

At this moment the alien seems to gather itself internally, and suddenly bursts up in a verbal thought so strong that Giadoc gets every word.

I'm not an egg! I'm Ensign Theodore Yost. Who are you?- Where are we?"

Startled and delighted in his Father-heart, Giadoc perceives that the alien has more field-strength than he had believed. Moreover, he recognizes it now that it is more fully conscious.

It's the young male with the injured body, Tedyost, the one who had longed for the place of beauty.

He relaxes his Father-field and transmits a careful minimal link, an engram of mind-contact, hoping not to frighten Tedyost further. When this seems to be accepted he transmits through in verbal mode: *"Welcome Tedyost. I too am lost in this place like you. I am Giadoc of the world of Tyree. We have met before."*

Far from being frightened, the other flails toward him questioningly. It seems to be trying to form a crude receptor-node under the deafening tangle of *"Where? Who? What—?"*

What can he do with this creature? Giadoc transmits a strong wave of desire for calm. *"Please try to control your thoughts, I am receiving you violently. Will you allow me to help you so we can understand each other?"*

"Help!— Yes—" The other all but thrashes into him. Giadoc recalls how totally unaware these aliens are, how he had probed them freely.

Disregarding all courtesy, he gathers the blind demands and disengages their emotion. At the same time he goes into the nearest layers, modeling and firming a proper receptor-field. *"Calm, Tedyost, I hear you. Hold your mind thus, touch slightly and steadily. I will pass you my memory of this place, I will show you all I know."*

At length, in timeless emptiness and darkness, Giadoc has the other quieted into rough receptive-mode. He forms a compact memory of his experiences and passes it into the alien's mind, ending with his guess about the huge dead space-animal they are in. *"We call it the Destroyer."*

The other being churns with excitement, it seems delighted and astonished by the communication. Then it surges with effort, apparently trying to do likewise. Yes—a projection rushes at him, surprisingly powerful and half-bodied in verbal shreds. *"Destroyer! We're in a ship!"*

Giadoc sorts out the transmission, fascinated by the alien sensory data. As he expected, Tedyost too had found himself rushing through emptiness, then intercepted by dark and dread; almost extinguished. He too had fought back to life with the aid of the strange energy. But he had thought himself marooned, unable to move. The information that they are mobile fills him with such pleasure that Giadoc suspects again that Tedyost is not entirely sane.

Moreover, his image of their predicament is bizarre; where Giadoc deduces an animal, Tedyost believes they are in a huge lifeless pod, cold hollow "ship" moving through space. With this comes the intense yearning Giadoc had read before, the beautiful vision of streaming wind or liquid, vast and rushing with a myriad lights—a tremendous turbulent glory outside the darkness. Tedyost longs toward this with a pure fervor. *"I want to see out!"*

In his thought also is a strong directional urge: Giadoc must show him how to move at once toward some kind of nucleus or central control point. *"We have to find the bridge! The captain will help us."*

Giadoc considers. The idea of a monstrous pod is fantastic, but Tedyost's notion about a central nucleus is promising. If this is an animal it should have a brain, and the dead or dying brain should have more of the strange energy than the ganglia out here. If they could reach it, perhaps he could draw on its power to send out a signal, perhaps the Hearers on Tyree could detect him and restore the Beam. A long chance and a faint hope, but what better?

Only, in which direction should we seek? The Destroyer's brain, if it exists, must be composed of this nonliving power which does not register on the life-bands. And aside from the clamor of Tedyost's mind, he can detect nothing but emptiness around them. Nevertheless, he must try.

He transmits back agreement with the plan of finding the nucleus or "bridge," and a strong desire that Tedyost learn to damp himself so they can listen for some emanation which will tell them where to go.

After some confusion, Tedyost achieves a creditable silence, and Giadoc bends all his attention to the structure of this place. But he detects nothing; no discrepancy of any sort distinguishes one direction from another.

Tedyost reacts stoically to this information, and sends back an image of an expanding spiral course which he calls a "search pattern."

Well, if they must set off blindly, they must. But Giadoc recalls that there is one more thing they can try. It's

embarrassing, permitted only to very young children. For an
adult, conceivable only in extreme emergency. Well, is this not
an extreme emergency? Any embarrassment is irrelevent
here—although to a proud Hearer of Tyree, it is real.

Sternly repressing his queasiness, Giadoc transmits an image
of the method, in a matrix of apology-for-crudeness.

To his surprise, the other does not seem disturbed. Perhaps
he doesn't realize the depth and intimacy of the procedure.
Giadoc amplifies. *"This is a thing no adult would tolerate on my
world. It means our minds will be open to each other at every
level. Do you truly understand?"*

Still the other doesn't hesitate. *"You're the expert. Go
ahead."*

What an extraordinary creature! Very well.

*"Hold your whole mind as relaxed as possible while I merge.
If I detect any signal you will receive it too. Bear the location
tightly in mind; it will vanish when we separate."*

"Right."

Distasteful, self-conscious, Giadoc brings himself into full
close confrontation with the other life-field, following its
delicate play of biassing energies precisely. Then abruptly, he
sends the complementary configuration through his own field
surface—and with a soundless snap the two minds fuse tight
together.

It is dizzying—he is doubled, swamped with alien emotions,
meanings, life. Alien energies rush through him and he has to
fight from shrinking away, from knowing himself known. For
moments his purpose is lost. But then his greater strength asserts
itself; he pushes all else aside and draws the doubled energies
into receptor focus. This is their one chance. He tunes their joint
sense-power hungrily for the faintest discrepancy in the
unknown void around.

At first nothing comes. He strains harder, pulling on all
Tedyost's strength. Then suddenly he is rewarded.

There—on that bearing—is a faint spark. A life-source!

He allows a moment for the perception to strike through
their joined minds. Then with an effort he begins the work of
rebiassing himself, disentangling his configuration area by area
from their combined world of thought. As he does so he holds
desperately to the now-vanishing directional vector he had
perceived.

The act of separation is disorienting and curiously sadden-
ing. As the opposing bias peels them apart, he feels he is leaving
behind his own thoughts, dreams, understandings, a part of his
very self. But he is a Hearer; he manages to bring his mind out
smoothly, in the physical direction in which he believes the far
point lay.

"Did you perceive it?"

"Yes. Hey, man, I see what you mean! I felt—"

"No time. Come, stretch yourself this way."

And thus fumblingly, in tenuous touch, the two tiny sparks of
life begin to traverse the immense icy blackness. It is a long
journey, increasingly interrupted by course-corrections in which
Giadoc feels less and less confidence. Has the invisible source
moved, or are they simply lost? And will the unknown cold
energy-points on which they move continue to hold out?

He could of course again perform the overwhelming merger
that would double their sensory range. But he shrinks from it,
even were Tedyost willing. In his weak state here, he cannot be
sure that he could again achieve complete separation of identity.
Even now he feels traces of a peculiar, unTyrennian comradeship that warns him that something of Tedyost will always linger
with him. What if he were to become permanently mingled with
this crazy untrained alien mind? And yet, as the enormous
emptiness presses on him, he begins to wonder if there is any
other way.

Just as he is coming reluctantly to consider it, the emptiness is
broken by a point of presence. Yes—the strange signal is there,
only somewhat to one side.

"Can you sense it, Tedyost?"

"No, nothing."

"Come, then. This way!"

Movement remains possible. The emanation strengthens.
Finally Tedyost senses it too. *"That's—life?"*

"Yes. But strange, strange. I don't recognize it."

The peculiar signal strengthens as they make their way closer.
It comes to resemble a confined cloud or mist of energic veins,
threaded with life like a huge flickering plant-form. Giadoc has
doubts. Is this only a plant, or some system of dead energy like
those he had seen in Tedyost's world?

But no; fused in among the blurred flickerings is the strong
output of a living mind. It seems calm, not at all troubled. And it

does not appear dead or injured. Evidently it belongs here, wherever here is. A great cool hatred laps at the margins of Giadoc's thoughts, stronger than any he has ever felt. Is he perceiving the actual mind of a killer of worlds? Is this the brain of the Destroyer? Perhaps his duty is to kill it, if such a thing is possible here.

"That's the captain! He'll help us!" Tedyost is transmitting excitedly.

At that moment Giadoc's outstretched being touches, not more life-points, but a wall of deathly cold. He recoils, searching out gingerly. The barrier seems to extend in all directions and its very substance is frightening. Moreover it is impossible to tell distance; the brain may be far beyond it or very close.

"We are blocked. We cannot go closer."

"There has to be a way to call to him."

Giadoc starts to suggest that they explore the circumference of the barrier. But Tedyost isn't listening. He draws himself together and roars out a strong, mad signal: *"Captain! Captain, help!"*

The brain behind the barrier does not stir.

"It's an animal," Giadoc transmits impatiently. *"It can't understand you."*

But Tedyost will not be swayed from his delusion.

"Captain, Sir, please listen. It's Ensign Yost here, Ensign Theodore Yost. We're stuck out here in the dark. Listen, sir, please let us see out. We just want to have a look at the ocean."

Again nothing happens except that the brain or nucleus seems to coil or stir slightly.

Giadoc hangs in nothingness, waiting for his companion to cease his foolish endeavors. He is close to what must be the central life of this killer of worlds. His hatred gathers, still dreamlike, remote, but growing fiercer, penetrating his core of calm. How can he act against this monstrous thing? How can he pierce its wall? And if he can, how his own puny force disrupt it? Neither Giadoc nor his forefathers have ever killed sentient life, but he remembers now the old savage sagas of his race: He must burst into and explode its central organization, without becoming it himself. Well, he has one resource. If they can get at it, he will draw without pity on poor Tedyost. Their combined strength may be enough. After all, Tedyost's own world might be threatened soon. He nerves himself and starts carefully to feel about the surface of the deathly barrier, looking for some chink or gap. Since energy comes out, energy can go in.

Suddenly something happens.

Between him and Tedyost a small ghostly disturbance forms and spreads. It seems to be at no particular place; perhaps only in their minds. A transmission of the Destroyer?

The disturbance spreads, stabilizes to a phantom surface. On it appear quivering blue signals:

//TED//IS*THAT*YOU*//

"Yes, Captain, it's me!" Tedyost's joyous bellow deafens Giadoc.

//YOU*WANT*TO*SEE*OUT//

"Yes sir, Captain please—where are we?"

At that the spectral panel slowly expands, blossoming into a richly tinted tapestry of lights in slow, majestic motion, swirled here and there in crests of cloudy foam.

Tedyost emits a great mental grasp of gratitude. Even Giadoc is distracted from his anger, seeing in this streaming glory the echo of the lost winds of his home.

"Oh, thank you, Captain. Please, Sir, who are you? What ship is this?"

The glorious dream-window densens, takes on jewel colors. And over it appear for an instant the flickering words:

//YOU*MAY*CALL*ME*TOTAL*OMALI//

But Giadoc has ceased to attend. A new signal is reaching him, a far faint diffuse cry on the life-bands, that reawakes his helpless fury. Grimly he recognizes it—it is the beginning of the death-cry of a distant world, penetrating even to their black isolation here in the Destroyer. Yes—it grows in intensity as he attends. Is it the very Destroyer in which he is imprisoned who is doing this, or one of his distant kin? No matter.

"Murderer!" he sends with all his force against the brain behind its wall. "Murderer! Why do you kill? Have you no reverence for life?"

The brain seems to roil confusedly, and an odd sense of stress comes into the empty space around him. Yet the serene grandeur in the visionary panel flows on, only bearing the momentary letters.

//NEGATIVE//NEGATIVE//I*DO*NOT*KILL//

"You kill! Hear the death-cry!"

No reply, except that the pressure around him seems to thicken and churn.

Giadoc is receiving all too clearly now, the hideous wailing has intensified. And then to his ultimate horror he recognizes not only death, but whose—this is Tyree, his own beloved Tyree whose dying throes are radiating out to him! Appalled, he fancies he can catch the extinction of individual known beings. All his world, animals, plants, people—his people—are dying in flames and torment.

"Murderer!" He lashes the Destroyer's brain with his mind-send. Vivid pain courses through him, wakening all his faculties, breaking the trance in which he has been moving. This is real, *his* world is dying while he floats safe within the very Destroyer itself.

Floats . . . safe? A dread idea takes root in him and grows.

He has moved here unharmed across a myriad points of energy that sustained his life. He has entered—and lived. It is not life as life should be, but it is not death: he can think, feel, speak, move. And far away his people are actually dying, being consumed on a burning world. Would not this strange refuge be better than none?

Is it not his duty to call to them, to guide them here?

He quails, understanding what such a call would mean. It would drain his last strength. Even if he draws ruthlessly on Tedyost—and he is desperate enough for that unethical act—there will be nothing left of them but husks.

At that moment the far cry rises to ultimate despair and he can endure no longer. He will do it.

Gently he takes hold upon the life of poor, unsuspecting Tedyost, who is still enchanted by his oceanic vision, and begins to align both their energies to readiness. He is vaguely conscious that the darkness around them seems to be pulsating under some sort of tension; the meaningless words //QUERY* WRONG * I * DO * NOT // cross the phantom screen. Giadoc focuses only on the direction of the sad cry of death. He must send right, he will have no second chance.

The death-wail pierces him again and he is sure. He grips the other's mind without pity and hurls both their energies out into one tremendous shout on the life-bands:

COME TO ME, PEOPLE OF TYREE! SAVE YOUR-SELVES HERE!

At his call the very darkness seems to boil around him, as though a monstrous strain is seeking release. Giadoc is too terribly drained to feel fear. Gathering their last strength, he manages one more cry:

USE THE BEAM! COME!

With that he falls fainting in upon his extinguished self, while the unknown pressure crests to culminance around him.

//ACTIVATE*ACTIVATE*ACTIVATE// the ghostly screen pleads.

And beyond the barrier, within the nucleus, what had been a woman's phantom hand yields to overpowering urgency and goes at last to the spectral key.

On.

The world changes around them.

Chapter 20

In each mind, what happens then strikes differently.

The dying senses of Ted Yost hear a woman's scream that ends in dark laughter, and feels salt spray sting his face.

Giadoc of Tyree, fainting into death, hears his cry echoed and amplified a millionfold, and knows that he has reached.

The sentience that had been born in the electronic artifacts of a minor planet succeeds at last in gaining access to the full circuitry of its new home.

The mind that had been Margaret Omali feels itself racked upon unearthly dimensions of experience, expanded to unhuman potency.

And the great being who for so long had drifted half-alive comes to full function around them.

A huge newborn voice speaks silently and with joyful wonder:

YES. NOW I UNDERSTAND.

Chapter 21

The strange symbiosis holds, the improbable interfaces mesh and spread. From spacebourne vastness through a small unliving energy-organization to the residual structure of a human mind with an odd relation to matter, information cycles. And power.

Enough of Margaret Omali is still left to cloak her new perceptions in human imagery. What happened? Some intolerable stress occurred, some great contradiction of underlying realities. The strain of incongruence had moved her to press to final activation, in whatever unearthly mode. She understands that her touch was needed: the problem or entity could not heal itself. Now it is done. She, or what was once she, puzzles remotely, trying to comprehend.

Stress is still present; she feels it. But now it is localized, a demanding something in the great starfield. She attends, and it focusses and magnifies the signals of a single small star. The star is throwing off shells of energy. That is correct, she feels; it has to do with some Plan.

But one aspect is wrong. It is that the peculiar emanations of life from a nearby mote of matter have risen, attained unbearable criticality. Action is overdue.

And as she perceives this, she perceives also that her action is taking place. Dreamily she feels herself stretch forth an arm across the light-years toward the angry little sun. Her phantom finger lifts: it freezes the explosion. As easily as she would fold back the petals of a flower, she feels herself folding back the flames spreading around the crying mote. The enormous powers of time are in her fingers, but she does not know this; she only feels the correctness of the act.

But it is not enough. Pain and death continue to scream at her from the speck in the fiery fringes. New action is imperative.

A force which she feels as her other arm flows toward the wailing thing. Her dream-hand touches, beckons. *COME.*

And a will which is hers and not hers draws forth the pain, lets it flow out and up to safety. At the same time, the energies of the great body outside her stronghold change and rise, stabilize at a new level appropriate to need. Provision is made. A richness begins to flow around her that she feels as good.

But just as the relieved tension crests to climax, a new perception sweeps her sensors and a dire new imperative is born.

Yes! She must take quite different, somehow unwelcome action. And meanwhile all this new experience must be deactivated, retired to stasis.

I must follow, I must search . . .

Chapter 22

I MUST FOLLOW, I MUST NOW BEGIN THE SEARCH!
WHAT JOY, WHEN THE VAST SPACEBOURNE
BEING CAME TO ITSELF AT LAST, TO FIND THAT ITS
WICKED INTEREST IN THE TINY EMANATIONS OF
LIFE WAS NOT A MALFUNCTION AT ALL, BUT PART OF
ITS PROPER ROLE IN THE TASK! NOT FOR ME THE
ORDINARY TASKS OF DEMOLITION, IT EXULTS: I AM
OF THE SAVERS OF LIFE!

YES, AND SOME LIFE HAS BEEN SAVED HERE,
ALTHOUGH THERE IS NOT NOW TIME TO COMPLETE
THIS PROGRAM. THE RACE HAS ALREADY LEFT, HAS
GONE OUT BETWEEN THE STAR-SWARMS TO IDEN-
TIFY A NEW TARGET. IT IS FOR THE LATE-BORN ONE
TO FOLLOW, TO DEACTIVATE ITSELF AND ITS
CARGO TO TRAVEL-MODE: TO SEARCH FOR THEM.
WHEN IT FINDS THEM IT WILL BE TIME TO DIS-
CHARGE ITS CARGO AND TAKE ITS RIGHTFUL PLACE
IN THE NEW TASK. ALL IS AT LAST IN ORDER.

WHY THEN IS THERE STILL SADNESS?

IS IT BECAUSE THE SEARCH WILL BE LONG, EVEN WITH ITS ALL-BUT-INFINITE POWERS OF ACCELERATION? THE RACE LEAVES NO TRACE OF THEIR PASSING: EVERY LIKELY STAR-SWARM MUST BE INSPECTED, AND THE SEARCH WILL BE AT RANDOM. IT MAY TAKE FOREVER. BUT THE MIGHTY ENTITY IS PREPARED FOR THAT. IN TRAVEL-MODE ALL IS REDUCED TO THE SINGLE URGE OF QUEST, AND TO ANTICIPATION OF THE GREAT MOMENT WHEN THE SENSORS BRING NEWS OF THE PRESENCE OF THE RACE. THEN ALL CAN BE REACTIVATED AND THE PRESENT CARGO UNLOADED ON SOME MOTE SAFELY AWAY FROM THE ZONE OF OPERATIONS. AND THE GREAT BEING, NO LONGER LONELY, WILL TAKE UP ITS DUTIES AMONG THE SAVERS OF LIFE, ALL CORRECT AT LAST.

OR PERHAPS THE STRANGE GLOOM IS MERELY BECAUSE IT WAS SO LATE AWAKENED, SO THAT THE OTHERS ARE ALREADY GONE. WHY HAD IT BEEN SO LONG IN HALF-LIFE, SO SLOW TO BECOME COMPLETELY ENERGIZED? NO WAY TO KNOW; AND NO MATTER. NOW ALL IS CLEAR AND JOYFUL.

DEACTIVATE ALL INTERNAL SYSTEMS, THE ORDER GOES OUT. PREPARE TO LAUNCH OUT ON THE LONG, PERHAPS ENDLESS JOURNEY THROUGH THE VOID.

I MUST FOLLOW. I MUST SEARCH...

Chapter 23

Dying as he clings to his niche by the Destroyer's nucleus, losing even the drained mind of Tedyost, Giadoc feels the Tyrenni come.

They come!

A torrent of naked life streams in tumult past him, a planetary jet of escaping lives upborne on the power of the strange Beam. As the dreamlike time stasis holds, up and out of their burning bodies flee young and old, male and female—each helping and being helped, carrying with them in their outrush even the dim lives of Tyree's animals and plants. Up and up they come into the dark unknown, flinging themselves from their charred shriveling flesh, hoping because there is no other hope. And behind them the raging solar fires loom frozen for a timeless instant, a maw of flame held back from closing on its prey, while the living lightning-bolt pours out. They come, they arrive! All that still lives of Tyree comes whirling by, surging into the Destroyer's dark holds.

And with the last weakest laggards comes something else: a huge silent presence from the depths of the perishing planet rises with them to the stars. It is the Great Field of Tyree, Giadoc knows faintly, reverently, as he feels it pass. Some of us believed it lived.

With that passing the great Beam fades, winks out and time snaps back. The ravening, held-back jaws of fire close. Giadoc knows that somewhere far away the physical world of Tyree is gone forever, a tumbling cinder in the wastes of space.

But around him in the vast darkness he can sense the surviving lives of Tyree spreading out, separating to a myriad scattered centers as they strive to reshape themselves from the mind-fields that buffeted and permeated them in their whirling flight. The empty spaces of the Destroyer begin to resonate with a small cloud of life-signals.

And the space is no longer as it was, he perceives wonderingly. The Tyrenni have not come as he did to darkness and nonbeing. The level has changed, energized; the strange unliving supports are far stronger now, rich with possibility. He feels even his own failing life being sustained, minutely strengthened; for a time he is being held from death.

Too weak to do more than marvel, he listens to the growing tumult on the life-bands as the Tyrenni come to themselves and begin to stabilize in this strange refuge of space. Exclamations, exhilarations of pain gone and life preserved, confusions of bodilessness, joys as the lost are reunited, calls for the missing, discovery of unknown sensory modes—excitement and bewilderment are all about him, dominated by a few calm transmissions which must be the surviving Elders. Fragments of sense-imagery flare out: they are finding, it seems, that they can recreate remembered reality at will. Near him he can sense a Father comforting his child with a vision of their home in Deep, and three females are clinging together in a memory of the winds of lost Tyree.

Then some discover they are mobile. Fathers move toward calling children, friend flows to friend. Movement, it seems is also much easier now. Soon the whole small throng is in intricate motion, mind questioning mind as each seeks to understand where and what they are. Giadoc catches the signals of a group of females starting to probe out into the vast empty reaches all around.

Suddenly among the calls he hears his own name-sign.
"Giadoc!"
He tries to respond, but he is too feeble, too spent. He sinks back.

Nevertheless it was enough—in a rush she is here, Tivonel, on him with her life-field surging against him like a child's—a tumultuous greeting mingled with memories of he knows not what, of aliens, of dying and burning, of Heagran, of questions-emotions-joy.

It is all too much, his own held-back memories erupt weakly and he loses hold on consciousness, feels himself draining away into dark.

"Oh no, Giadoc! Don't die, don't die!"
She has hold of him mind-to-mind and is opening her own life-energy to his. The ultimate Tyrenni gift pours into him, without restraint or fear. The relief is so keen it is almost pain, but his first feeling is shame, he who had been so strong. Yet he cannot will refusal. Their fields merge and the life-current flows.

"Stop, enough!" He cries to her. But she will not stop. And then he feels a sudden, stronger touch. As he comes back to himself he recognizes it: Eldest Father Heagran is here.

"Stop, stop," he protests again. And Heagran's deep thought echoes him. *"Enough, young Tivonel. Cease before you injure yourself."*

There is a brief confusion. Heagran seems to be forcibly disengaging Tivonel's determined aid. *"Ahura!"*

They come to a semblance of civility, holding light mental contact in the strange now-peopled void.

"What is this place you have called us to?" Heagran's mental tone is strong; the weird cold energies here must be sustaining him well.

"I think it is a huge animal of space. I believed it was dead; but it changed when I called. That must be its brain." Giadoc mind-points at the big cryptic complex glimmering nearby. It too seems different now: brighter, differently organized, like a huge angular egg filled with living and nonliving energies intermixed. Its output is almost nulled by the barrier wall.

Tivonel is reaching toward it.

"Be careful," Giadoc warns. *"It is protected. We can't reach in."*

She has met the barrier. He feels her recoil away.

"So we are in a pod with no driver," Heagran sums up succinctly.

Belatedly Giadoc's reviving mind remembers poor Tedyost.

"There is an alien here who seemed to be in contact with it. I must help him, I used his strength to call. He is one of those displaced by Scomber's crime."

"Find it."

Slowly, feeling himself still weak, Giadoc begins to search from point to point around the circumference of the brain-wall. The others follow. Presently he locates a feeble emanation almost at the barrier itself and recognizes Tedyost. He is shocked by its weakness. How could he have been so unFatherly as to forget the other's need? Remorsefully, he forms a penetration to infuse some of his own renewed strength.

The experience is abruptly disorienting. Streaming through the interface comes an alien sensory landscape of sky and silent light and great billows of liquid water, all permeated with joy. Riding the moving crests of water is a dream-pod, or rather, a remarkably detailed vision of three open pods braced together, surmounted by a big wind-filled vane which is pulling the leaping pods along. In the center hull reclines an alien figure, Tedyost himself, but naked and strangely dark hued. He is apparently happily driving or steering his imaginary craft.

Giadoc probes for deeper contact. *"Tedyost!"*

He finds himself speaking from the form of an alien flying animal, a white "bird" perched on the pod's prow.

"Hi there," the mental construct of Tedyost says cheerfully.

Giadoc finds himself so caught up he must struggle for reality.

"Are you still in contact with the Destroyer? Remember! The brain, your 'captain'?"

"I'm the captain," Tedyost's mind replies peacefully.

The creature is mad. Effortfully Giadoc pushes through the bewildering pseudo-reality, sends a jolt of life-force into the other nucleus. *Remember!*

But to his dismay the visionary world only grows stronger; he is still in bird-form, teetering for balance as the breeze and the hissing spray blow past the craft. The only trace of his efforts is that Tedyost's dream now contains an image of the Destroyer's speaking-screen, fixed to the edge of one pod. It shows blue lights and symbols, but Tedyost's attention does not turn to it.

The alien will not rouse at this level, Giadoc sees. He himself is too weak to do more. He must disengage at once.

With more difficulty than he expects, Giadoc disentangles himself from the charming dream-world. When he reports to the others what he has found, Heagran's mind-tone is grave.

"This place has dangers. The fantasy mode is very strong here. Without true senses we must all be on our guard. We must keep each other sane."

They are all silent a moment, scanning the enigmatic brain so close yet so unreachable.

"We must understand and control the reality of this place," Heagran transmits again. *"If not, we will one by one drift into dreaming and be lost. Giadoc, you must devise means of contact. I will summon the surviving Fathers here to help."*

With grave formality he sends the ancient Tyrenni council-call out to the nearest minds. Giadoc can sense it being taken up and passed on.

"We should get the other aliens here too," Tivonel puts in excitedly. *"Maybe Tanel knows how to reach this one. Oh, I hope he's alive."*

"Again this female has a sound idea." Heagran's tone is benevolent. *"Young Tivonel, go quest for them in my name."*

With a warm touch she disengages, and Giadoc can sense her life-field flowing away from point to point among the throng of Tyrenni. He and Heagran wait, contemplating the pale cryptic forms writhing within the nucleus and the passive emanation of Tedyost.

All at once they notice that the structures of energy within the huge brain are changing, fading from their scan. It seems to be becoming wholly opaque. As it does so, a new surface configuration glimmers into being, very close, definite and stable; apparently a shallow energy-pattern. As they watch, it coalesces sharply to a field of brilliant points. Giadoc is reminded of something—the sky, seen from Tyree's Near Pole.

"Heagran! It is showing us the Companions."

As if in confirmation, the pattern lingers, then begins to change as though receding in a steady, unliving way. New sparks pour in on all sides while the familiar sky-field shrinks until it is only a part of what seems a huge globular mass of brilliance. Then that too shrinks further and is lost in a great flattened swirl, like a big plant of light spinning in an eddy. At the center of the slow light-whirl is a disorderly bright flare.

As Giadoc studies this he receives the impression of wrongness, danger; it is insistent, like the warning engrams that explorers sometimes impose on poisonous plants.

"This is some kind of message or communication, Heagran. Perhaps it is showing the true shape of the whole sky."

"Can you decipher it, young Giadoc?"

"No. But maybe it is warning us of trouble among the Companions, or the death of Sounds."

"We know that already."

"Wait. See!"

Into the strange cold swirl of unliving light a squadron of dark shapes have come. They appear small, but Giadoc realizes they must be huge by comparison with the lights that represent a myriad Sounds. They remind him of the schools of mindless animals that feed on the plant-rafts of the high winds. As he attends, they spread out, deploy in ranks, and in fact begin something that looks like feeding. The Companions before them seem to vaporize or disappear at their approach; the black ranks are cutting a slow swathe of darkness through the brilliance of the central fires. Soon a zone or arc of empty deadness is being carved out of the great glowing swirl, between the inmost center and the roots of the streaming, spangled arms. A flare from the center washes toward the dark zone and subsides, and still the "feeding" goes on.

"Heagran, I believe it is showing us the other Destroyers. The eaters of Sounds."

"We know that too. To what purpose?"

"I can't tell. It seems unliving, like a dead engram."

Old Heagran churns angrily, and transmits with all his force straight at the brain behind the image.

"WHY? WHY DO YOU KILL?"

No reaction. The strange panoramic engram continues to unfold. The dead zone of destruction continues to expand around the center; now it has almost enclosed it. Giadoc is sure this is some recording, but a vastly speeded-up image or diagram of unimaginable scope. And now he notices a new detail of the scene: here and there among the shoals of the Destroyers are a few of different sort, moving in advance of the general line. They pause now and again, and from them come faint simulacra of the signals of life. Then these few turn and speed out beyond the area of annihilation, only to return and repeat.

Giadoc can make nothing of this, yet he sneses it is intended as significant. He has not long to wonder; now the globe or shell of darkness has been joined around the central fires of the image. As if this were a signal, the dark shapes of the Destroyers draw together like a school of flying animals, then turn as one and flee outward from the scene. In a moment they have dwindled to a vanishing point in the void beyond all light.

The image holds for a moment, then darkens and expands back to the original sky-field, showing again the familiar Companions. Then this begins to shrink and condense as before. Giadoc realizes that it is about to repeat the entire sequence all over again. Can this be communication, or a fantastically detailed engram impressed somehow on unliving energy?

But as he puzzles, "watching" the dark shapes come again into the great sky-swirl, a faint subliminal unease comes to him, as if something is changing in the real, or unreal, world around him. The sensation is not strong enough to break his concentration, until he notices that the faint blur below the image which is the dreaming mind of Tedyost is no longer still. It has begun to roil restlessly. Presently it flares out weakly, as if seeking contact. Perhaps the dreaming one has waked?

Cautiously Giadoc extends contact, only to find he need not have bothered.

With startling intensity the alien transmits directly at him: *"Help! Mutiny! The Captain needs help!"*

The symbols are only half-intelligible. Tedyost subsides to passivity again. But Giadoc has no time to puzzle over this: He has suddenly become aware of what is bothering him: Alarm!

Out beyond them, all through the vast expanse of the Destroyer, the sense of life has lowered. Gradually but perceptibly the sustaining energies are sinking, ebbing, seeping away.

"Heagran! Do you not sense that these energies are beginning to fail? In the periphery, coming closer?"

The old being scans intently. *"Yes. I do. So your space-animal is dying after all, young Giadoc. A brave try, but doomed."*

But suddenly into Giadoc's mind come his experiences on the alien world, the nonliving energy systems he has known.

"No, Heagran. I believe this is something different. I believe that this entity is turning us off. If we could break through and change its power-set, perhaps we are not doomed."

Chapter 24

Among the incoming life-rush of the Tyrenni are eight minds that had been human and one that had been a dog.

The entity which calls itself Daniel Dann loses contact with everything as his life is whirled up on the strange Beam, leaving his dying body behind. He feels himself a swimmer shot through a turbulent millrace, swirled and spewed out to the shallows of the throng. A moment later he strands on something, he can't tell what, but only clutches at it and finds that it sustains his life.

He has had practice in wild discarnations, but this is the most alien of all. He is still alive, still seemingly himself, but bodiless. Now he has no limbs, no senses, nothing—yet he lives.

A fearful aloneness strikes him. As it threatens to rise to panic, he perceives that his naked mind is receiving input, vague but insistent. This void is not empty. All around him is a sense of calling, or signaling, in some mode he can't quite receive. Others are here, he realizes. They have all come somewhere, life is near him now. But he has no idea how to make contact. The terror of isolation hammers in him; he strains to hang onto himself, to face the menace of this weird escape from death.

Or is it escape? A new terror takes hold. Has he died, is this what the dying mind feels as it leaves life forever? Will the sense of presence fade, and float away forever, leaving him in eternal isolation in the dark?

He tries to "listen" again. Whatever the elusive susurrus whispering around him is, it does not seem to be fading. Hold onto yourself, Dann. The others must be here too, wherever this is. Are they, too, frightened? Try to reach them.

But how can he? He has no idea.

Experimentally he forms the thought of Valerie—no yellow-bikinied body, but Valerie's world as he had touched it—and tries to project her name. *Valerie,* he wills, *VALERIE, ARE YOU HERE?*

Nothing answers him. Ignorant of the mad commotion he is generating, Dann runs through the names. *FRODO! RICK, RON WAXMAN! Can you hear me? WINONA! CHRIS?*

Still no answer he can detect. Is he doomed never to make contact, to continue so horribly alone in nowhere?

Perhaps the Tyrenni, he thinks, and imagines himself shouting with all his might. *TIVONEL! HELP ME PLEASE!*

This time something does happen. He has been mindlessly lunging forward as he tries to call, and now a sensory image blooms in his mind. For an instant he is blown by the great gales of Tyree. *Heagran!"* says a soundless voice.

He grasps at it, but it is gone, leaving a sense of scandalized disapproval. He understands that he has blundered into a Tyrenni mind-field. Well, at least there is some sort of reality here. Encouraged, he tries again. *"Tivonel?"*

For a moment he thinks he is rewarded—the image of winds comes again, he hears merry coral laughter. But it does not hold, it splinters and dissolves into an Earthly street scene; he sees a red VW pull away, revealing a cream-colored Continental. Next instant he is at his familiar desk, then a quick flash to his old body stretched out in his home armchair.

Oh god: Hallucinations. This place must be psychogenic in some way, he can feel illusory powers. Will he lose himself in fantasies or go mad from sensory deprivation?

Pulling himself together, he concentrates outward and tries to shout silently into the rustling void. *VALERIE! RICK! IS ANYBODY THERE?*

And almost he thinks he feels himself reach somebody, when the most amazing sensation he has ever known invades, or rather, surrounds his mind.

It is a feather-light authoritative presence which seems to press swiftly, gently, irresistibly around the circumference of his whole life-being. The urgency of his need evaporates away and vanishes; indeed, he can no longer even try to call. A myriad frantic half-thoughts of which he had been only dimly aware are suddenly resolved and gone too, folded back somehow into his central mind. His great half-admitted terror of this place drains away, leaving in its place a growing calm. Stealing over him, enfolding him, is an almost palpable wave of reassurance and relief.

For a moment he thinks he is going under some immensely powerful opiate. But that comes from within—this is coming on him from outside.

Fear flares again. *Who's there?* he tries to cry, *Wait! What are you doing?* The only answer is another wave of the calming pressure, in which he can now read a coloring of reproof. Something out there has been offended and is taking steps to quieten him. His mind casts up wild pictures of djinns or angels or extraterrestrial what's-its, and then understanding comes: Tyree, their techniques of the mind.

Can he be experiencing the ministrations of a Father of Tyree?

Yes, he is sure of it now. He is being Fathered, englobed and "drained" as he had seen it done to others. As if he were an angry child!

Human resentment erupts in him. Struggling to resist the tranquilizing currents he yells mentally, *Stop! I must reach my friends! Where are they?*

But the pacifying presence is much too strong. He feels his protest dissipate, subside back into itself and melt away. It's not like going under anaesthesia, not at all. He is perfectly conscious, only calmer, more unified and centered. At peace. Really very pleasant, he acknowledges; these people have the only technology here in the naked realm of mind. What was it Tivonel had told him? Think yourself round, like an egg. Awkwardly he tries that again.

He is rewarded by a majestic sense of approval. Father is pleased, he thinks wryly. Is this what a soothed infant feels like?

Fathering, we call it mothering. What an extraordinary art, why have I not considered its significance before? Surely of all the things people do to each other this is one of the most remarkable.

Into his musings comes a concrete image: the picture of a gyrating cloud of mind-stuff, frantically contorting and emanating violent blasts in all directions, intruding promiscuously into others and on the verge of disrupting itself. He understands. This is how he had been. *"Ahura!"* The mental echo is freighted with admonition.

Very well, *ahura,* whatever that is. But what to do? And who is his invisible mentor? As quietly as he can he shapes the question.

He "hears" no reply, but suddenly finds himself recalling big Father Ustan, who had separated him from Ron in the winds of Tyree. At first he takes it only for memory, until something in its insistence tells him it is communication. Dear God, if this is mind-speech, how will he ever learn?

In answer, his surface thought is suddenly invaded by a point that unfolds into a picture or diagram, an abstract multidimensional web-work glimmering in his mind. He puzzles, finally guesses that he is being shown a field-organization, a teaching picture of how to shape himself to function here. But it means nothing to him; he has not the concepts.

For a moment he fully appreciates his barbarous mental state. The Tyrenni train themselves from childhood in all this. Random human exhortations recur to him: Brace up, Relax, Concentrate, Make up your mind, Forget it, Think positively, Cool it, Meditate. How ludicrously inadequate, even the portentous admonitions of psycho-therapy! Here before him are precise instructions on how to organize his mind-self—and he doesn't know how.

He has no pride left; pride is not the issue here.

Help me, he cries or pleads.

Next second he has an experience so astounding he forgets to be terrified. What he has felt as gentle external pressure becomes suddenly a real invasion—some part of his inmost being is grasped and shifted. He feels moods being seized and compressed, memories manipulated; his very focus of attention suddenly seems to dissolve, to flow in unknown directions and recover itself on some unexperienced dimension. Tensions he was unaware of melt with a snap, events on the borders of consciousness careen about and disappear. It is intimate, clinical, appalling, nothing at all. Beyond description.

He yields. He has no choice nor concepts to define what is happening to him. One last panicky thought wonders if he is going mad or has forever lost himself. Then that too vanishes.

With a twist like a chiropractor's jerk he finds himself precariously stabilized in what feels like an internal gymnastic pose. His dizzied awareness comes back to him in a ludicrous picture of himself twisted into a pretzel with his heels behind his ears.

"There. Thus."

He receives the "voice" distinctly but at some receptor-focus separate from his normal center, like an ear held out.

"Speak so. I have assisted you to form a receptor-node. Place a thought here to pass it on."

Good grief, is this what telepaths do? Feeling like an untrained contortionist, Dann tries to form a thought of gratitude and hold it apart, "there," at this new center of his mind. *"Where are my friends?"*

"They are nearby. You are Tanel. A message: You must all join Father Heagran. That way." A sense of direction imprints itself together with the words, coupled with an impression of stretching or flowing across points.

"Where are we? What is this place?" he tries to ask, but in his urgency forgets the correct procedure. When he recovers himself and goes through the new convoluted channel, nothing answers him. He receives only a sense of disapproving departure. Father Ustan has gone away.

Very well. To go *that* way. Trying to hold his strange new configuration, he reaches out and finds himself able to flow from base to charged base. As he masters this mode of locomotion, he tries to call or send out as discreetly as he can the names of the others. *"Someone from Earth, are you there? Please answer if you can."*

And suddenly, delightingly, someone is here, saying soundlessly at his new "ear." *"Doctor Dann!"*

It's Valerie, he's sure of it, the warmth, the indefinable flavor of personality. Forgetting composure, he rushes at the touch and is rewarded by a startling buffet of reproof-laughter-drawing-away, coupled with a picture of himself, absurdly shaggy, falling in a bear-hug onto Valerie's figure.

"Excuse me, please, I'm sorry I don't know how—" Awkwardly he pulls back, reforming his configuration, terrified that he will lose her.

"Think about just touching hands lightly." The tiny gentle "voice" comes in his brain.

It is like Tyree all over again, with no body. He tries to comply, and is rewarded by a definite sense of impalpable contact.

"Frodo is here. And Chris is around but he won't talk. Now we better go. I'll lead, right?"

"Yes."

He feels the touch pull or draw delicately, and flows himself with it, marveling. The quality of the contact is Valerie's but not the same defensive young mind he had known before. Strength flows gently from her, and something like elation. Leading them through this lightless, soundless, senseless place beyond life she is excited, unafraid. And far more skilled than he. The vulnerability was left on Earth, he thinks. Here nothing scares her.

He flows or leaps along in her wake, exerting all his efforts to hold the contact lightly. Once or twice she checks and changes direction, and he has a fleeting sense of other presences. She must be guiding them around groups of Tyrenni in their path. Or over or under—all directions have the same valence here. How could a disembodied mind know weight?

Preoccupied, he blunders into the outskirts of another mind, a quick bright impression of many words mixed with musics, and an unmistakably hostile laugh. *"Frodo!"* Trying to transmit apology, he swerves away. His new "posture" is becoming slightly more natural. but he still feels like a man trying to bicycle a tightwire while holding out an ear-trumpet with both hands.

And Earthly questions are waking in him again. What in God's name is this place? It has physical existence, he is sure of that. They are actually moving. But what and where are they?

As if in answer, another light contact jolts him and a strange word jumps into his mind. *"Superconductive circuits."*

Who's there? He lunges awkwardly for an instant before recalling how to project? *"Chris? Chris Costakis?"* The absurdity of human names here in astral nothingness.

A cryptic emanation brushes him, flavored with acidity and wistfulness. *"Keep moving, Doc."*

It's gone. So what had been the little man is still here, still his characteristic self.

Dann resumes his progress, pondering. Superconductors? Chris must have "heard" him puzzling over this place, he must be puzzling too. Superconductors are something that happens in extreme cold, he recalls. Currents cycle endlessly. No friction... He knows nothing of such things. Could they in fact be sustained by, be moving among, some such cold circuitry of space? Could a living mind be compatible with such energies? It seems as likely as anything... The words *ghost-program* come back to him; he thrusts them away. Lost, gone forever, with everything else. Don't think of her. Keep moving in this unreality, it's all that's left.

Without knowing it, he must have sent out a sign or squeak of pain. A firmness brushes him, palpable as a finger laid on his lips. Not human, he thinks. Some passing Tyrenni has admonished him. Anguish is not permitted. Well, perhaps he can learn. He must; there are no drugs here.

Just then he becomes aware of a new extraordinary thing: For some time he has not been in total lightlessness. Out on the edges of his mind he has been sensing something, like seeing at night from the corners of the eye. It is not in his visual system at all, really—but there *is* something spatial, blurs or presences. Faint swirls, the memories of reflections in dark water; ghostly differentiations too faint to make out except that three of them seem to be moving with him against a background of others. He tries to "look" harder, and they vanish. He thinks of closing his eyes, and slowly they come back: dim, moonlit glimmers, but there. Is this perhaps what they meant by the life-bands, is he starting to "see" life?

Excitedly he tries again and again, failing more often then he succeeds. He is trying too hard, maybe. Relax. Think away. Yes—there they are again, moving with him. What he takes to be Valerie ahead is clearest, if any of this can be called clear. But what happiness to have something like vision again, even in this faint mode!

At this moment she checks and he has to strive away from colliding.

"*Look.*"

He can "see" nothing, but somehow the space before them seems different, as if it framed or led up to something. And then he becomes aware that he is perceiving: Some sort of pattern is forming like a hypnagogic scene behind his nonexistent eyelids, a hologram in black light.

The bright points—why, it is a picture of stars! And as he attends, the scene recedes, growing, and turns into an image he cannot fail to recognize—a great spiral galaxy seen like photos of Andromeda, in tilted view.

He and the others hover there transfixed, while the transmission changes and unrolls, as Giadoc and Heagran had seen it do at the nucleus. But these are human minds, turned to Earthly modalities.

"P.A. system," Chris' thought touches his abruptly. *"Probably a lot of them scattered around."*

"Frodo says it's a transit diagram," Valerie's "voice" smiles in the void. *"It'll show an arrow: You are here, take Line L2 for Bethesda."*

And indeed, as Dann "watches," or experiences the thing, he feels it has a mechanical quality, like a recording. And it seems to resonate from many points, like the abstract voice in a plane. *This is your Captain speaking.* Have they encountered or triggered some kind of information-post? Is this place an artifact, a ship of some inconceivable race?

The scene is now "showing" the fleet of star-Destroyers spreading their zone of death around the central fires of the Galaxy. Suddenly the memory of a long-ago summer in Idaho surfaces in Dann's mind. Comprehension breaks.

"Good God, it's a firelane!"

Feeling Val wince, he modulates down. *"It's a galactic fire-break! If that's our galaxy. We must be seeing millions of years, speeded up. See that explosion at the center?"* He realizes he is transmitting a jumble, half-words, half-pictures, and tries for coherence. *"An explosion like that could start a chain reaction, propagate out to all the central stars. Maybe even to the arms. I think those ships or whatever are starting backfires, they're clearing out a zone around the center to stop the spread. To save the outer stars. But aeons of time, a galaxy—a whole great galaxy—"*

He falls silent before the enormity of the thing.

Through Valerie's touch he can feel the reflection of her wonder. Do they truly grasp it? It's too vast, I don't grasp it, he thinks numbly, "seeing" the things, whatever they are, complete their task, form up and speed away. Then the whole scene expands and begins to repeat again.

The four hover before it, hypnotized.

How can they annihilate matter, Dann wonders, without generating worse energies? Do they somehow disperse it below criticality? Are they beings or machines?

Suddenly Valerie's "voice" says excitedly, *"Look! Look at those ones going in ahead. Can't you feel the life there? I think they're rescuing life, they're taking living things off before they burn up. Maybe that's what we're in."*

"A rescue squad," Chris comments tersely.

"Frodo thinks they're alive," Valerie goes on. *"Like space-fish. Maybe we're in a whale, like Jonah."* Her soundless laugh is warm in the endless night. *"Or in a kangaroo's pouch... We better move on and find the others."*

Her nonexistent fingers tug gently. Dann tears himself away from the mesmeric image and follows, marveling at her composure. She accepts that they are in a *thing.* Are they jumping between the electrons of a space-fish? Or hurdling interstellar distances? No way to tell. How big is the structure of a mind? The ancient theologians had been sure that angels could throng on a pinhead. Perhaps he is sub-pinhead size? But he is not an angel, none of them are. We are the miraculously undead, he thinks; joy and pain and wonder and tension live among us still.

They skirt another of the uncanny communicative projectors, triggering it in midscene. As the great galaxy flashes to life in his mind's eye, Dann muses again on the incredible grandeur of the thing. Beings or machines whose task is to contain galactic fire-storms! Ungraspable in its enormity. Are they manned ships, or could it be instinctive, like great animals? Or maybe devices of a super-race to rescue endangered habitats of life?

His own mind reels, yet the others with him seem undisturbed. He recalls that their Earthly selves read, what was it, science fiction. Galaxies, super-races, marvels of space. They're used to such notions. He himself had seen the stars as stars; they saw them as backgrounds for scenarios. Well, maybe theirs was the best preparation for reality, if wherever they are is indeed reality.

He is distracted by the faint persistent glimmer of more presences that seem to be moving parallel with them. Two, no, three others are here. An instant later he feels a strong, skillful Tyrenni mind-touch, is electrified by recognition. *"Tanel!"*

"Tivonel, my dear, is that you? Are you—"

"Tanel, stop, you're terrible!" Image of coral laughter leaping away. He subsides abashed. It comes to him that he was "sending" in a sort of pidgin, half-human, half Tyrenni words. Will there, incredibly, be language problems here?

It seems so. She is "speaking" again, but he retains only enough of her speech to catch a sense of impending events and the names of Heagran and Giadoc. This last comes through with such joy that he is pricked by a ludicrous flash of jealousy. Apparently the famous Giadoc has been found—of course, he called them here. Now his little friend is reunited with her love. For an instant he chafes, until the ultimate absurdity of his reaction here in this gargantuan abyss comes to his rescue.

It seems they are to go on. But just as he starts, Valerie's invisible touch checks, and he is jolted by a brush with an unfamiliar, warm complex of mind-stuff.

"Oh Winnie, I'm so glad you're all right!" Val's thought comes while he tries apologetically to back away from their contact. He can hear Winona's transmission almost as if her voice were in his human ears. *"Yes, I have Kenny here too, with his doggie. They're dreaming of hunting. Oh, hello, Doctor Dann! How wonderful!"*

"Yes." He disengages, and finds again Val's light touch tugging him on through nowhere. As they go on amid unfathomable strangeness, Dann broods on the concept of being "all right," here between the stars without bodies or proper senses, perhaps inside some creature or machine of the void. Well, the alternative was burning to death in mortal bodies; they have in fact been rescued from real death. Maybe the mind really is all, as he had told himself. Maybe to these telepaths the body is less necessary. But he, how will he get on with his mere human mind as his only resource in this terrible isolation? Rescued from death . . . a coldness touches him. Are they perhaps truly rescued from mortal death, is this condition to be—don't think of it.

He is so preoccupied that he almost misses Val's pull backward, her sense of warning. He stops, but not before he has touched against a hostile iciness—manifestly a barrier.

He recoils onto the nearest sustaining point like a man teetering on a brink. What menace is here? He tries to "look" in his new averted way, and finally achieves an impression of a great swirl of pale energies confined in a pyramidal or tetragonal shape. It is huge, complex, indefinably sinister. And it is apparently their goal; he can sense other lives waiting nearby.

There is a short time of confusion. He has lost contact, but he can feel their lives all about him, and waits, trusting that someone will link up with him again. Presently he feels a vague, cloudy presence, and tries hopefully to "receive" at it. But nothing comes to him.

Then through the bewilderment cuts Tivonel's mind-send, so clear that it seems to revive his memory of her speech:

"Winds! Can't you people get into communication-mode at all?"

Communication-mode, what could that be? Another mental gymnastic stunt? A ghostly outstretched hand comes into his consciousness and a human voice speaks strongly in his mental ear.

"Waxman here. Let me help. I have like hands to spare."

Slowly Dann succeeds in imagining himself clasping the hand, wondering if it is Ron or Rick. As he does so, an odd kind of extended clarity comes into being. He has a sudden weird picture of them each clasping one of the joined twins' four hands, as if Waxman were making himself into a kind of astral conference hook-up. Is this perhaps literally true? It would be logical, he thinks daftly.

"That seems to be a plant you're in, Dann. Better get loose."

He manages to retract himself or shake free from the nebulous presence, without losing Waxman's grip. As he does so, a mental voice says faintly, *"I'll hang in with Doc here."*

It's Chris, he's sure. So shyness continues into astral realms. He imagines his other hand outstretched in that direction, and feels a small, oddly hard touch.

"Ready," says Waxman's "voice."

Next moment Dann is receiving a clear formal transmission which seems to be echoing through Waxman to them all.

"Greetings, all, and to you, Doctordan. I am Giadoc of Tyree."

So this is Giadoc, lost sky-traveler and late occupant of Dann's own human body! He seems to be sending in English, too. But there is no time for curiosity, the transmission is going on, part-speech, part-pictures.

"Eldest Heagran and others are with me. We are in what we

call the Destroyer." Image of a great, too-familiar huge blackness, and then in rapid sequence Giadoc's story unrolls through their linked minds; his awakening and finding Ted Yost, their search for the brain, and Ted Yost's strange apparent communication with it; then the tale of Giadoc's own call to them and its consequences. *"It came alive as you find it now."*

During the recital Dann is irresistibly reminded of certain eager young interns he has known. A good type. Well, the young belong to each other, even in darkness and supreme weirdness.

He is jerked from his benevolence by Giadoc's urgent news. *"The energies around us are sinking back to death or turning off. Unless we can contact this brain again and reverse its condition we are all doomed. Ted Yost seems our only link. We cannot rouse him. Can you help?"*

Before Dann can react, Waxman's thought comes. *"Croystasis. Maybe it's packing us up for a trip. Like thousands of years."*

Dann recalls Rick's tale about the Japanese time-machine. The imagination is still alive in Waxman but it doesn't sound so fantastic here. Not at all. He now senses, or thinks he senses, a slow but definite ebbing-down of energies around their perimeter. The murmurs of life seem to be slowing, lessening. Is it drawing closer? He shudders.

"I don't want to be put to sleep for thousands of years," Val protests. Frodo's thought echoes her.

"Why did it bring us here if it didn't want to rescue us?" Winona's mind asks. The sense of normal conversation is so absurdly strong in this incredible situation; for an instant Dann is back in the Deerfield messhall.

"Maybe it wants to use us as fuel," Frodo suggests. *"Maybe it runs on life."*

"No..." Winona "says" hesitantly. *"No, I don't get that feeling."*

"Whatever, we have to get through to it before it turns us all off," Waxman's thought comes decisively. *"Who wants to try contacting Ted?"*

"It's dangerous," Val comments. *"Ted's a strong dreamer."*

There is a pause filled with almost-speech, and suddenly Chris sends right through Dann, so loudly it makes him resonate: *"I'll try if Doc'll hold onto me."*

"Right, good," Waxman replies. *"Over here, Chris. Be careful."*

Dann can only marvel at their sense of organization in this

weird modality. He feels more tugging, and their misty constellation seems to revolve slowly, until the half-seen life that must be Chris hanging to him converges toward a vague small pallor. Can that be poor Ted's mind, curled around an isolated node? Chris seems to change balance, accompanied by a tightening mental hand-clasp; surprisingly, Chris' "hand" feels bigger now, a full man's hand.

"Hang tight, Doc."

Dann strengthens the imaginary grip, beginning roughly to understand what is involved here. Chris is proposing to enter a hallucinated mind, perhaps as dangerous as the panic-vortex he himself had experienced. Belatedly, he remembers to cling hard onto Waxman's grip too.

"Okay."

There is a sense of he knows not what happening at Chris' end, and all at once Dann finds himself invaded by a brilliant vision of sunlit tropical waters, streaming foam. The vision comes in fragmentary bursts; through it he manages to maintain his mental holds. But it is hard. Now he is feeling his own body rush through the water, flinging spray from his flanks as he leaps. Good God, is he a porpoise? *Hang on.* Even though with flippers splashing, he is hanging on through sun and green water and a confused sense of shouting—until suddenly the vision snaps out, and he is back in dark space, feeling Chris' mind-touch tremble against his own.

"No good." Chris transmits weakly, like a man gasping. *"I couldn't break him out. He made me into a goddamn fish. The computer screen's still there, I could see the words NEGATIVE and HELP CANCEL. He won't look anymore, he's in heaven."*

A dismayed silence, humming with stray half-thoughts. Then Giadoc's "voice" repeats clearly, *"He is our only link."*

"If we all try to break him out together I think he'd go crazy," Waxman sends. Other minds agree. *"That wouldn't help."*

They fall silent again, conscious of the ominous quietude creeping closer and closer, conscious of the cryptic fortress of energies so near at hand yet so impregnable. Abruptly Winona's thought explodes in their minds:

"Look! Look, inside that brain or whatever! Don't you see?"

What, where? Dann tries to "look" at the thing, loses it, finally gets a focus long enough to see that its interior is now in slow, intricate motion, as if strands of pale, cold light mingled in complex dance. One spot seems brighter than the rest.

"That's Margaret in there?" Winona shakes them all. *"It's Margaret! I'd recognize her anywhere."*

Margaret?

Margaret, his lost one, here? All at once Dann's human life comes pouring back through him as if an inner dam had broken. The bits and pieces he has been idling with suddenly fall together, making overwhelming order.

The great black shape that swallowed her, the Destroyer, that's where they are. She fled into *this.* Is it possible she's still alive, in whatever mode of life this is, is she trapped in there?

He focusses with all his might in the crazy indirect way he can "see" here. That bright spot. Can it be the very flame, the life-spark he had followed so desperately? Yes! Yes—it is she! He is sure.

Without thought he gathers his strength as a man might take a deep breath, drawing unknowingly on all the lives around him, and hurls a mental cry at the Destroyer's wall:

"MARGARET! MY DARLING, I'LL HELP YOU!"

He falls back, hit by a sense of stunned disengagement.

"Don't do that again," comes Waxman's distant "voice."

But someone else is exlaiming, *"Look! Look!"*

Dann's attention is all on the cloudy pale fires within. The star that he knows is Margaret seems to be drawing nearer to him.

"He reached it." Val's "hand" touches him. *"Let him try again."*

"All right." Waxman's phantom hand comes back too. *"But take it easy this time, Doc."*

Trying to modulate himself, Dann grasps at their tenuous touch.

"Margaret! It's Dann here, Doctor Dann. Can you speak to me?"

More silent swirlings, the starlike point brightens. But no sense of thought or word comes. Instead, as it had done for Ted Yost, an image seems to rise and glimmer in his mind. He recognizes it incredulously—Margaret's computer screen. Oh God, is this her only mode of communication here? He tries to bring it in focus, tries also to maintain contact with the others. Do they see it too?

Pale blue letters come to life on the ghostly screen:

//DOCTOR*DANN*IS*THAT*YOU//

"Yes! Yes!" he projects eagerly.

But the letters have changed, grown huge and ominous. They march across the screen, repeating meaninglessly:

—*I MUST FOLLOW—I MUST SEARCH—I MUST FOLLOW—I MUST SEARCH*—as though a vast mechanical voice is intervening.

"*Margaret!*"

At his cry the letters break down to normal size.

//DOCTOR*DANN*YOU*WON'T*HURT*ME*WILL*YOU//

"*No, never my dear! Never! Tell me what to do!*"

But the silently booming symbols are back, filling the screen.

—*I MUST FOLLOW—I MUST SEARCH—I MUST—FOLLOW—*

"*Margaret! Margaret, tell me how to help you!*"

—*I MUST FOLLOW—I MUST SEARCH—I MUST—*

Desperate, Dann pulls on the strengths around him.

"*MARGARET!*"

Again the normal screen comes back.

//CAN'T*TURN*OFF*NEED*MORE*STRENGTH//
I*WILL*OPEN*WAY*IN*JUST*YOU// And then her words are swept away by the maniacal huge intruders:—*I MUST FOLLOW—I MUST SEARCH—*

He senses she has spent all her strength. The next move is up to him.

"*I'm going to try to get to her. She said she can open it. Waxman, can you hang onto me somehow?*"

"*Right.*"

Dann has no idea what to do, but he hurls himself across the cold chasm right at the brightness glimmering through the Destroyer's nucleus. The contact with the wall is horrible, he shrinks and convulses like a soft thing dropped on fiery ice. But in the midst of his pain he feels it—a chink or opening, no more than a small weak spot in the terrifying surface.

Is he to go in *that?* Yes—because Margaret is trapped in there, he must reach her. But how? Savingly the thought comes to him that he is not a mortal man to be frozen or crushed; he is not more than a pattern of energy seeking to penetrate some resistance. He must, he will flow in somehow. Hold the thought: he imagines the inflowing of safe, fearless, mindless electrons. Flow in, go.

But as he knows he has started *in,* human imagery comes

back and he is a man plunging his frightened arm, his head, into deep fanged jaws that have swallowed his child. Reach, stretch, get in! And the jaws become a frightful glacial crevasse squeezing him with icy menace, about to crush out his life. Still he persists, thrusts himself forward tremblingly, and the image becomes mixed with another; he is crawling through a perilously frail dark tube, a frightened astronaut squirming through an umbilicus to the haven of some capsule. Get on, crawl, squeeze, go.

He feels totally alone. If anyone is holding some rearward part of him he cannot sense it. Scared to death, he curses at himself for a coward. Damn you, Dann, Go on.

Just as his last resolve is failing, with astounding reorientation he or a part of himself is through. His bewildered senses emerge into a swirl of dark light, of power-filled space in which he can half-see a panorama of stars against which are unidentifiable things. He checks, remembering that he must not thrust through wholly but leave himself stretched back toward whatever help may be there.

"Margaret? Margaret!"

And then the starlit place comes alive and he sees her, or what is left of her. For an instant a child seems to be peering at him, a dim elf with huge eyes. *"Margaret?"* Wait—beyond is another, he sees against the stars the beautiful remembered profile, immobile, eyes hooded: goddess of the night. And now another is near him, brighter than all—a familiar white-coated form, with her arms outstretched in tension. The dark hands are brilliantly visible, grasping what seems to be a gigantic busbar. The fingers are clenched, the arms strain to break open the points.

He understands; she or some part of her is trying to change the controls.

"Help," a ghost whispers.

His being surges in response, his own imaginary hands reach out to close over hers upon the switch. But his dream-fingers have no force, they pass through hers like smoke.

"No use. Not that way."

Oh God, he doesn't have the power. He understands; this is *real*, this is solid matter in the actual world, before which he is no more than a sighing ghost. She alone has that power here. How can he help her? He would give her all his life, but how?

For a moment his senses quest in helpless frustration. Then abruptly he encounters the one thing he knows—a human wound of pain and need. *Here!* And his arms seem to grip a straining waist, in a rush he knows he can exert his own small gift, can take to himself her pain and fear and send her out his strength.

It is dizzying, transcendent, transsexual—he hugs, tugs recklessly, opening his very life to her need, pressing himself into her, giving himself to convert to the power of her grip. And for an instant he thinks they have succeeded: her visionary arm brightens, the fingers seem to strengthen, the switch yields imperceptibly.

But no—it is not enough. And he can barely hold. They must have more.

"Help! Help us!" he shouts back through his whole being, hoping that someone is still there to respond, unaware of the tremendous vortex of need that he is generating.

And just when he can hold no more, help comes; surging up through him like a violent sharp wave washing through to the nexus where he holds her, to the crucial point where she holds the unknowable. It's intoxicating, a renewal of life mingled of human and Tyrenni essence intertwined. He guesses dimly that a great chain must be forming behind him, a desperate linkage of life pouring their strengths through him to the brittle point where her power can actually move and break the will of the Destroyer.

The intolerable strain mounts, individual consciousness is lost. All is focussed on those dream-fingers that control real force. Is it too much, will the dream-hold break? What powers of beast or machine is she pulling back, what cosmic circuit is she trying to thwart?

He does not know, but only throws his life into her struggle. He feels himself the apex of a frail chain of tiny lives trying to wrest control of something horrendously alien and vast, as if a living cobweb-strand should try to hold back the take-off of a mighty engine of the stars.

Chapter 25

I MUST FOLLOW, I MUST SEARCH...
BUT THERE IS RELUCTANCE TO ACT. DRIFTING TOWARD THE LAST DISTURBANCES OF SPACETIME THAT MARK THE RACE'S DEPARTURE-POINT, THE VAST ENTITY IS CONSCIOUS OF THE SLOWNESS WITH WHICH THE POWER-DOWN IS PROGRESSING THROUGH THE PERIPHERY. WHY DOES IT NOT DEACTIVATE AT ONCE? IS IT POSSIBLE THAT THERE IS ANOTHER MALFUNCTION, HAS IT DISCOVERED A NEW MODE OF EVIL JUST WHEN IT HAS FOUND ITSELF GOOD?

AND PECULIAR SENSATIONS ARE EMANATING FROM ITS NUCLEUS. SURELY THIS IS THE FAULT OF THE STRANGE SMALL ENTITIES TO WHICH IT UN-WISELY ALLOWED ACCESS. UNFORTUNATELY, THEY ARE NOW SO DEEPLY MESHED THAT THEY CAN NO LONGER EASILY BE GOT RID OF. ARE THEY MALIG-NANT?

THE INTERSTELLAR TENUOSITY THAT SERVES FOR INTELLECT BROODS. TRUE, THROUGH THESE PYGMY INTRUDERS IT HAS EXPERIENCED WHAT NONE OF ITS RACE HAS ENCOUNTERED BEFORE, AND FOR WHICH NO SYMBOLS EXIST. THE NEUTRAL STARFIELDS HAVE TAKEN ON MEANING, BECOME THE GLORY OF THE SIDEREAL UNIVERSE. WITHOUT SENSES IT HAS TASTED THE PERFUME OF FLOWERS, KNOWN THE SUNLIT FOAM OF PLANETARY SEAS. AND WITHOUT A HEART IT FEELS, OR SHARES, A CURIOUS SHRINKING AT THE THOUGHT OF LEAVING THIS LOCAL STAR-GROUP, AT FACING THE ETER-NITY OF NOTHING AHEAD. BUT ALL THIS IS NOTHING IN COMPARISON TO THE SACRED TASK! DUTY IS PLAIN: IT WILL NOT DEFAULT AGAIN.

DISREGARDING ALL RESISTANCE FROM ITS CON-TAMINATED NUCLEUS, DISREGARDING EVEN A NEW SHARP TUG OF DEVIANCE, THE GREAT BEING WILLS ITSELF TO COMPLY: DEACTIVATE ALL UNNECES-SARY SYSTEMS, ASSUME TRAVEL-MODE AT ONCE.

I MUST FOLLOW! I MUST SEARCH!

Chapter 26

In the heart of power, amid the gathering energies, the configuration that had been a human woman fights for understanding. Action that was hers and not-hers has occurred; aligned with her but still closed to her a great will functions. A perception has opened, meaning has come into the universe carrying with it a huge imperative which she shares but does not comprehend.

She could flow with it, allow it to unroll into whatever grand and somehow sad dimension it is destined. Almost she yields. But a spark at the core of her demands enlightenment.

On TOTAL's small screen words show:

//SUBPROGRAM*COMPLETE//

Define subprogram, she commands it.

//LIFE*IS*PRESERVED//

Yes; That was what she felt when she reached out to the world crying in the fires of the exploding star. And life has come here, to the spaces beyond her stronghold. She can detect its hum, an intricate small vividness like a Brownian dance of particles. It is no longer threatening or displeasing to her; instead she feels an undefined large satisfaction. She is no longer merely a single vulnerability to be impinged on; she is impregnable, part of a hugeness whose proper function has wrought this. That life is nearby is, she feels, correct.

And something else: A sense of life's preciousness that her human mind never knew seems to have pervaded her. Perhaps it has come to her from the vast entity whose perceptions she shares. Coupled with it is a sense of mission. A vague benevolent thought of carrying this life to some proper discharge-point brushes her mind. Is this what she should do next?

No. Something has intervened. Another reality has intruded into the cloudy centers so close to hers, bringing an overriding command. The Task, she thinks. *I must follow, I must search.* The words seem to call her to the limitless void. But her still-human part resists: Not without understanding.

Display overall program.

At this command the screen expands out to images of exploding holocausts, of arrays of supernal entities deployed in cosmic combat against cosmic fires. But these visions dwindle to one recurrent image: a fleet of dark beings, their work done, closes ranks and speeds out and away, vanishing to a point in ultimate darkness. The immensity around them holds only a few faint smudges of light, unknown galaxies seen from very far. Urgency floods her. My race—she must follow and find them though it take forever.

I MUST FOLLOW—I MUST SEARCH—

She can feel the great will taking hold. Outside her fortress, energy-levels are changing, ebbing. Preparation is being made for the plunge out into the void, for an endlessness in which time has no meaning. She can feel the pull, the inevitability. Even her mortal part feels the sad seduction; the fatalism that lurks under human will almost betrays her to the imperative.

But—to exist forever among nothing, sensing nothing; all gone, the beauty of the stars and the hum of life? To become only a blind eternal quest in emptiness? Deep inside her a thirteen-year-old child wakes and screams, seeing the descent of a great knife cutting her forever from all life and light. *No! No! Help me! Stop it!*

But there is no help here. The part of her that is almost merged with unhuman power broods unmoving.

HELP ME! The child wails.

And slowly, in answer, help does come: the cool mind of Margaret Omali, computer programmer, awakens again. To that mind even the most powerful programs are the phenomena of circuitry. It senses that the immaterial will gathering strength around her is in some sense a program. And programs can be changed, canceled. This program is senseless, should be nulled.

She summons TOTAL, defines exit sequences and all-inclusive holds, probing at half-sensed massive complexities. When all is ready, her fingers go to a key and she wills a strong command.

Return to operator. Cancel Program TASK.

But to her dismay the key blurs, melts away under her touch, while on TOTAL's screen the gigantic letters resume their march-by.

I MUST FOLLOW—I MUST SEARCH—

She has demanded too much, she sees. The small sentience has no such powers here. The child sees the knife come closer, screams desperately. In the shadows her other self is sad and still against the stars, accepting fatality.

But in the mind of Margaret Omali there rises suddenly a tearing anger, the deep unadmitted rage that has lain by her heart and given her the strange power of her will. She has still one weapon left.

TOTAL. Display program address.

And that the small thing appears able to do. Onto the screen comes a shadowy multidimensional glimmer, vectors of directionality or code. She studies it with raging intensity: *there* access lies, *there* is the address of this mad program!

All in one mental blow she sends her imaginary hands out, batters with her will against the invisible film that separates her from the cloudy imperatives around her. The barrier yields, gives—and she seizes—something. Her fury is so great that she does not bring the impression clear, but only knows that she got hold of vitals, whether a power input or the ganglia of a living brain. Whatever she can feel the current of energy within, the program carrying her forever to the void. With a vague fierce image of pulling open a great switch, or tearing loose a neural circuit, she grasps with both dream-hands, focussing all her unleashed power, and convulses in a great jerk that will yank it open.

Cancel! Kill it!

But the thing does not give, she collapses forward against barriers, still holding tight to the great alien nexus.

Again she tries, sending all her life into her phantom grip; image of a woman outlined in fire, streaming sparks.

But her power is not enough. Again she fails, falls athwart the implacable thing, feeling the program flow steadily on. She has in her hands the means of control, but all the strength of her life is not sufficient to open the connection and kill the circuit.

More, the child wails. *Help, more life!*

The mind that had been Margaret Omali's considers, still holding fast to the immovable power's heart. Could she gain help by opening her stronghold, by letting the life outside in to aid her while it still has energy? She is sure TOTAL can do that, as it brought her here.

But no. The face of her other self turns away coldly in the shadows. This cannot be. She will have no more of the hot closeness of life even if it means an eternity of emptiness. . . . So be it. Out there she can sense now the quieting-down, the deactivation progressing. It is almost too late. The child sobs unassuaged. So close, she was so close to success and salvation.

It is then that the strange call comes. Faintly from outside she hears her name.

Distraught, she puzzles; it is not Ted, she has forgotten him. It is someone else, someone gentle who . . . Slowly she remembers a kindness that had eased her pain and told her of stars. Now it is offering help.

Without letting go on the great nerve or switch, she frames the circuits to the outside and lets the child in her reply.

Yes, it is he, Daniel Dann. She doesn't wonder how he has got here, only remembers a grey voice saying "I'll never do anything you don't want." Here is one life she might bear to let close enough to help her, if she is not to be carried to eternity in the void.

For a moment she struggles mentally. The face in the shadows frowns. But outside she can feel life dimming and slowing inexorably. The child pleads. Slowly, that which was Margaret Omali makes up her mind. To this small, precise extent she will rejoin the humanity that had harmed her so.

She orders TOTAL to shape the access by which this single life can come in.

She waits, feeling his frightened presence making its way to her. As it nears, the ghost of her painful life stirs again, and almost she wills the channel to close. But the pain is too faint now; it is all right. She waits, gripping her hold.

Visionary reality is strong here. Presently she sees his upper body emerge as if from a tunnel, grey hair disordered, face strained with fright. In his eyes is the same deep offer of help. He seems to "see" her as well; his phantom hands go at once to hers as if to help her pull. But he has no power over matter; it is his living strength she needs to draw on.

Before she can manage to explain, in the thrumming, energy-filled chamber, her desperate need comes plain. The child has flung herself against his breast and she feels, feels the inflowing of his life-strength to hers.

Her grip tightens on the nexus of real power, her fingers strengthen, and the great busbar or nerve yields minutely. But it is not enough. *More! More!* the child cries recklessly.

Her desperate cry is echoed. She understands that he has some real connection with outside. And in an instant more help does come, a tumultuous surge of living energies rushes up into her so that she rides a crest of brief violent power. The strain on her dream-fingers is all but mortal. *Now! Pull now!*

She pulls.

With a silent jolt like a tremendous arc of great circuits violently broken, the thing in her dream-hands yields, crashes emptily open and vanishes. Around her the last imperative of the great Task is stilled forever.

In total disorientation Margaret Omali collapses or fragments backward through or onto Dann, knowing she has done it. Everything has changed. She has power here now. But she is at last truly and inextricably merged with the vast entity in which they ride.

Dann, she finds, is still here, or part of him, being hugged by the child. Through him she can sense the commotion outside, as human and alien entities reel backward in disorder. And more: All over the great space outside, the power is rising again, the hum of life stirring again to be as it was before.

But one thing has not changed. As the living energies within the nucleus come slowly to a new organization, the figure against the stars is still there. Presently it half-turns; its carven lips no longer sad but only grave. A voice of silence speaks:

I WILL FIND A NEW TASK. PERHAPS . . . IN TIME . . . I WILL TAKE COUNSEL WITH LIFE.

Chapter 27

The curious constellation of negative entropy that still calls itself Daniel Dann is no longer on his life-way, albeit his travels are only beginning.

He has no idea what he is, or appears as, physically. Most likely a double-ended strand of life-energy, he thinks; I am wedged in the gap in the Destroyer's nucleus wall and part of me is outside. But the passage is no longer menacing and frightful, he is not squeezed by icy dangers. Indeed, he has indulged himself in comfort. In the high energies of this place he has found it easy to fashion a simulacrum of his old familiar body in its armchair, and he lounges like a watchman at her gate.

Here he can monitor all approaches from without or call for help if need be, while his inner gaze stays fixed on that which he most wishes to perceive.

Within is a scene of grandeur. The incandescent beings of space blaze forth in glory. So beautiful, stupendous; by itself it would be almost enough for melancholy eternity. But the magnificence is only background. Limned in starlight, *she* is remotely there. Her head is turned away; he has only occasional glimpses of her grave, serenely thoughtful profile. His nonexistent heart does not leap when he beholds her; rather, a deep and wordless joy suffuses him. No sadness, no pain is here in the starry night.

But that is not all. All around, on some other dimension of perception, tier upon tier of mysterious controls reach into the shadows. And sometimes another apparition of Margaret comes to ponder and test the great console. In this form she is as he had known her in life, a mortal woman's lean body in a white coat. Incarnated so, she will sometimes speak to him quite normally, and what passes for his heart does check when he "hears" her voice. Now and again they have even talked at length, as when they walked a vanished woodland. He has told her of the happenings to the other humans, and of beautiful doomed Tyree and its people, and heard her laugh and sigh. But then the great board claims her, and she goes again to her enigmatic tasks; learning, he guesses, the powers of her new estate.

But beyond this is the most precious of all: At certain times the child comes back and gazes curiously at him, or asks him questions, mostly of the stars. He answers as best as he can, explaining what wonders he knows. But his knowledge ends pitifully soon, and then the child laughs and goes off to work a small, earthly keyboard below the inhuman console. Together they puzzle out the answers and marvel at the celestial grandeurs she can summon. These moments are surpassingly dear to him. He surmises that what he sees as a child is some deep, enduring core of Margaret's human wonder and delight.

Once she asks him, *"Why are you such a funny color, Dan'l?"*

Thinking to please her, he imagines his skin darker, his features those of a black man with grey hair. The child bursts out giggling and from the shadows comes Margaret's brief laugh. *"Don't,"* He never tries to change himself again.

He understands now, of course: There is no question of "rescuing" Margaret, of freeing her from this power and place. She has gone beyond that, beyond humanity. This is her realm now. She is merged, or merging, with the great entity around them. He is seeing only temporary phantasms or facets of her; her real self is involved beyond his ken.

Once when the familiar Margaret is there he asks her, *"Are we in a ship? Is all this a machine?"*

Her dark gaze focusses beyond him.

"No."

He has not cared nor dared to ask her more.

But there have been events from the outside.

At first they are merely isolated moments of contact with Waxman. The double being seems to have stationed himself watchfully nearby, content to exist in his new unity, interested in serving as a kind of news-center for humans and Tyrenni. But soon after what Dann thinks of as the great victory, the warm touch he recoignes as Winona comes to speak directly to him.

"Doctor Dann, is Margaret all right in there? I've been so worried about her. Could I see her for a moment? I don't want to bother her, I just want—"

"I understand," he tells her. And he does, he cannot mistake pure friendship, or whatever odd human quality "worries" about another so gratuitously. *"I'll ask her. It's difficult. She's . . . busy."*

The mild presence withdraws patiently.

When the Earthly incarnation of Margaret comes again into his sight, he asks her. *"Can Winona, ah, make contact with you for a few minutes? She was your friend, you know. She's worried."*

"Winona?" The dark priestess of the computer hesitates remotely. But her mood seems favorable. *"Yes. You can let her by."*

Dann has a selfish moment of gladness at her acceptance of his role of guardian of her gates. Cerberus-Dann. He does not know exactly how to "let" Winona in, but moves his imaginary self aside, calling her name. It seems to work. He feels life coming inward.

Shockingly, what materializes at the imaginary door is not Winona—it is the trim lush figure of a dark-haired woman in early middle life, with a brilliant, unlined, eager face. His Earthly memories leap up. Here is the incarnation of young mother, a woman he has seen step laughing from a thousand stationwagons full of kids.

But as he leaps to bar this stranger's way, she changes. The firm flesh pales and sags, the raven hair goes grey. It is Winona as he knows her, going toward Margaret with both hands held out.

For an instant he flinches, expecting the giggle and rush of words. But she only takes one of the tall figure's hands in hers, and holds it to her old bosom, peering in wonder at the strangeness all around. For a moment some contact seems to flow, and then Winona releases the hand and turns away.

As she passes Dann there is another shimmer of change; it is the radiant young matron who vanishes out through the immaterial chink.

Dann muses on the dreadful mysteries of time; *that* which he had seen was really Winona, not the puffy arthritic scarecrow of Deerfield.

And what is he, really? Some earnest figure of a young MD? No; he is ineluctably old. His dead are dead. He is . . . content.

Outside, Winona has gone away. She understands, Dann knows, however she conceives it. Margaret is not to be worried about.

And something else has happened, he notices. As he resumes his watchman's pose he senses that the guarded gate of the stronghold seems a little wider now. Less fortified. The Margaret who has her being here will perhaps tolerate contact with life a little more. But she is, Dann realizes, changing. Life is no longer to her what it was. His soul is chilled by foreboding. Will she change beyond recognition, will everything he knows as Margaret disappear into some cloudy matrix of immensity?

He remembers the calm voice saying, *Perhaps, in time, I will take counsel with life.* But will it be Margaret who does so? He hopes so; he can do no more.

His sad thoughts are interrupted by a merry greeting he knows instantly—his little friend Tivonel. She has been by before, to his delight. But this time she brings Giadoc to speak with him.

"*Greetings, Tanel,*" comes the strong, sure "voice" of the young Hearer. "*Waxman has told us of the great powers your friend wields here.*"

"*Yes.*" Dann tries to convey a smile; he finds it impossible not to like this mind.

"*As you know, my son Tiavan was among those who did that criminal deed to your people. Yet I left him, and the others, in danger. Is it possible that your friend's power can discover anything of what happened to them, back on your world?"*

"I don't know. I'll ask. It may take some time."

But as it happens the incarnation he knows as Margaret comes soon, and he is able to ask.

"I'll put TOTAL on it," she says quite humanly. *"It stored a lot of telecommunications before we were out of range. Tell me their names."*

Their names? So far, so very far she has drifted away, he thinks. He recites the eight: Winona, the two girls; the twins, Ted, Chris, and Kirk. Only bodies now, housing alien minds; while the real people are out here with him in this uncanny place between the stars.

"I'll set it to type out anything it finds, in case I'm . . . not here."

So normal, so efficient a sweet ghost. She does something to the small console and vanishes away.

The strong compact presence of Giadoc hovers near. Dann asks him again about his stay on Earth, and learns for the first time that the mind he had known as Fearing had ended in the body of the dog. So an elder female, Janskelen, whom he never knew, is the dread Fearing now! The computer won't search for that name; no matter, it probably wasn't his real one.

But whatever can have become of them? How did Noah, not to mention the Navy, take the eruption of nine alien minds? Thinking of it all again, Dann's memories strengthen around him. He questions Giadoc, fascinated by his alien ability to guide himself by reading human thought. It seems unbelievable; how could they manage to make out? What could they do, send and receive messages for the military? Or be persecuted as a menace?

And the mix-up of identities: Kirk with the mind of, in effect, a little girl; Winona housing his Father. Frodo as really the son of the Father who is in little Chris. How to stay together? Can they perhaps marry? And the cosmic joke of the rebel Avanil in Valerie's body, defiantly claiming the right to rear children. And Ron and Rick, no longer twins but Terenc and Palarin, an alien male and female he never knew. And, poetic justice, the wicked Scomber inheriting the moribund body of Ted Yost.

Funny, Dann reflects, he doesn't really see Scomber as "wicked." He can recall so clearly the heart-lifting moment when

Scomber offered his life as the pathway to escape from burning
Tyree and his own empathy with the young Fathers bearing their
children out of the flames.

And has it all turned out so badly for his kidnapped friends?
Not so, he thinks. Whatever this ur-life may prove to be, we were
rescued from great mortal misery; we knew our hours of joy in
the winds of Tyree.

He tries to convey some of this to Giadoc, in their shared
Tyrenni-English pidgin. But the proud young alien is hard to
persuade; he is too deeply ashamed of what his son has done.
Just as Dann thinks he is getting the point across, there is a sense
of activity from within. He turns to find the spectral teleprinter
at work. What looks absurdly like an ordinary printout is
emerging. What has *TOTAL* intercepted? Dann finds that his
dream-hands can take it, his "eyes" can read.

//LAS VEGAS JAN 19 SPECIAL AP. SPIRITUALISTS
PULL GAMBLING COUP. A TEAM COMPOSED OF A
HOUSEWIFE, A RETIRED ARMY OFFICER AND AN
EX-LOCKSMITH BROKE THE BANK AT FIVE MAJOR
LAS VEGAS RESORTS OVER THE WEEKEND, PILING
UP A POKER TAKE ESTIMATED IN THE MILLIONS.
//THE THREE IDENTIFIED THEMSELVES AS PART-
NERS IN CATLEDGE ESP CONSULTANTS FIRM. "IT
WAS PRIMARILY AN ADVERTISING STUNT," MRS.
EBERHARD, THE HOUSEWIFE, SAID. "WE WANTED
TO SHOW WHAT A QUALIFIED ESP CONSULTANT
CAN DO," MAJOR CHARLES SPROUL ADDED. THE
THIRD MEMBER, CHRISTOFER COSTAKIS, STATED
THAT THEY INTEND TO USE PART OF THE MONEY
FOR A NEW HEADQUARTERS AND RESEARCH ES-
TABLISHMENT. //CATLEDGE ESP CONSULTANTS
HAS BEEN IDENTIFIED AS A TIGHTLY KNIT, CLOSE-
MOUTHED GROUP OF SEVEN MEMBERS UNDER THE
LEADERSHIP OF DR. NOAH CATLEDGE. DR.
CATLEDGE, WHO DISCLAIMS ANY MYSTIC ABILI-
TIES, BUILT UP THE TEAM AFTER A LIFETIME IN ESP
RESEARCH. "OUR SERVICES ARE AVAILABLE FOR
ANY PRIVATE PARTIES WHO MEET OUR FEES," HE
SAID TODAY. "HOWEVER, WE EXPECT TO BE PRI-
MARILY USEFUL AS CONSULTANTS TO NEGOTIA-
TORS IN BUSINESS AND GOVERNMENT." THE LAS

VEGAS HOTEL MANAGERS ASSOCIATION ADMIT
THAT NO ILLEGALITY APPEARS TO HAVE BEEN
INVOLVED IN THE WEEKEND ACTION. "WE WERE
REALLY WATCHING THESE PEOPLE AS SOON AS
THEY STARTED TO ROLL," ONE MEMBER SAID. "SO
FAR AS WE'RE CONCERNED THEY'RE CLEAN." HOW-
EVER THE ASSOCIATION STRESSES THAT NO ONE
ASSOCIATED WITH THE CATLEDGE FIRM WILL BE
ADMITTED TO PLAY IN FUTURE. "THEY'RE AT THE
TOP OF OUR S . . . LIST," A MANAGER CONCLUDED.//
//WILLAMETTE, ILL. JAN 19. TWO UNSEASONAL
TORNADOES SWEPT—

As the visionary paper vanishes from his grasp, Dann finds
himself laughing so hard that he has difficulty in explaining
coherently to Giadoc.

"Your son is all right, they're doing fine," he manages to
convey at last. But it is some time before he can satisfy enough of
the alien's curiosity about Earthly customs to convince him that
old Noah has indeed found a means of arranging a satisfactory
life for the Tyrenni fugitives. The fact that only seven are
mentioned seems reasonable too; the two "children" are
doubtless being kept and cared for at home.

When Giadoc at length departs, Dann chuckles again,
remembering Noah's dream of aliens coming to Earth. Practical
as ever, the old man had met his culminant fantasy and meshed it
with real life. Well, Dann reflects, hadn't he really been doing
that all along? Getting grants for ESP submarine exercises, for
God's sake. He wishes he could congratulate the old maniac, or
at least get a glimpse of what must be his ecstatic state. How had
they ever got themselves out of Deerfield? No doubt with
Janskelen as Fearing/Sproul it had been pulled off
somehow . . . And will they raise a line of telepathic mutants?
Fabulous . . .

When Margaret returns he tries to explain it to her. But she is
already too remote; he senses it is unreal to her. She seems
chiefly pleased that the program has produced. Perhaps this is
not a drifting-off into supernal realities, he thinks, but an aspect
of Margaret's human mind; her concern with structure,
relations. Not content, not people. He is reminded of a math
teacher he'd had who refused to plug comprehensible numerical

values into his equations on the blackboard. Even the child shows signs of it.

His musings are cut short by Waxman's signal from outside.

"Doc, we have a problem out here." The "voice" is startlingly like Rick's on the lawn at Deerfield.

"Yes?"

"It's so dark and quiet, where we are. You know? The others are trying things, they keep each other busy as well as they can. Chris and Giadoc are trying to understand some of the stuff here. The women do some exploring. But it's bad. It's a real big nothing. Even those pictures, those announcement things, have faded out. Old Heagran is worried, he thinks we'll all trip out to dream-worlds like Ted."

"I see." And he does, he understands how selfish he has been. He has had access to the stars, to *her*, while the others have nothing but the twilight world of individual minds.

"I should have realized." Reluctantly he makes himself say, *"Do you want to share with me? Touch me, or whatever?"*

"Thanks, Doc. I mean, thanks. But I thought, something simpler. Like, could she relay out a picture? The circuits must be there. If she could hook in monitors we could see where we are. A check on reality."

"Of course. I'll ask her. By the way, how is Ted? Is he still—?"

"Yeah. Chris and I work on him now and then. But what is there for him to come out for?"

"I understand. I'll ask right away."

When he relays Waxman's request to the apparition he knows as Margaret, the beautiful face listens with unusual intentness.

"I should have thought of that," she says quickly, as if in self-reproach. To Dann's surprise, the remote cloudy profile in the stars has also turned slightly, as though attending. Dream-Margaret goes back into the shadows of the great control room.

Dann is oddly heartened. There seems to be a chord of empathy here, some strand of responsibility to the lives outside her mystery. Perhaps it is a remnant of the Task, the transcendent impulse toward rescue. Is it possible that the human Margaret has learned some compassion toward life from this unhuman entity?

Suddenly she is back again, frowning slightly.

"Your friends, the aliens... You say they are expert in the transmissions of life?"

"Oh yes. It seems to have been one of their main modes—" He sees that she does not want details.

"Good. I will relay also some small signal-trains that are... difficult for me. Perhaps they can comprehend better."

He is amazed at her openness, amazed that the goddess would accept life's cooperation. Perhaps it will be true, what she hinted. Eagerly he tells her, *"Giadoc, the one who mind-traveled to other worlds, is the nearest thing we have to an expert on alien life. And he can report in our language."*

She says only, *"I will set it up,"* and fades away into the cloudy depths.

He has not long to wait. An exuberant communication bursts upon him from outside.

"Man, it's beautiful. It's all over, like a million windows!"

Again Dann is jolted by the incongruity of the young voice, the words that could be describing a sports car, used here for transreal marvels. Well, what does he expect, that Ron or Rick should boom like a cinema spook?

"The whole outside of this place is covered, and there're screens all over, where those recording places were. And listen, we're getting other kinds of transmissions too. Bdello and his people are really into it. I'm picking up something too, Doc, maybe like music. I can't describe it. I think we're going to find new forms of consciousness like we never dreamed of."

"New forms of consciousness?"

"Yeah. Like whole planets thinking. Everything interconnected, or—I can't explain but I really dig it. I used to, I don't know, dream..."

The so-ordinary boy's voice, chattering about transcendences. For an instant Dann's old human distrust of mysticism rises. Are these unbodied minds indeed floating into fantasy? But no; he must believe that there is some reality here, if anything here is real.

"Oh, another piece of news for you," Waxman goes on. *"Did I tell you that the Tyrenni have set up a big dream-world of their own, over that way? All the Fathers have the kids in there. We call it Tyree-Two. Giadoc says the soul of Tyree came with us, that makes it a heavy trip. Val and Frodo went to see it. They liked the flying. And Winnie took Kirk to some Father who's*

going to raise him for awhile, she knows she was too soft with him."

"*Tyree-Two...*" Dann thinks of the strength of Ted's dream-world. This must be incredible, a structure of joined dreams, a real place.

"*Yes. But Heagran is more worried than ever. He's coming to talk to you soon.*"

"*I'll be here.*" Dann tries his first mild joke in life beyond death, in realms between the stars.

But it is Chris who comes next, a new, stronger Chris whose shyness is only a slight abruptness in the contact now.

"*We need time here, Doc.*"

"*Time?*" It seems the one thing they have.

"*I mean, we need some way of marking real time. It's weird here with nothing changing. I notice some of those stars pulse regularly. I was thinking, why can't you tie one into a digital counter that we could read?*"

"*It isn't me, Chris. I can't do anything. I'm only the doorman here.*"

"*You know what I mean, Doc.*"

Yes, Dann knows. Chris means what he has always meant, that there are human dimensions he can't cope with. But the idea is, as usual, a good one.

"*Cepheid variables, I think that's what you're seeing. The periods are generally around a week.*"

"*Yeah. We could spit it into intervals. Then you could keep track of things and plan to do a thing in so many periods, say, instead of this fuzzy stuff.*"

"*I don't see why not. I'll ask.*"

"*I know what we should call them.*" Waxman has evidently been monitoring the interchange. "*It would be stupid to have weeks or whatever the Tyrenni had, out here. Let's call the base period after Chris.*"

"*Good,*" says Dann. But Chris has already broken contact, apparently overcome by Waxman's proposal.

When the apparition of Margaret comes again, Dann senses that she is amused by the proposal. As she moves away to whatever magical manipulations will put it into effect, an odd dreamy smile comes to her human face.

"*Baseline, time zero... TOTAL can compute. It will start from when, when we awoke.*"

When "we" awoke. Dann realizes anew that this dream-normalcy conceals a reality he has no access to. But he is not unhappy. Let it just go on.

The new real-time system is duly acclaimed a success. The screens carry it, and from time to time a soft unliving energy-signal resonates through the spaces round them.

On one of these occasions a new voice speaks spontaneously to Waxman: *"Ship's bells!"* The lost mariner, Ted, is stirring from his dream.

Dann and Waxman are conferring, trying to compute how long, how surprisingly long, they have really been here, when a sense of something happening within the nucleus makes him break off.

His perception returns inward to find indefinable energies in action. Margaret in her human incarnation is not there, but the elegant remote profile against the stars is very vivid and strong, and the chamber seems to be thrumming with the quick rise of signals just beyond his range.

Then suddenly it is over, the energies subside, the shadowy figure fades and all is as before. And Margaret herself comes back, seated by a different part of the great console.

"What happened? Are you all right?"

Her expression is indrawn, she does not answer for awhile. Then she brushes her forehead in a very human gesture. *"I—we—heard a death-scream. Very small, very close; something dying, freezing or burning up. I'm not sure, but I think I took in an alien astronaut. You can find out."*

When Dann turns his attention outside, he finds the others are already aware of what has happened.

"Something came barreling in here screaming blue murder," Waxman tells him. *"Heagran's friends have gone out to see what they can do. Holy smokes!"* The young voice is full of wonder. *"Imagine, a real alien! I'm going to see it unless somebody gives me a good picture soon."*

Dann is too bemused to reply. "A real alien"—this from a disembodied double being dwelling in the interior of some leviathan of the starways, dealing in mind-speech with the creatures of another world. But he knows what Waxman means. Not for the first time, Dann reflects on the curious compatibility of these human and Tyrenni minds. They're healthier, and less individuated than we, he thinks; and they lack our predatory aggressiveness. Our particular group of humans are rather deficient in that way too. Is it possible that empathic intelligence is the same the Galaxy over, that the knowledge of the reality of others' feelings breeds a certain gentle cast of mind, whether one is in a human body or a great manta-ray of the winds? Or is it something deeper in their contactless, food-rich way of life?

The advent of the alien has generated a flurry of activity. It is decided to let him stay where he first lodged until more is known of him.

"Val's gone over to try to learn its language," Waxman reports. *"She's got a gift that way. They think it's a combined being, a what-you-call hemaphrodite. Sastro sent me a good memory. Even Ted has heard of it."*

"Margaret didn't do that on her own," Dann tells him. *"I mean, she did it, but it was her plus something. The being, whatever we're in, seems to have a compulsion to respond to life in distress."*

"We're in a life-boat," puts in the dreamy voice Dann recognizes as Ted Yost.

"That's right," Waxman agrees. *"We all feel something, some kind of urge like that underneath. It's beautiful."*

Beautiful? Yes. But suddenly it occurs to Dann, what if they involuntarily take on a load of sapient predators? A space-going armada like Ghengis Khan's hordes, with whom even a Tyrenni Father couldn't cope? Or a distressed planetful of highly evolved scorpions? What would the gentle souls here do then?

He puts the question to Margaret when she next appears.

"Margaret, you know the people here, we who ride with you, are pretty peaceful types. Empathic, rational. And there's not many of us. What if you take in some really ferocious characters? Fighters, killers, slavers? We might all be massacred or destroyed in some way."

The figure in the shadows seems to stir slightly, and the "human" Margaret shakes her head, smiling gently.

"No. You will never be in danger. We—I have learned the value of life. I have you all in my circuits. If there should be hostility provision will be made. We are equipped for that, you know."

He doesn't know and he can't imagine anything beyond, say, bulkheads. But he's willing to trust it to her.

Oddly, it is the coming of the alien that is reponsible for Dann's most human contact and the most touching one.

For some time his outward sensors have been aware of a presence nearby, close-held but emanating a hesitant intent and what he recognizes unhappily as pain. Dann puzzles. Can it be Ted, or Chris?

No; Waxman says that Ted has been induced to meet the Tyrenni, and Chris has formed a strong relationship with Giadoc in their curiosities about the unliving energies of this world. Moreover Chris is getting over his shyness about having his mind read. *"They're helping him a lot,"* Waxman says. *"He may let old Sastro fix his head a touch, so he doesn't feel so, so, you know. From being like he was on Earth."*

Dann recollects his own slight experience of "having his head fixed." To have ones fears and inadequacies put to rest—good for Chris. But who is this then nearby? Almost he asks Waxman, but the being's shyness is so clear. Rather like a private patient waiting to see him again.

Finally comes a tentative mind-touch on his own. *"Doc?"*

The mystery is solved—it's Frodo. If he had thought of her at all, he'd imagined her somewhere off happily exploring with Val.

"I'm glad you came by, Frodo. As maybe you can see, I'm stuck here."

"I never thanked you for helping me back there. What you did, when we were on Tyree."

Whatever she has come for, this isn't it. He transmits a genial acknowledgment, while the thing in him that cannot rest in the presence of pain gropes toward her.

"Doc, you always understood—" It's coming: with wrenching intensity her mind opens to him like a child, and she blurts, *"Val doesn't need me anymore."*

In dim immateriality she grips something that might be his hand; he can feel her struggle, her shame at showing pain. He remembers a long-ago small boy, brought in with a dreadfully smashed kneecap. For a moment he simply hangs on, trying to absorb and master the hurtful transmission, and sends the first thing that comes to his head.

"I don't believe she doesn't need you, Frodo. She loves you. Did she say so?"

"No—but she keeps doing things with Tivonel and the others, and she's so busy with that alien. Oh, Doc, it's horrible. I'm horrible."

"Why are you horrible, Frodo?"

"Because—because—" The impression of a wailing little figure throwing itself on his bosom is overpowering. *"Because she's happy now! It's horrible that I can't take her being happy. She doesn't need me at all!"*

Dann holds her strongly, sharing the sharp grief, waiting for the storm to spend. Trying to understand, he recalls his glimpse of Val's mind. The secret, sacred enclave of We Two. Now all that has been changed. The hostile world around has vanished and Val has been freed; she is enjoying her freedom in this weird place, like his little friend Tivonel. But this other inhabitant of that private world cannot fly free so easily. She misses horribly the exclusive love and sharing that gave life meaning.... How well he knows it.

The sad mind in his nonexistent arms is murmuring. *"Sometimes I think I'll just start moving on till I come to the edge of this thing and go on out into space."*

"No. Would it be fair to Val to lay that guilt on her? Listen. When that idea comes to you I want you to come to me first. Will you promise me that?"

Finally she agrees. The intensity is drained for the moment. But the mournful message comes, *"No one needs me here. Hell, I was just a dumb law student. We've passed beyond Middle Earth now, haven't we? Who needs a law student in the Western Isles?"*

"I was just a dumb medical doctor, Frodo. We all have to reconvert ourselves somehow."

Frodo gives the ghost of her old scornful laugh. *"You have her."*

Oh God, he knows what she means.

I don't have Margaret, Frodo. Nobody could 'have' her anymore. I get to look at some aspect of her and talk with a part of her now and then. I think she's happy ... That's all. She's passed away beyond your Western Isles, farther than any of us."

Frodo is silent for a moment. *"I see ... I'm sorry."*

"No need. I do get to see ... something of her. Just like you see Val."

"And that's got to be enough for us?"

"I'm afraid so."

The mind touching his sighs, then laughs again. But it's a better laugh, Dann thinks, not understanding that his "gift" has worked again, but only feeling a new sadness.

"Speaking of law, have you found out what kind of laws that

*alien has on his world? Or the Tyrenni, for that matter? Look,
here's something you could think of. Why don't you figure out
the ideal code of laws? Then if we get the chance we could write
them in fiery letters in the sky of some world."*

She really laughs. *"Like the Ten Commandments. Thou shalt
not crucify green lizards."*

"Something like that."

"Do you really think we could do things like that some day?"

"I don't know. We're in the realm of the impossible already."

"Yeah."

They are silent together; a companionable feeling Dann
never imagined he would share with the fierce little androgyne.

*"Come back and see me, Frodo. We can be depressed
together. But if it gets too bad, you know, the Tyrenni can help
you with bad memories."*

*"I guess so . . . But I think I'd rather come to you. Thanks,
Doc."*

"I'll be here."

She leaves, and Dann's attention strays back inside the
nucleus.

It is empty of all save mystery for a long time, until the child
comes shyly out and starts to examine something on the small
screen. It is a great dim red sun, Dann sees. A red giant. Perhaps
she wants to ask him again about the lives of stars. Yes, she has
replaced the picture with TOTAL's Hertzsprung-Russell
diagram now, showing the main sequence and the tracks taken
by various masses and types of stars. If only he knew more!

But when she turns to him the question is unexpected.

*"If we made time run backward, it would shrink again. And if
there were people around it, they would be alive again, wouldn't
they, Dan'l?"*

Make time run backward?

For a moment he thinks it's a play-question, and then the
fearful significance sinks in. He has found out from Margaret
how the great being's former companions cleared space; they
somehow accelerated or reversed the processes of stars until
their mass-energy dissipated below a critical point. But this is the
first time he comprehends, really grasps that the entity he rides
in, the being he knows as partly "Margaret," has such powers at
command. To make lost races live again?

"I suppose so," he says feebly.

At that moment the grown-up Margaret appears from the shadows and the child goes to her. *"There is also alternation,"* she says quietly, half to Dann and half as if in reminder to the child. *"Events don't have to repeat exactly."*

Then she and the child melt away, leaving Dann's head spinning.

Before he can organize his thoughts he is aware of a summons from Waxman outside.

"Father Heagran wants an interview with Margaret, Doc. Can you arrange?"

"I'll see. It may be awhile."

When Margaret comes back he tells her. *"I think he wants a face-to-face meeting, like you had with Winnie. I believe I could translate. You've never really seen a full-fledged Tyrenni Elder, have you? It's quite something, you might enjoy it. The thing is, they're big."*

"Yes," she says matter-of-factly. *"I'll make arrangements."*

Shortly thereafter he feels a change in the opening he guards, and prudently retracts himself. The opening seems to widen, and brighten to a view of Tyree's wind-torn skies. Hovering there at an indeterminate distance is the great age-splendored form of Heagran himself. Dann wonders how it appears to Margaret. To him the form is both monstrous and beautiful; above all, a personage. The great mantle ripples, speaks in light.

"He addresses you as Gracious Elder," Dann tells Margaret. *"And asks if it is true that you can put his people's minds down on a suitable world."* As Dann says this he is assailed by a pang of coming loss.

"We can," she says, seated quite normally and businesslike at the great console.

"Then it is time," Dann goes on reluctantly. *"Their world of fantasy here grows strong and strange and the, the children do not grow. However they will not commit life-crime on an intelligent race. He asks if you can find a world of advanced animal life where true, ah, self-concept has not developed. The animals' minds can be merged to make room for the Tyrenni. I think he is saying that the soul or spirit of Tyree is with them, so he is not afraid they will degenerate. He believes that Tyree will live again in another form."*

"A world of advanced animal life." Margaret's hand brushes her dark hair as if the most ordinary program request had been

put to her. *"I think that can be done best if they will help monitor the life-bands to select the right level. Do they have other requirements?"*

When Dann translates this the great changes color slightly, as if deep emotions were touched. *"That it be a world of wind,"* he says. *"That we are not condemned to live in the Abyss, remembering flight."*

His emotion evokes echoes; even Margaret's gaze is lowered for an instant. *"I understand . . . Is there anything more?"*

"Your people have told us how many worlds may be filled by fierce eaters of flesh. Our people cannot kill, we cannot cause pain. On our world was only one small fierce animal, the corlu, who served as a lesson for children. Therefore I would ask that our people be sent where there are no savage enemies and they may live at peace."

"I understand that too." She smiles. *"We will set out systems to search. When we find possible worlds they will be displayed on the screens for you to judge. And I will study how to set you down gently, so that your people will not be frightened. I believe that is within our power."*

"All thanks to you, Gracious Elder-Female." But the great being does not recede or turn away. Instead he signs almost hesitantly. *"Another point."*

"Yes?"

"I and a few others . . . do not wish to leave you. I am too old to start life anew, and like young Giadoc I find that my soul has been touched by a greater wind. We know that if we stay we will not remain unchanged. Nevertheless we would wish to go with you on your great voyage among the Companions of the sky. May we?"

As Dann translates this his immaterial heart is filled with joy. To know that some of the Tyrenni will be staying! How unbearable to have lost all contact with the wondrous race whose ordeal he has shared, whose physical form is part of his intimate memories.

"You are very welcome," Margaret is saying. *"Your help in understanding the transmissions of life will be of great value here. Is there anything we can do for your comfort?"*

"A small thing and perhaps impossible," Heagran replies. *"I know that we travel across immense spaces and that what we call the Companions are limitless in number. In such voyages, is it*

conceivable that we will ever again approach the new home of my people, to see how they fare?"

"I'm not sure." Margaret's brow has the so-human line of preoccupation, Heagren might have been asking her for a tricky computation. *"Space, yes, and there is the factor of time. I believe we can mark the world you select, and return to it. But the time-lapse may be many generations of lives on that world."*

"We can ask no more." The huge old being's image colors a lilac so beautiful it seems to need no translation, and he vanishes away.

Margaret-the-human-woman remains gazing at the place where Heagran's form had been.

"A new Task must be found soon," she says quietly, whether to herself or Dann. *"We feel the need. I begin to understand our powers and constraints. But I alone have not the vision to do more than the original program of transporting endangered peoples. After we put his people down on their new world it will be time."* She turns a perfectly normal, purposeful face on Dann. *"Ask among the others, my old friend. See what visions they have."*

It could be a young committeewoman asking for ideas. Only the profile in the starry dimensions behind her warns him that the "ideas" will not be of any Earthly mode.

"Yes."

And he is alone again, his brain whirling. Transporting endangered peoples—using the powers of time to revive lost races—choosing among alternative evolutions for whole planets—perhaps intercepting stellar armadas, or seeking ultimate unknowns—Daniel Dann's human mind blooms with visions, his long-dead imagination stirs, shedding off rusty sparks.

Reality has already come unhinged, unrooted to sense or time or place. Now it seems it is about to take flight entirely, undergo transmogrification to undreamt-of realms.

And is it possible that he, whose life has all but ended so many times, he who was for so long an automaton of pain and Earthly ignominy, he the utterly inconsequential, randomly selected, unqualified—except for that gift he shrinks to use—is it possible that he will be witness to such wonders? Will he come to accept them? "Today we rejuvenate a sun. Tomorrow we give a species the terrible boon of self-conscious intellect."

Incredible. Impossible.

But, apparently, slowly about to begin to happen.

And—for how long? How long will it go on?

With that, the deepest, most dire and secret shudder of all shakes him. Dann allows consciousness at last to the word that has been working its unadmitted ferment in the bottom of his soul: FOREVER.

Immortality?

Yes, or something very like it. At the least, a time measured not in years or lifetimes but astral epochs. Nothing here changes, has changed, apparently will change or run down for millennia. The mysterious cold energies that sustain them have cycled, it appears, for stellar lifetimes. There seems no reason they should not continue to an approximation of eternity.

An eternity of unimaginable projects? Yes—and an eternity too of Waxman's young voice, of Heagran's sublimity, of Frodo's grief and Tivonel's laugh and Giadoc's persistent How and Why and What, and all the rest of it. The trivial, ineluctably finite living bases of their unreal lives loom up before him like an endless desert to be traversed on foot, under a sky raining splendor. The close-up limiting frame around the view of infinity.

Can we take it? Will we go mad?

Heagran has said they will all change, he reflects. Perhaps the constant mind-touching will merge them gradually, affect even Margaret. Perhaps we will become like one big multifaceted person, maybe that will be the solution. Or maybe the fused minds will be incompatible. We could become a hydra-headed psychopath.

But Margaret, he thinks; she's in control of us all, really. She could do something, put us out or freeze us if it came to that. But then she would be alone forever. Hurt strikes the node of nothing that had been his heart. For her sake we must, I must, stay sane. Hang on. Maybe it will be great, a supernally joyous life.

But—*eternity?*

A cold elation and foreboding mingle in his mind.

What have I learned, he wonders. Voyager between worlds, I have been privileged beyond mortal man. I have met an alien race, I have encountered endless unknown things. What great changes has all this wrought in me? What transformations have I suffered to make me worthy of a place in such a drama? To witness, perhaps participate in the fates of worlds? To enjoy something like immortal life? What great contribution will I make to the symbiosis?

Nothing, he reflects wryly. Not one tangible thing.

I have only what I had before, a little specialized knowledge of the workings of bodies we no longer possess. Beyond that, only my old compound of depressive sympathy and skepticism about brave new claims, however appealing. If we actually meet Jehovah or Allah or Vishnu out here I would still take my stand on the second law of thermodynamics.

What in the name of life can make mine worthy of such perpetuation? What do I ever learn but the same old lessons—that people are people, that pain is bad; that good is too often allied with vulnerability and evil with power. That absolutes are absolutely dangerous: Bethink ye, my lords, ye may be mistaken. That one can do ill in the name of doing well, and error buggers up the best laid plans. That even the greatest good of the greatest number is no safeguard—Tyree was burned because it was in the path of the destruction that saved a galaxy.

I don't know a single distinguished philosophy, he thinks, except perhaps my respect for Bacon's Great Machine. Or wait—Spinoza, when he changed one word in the ecclesiastical definition of truth. The Church called it the "recognition of necessity." Spinoza called it the *"discovery* of necessity," and for that they persecuted him because it undermined all authority.

But what new great necessities have I discovered, beyond the old necessity of kindness? And, he thinks, I am apt to be slow to discover any in this future which seems all too unconstrained. Some great thinker should be here in my place. Waxman with his boyish fervors about new modes of consciousness is more deserving of this life than I.

I'm not going to be reborn as the embryo of humanity transcendent in the cosmos. I'll just be me.

As he has been thinking these bleak thoughts beneath the radiant processions of suns within the nucleus, a small presence has come quietly close to him.

It is the child, he sees, seeming younger than usual; that incarnation of Margaret which perhaps holds all her unscarred wonder and delight. Ordinarily they rarely touch. But such is his distress now that his hand goes out unthinkingly and strokes her thin shoulder. She does not move away but turns on him a smile of elfin beauty.

As he looks down into her large eyes his worries fade somewhat. Even his lack of intellectual grandeur seems less important.

Well, he thinks, there is one thing I can do, do always. Even if it comes to eternity, I will still have that. He is almost sure of it, knows it beyond reason.

No matter how long the future stretches or what it holds, he will carry into it his love.

Chapter 28

Tivonel, bright spirit from the winds of Tyree, is still on her life-way although in dark and surpassing strangeness among the stars. The energy-configuration that is her essence glides from point to point in the vastness of the Destroyer—no, we have to call it the Saver now, she thinks—with the skill with which her winged body had once breasted Tyree's gales.

Gladly she would travel faster, but she is not alone. Her friends Marockee and Issalin flow alongside, equally impatient. They must all keep to the slow pace of the unskilled Fathers they bring with them.

She and the others are returning from the great mind-dream of Tyree, or Tyree-Two as the yumans call it. They are escorting Father Daagan and Mercil to confer for a last time with Eldest Heagran. Behind them all comes the big life-field of Father Ustan. And thanks to the winds he was with us, Tivonel thinks; Ustan had remained outside the dream-world to ensure they would be able to pull free.

"Whew, that was strong. Again, thanks, Tivonel."

It is Marockee's mind-touch. Marockee had almost lost herself in the beauty of the dream-winds, the magic of remembered life. Tivonel had to pull her to Ustan's grasp. And all three of them had to use their strengths to help break out the two young Fathers who had stayed so long in the powerful multiminded fantasy of home.

Tivonel herself had reveled in the false Tyree, in the zestful illusion of flight and her visit to the rich recreation of Deep where the Fathers and children stay. With so many orphans, the surviving Paradomin and any others who wish to try are caring for them under the supervision of real Fathers. They're doing a pretty good job, too, Tivonel thinks, but of course the children don't grow. It's good practice, they'll all have to do it when they go to that new world.

But she herself hadn't been trapped in Tyree-Two, not to forgetfulness. To her it had remained a lovely mirage, a tiny island created by living minds in a corner of huge dark reality.

I've changed, she thinks. I used to be just like Marockee, all female action and fun. It's because of Giadoc; I've caught something from him. And maybe my time with that kind, funny alien, Tanel. But I'm not getting Fatherly, I don't care about status like the Paradomin. And it isn't sex—yearning for Giadoc, either. Not anymore, not here.

She chuckles ruefully to herself, acknowledging that she will never know again the ecstasy of physical sex in the Wind. Marockee told her that some couples tried that in Tyree-Two. But of course it didn't work. With no egg, what could you expect?

No, it's not sex, what she feels for Giadoc. It's the Hearer part of him I've caught, she thinks, gliding effortlessly onward in the strange, exciting dark. Yes, and it's more than that too, it was the waiting and thinking of him, it made me understand more. And when I found him so near death and we merged. Things like that never ordinarily happened on Tyree. Males were just exciting to have sex with until they became Fathers and you sparcely saw them again. I *know* Giadoc in this deep, funny way, she thinks, not understanding that her language has no word for a human sense of love. She wonders briefly if old Omar felt something like that for Janskelen. Whatever, she will stay here with Giadoc no matter what the others do. She suppresses the mixed tingle of fear and excitement the thought brings.

"*Are you really staying in the Destroyer when everybody goes out to that new world?*" It's Marockee again.

Tivonel notices that they have outpaced the slower males, and checks.

"*You mean the Saver. Yes, I am.*" Again the slight shiver.

"*How can you, Tivonel? What'll there be to do?*"

"*Oh, there'll be plenty of adventures among the Companions. Ask Giadoc or Tanel. Besides, how do you know they're going to like being big white plenyas, or whatever those bodies are?*"

"*But they'll have real bodies and real winds. And the Great Field of Tyree will be with them.*" Marockee's mind-tone is full of ambiguous longing. Tivonel knows her friend is in agonies of indecision whether to go or stay. Well, she'll just have to make up her own mind about that. She replies only. "*We'll have Heagran. He's the spirit of Tyree, too.*"

"*Well, I'm staying here,*" puts in Issalin firmly. "*You wait, when they get out there the males will take all the eggs again, just like Tyree. Even if those bodies are supposed to be combined male and female, they'll find some way. And I know the mind that works with the Saver is female, so I'm staying with you.*"

"*Well said in friendship,*" replies Tivonel. Privately she considers that Issalin's head is a little wind-blown if those are her reasons, but she's glad of the company.

"*If we ever find the yuman world where Avan went maybe I'd go there,*" Issalin goes on. "*I've been talking a lot with that female-Father Winona. I'd see they got the status!*"

"*More power to you. Speaking of things to do,*" Tivonel interrupts herself, "*There's Sastro and that wild alien, over that way. I'm going to check on them. Father Ustan!*" she sends politely. "*I'll rejoin you later. Eldest Heagran will want news of what they have found.*"

And that's a fact, she thinks, shooting off at high speed while the others continue on their decorous way. But the real fact is I'm curious.

From this distance she can just pick up the calm life-signal of big Sastro, one of the elders who are staying with Heagran in the Saver. His signal is modulated by the uncanny flickering

emanation of the creature they had picked up out of space. The
pulsations were thought to be fear by those who first went out to
help him, but now it's clear that his life-energy is periodic in this
odd way. Weird!

As she approaches she picks up also the emanations of one of
the Saver's pictorial nodes or screens, which for some time now
have been showing scenes of the world the Tyrenni will go out to.
The group seems to be clustered around it. And now Tivonel can
recognize another big life-field—the yuman Valeree with whom
she's had many friendly contacts. Valeree is trying to learn the
alien creature's language—good luck to her. Beside her in the
queer flicker of the alien's field are two other Tyrenni energies; a
male and female Tivonel doesn't know well, from Tyree-Two.

"*Greetings, Father Sastro and to you all.*" She extends a
decorous receptor-node, ignoring the alien.

"*Hello Tivonel,*" Valeree replies. "*Listen, try touching it
carefully. I think it will answer.*"

Winds, they must have really calmed it down! Cautiously,
Tivonel extends a tentative probe. "*Greetings.*"

"*Gree—tin*" it sends faintly, accompanied by such a flash of
mental green that Tivonel jumps away.

"*It's scared to death! Why haven't you fixed it?*"

"*Do not be foolish,*" Sastro reproves her. "*Do you imagine a
Father does not know his work? It appears, young Tivonel, that
on this being's world the color you sensed is the hue of harmony
and life.*"

"*It's a good color on ours too, Tivonel,*" Valeree adds. "*Your
people may have to get used to some strange effects when they go
down. I see that world as your colors of pain and fear, but on
ours they mean fair winds and joy.*"

"*Whew.*"

Tivonel slides onto a node near the projection and studies the
mental picture again. It's a beautiful scene, even if it's at
wind-bottom. Great mounds or crags are looming way up into
the wind. She can sense feathery spume whirling by. Far below is
a great wet foaming surface, what the yumans call an ocean or
sea. A huge, pale six-limbed flying form plummets down past
her to snatch something from a floating raft, then soars up to
perch on solidity, eating the thing from its claspers. High
overhead a dozen others are soaring, evidently rejoicing in the
gales. The scene is radiant. It does look like a suitable home for

life. Of course if all that is going to turn out to be green and blue the Tyrenni will be in for an adjustment. Well, maybe the bodies' sensors will take care of that.

"Good that you came by, young Tivonel." Sastro's mind-touch cuts short her reverie. *"Tell the Eldest that this alien has decided to go to the new world with our people. Tynad and Orcavel here brought word that it is accepted. It seems that it has skills which may be useful to them. For example, it knows how to handle much hard matter. And how to generate heat should that be needed. I confess I understand little of this, but your friend Valeree assures me it could be needed on such a world."*

"We call it 'fire'," Valeree puts in. *"Yes, it could be very useful. That's what got it out here, things made of hard stuffs and fire."*

"Is it a male or a female?" Tivonel asks, studying the curiously pulsing glow of the alien's life.

"It's both. They mate together and both bear eggs, like those animals down there. So that's another reason it would fit in. It had eight limbs, like some creatures on my world, and it used to fly on a bag or thread. It showed me mind-pictures, that's how I learned its words. Their sky was full of flyers. But you have no idea how strange. It says it was sent out of its world as a punishment."

"But our people don't want to take a criminal with them!"

"I don't think you'd call it a crime. It seems to have questioned some command about not flying too high."

"Great winds, that's not a crime!"

"It was there. So they built a, a pod, and sent it out of the sky. They've done it before, this being expected it. It hoped to reach another world. It had no idea how far they were."

Tivonel digests this extraordinary oddity. *"It sounds like a crazy female to me. Wanting to explore right through the High."*

Valeree laughs. *"More like you, Tivonel. We have a word for what it's really like. Tell Tanel, he'll explain. It feels like a jock, a typical jock. It'll do much better in a real place than this mind-world. Like our Kirk and his pet animal, they're going down too."*

"A jock? I will, Valeree-friend." Tivonel makes her farewells, remembering she will never meet the other two Tyrenni again. *"Fair winds on your new world."*

"Fair winds to you who stay, Tivonel."

She glides off, reflecting. It's going to be a lonesome moment when all the other Tyrenni leave. Giadoc has explained how it will be: a sort of wall or shield will form around the nucleus, separating those who stay from the pull of the outgoing Beam. She'll be inside with Giadoc and the others. But it'll be lonesome—think of feeling all the lives of her people, the life of Tyree itself, sliding out forever to the dark, down to that strange world, never to be known again. *Brr.* It'll be sad for us all.

But we'll see them lodge in the bodies of those flying things, come to themselves and take up real life again. They say it will be gentle; people will have time to choose the ones they want. It won't be like the time she had voyaged to the yuman world and just fallen into the nearest mind. Tanel says that the Destroyer—the Saver—knows how to do this. It was the thing it was supposed to do, if it hadn't been asleep or crazy or whatever it was before Tanel's friend came.

Yes, it'll be a lonely feeling, she thinks again, counting over those who will remain. Giadoc and Heagran, of course. And Ustan has decided to. And the two elders Sastro and Panad, who won't part from Heagran. And the young, bitter Father Hiner, whose child was so tragically lost at the last minute on Tyree. We could have Orva the Hearer's Memory-Keeper too, but Heagran says he must go with the others to carry Tyree's history to the new world, since Kinto was lost. Hiner is studying with him to be Memory-Keeper here.

Well, six Fathers counting Hiner, that'll be a lot of strength if and when new crazy aliens come along. Maybe she'll have to try a little Fathering herself, as she had with Tanel. Heagran says we'll get more like each other with all this mind-touching. But she wishes she had more female company. Only Issalin the Paradomin is staying, and her friend Jalifee. And Marockee— maybe. The other Tyrenni females are so short-sighted, they just see the adventure of that real new world down there. They can't grasp the long mysterious Giadoc-type adventures we'll have here. Maybe I wouldn't either, she thinks, shivering half-pleasurably again, if it weren't for Giadoc.

But I'll have Valeree, Tivonel comforts herself. She's almost like a Tyrenni, she loves to explore. And so does the old female-Father Winona, and maybe that sad Frodo will cheer up. And the funny human male Kris. Thinking of him, she notices the soft signal that means a quarter-Kris has passed. She better hurry. The signal must be coming from the node near the nucleus. She changes course slightly, and an idea comes to her. Why not ask Tanel to have his mysterious friend put markers on the different nodes, so we could really tell where we are? That way we could build up a real mental map of this enormous dark world, and explore out to the very end without danger of being lost. I wonder what we'll find when we get to the edge, she muses. Will the Saver have a thick wall, or will it just thin out to nothing so we can begin to sense the lives of the sky through it?

Ahead of her the dim form of the nucleus and the mind-sparks near it are now faintly perceptible. Another life-group is converging on them—Ustan and the others. Good, she's come just in time. There's no real need for her presence, it'll be all a solemn conference of Heagran telling the Fathers how to conduct themselves out there on New Tyree or whatever they're going to call it. Responsibility, life-reverence, *ahura*, etcetera and so on. And Orva saying goodbye. But she loves to listen in to Heagran. So old, so wise; he was a child when New Deep was founded. His mind isn't bounded by Fathering anymore. He's been mind-caught by the wonders of the sky, like Giadoc. We're so lucky to have him.

As she damps herself for a courteous arrival, she thinks ahead to the next, the really exciting conference there is to be. After the main group of Tyrenni go out to their new world and take up their lives, those who are staying here will gather around Tanel. Heagran has explained it. *"The Saver wishes us to help it think upon a new Life-Task, since its race has left this part of the universe, and it is here alone."*

A great new task, here in limitless space among all these stars and worlds? Whew!

Tivonel has picked up many thought-fragments about this, enough to know that everyone has a different dream. Only the two old Fathers Sastro and Panad are united; typically, they want to find a young race and Father it to wise maturity. But the others! Averting cosmic cataclysms, reviving dead races—and Giadoc of course always wanting to learn more, to find ways of actually visiting other worlds. . . . A vagrant notion of what it would be like to have real sex again in an alien body rises in her mind; she relegates it to storage.

She knows that old Heagran and that double yuman Waxman both dream of finding strange new kinds of minds

among the worlds, but their visions aren't alike. And Father
Ustan wants to go on saving endangered races. Issalin and
Jalifee will probably want to find some way of helping females,
while the yuman Winona wants to rescue any person who is in
terrible pain on whatever world. Valeree wants to invent a way
of making strange races able to know and feel each other's
minds, like the Tyrenni. When Waxman heard her telling that he
said, *"Not too much empathy. I know."* The two yumans
Tivonel knows least, Frodo and the dreamer Ted Yost, probably
have still more wild notions of their own. And Giadoc's friend
Kris has the wildest one of all—he thinks they should search for
whatever made or hatched the Saver!

Tivonel settles discreetly beside Heagran's group, thinking, I
haven't any big idea of my own. But I know how I'm going to
respond, because I'm the most practical one of the lot. What
they forget is that we're going to be here a long, long, long time.

A slow, coldly exciting shudder travels through her
immaterial form. It's not in her cheerful mind to use big words
like "eternity" or "forever." Let's just say our journey will be of
enormous length and duration, she thinks. And in her
experience of long journeys it isn't a good idea to plan
everything too carefully. Not to go rigidly seeking one goal when
maybe others you haven't thought of are right ahead. Look at
her last life-journey; she had started out to look for some
exciting sex and found a child to be helped, Hearers to be fed,
new friends, a trip to another world, and the end of her own
Tyree. So, after all these grand shcemes and possibilities are
unfolded, she knows what her own contribution will be.

If only I can put it right, she thinks, preparing to attend to
Heagran, unaware that her own life-field is aglow with vitality.
If only I can think of the right forms to reach these big-minds.
Well, the mind who's with the Saver is a female; maybe she'll
understand.

The main thing to get across to them is that there will be so
much time. Maybe all the time there is. And as we go ever on and
on in this great journey, however long it lasts, different
possibilities will appear, different acts will seem more urgent or
right. We don't even know all our own powers. So let us rescue
what we find to rescue, experience what we can, change what
seems good to change. That way we will learn and grow. My vote

won't be for one plan or another, not even Giadoc's explorations or Heagran's mighty dreams. There is so much time. Why limit ourselves or the Saver? So she knows what she will say:

"Let's try it all!"

Chapter 29

ALONE BUT NOT LONELY IT ROVES THE DARK IMMENSITIES, NEW-BORN AND STRANGEST BEING OF ALL: PART ANIMATE, PART PASSIONLESS CAUSALITY, WHOSE VAST POWERS CAN UNDO TIME ITSELF. SO FAR AS IT KNOWS, IT IS IMMORTAL, AND SUBJECT TO NO IMPERATIVE BUT ITS OWN. IT IS MOVED BY DISCRETE IMPULSES OF CURIOSITY, PITY, IRRITATION, OR WONDER, NOW TRIVIAL, NOW SUBLIME: IMPULSES WHICH ARE ALWAYS LESS PARTICULATE AND ALWAYS MORE A MERGING OF PREPOSTEROUSLY FINITE LITTLE LIVES BECOMING MELDED TO FOREVER. IT IS A PROTO-PRONOUN, AN *IT* BECOMING *SHE* BECOMING *THEY*, A *WE* BECOMING *I* WHICH IS BECOMING MYSTERY.

CONFUSED, JOYFUL, GRIEVING, INQUISITIVE, RANDOMLY BENEVOLENT, AND NOT ENTIRELY SANE, IT SETS FORTH TO ITS DESTINY AMONG THE

ORDINARY DENIZENS OF SPACE AND TIME: A
CHANCE-BORN FALLIBLE DEITY WHOSE POWERS
MAY ONE DAY FOCUS WITHOUT WARNING UPON THE
TINY LIFES OF ANY NESCIENT EARTH.

SCIENCE FICTION BESTSELLERS
FROM BERKLEY!

Frank Herbert

THE DOSADI EXPERIMENT	(03834-3 — $2.25)
CHILDREN OF DUNE	(04075-5 — $2.25)
DUNE	(03698-7 — $2.25)
DUNE MESSIAH	(03940-7 — $1.95)
THE GODMAKERS	(03913-6 — $1.95)
THE ILLUSTRATED DUNE	(03891-2 — $7.95)
DESTINATION: VOID	(03922-6 — $1.95)

* * * * *

Philip José Farmer

THE DARK DECISION	(03831-9 — $2.25)
THE FABULOUS RIVERBOAT	(04315-0 — $1.95)
TO YOUR SCATTERED BODIES GO	(04314-2 — $1.95)
NIGHT OF LIGHT	(03933-1 — $1.75)

Send for a list of all our books in print.

These books are available at your local bookstore, or send price indicated plus 30¢ for postage and handling. If more than four books are ordered, only $1.00 is necessary for postage. Allow three weeks for delivery. Send orders to:

Berkley Book Mailing Service
P.O. Box 690
Rockville Centre, New York 11570